Dear reader,

Being a writer was never a path I thought to walk, yet here I am, a full five years after I started writing the book before you. As an avid reader, I've devoured books across multiple genres for as long as I can remember. I marveled at the worlds master authors weaved, and swooned at the poetic prose that brought character and plot together.

Yet I found myself restless, searching and searching for that one book I couldn't find. An epic fantasy built on the stones of non-Western civilizations, with a female lead born from my background. Toni Morrison once said, "If there's a book that you want to read, but it hasn't been written yet, then you must write it." And so, I started to write.

I know not every book is for every reader, but I hope this book brings you as much joy in reading as it brought me in writing. This series consumes my every thought, and I cannot wait for you to read what I have in store for it.

Thank you so much for taking a chance on it.

With all my love,

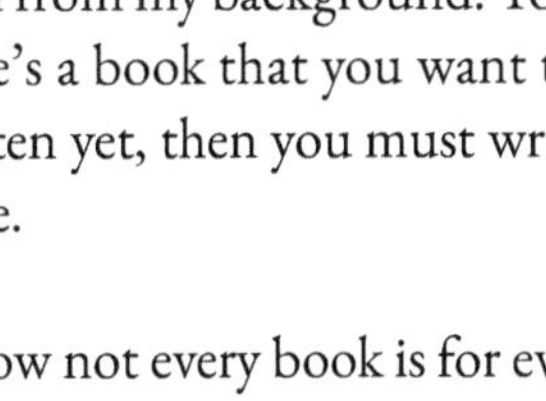

FAYE OLIANDER

A LEGEND IN THE SKY

the
GEMINI STONES
Book One

CONTENT WARNING:

This book contains content some readers may find triggering. For a full list of potential triggers, please visit: fayeoliander.com/alits

Cover illustration and design © Cynthia Conner
Map and heraldry © Moreno Paissan and Angela Gubert Art
Character art © Nebraska JC Illustrations

Interior art sourced from various contributors at Depositphotos, Adobe stock, and CanvaPro

Set in EB Garamond and Meritta Serif

Editing by C.B. Moore and Melanie Underwood

ISBN: 978-90-834986-5-2 (eBook)
ISBN: 978-90-834986-1-4 (Paperback)
ISBN: 978-90-834986-9-0 (Hardcover)

GRASSQUIT
BOOKS

To my Heavenly Father, without whom I'd be nothing. You have all my failures, you have all my victories.

Story Guide

LANGUAGE

PRONUNCIATION GUIDE

Æther ꩜ *Ee-thur*
Ænunaki ꩜ *Eh-noo-nah-kee*
Karuiles Siunes ꩜ *Kah-roo-les Syoo-ness*
Naila ꩜ *Nigh-lah*
Phæralei ꩜ *Fa-ruh-lay*
Rē ꩜ *Ray*
Š ꩜ *Sh*

DICTIONARY

Æther ꩜ *the Lemaï's sacred power of flames*
Baba ꩜ *dad (informal)*
Camoda ꩜ *a large, hoofed mammal that inhabits the deserts of the Midlands*
Dogan ꩜ *little brother*
Doran horse ꩜ *a special breed of horses, bound by æther to shadowreapers*
Feylana ꩜ *female (girl/woman)*
Gavana ꩜ *an informal title used for those people consider the best/the strongest*
Helicoprion ꩜ *spiral-shaped jaw shark*
Iluna ꩜ *two of moons (Lemuria's binary moon)*
Karuiles Siunes ꩜ *literally: seven titans. An ancient species of giant serpentine dragons*
Lai ꩜ *no*
Lugal ꩜ *male (boy/man)*
Šaltana ꩜ *princess*
Šar ꩜ *emperor*
Šargon ꩜ *crown prince*

To my Heavenly Father, without whom I'd be nothing. You have all my failures, you have all my victories.

CONTENTS

SCROLL I
An Unlikely Event

SCROLL II
A Song Within the Storms

SCROLL III
Bound by Blood

SCROLL IV
A Legend in the Sky

Story Guide

LANGUAGE

PRONUNCIATION GUIDE

Æther ⸎ *Ee-thur*
Ænunaki ⸎ *Eh-noo-nah-kee*
Karuiles Siunes ⸎ *Kah-roo-les Syoo-ness*
Naila ⸎ *Nigh-lah*
Phæralei ⸎ *Fa-ruh-lay*
Rē ⸎ *Ray*
Š ⸎ *Sh*

DICTIONARY

Æther ⸎ *the Lemaï's sacred power of flames*
Baba ⸎ *dad (informal)*
Camoda ⸎ *a large, hoofed mammal that inhabits the deserts of the Midlands*
Dogan ⸎ *little brother*
Doran horse ⸎ *a special breed of horses, bound by æther to shadowreapers*
Feylana ⸎ *female (girl/woman)*
Gavana ⸎ *an informal title used for those people consider the best/the strongest*
Helicoprion ⸎ *spiral-shaped jaw shark*
Iluna ⸎ *two of moons (Lemuria's binary moon)*
Karuiles Siunes ⸎ *literally: seven titans. An ancient species of giant serpentine dragons*
Lai ⸎ *no*
Lugal ⸎ *male (boy/man)*
Šaltana ⸎ *princess*
Šar ⸎ *emperor*
Šargon ⸎ *crown prince*

Suyarmašu ⸙ *sea goat*
Sengan ⸙ *older brother*
Ut Asanatæ ⸙ *literally: the immortals; an elite unit of warriors from Crishire*
Yana ⸙ *yes*
Yelud ⸙ *child*

PHRASES

T'ilaa ni gloria ⸙ *glory over you (a battle cry)*
T'alfera ana emaya ⸙ *would translate to: you have brought me joy; thank you*
Nirihim no Nalahai ⸙ *Heir of Elysium*

TIME PERIODS

One winter / one summer ⸙ *one year*
One moon ⸙ *one month*
One sun ⸙ *one day*
One bell ⸙ *around 70-75 minutes*
One chime ⸙ *around 15-20 minutes*
One tinkling ⸙ *around 1-5 minutes*

THE KARUILES SIUNES

⸙ The Azag of Helath

SOCIAL HIERARCHY

I. **THE LEGENDS** (deities)
- I. Major gods
  - i. Ishtar
  - ii. Marduk
  - iii. Sin & Shamash
  - iv. Nergal
  - v. Enki
- II. Minor gods
- III. Demi gods
  - i. Lamaštu

II. **THE ŠARS** (emperors; pages xiv - xv)

III. **THE PRINCES**

IV. **THE COURT OF ELDERS**

V. **THE IMPERIAL HAREM**

VI. **THE NOBILITY**

VII. **THE GENERALS**

VIII. **THE PRIESTESSES**
- i. Nergayla ꩜ *Head Priestess*
- ii. Sêra ꩜ *High Priestess*
- iii. Khaylūm ꩜ *diviner*
- iv. Heka ꩜ *Senior Priestess*
- v. Hierodula ꩜ *Junior Priestess*
- vi. Learlings ꩜ *apprentices*

VII. **THE SCRIBES**
viii. The Imperial Scribe
ix. The Senior Scribe

x. The Junior Scribe
xi. Learlings ↫ *apprentices*

IX. THE ARMED FORCES

I. Elite Units (each empire has a unique name for its special forces)

i. The Shadowlands ↫ *Shadowreapers*
ii. Crishire ↫ *Ut Asanatæ*
iii. Gudea ↫ *Keshig*

II. Cavalry

i. Vigiles ↫ *infantry*
ii. Watchmen ↫ *local law enforcers*
  i. Il-Ragab ↫ *crisis managers*
iii. Sentries ↫ *guards*
iv. Whisperers ↫ *spies*
v. Hired blades ↫ *mercenaries*
vi. Learlings ↫ *apprentices*

X. THE UPPER CLASS

XI. PEDESTERS (peasants)

XII. SLAVES

i. Indentured servants
ii. Forced laborers
iii. Blood slaves

The Winterlands

The Empire of Skeldor
From the void we fell, to the stars we rise

THE SILVER ŠAR

The Empire of Jodrir
In strength, we take flight, through ancient woods and endless night

THE ICE ŠAR

The Empire of Syeon
Where wisdom lights the way and guides the heart each day

THE GRAY ŠAR

The Elderlands

The Empire of Crishire
Through reason or by force, we find our power in every choice

THE RED ŠAR

The Empire of Numidea
Guided by Wisdom, Driven by Courage

THE FIRE ŠAR

The Shadowlands

The Shadowlands
The wind blows to move us forward, not so we can stand still

THE SHADOW ŠAR

The Summerlands

THE IRON ŠAR

THE BONE ŠAR

THE BLACK ŠAR

The Midlands

THE GOLDEN ŠAR

THE WHITE ŠAR

We are all visitors to this time, this place.
We are just passing through.
Our purpose here is to observe,
to learn,
to grow,
to love…
and then we return home.

— AUSTRALIAN ABORIGINAL PROVERB

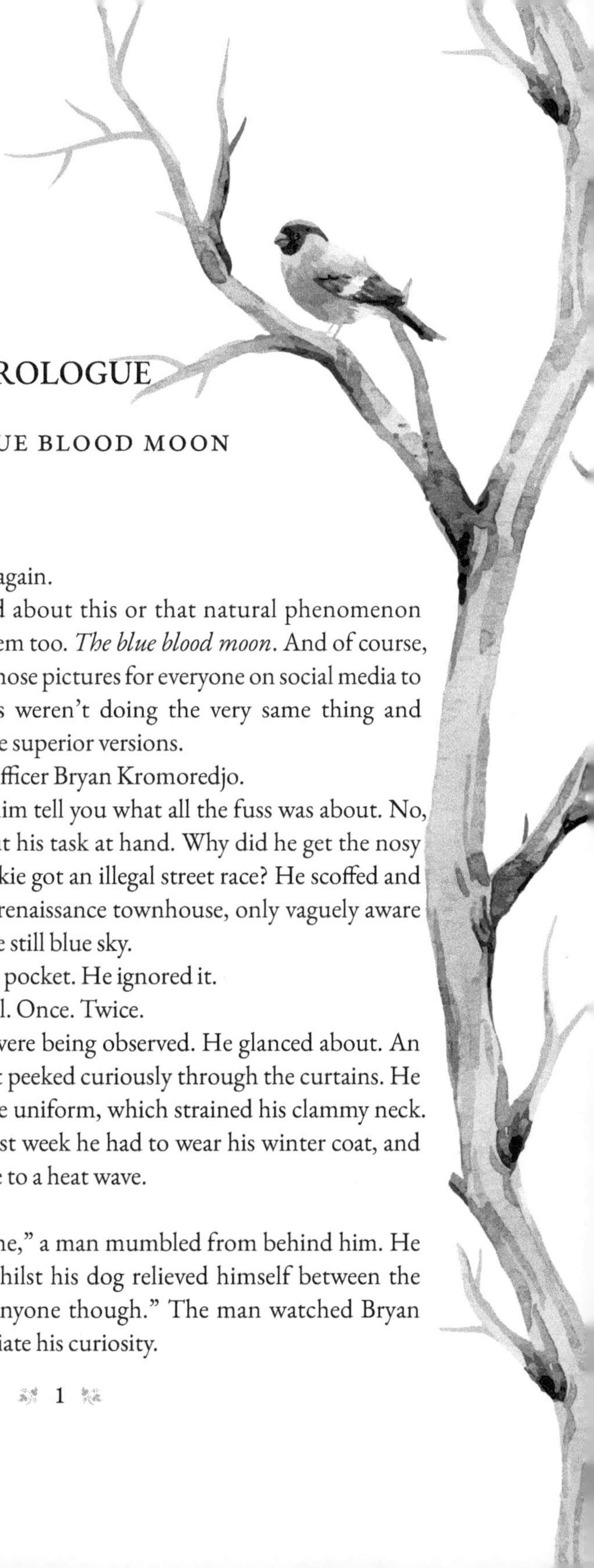

PROLOGUE

THE BLUE BLOOD MOON

IT WAS one of those days again.

Where people gushed about this or that natural phenomenon because the news told them too. *The blue blood moon*. And of course, they had to make sure to post those pictures for everyone on social media to see. As though their mutuals weren't doing the very same thing and photographers didn't eternalize superior versions.

All of that bypassed rookie officer Bryan Kromoredjo.

He couldn't for the life of him tell you what all the fuss was about. No, *he*, was too busy moping about his task at hand. Why did he get the nosy neighbors when his fellow rookie got an illegal street race? He scoffed and ascended the stairs to the neo-renaissance townhouse, only vaguely aware of the red orb painted upon the still blue sky.

His phone buzzed inside his pocket. He ignored it.

Instead, he rang the doorbell. Once. Twice.

His skin prickled. As if he were being observed. He glanced about. An elderly woman across the street peeked curiously through the curtains. He loosened the collar of his police uniform, which strained his clammy neck. Bloody Dutch weather. Just last week he had to wear his winter coat, and now this week crept eerily close to a heat wave.

He rang again. No answer.

"He keeps to himself, that one," a man mumbled from behind him. He took a drag of his cigarette whilst his dog relieved himself between the hydrangeas. "Never bothers anyone though." The man watched Bryan sneakily, perhaps hoping to satiate his curiosity.

Bryan smiled inwardly. People were so transparent. "Does he now?" Was all he said, not hinting whatsoever that several neighbors had complained about midnight noises.

It wasn't the first time they'd called about the man. Just two days ago someone had alerted the fire brigade, claiming the house was set alight. When the fire brigade met with a perfectly intact townhouse, the nosy neighbor had mumbled they must have been confused with the first sighting of that red moon or something, something. He shook his head. Crazy people. First, it was that stone in Genghis Khan's newly discovered tomb, now it was some moon.

Bryan just wanted to warn this Philippe Jang and be on his merry way. But after ringing the bell once more, he supposed he'd have to postpone the task to another day.

His phone buzzed again.

This time he messaged back.

When he looked up, the man still watched him expectantly.

"Gotta go," he said conversationally instead of satisfying the man's curiosity. "My twin is throwing a party."

And was he in need of one. Contrary to his twin, who was an up-and-coming soccer player, he had to deal with *this,* and sleepless nights due to his newborn son.

The man smiled. "Barbecue?"

"Nah, midnight swim at Nesselande Beach."

The man saluted him and dragged his dog away. After one last look at the townhouse, Bryan, too, left. Unaware that the blue blood moon wasn't the only thing following him.

SCROLL I

AN UNLIKELY EVENT

Oh, woe, the fledgling night songstress doesn't know its own strength,
The manifold peril she endures on her quests of endless length,
Be warned, the dull feathers and petite frame will deceive many a fool,
Out of her wee body comes a song more powerful than many a tool,
But before all, she must leave the security of her mother's perianth.

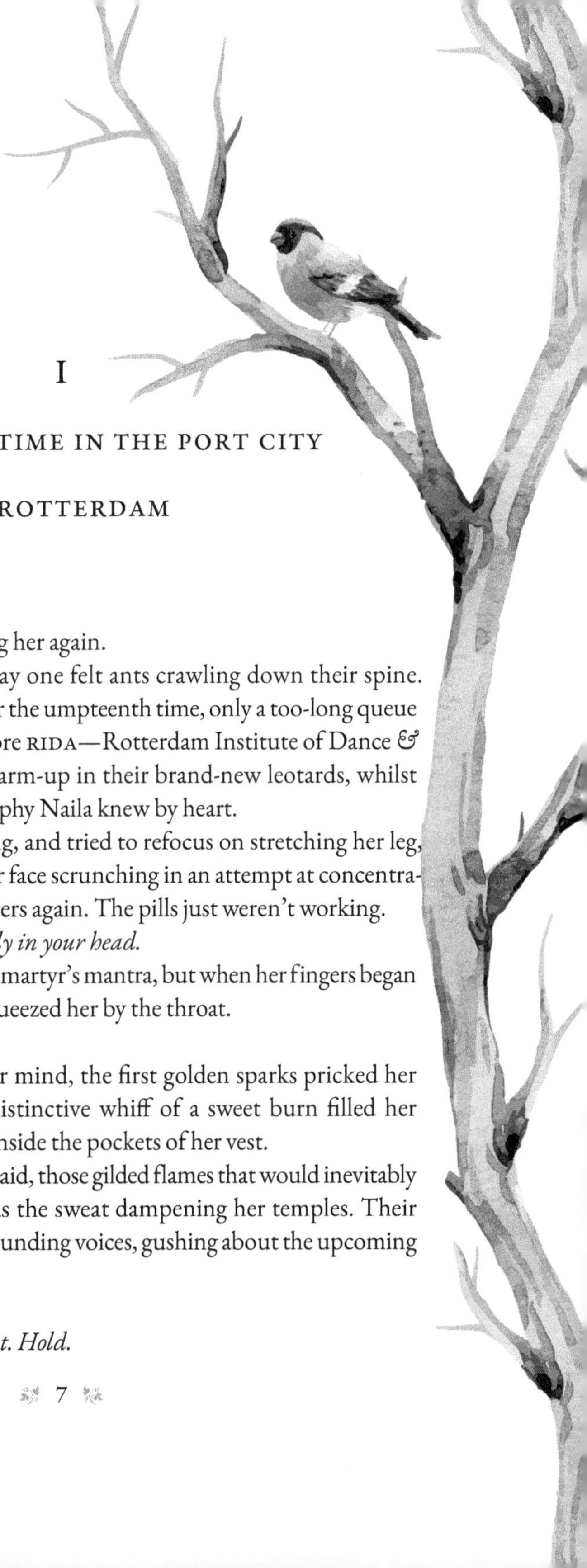

I

ONCE UPON A TIME IN THE PORT CITY OF ROTTERDAM

SOMEONE WAS watching her again.

Naila knew it the way one felt ants crawling down their spine. When she glanced up for the umpteenth time, only a too-long queue of aspiring dancers waited before RIDA—Rotterdam Institute of Dance & Arts. A couple of girls did a warm-up in their brand-new leotards, whilst others rehearsed the choreography Naila knew by heart.

She shook off the odd feeling, and tried to refocus on stretching her leg, the golden-brown planes of her face scrunching in an attempt at concentration. She'd have to call Dr. Peeters again. The pills just weren't working.

It's only in your head. It's only in your head.

She repeated the words like a martyr's mantra, but when her fingers began to burn, the claws of horror squeezed her by the throat.

No, no, no. Not right now.

Even as the thought left her mind, the first golden sparks pricked her fingertips, and the chilling, distinctive whiff of a sweet burn filled her nostrils. She thrust her hands inside the pockets of her vest.

No matter what Dr. Peeters said, those gilded flames that would inevitably encase her fingers felt as real as the sweat dampening her temples. Their sizzling rang as true as the surrounding voices, gushing about the upcoming auditions.

She sucked in a deep breath.

Breathe in. Hold. Breathe out. Hold.

The sparks in her fingers retreated back to a slumber. *Thank heaven...*

She slapped her cheeks for good measure. A girl in front of her cast her a curious look. Naila's heart sped up. This was it. A chance to make a friend.

"Hi," she said, nervously.

The girl smiled. "You're so pretty! Like a doll. I'll bet they choose you."

Her cheeks heated. She was quite relieved her brown skin prevented her from blushing. But then the girl's eyes went up, up, up. Like everyone who met Naila for the first time, her gaze briefly rested upon the two little marks etched between her eyebrows.

The markings she had been bullied for during her whole childhood.

Those markings she *hated*.

The girl's friend turned around and her eyes widened when she saw who she talked to. She pulled her by the arm, away from Naila.

Naila swallowed back her disappointment.

Around her, everyone chatted excitedly whereas she stood there alone... Unwanted.

Her scars were odd, she knew that. Her mother said they were no more than the remnants of an unfortunate childhood accident, but she didn't remember it. Then again, everything before her fifth year was a haze. Still, what person had a diamond atop a lying crescent moon the color of mother-of-pearl carved upon their forehead?

No, Naila, don't go there.

And then there were her eyes, which added even more to her unusual appearance... Because, sometimes, when she was really upset, her bright brown eyes flashed liquid gold. Her mother had said so herself.

"Folie à deux," Dr. Peeters had called it, "It's no more than a delusion shared by two."

Naila forced herself back to the present, in time to hear the whispers before her.

"My friend went to school with her. They say she has a shrink."

A gasp.

She averted her eyes, tuning out their gossip about *her*. If she didn't, she was sure to snap at their rudeness. She sighed. They didn't understand. No one did. Only Philly... She pulled her phone out of her pocket. Still no reply from Philippe Jang. Worry gnawed at her. *Where are you, Philly?*

Her fingers sparked anew around her phone.

Why were her flames so out of control today? She forced herself to focus on her breathing once more. Fortunately, or perhaps unfortunately, the surrounding girls were too busy striking poses for their phones to notice the skittish girl in the corner.

When the heat in her fingers finally retreated, she adjusted a stray curl behind her ears with trembling fingers. She fidgeted with her blood-red *fayalobi* hair clip—the national flower of her motherland Suriname, a former colony of the Netherlands. The heat and humidity had invited frizz into the full length of her long curls, courtesy of her sub-Saharan African ancestors.

Meanwhile, the screen plastered on the building interchanged RIDA's logo with a news report that'd been recycled ad nauseam:

> *The death toll in the explosion at Nesselande Beach two weeks ago has risen to ten, according to the latest count, and two more are still missing: twins Bryan and Patrick Kromoredjo. The police claim to have no clue as to who the perpetrator is, but insiders say it's an act committed by foreign terrorist organization—*

"Naila Wilhelmina Groenhart," a voice boomed.

She jerked up, stroking her compass pendant as if it could give her luck.

A woman with scarlet lipstick and cat eyeglasses looked up from her notepad. "You're up."

Naila squared her shoulders and pranced toward the woman with a confidence she didn't feel, ignoring the gossiping girls. Change your thinking, you'll change your world, she reminded herself.

If only she could make her flames see reason too.

THE SKY was well on its way to the night when Naila reached her apartment complex. As she walked to the door, her gaze drifted upward, but she pouted in disappointment when the only thing that met her were the angry, dark clouds. When she was a little girl, Philly taught her how to spot the constellations in the night sky. He said you had to pay close attention to them, because the stories of the future were already written in the stars. Naila didn't believe him, of course, but ever since, she was intrigued by the celestial bodies.

Her fingers brushed over the polished surface of her compass, hanging from her necklace. When she and her mother moved, Philly gave her her father's moonstone compass he had found—much to her mother's displeasure. Even now, it was still her most prized possession.

The rumbling of a scooter faded into the distance whilst she took to the stairs. As she stuck her key into the lock, shivers crept up her body. She glanced over her shoulder to the street below, but only a few cars drove by.

Still, she couldn't shake the intense feeling someone was watching her again... like a deer being hunted. When Naila opened the door, she noticed, to her surprise, her palms were sweaty. She quickly closed the door, exhaling in relief. *Bigi Pokoe* music hummed in the living room.

Something furry rubbed itself against her leg.

"Wha—" When her eyes took in the offender, she pressed her hand in relief upon her heaving chest. It was her tabby cat, Tigri. Smiling, she picked up the cat to cuddle it, giving him the attention he craved.

"Hey, boy, did you miss me?"

Tigri nuzzled against the collar of her jumpsuit, purring softly.

"What's that?" she said, as if the cat could understand her. "Are you asking how my audition went? How attentive."

"Nene?" Her mother peeked into the hall, her locs styled with a head wrap. For once, there was no paint swiped across her cheek. "There you are!"

Her cheeks burned, ready for her mother scolding her for make-believe talking to animals again. But Wilhelmina 'Willa' Groenhart rushed to Naila and took her face within her brown hands, as if to assure herself no harm had come to her daughter.

"Hey."

"Don't hey me. Didn't you hear what happened at Nesselande Beach?"

Naila rolled her eyes which earned her a stern look. "I doubt I'm the target of some terrorist, Ma."

"You don't know if they're terrorists."

Naila opened her mouth to protest but Willa waved dismissively. "How did the audition go?"

At once a kaleidoscope of butterflies unleashed themselves in her stomach. She kicked off her shoes and followed her mother to the living room, passing all the family portraits her mother had painted... where one person was painfully missing. "I did my best."

"Of course you did." Her mother smiled, pouring her a cup of tea. "They'd be crazy not to select you."

Naila nuzzled on the fullness of her bottom lip. "They asked for my medical history."

Her mother's hand froze mid-air. She carefully put down the teapot. Stroked an invisible crease out of her skirt before meeting Naila's eyes. "Well, you're doing better now. Have you told them that?"

Something snapped inside of her. "Doing better? Doing *better?*" She laughed humorlessly.

Her mother shifted in her seat. Good. For once she was the one uncomfortable. "Well, Dr. Peeters said you're making progress."

Because she lied. Told him all he wanted to hear so she could quit those dreaded consultations. She met her mother's gaze squarely. "Who cares what Dr. Peeters says."

"Nene!" Willa pursed her lips. "I will not have you speak about the doctor with disrespect."

Naila lowered her gaze to her hands. Rebelliousness made way for sadness. "They feel so real," she whispered. Her eyes blurred with hot tears. "Why do these flames feel so real?"

Her mother tugged her into a hug.

She made no attempt to stop her tears from wetting her mother's dress. "Philly saw them... You said you saw them too."

"You know what the good doctor said," her mother soothed.

Folie à deux.

"'Tis a hard world we live in. If you don't cooperate with Dr. Peeters, earnestly I mean, society will keep their doors shut to you. I don't want that for you. You deserve better. Now is not the time to be stubborn." Her mother's voice trembled ever so slightly.

Naila stared blankly at the gold-framed paintings decorating the forest-green wall. Tigri licked his paw near a dear one: the only one of her and her father. Except *his* face was burned away.

She stroked her compass pendant. "Tell me about my father."

"Naila..." Her mother rarely called her that.

She untangled herself from her mother's embrace. Her chin lifted in defiance. "I'll be eighteen in a few hours. I deserve to know who he is."

Her mother's face crumpled in pain.

A part of her felt guilty, but a far larger part was beyond frustration. Why all the secrecy?

"He gave me you and then he died. That's all you need to know."

Naila shot up, "Ma, seriously—"

The house phone rang. At once, all three of them, Tigri included, stared at it, wide-eyed—RIDA.

Her mother's eyes glittered with excitement. Dancing was the one thing she and Naila agreed upon. "Go on, pick it up."

Naila's heart fluttered wildly, missing a beat here and there, as she dashed to the device. Today would change her life forever. She sidestepped Tigri, much to the cat's displeasure. It gave her an offended meow and walked around the table to nestle against Willa's slippers instead. She picked the phone up.

Her head felt light as a feather—waiting for the deciding words.

"Is it RIDA?" Willa's voice betrayed a nervous tremble. Even Tigri eyed her curiously.

Naila nodded as she heard RIDA's spokesperson speak.

"*Mi Gado, mi Jesus.* I'm so nervous, I might faint," Willa went on.

It seemed like ages before she finally ended the call. The anticipation of its content had frozen Naila to the spot. Her breaths came out in rapid movements as the life-changing words finally registered.

"Please tell me they accepted you," she vaguely heard Willa say in the background.

Naila played back the conversation repeatedly because somehow, she couldn't comprehend it.

Those words simply couldn't be true.

"Say something."

After a long moment, she slowly raised her eyes to Willa's, trying to hide the bitter disappointment spreading through her.

Willa's smile faltered. "What did they say?"

Tears blurred Naila's vision.

"I got rejected."

Three simple words yet they cut into Naila like a sharp, jagged knife. She couldn't breathe, couldn't think.

Rejected.

All her dreams crumbled to dust with one word.

Peculiar, how the bricks of life can collapse from one moment to the next, leaving nothing left to stand on. Nothing left to hold onto.

Willa clasped a hand over her mouth, her stricken face no doubt a mirror of Naila's own. Her mother's eyes glistened with unshed tears. She had to get away. *Now*. If she spent another moment seeing the devastation in Willa's eyes, she would break. Naila rushed out of the apartment, ignoring Willa's pleas all the way down to the street.

She clutched her compass pendant. *Philly*. She had to get to Philippe. He couldn't ignore her any longer. As she reached the tram station, her mind was so fixated on a future that would never be, she didn't notice how the sidewalk behind her darkened with the movement of a pair of shadows.

Silently.

Determinedly.

II

THE CURIOUS CASE OF PHILIPPE JANG

THERE IS magic in a rainstorm.

It can soothe nail-biting nerves and lull insomniacs into slumber, wash away remnants of the old, and make way for the unknown ahead. Naila savored the soft raindrops splattering her face. The weeping clouds spoke the words she couldn't find to say.

The wind blew her midnight curls behind her, making them impossible to distinguish from the dark of the night. Her jumpsuit got wet, but she found herself not caring. With the rain washing away her tears, a state of shock had opened its unwelcome door.

As she turned around the block, the clock of the old church marking Philippe's street struck ten. Two more hours until her birthday... Yet nothing. She felt nothing. RIDA had rejected her. The shock still hadn't worn off. She trudged past the brick houses from the early twentieth century—the few remaining after the city was bombed in the Second World War.

Even in the dark, she could see delicate flowers in the full range of pastels blossoming in the gardens. To think this little tree-lined cul-de-sac used to be her home too, long ago.

Still stunned, Naila stepped past the houses, her feet taking over from her mind.

Despite the weather, cheers came from the soccer field hidden behind the trees. It was there she'd met Philly years ago, and where he had told her the stories of the stars. She smiled wistfully. *Philly and his fairy tales.*

Her smile vanished. It was also where Philly would talk her out of her panic attacks when yet another hallucination of flames frightened her. And where he'd solemnly listen as she cried about other kids putting dog poo in her lunchbox again.

Her phone buzzed over and over.

She pressed away her mother's call, muted her phone, and sent a text.

> Staying with Philippe. I'll be back home when you're ready to talk about Pa.

She rubbed the shivers out of her arms and mentally brushed her guilt away. Her mother didn't understand. Naila knew she meant well, but her secrecy and overprotectiveness suffocated her.

A flash of lightning lit up the sky just as she reached Philly's house. The driveway was empty, and the lawn looked like it hadn't been mowed in weeks. She frowned at the closed curtains. Not a single light burned inside. Unease washed over her. Why hadn't he answered any of her calls?

She glanced over her shoulder. Aside from a rumbling car passing underneath the streetlights, there was no sign of anyone else about. She strode to the front door. Naila always wondered why Philly chose to live in this quaint townhouse.

It was a rather mundane place for a young man as remarkable as wildlife photographer Philippe Jang. He had seen the most alluring beauty and lethal dangers of the world: from the rainforest of Congo to the ice sheets of Antarctica. Every trip of his was an adventure.

She trudged across the lane to the back garden. The curtains were closed there too, although a window was left ajar. Not expecting anything, she took her phone—ignoring her mother's missed calls and capitalized texts—and called Philly. The faint sound of his ringtone came from somewhere inside the house.

Nobody answered.

Naila gnawed on a nail, her pearly nail polish fragmenting in her mouth. It was unacceptable to enter his house uninvited, but what if something was wrong? So many times, debt collectors found people lying dead in their rooms.

Looking around to see if curious neighbors peeked out of their windows—she didn't want a criminal record, thank you very much—she opened the window and crawled inside.

The musty house was utterly silent. Atop the mahogany dining table rested Philly's cell phone, amid scattered newspapers and his open laptop. Several pens rested on the newspapers, while some had fallen on the carpet tiles. *Odd*. The place was usually neat whenever she visited. You couldn't spot a hair on the floor, and the air always had an elegant, balsamic aroma.

Naila went to the table, curious to see what Philly had been reading. Her fingers brushed over the newspapers' headings. They were articles about the Nesselande Beach mystery. She frowned. From what she knew, the police didn't solve the case yet, giving conspiracy theorists a field day. Especially with the spiral-like imprint left next to the deceased victims. She had shrugged it off and moved on. Apparently, Philly had not.

She glanced to the back of the room, at the door leading to the stairs.

"Philly?"

She sighed and turned to leave, when a sound froze her in her tracks. Sure enough, she heard a rumbling noise again. It came from the basement where Philly processed his films. She tried in vain to rub the shivers out of her arms as she walked to the basement door. Her fingers paused on the handle, and after several deep inhales, she opened it and flicked on the light. It was times like these that she frustrated herself. Why couldn't she just turn and leave?

The rumbling grew louder and louder with every step Naila descended. She could no longer ignore her growing unease and hurried down the last steps. Her heart skipped a beat at the sight that met her. All thoughts of RIDA well and truly left her.

Philly struggled on the floor, tied to a support beam, with his mouth taped shut. There was something carved in the concrete wall behind him. Glass shards and dried flowers Philly had used in some of his photoshoots were scattered on the ground.

When Philly's gaze met hers, he shook his head wildly, but Naila rushed over to him.

She ripped the tape off his mouth.

"Why are you here?" Philly croaked.

His inky hair was disarranged and his eyes wide with horror. Yet even so, Philippe Jang emitted an effortless regality kings would kill for. His ivory skin was blemish free, his eyes the clearest jade. People always gushed that he looked like a Korean idol, but Naila disagreed.

Philly was simply ethereal.

She paused before working on the knot in the rope.

"Who did this to you?"

"You have to leave before they return. Go and call the police."

An icy cold crept up on Naila. "*They*? What happened, Philly? Don't tell me you pissed off some mobster?" Her fingers grew clumsy with bubbling nerves and it took her several tries to untie the knot.

"I didn't want to tell you like this, but time leaves me no choice."

His voice was hard and urgent, but to her relief, his eyes kept their softness. Naila studied them, waiting for the familiar twinkle of laughter to appear.

It didn't.

"I don't understand."

Philly's newly freed hands enfolded her trembling fingers. "Remember how I told you the story of the celestial maiden?"

"Who? Virgo?" Naila let out a chuckle, but it came out as more of a desperate gasp. "This is no time for fairy—"

"With her wings of gold, she wasn't only beautiful, but honorable and graceful," Philly interrupted her. "And well protected by many."

"You mean the Crow and the Serpent, and all the other constellations guarding her," she said matter-of-factly.

Philippe nodded and said, "Among others... But you see, the maiden had something of her own to guard and protect."

She studied Philly's features. His face was solemn, serious. Whatever was he trying to tell her?

"The diamond of Virgo," he murmured, "Never forget."

"Philly..."

"Your hallucinations, they are real, Naila."

Naila shook her head and whispered, "Stop it."

She couldn't handle this. Not right now. Not when she just *knew* that was the reason RIDA had rejected her.

Philly unfolded her fingers one by one and grasped a wilted lily off the ground. He put the flower on Naila's palm and gently tucked her fingers over its dried petals. "They. Are. Real."

"No."

But even as she said it, her body betrayed her. That treacherous fire she so feared surged through her nerves until it reached her fingers and erupted in a spark.

"No," Naila said, louder this time.

Her heart thundered in her chest, and a salty tear reached her lips.

The air sizzled.

A honeyed burn spread through the basement.

And all she could think of was, *no, no, no.*

But her power, this hallucination, had a will of its own. Gilded flames sprouted out of her pores and encased her fingers, her whole hand. The flames licked at the flower. Tentatively. Curiously. Until they'd completely covered the dying botanical with their gilded marks.

Naila squeezed her eyes shut, but it didn't stop her from feeling the inevitable. The dried, crumpled petals swelled until they were soft and lush again, like they'd just sucked in a breath of life. She opened her tear-filled eyes, and sure enough, a beautiful pink lily rested in her hand. As if it had just been plucked out of the fields in the early morn.

Philly twirled the flower between his fingers, studying it with a hint of reverie in his eyes. "I can see this too."

So Naila's mother had claimed once upon a time as well. *Folie à deux, folie à deux, folie à—*

"Why?" Naila choked on her words. "Why are you doing this to me? You know this can't be real. It's impossible."

Philly brushed a long, curly tendril from her tear-stained face and reached for her necklace and its ever-shimmering compass pendant; the only possession left from her father. Philly was the one who had defied Naila's mother and secretly bought the compass when she sold it at a flea market.

He had smiled a secretive smile when he had given it back to her, enfolding her fingers over it, and assuring her it would always point to the heart's desire, no matter where that might be—here on Earth or far between the stars.

Philly clicked the compass open. Like always, the arrow twirled round and round. No repair shop had ever managed to fix it. His lips curved into a sad smile. "In this infinite time with an infinite space, the impossible isn't only possible. It's also a certainty."

He let go of her hand and jumped up, glancing around the basement as if looking for something. For the first time, she truly noticed the carvings in the concrete wall: strange symbols forming a spiral. Not unlike the one that'd been burned into the sand of Nesselande Beach.

Her hands turned to ice. "Philly, you never answered me. Who are *they*?"

A sense of unease constricted her throat, cutting off access to air, never letting go. Her hands grew damp with cold sweat. Naila tried to inhale deeply, but her breaths came out fast, sharp and shallow.

Philly frowned in alarm.

He darted back to her and grasped her shoulders, stabilizing her. She tried to pull away, but speckles of black and white danced around her vision.

"Calm down, Naila, look at me, okay? Just look at me." He rubbed her arms in the soothing way he always did. A reassuring smile took shape on his worry-creased face. "Everything is going to be all right, but we have to find a way out first, okay? Then I'll tell you everything."

She gave a small nod.

Philly would know what to do. He always did. He'd always been her savior, her very own guardian angel.

A squeaking of the floor above cut off their conversation.

She thought for sure her heart stopped beating. When she turned to Philly, she realized that in the moment gone past he had dashed over to the basement's only window. Philly turned to Naila and pulled her toward the narrow window.

"Climb out of the window and run."

For a moment she was too bewildered to respond, but when Philly's eyes pleaded with her, she nodded.

Suddenly, it was eerily calm in the basement, as if even stray cockroaches were afraid to move. Before she had time to make sense of the situation, Philly pushed her to the side. A deafening crack reverberated through the basement moments before the concrete floor and walls shuddered. Below the window, a small hole broke the surface. Around it, the wall crumbled like toast, revealing glimpses of the neighbors' garden above.

An intense bout of fear shot through Naila's spine, numbing her brain to any coherent thought.

"Naila Stormhold?" a low voice whispered in a musical language Naila had never heard yet understood to the core of her soul.

Stormhold...?

Philly stepped to the front, in an effort to form a barrier between her and... and... Whatever *they* were, they couldn't possibly be human.

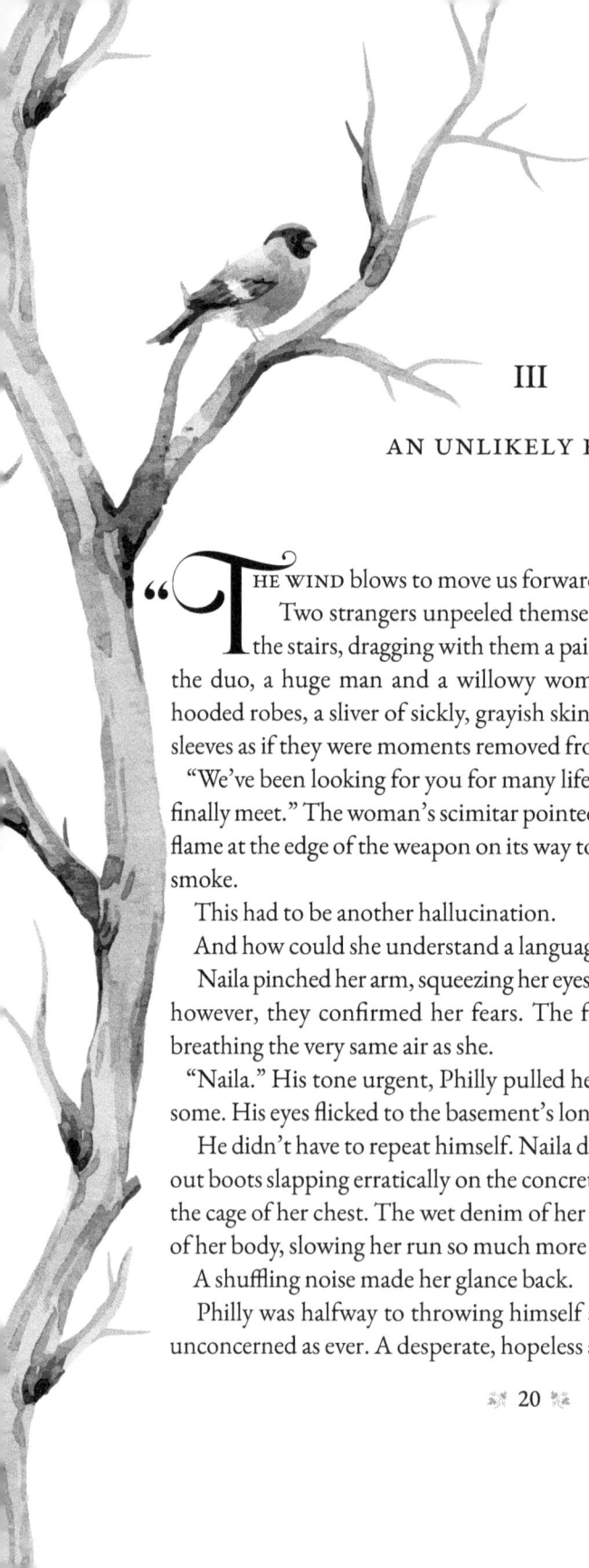

III

AN UNLIKELY EVENT

“The wind blows to move us forward, not so we can stand still.”

Two strangers unpeeled themselves from the shadows beneath the stairs, dragging with them a pair of hostages. While the faces of the duo, a huge man and a willowy woman, were hidden behind dark, hooded robes, a sliver of sickly, grayish skin peeked from underneath their sleeves as if they were moments removed from certain death.

“We’ve been looking for you for many lifetimes, Stormhold, and now we finally meet.” The woman’s scimitar pointed at the hole in the wall, a bluish flame at the edge of the weapon on its way to extinguish into a single trail of smoke.

This had to be another hallucination.

And how could she understand a language she’d never heard before?

Naila pinched her arm, squeezing her eyes shut. When she reopened them, however, they confirmed her fears. The frightening pair was still there, breathing the very same air as she.

“Naila.” His tone urgent, Philly pulled her attention away from the twosome. His eyes flicked to the basement’s lonely window. “Run for it. *Now.*”

He didn’t have to repeat himself. Naila dashed to the window, her worn-out boots slapping erratically on the concrete. Her heart thundered against the cage of her chest. The wet denim of her jumpsuit stuck to every crevice of her body, slowing her run so much more than she would have liked.

A shuffling noise made her glance back.

Philly was halfway to throwing himself at the pair, whose stances were unconcerned as ever. A desperate, hopeless action.

Surely, he knew it would be in vain? He didn't think of actually sacrificing himself... did he? *Oh, no.*

Naila froze in her tracks, leaving her standing no more than a few feet before the light of the window. Her only escape from the unpromising dark of the basement...

Philly lay upon the floor, his face creased in pain, as he grasped his shoulder. Blood soaked the whole of his white sleeve.

"Philly," Naila gasped.

All thoughts of running evaded her. She stumbled back to her friend. There was simply no world where she'd ever leave him behind.

Naila reached for Philly's sleeve, his hand, his shoulder, not knowing what to do. At last, she settled on pressing her hands against the wound to stem the bleeding.

"What are you doing?" Philly groaned. "I told you to run."

The hooded man pointed his flaming sword at Philly. "Nobody is leaving without me saying so. *She* is coming with us."

"I'm not." Naila's gaze darted from the pair to Philly and back. "Y-You've got the wrong one. My name is Naila Groenhart, not this Stormhold."

Naila clasped her bloodied hand over her mouth. She'd just spoken in the odd tongue of the strangers.

How? And why did no one, not even Philly, think this strange?

The man cocked his head.

"The *feylana* does not know what she is, Daena." The same musical highs and lows as his partner's underlined his otherworldly accent.

Daena stepped into the dull rays of the incandescent lamp, the man following suit. "Unexpected, indeed."

As the light unveiled the strangers' appearance, the remnants of food inside Naila's stomach threatened a backflow to her throat.

Underneath their robes, dark leather covered their necks and jawlines, finishing in a row of black metal fangs. Their grayish skin was covered from head to toe in strange scars—cuneiform characters, perhaps?

It wasn't only their strange attire that drew Naila's eyes, however, but also their unnerving eyes. She blinked once, twice, but her mind hadn't fooled her.

Ice-blue flames danced upon her attackers' irises. The very same flames that had burned around their scimitars moments ago. Flames, oddly reminiscent of the gilded flames that sometimes lit up her own eyes.

"W-Who are you? No, scratch that, *what* are you?"

Philly dug his fingers gently into hers, but whether it was to calm himself or her, she didn't know.

"Naila, they—" Philly grunted.

"Who we are is none of your concern," the man stated flatly. "Are you certain we have the right one, Daena? This one breathes and smells damsel in distress."

Naila flinched at the sharpness of his insult. How dare he? She may have cried countless times in private *after* her bullies' cruelty, but she had never cowered before them.

"The Shadow Šar is never mistaken, Colios." Daena narrowed her flaming eyes on him. "And we should try not making another mistake, after you almost got us exposed at that beach." Daena's eyes shifted to Naila's forehead. "Besides, she bears the mark of Ishtar."

That beach... as in... Nesselande Beach?

Naila squeezed Philly's hand.

The hostages behind Colios and Daena moaned and writhed. They were tied up, mouths duct-taped, like Philly had been. Colios pushed his prisoners forward, and they fell to the ground with loud thuds.

Their identical eyes were wide with fear and their similar masses of mahogany curls were soaked in sweat. *Twins.* The same ones plastered over the news as the missing victims of Nesselande Beach. Bryan and Patrick Kromoredjo.

"Colios..." Daena continued.

She said no more than that, but apparently, nothing had to be said. The flares in Colios' eyes rekindled, but his ashen lips tightened into a grimace, much to Naila's surprise. As if he didn't particularly enjoy what was to come.

Colios unsheathed a crystalline, hollow dagger from the broad belt around his tabard. It came alight, flaming tendrils moving around its edge.

Naila jerked back, but Colios didn't head for them. Instead, he stooped over Bryan and Patrick, who squirmed like worms in a can.

"Feel honored. Your sacrifice fuels the winds of fate," said Colios.

The cloth stuffed in Bryan's mouth fell away. He glared at Colios and barked a selection of choice swear words.

Colios thrust the dagger into Bryan's heart with one swift movement. Blood spattered on his midnight cloak and all over the concrete floor.

A metallic tang spread through the basement; the same nauseating scent that made Naila avoid anything to do with hospitals with a wide berth.

Bryan's heart pulsed his blood straight into the center of the dagger. With every heartbeat, his skin dried and crumpled, until nothing more than remains akin to a mummy were left.

The dagger's flames morphed from azure to royal purple to ruby until they were no more. At the top of the hilt, a single crimson crystal appeared.

Shiny, perfect, the proceeds of blood.

An ear-deafening scream echoed in the room. It was only when Philly pressed his fingers into her upper arms, she realized that scream was hers.

"Naila, get a hold of yourself. Do *not* show weakness before your enemy." Philly shook her again, and Naila nodded with a sob. By the time she forced her breathing to calm, Patrick lay dead on the floor...

And Daena hovered over *them*.

The woman pressed the tip of her dagger into the softness beneath Philly's Adam's apple. A drop of blood welled up and slid down his snow-white throat.

"No, please don't," Naila cried.

"Rise. Both of you."

Naila's hands trembled around Philly's good arm. Her eyes never left the murderous stranger or the accursed dagger threatening her friend.

Outside, the neighborhood clock tinkled. Once, twice, until it struck twelve. Happy eighteenth birthday to her.

"It is time," Daena said, her voice devoid of any emotion. "Open the gate."

The gate?

Colios sauntered toward the spiral carved in the wall. Within its center were two oval scratches, illuminated by the moon shining through the window, the perfect fit for his newly created blood crystals.

As soon as he pushed them within those crevices, the spiral shifted into a moving swirl. Faster and faster it spiraled until the center of the wall exploded into... nothingness.

It was literally nothing.

Just a swirling black hole in the middle of the basement, burning spiral markings onto the floor. The very same markings that had been burned into the sands of Nesselande Beach.

Naila whimpered. "What is that thing?"

Philly's mouth hardened. Daena pressed her dagger into his skin in a silent warning. "It's a portal through the stars... a road that leads to another world."

"Which world?" Naila whispered.

Philly's eyes met hers; an unreadable look hid within their depths. "The one that dreams and nightmares are made of."

That did *not* sound reassuring.

Without warning, Philly pushed Naila behind him, standing firmly between her and Daena and Colios, his features scrunched into a frightening scowl, as he evaded Daena's dagger.

Colios twirled his two scimitars in his hands, a determined expression etched on his scar-ridden face. The swords blazed into a blue inferno, as did his eyes.

Right before the two collided, Philly moved lightning fast to the side and shifted behind Colios. He kicked the colossal fellow toward Daena.

The woman, however, jumped before he hit her.

Colios crashed onto the concrete with a loud bang. If any neighbors were at home, they had no doubt heard the ruckus.

Naila clutched her necklace. Where did Philly learn to fight like that? She glanced about the basement for anything that might aid her friend.

Philly didn't stop. He threw himself at Daena. The woman's dagger flew into the air and clattered on the ground next to them.

"If you want her, you'll have to get through me."

"If you insist." Colios sharpened the edges of his blades against one another. "If it is a fight you want, it is one you will receive."

The crash hadn't put a scratch on Colios. He cracked his knuckles and brushed off some dust, as if plummeting into stone didn't at least break a bone or two.

Colios spat out a phlegm of blood. Red like Naila's. Somehow, this surprised her even more than him being alive after the crash. It made him seem oddly human...

Naila's gaze flicked to Colios, to Philly wrestling with Daena, to the dagger lying upon the floor. She darted to the weapon.

Before her mind came up with a plan, her hands took the lead, pressing the blade to Daena's throat. The same way the woman had done to Philly.

"Drop it," Colios ordered.

His swords pointed at Philly's back.

"Don't listen to him. Do it, Naila," Philly said, his eyes pleading with her. "Forget me and get out of here."

Naila's lip quivered. "What are you saying?"

"Do it, damn it. Now," Philly cried out.

"Do you want to die so badly?" Colios sneered. "There is no glory awaiting you in the afterlife."

"I do not care what happens to me. My only goal in life is to keep her safe."

The dagger trembled in Naila's hand. The thought of taking a life made her sick to her very core, even if it meant saving her own. And she knew full well if she killed Daena, Colios would kill Philly.

"Never hesitate," Philly whispered, but defeat laced his voice. He knew she'd never sacrifice friend or foe to save her own skin. "Even if it's someone you love. Even if it's me."

Colios grabbed Philly roughly by the neck and pulled him off Daena.

Naila still held the blade in her hands, still held it to her enemy's neck.

Daena studied her with a calculating gaze. "We mean no harm," she finally said, the harshness in her voice turning sweeter than sugar. She opened her palms in a peaceful gesture. Braided black metal twirled around her hands, the fingertips ending in metal claws. "If you do as we say, he shall live."

Naila's tear-filled eyes flickered to Philly in question. Philly shook his head and mouthed, *no.*

Her hands grew shakier. What was she to do?

Sirens blared in the distance, getting louder and louder with every second. Sure enough, alternating blue and red lights flashed outside.

Daena pinned Naila with a determined look. She slapped the dagger out of Naila's hand. Naila yelped.

"Daena, to the portal," Colios barked.

Everything went by in a flash. Daena jumped up like a graceful cat on the hunt. She grabbed Naila's arm and pushed her to the portal, whilst Colios seized a struggling Philly.

Daena murmured an incantation in a long-dead language, the words equal parts musical and haunting.

In the middle of the room, the sphere beat with the rhythm of a soundless heart, the surrounding air vibrating, reminiscent of the heated wind in an Arabian desert; the inside ever a space devoid of light... like the dark behind the stars.

So cold, so empty.

An endless night.

The beating sped up, faster and faster until Naila found she couldn't take her eyes off it. Her mind screamed to get away, but the portal's hold on her body was too great. This is how Proserpina must have felt when she was seduced by pomegranate seeds in Pluto's underworld.

The noise of a struggle snapped Naila out of her reverie. Without realizing it, the space between her and the black sphere had turned to nothing. Before Naila could distance herself from it, Daena pushed her hard, and she fell into the pit of darkness.

"Naila, no!" Philly yelled.

It was too late.

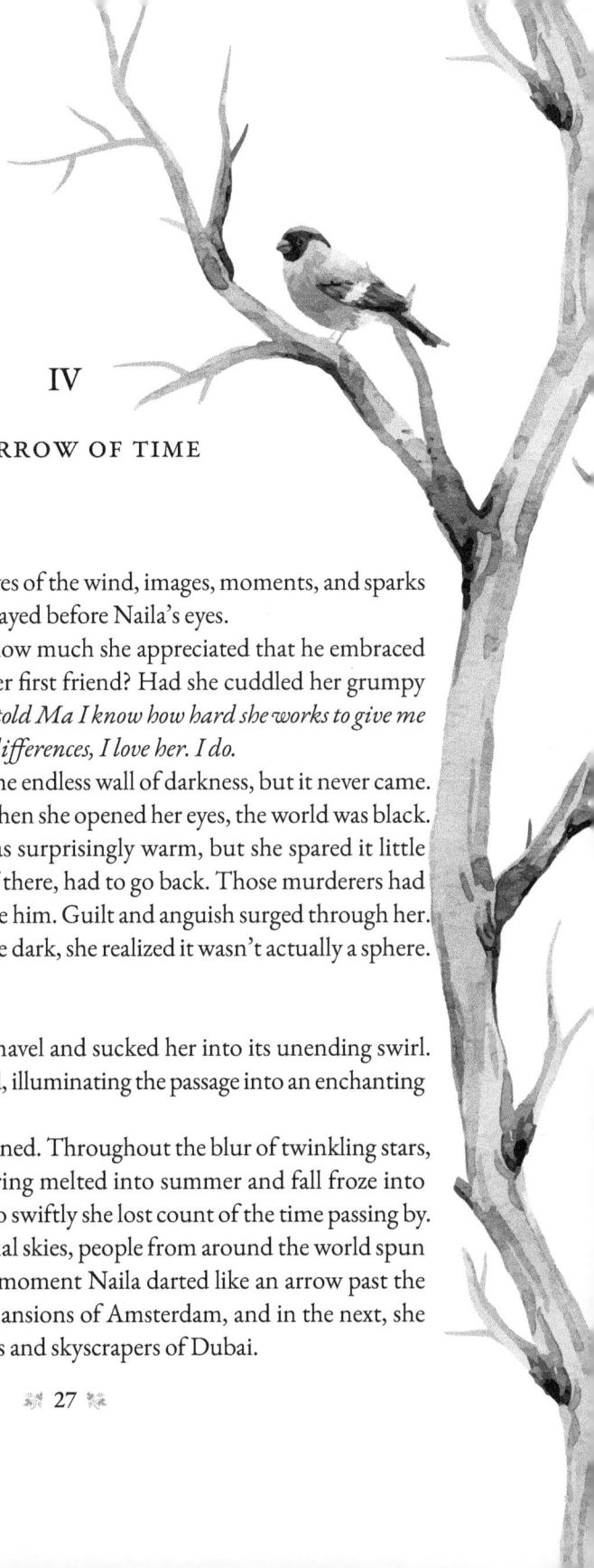

IV

AN ARROW OF TIME

LIKE THE ever-changing waves of the wind, images, moments, and sparks of memories yet to come played before Naila's eyes.

Did she ever tell Philly how much she appreciated that he embraced her into his life and became her first friend? Had she cuddled her grumpy cat Tigri enough? *I never even told Ma I know how hard she works to give me a better life. That, despite our differences, I love her. I do.*

Naila braced herself to hit the endless wall of darkness, but it never came. Nothing, she felt nothing... When she opened her eyes, the world was black.

The inside of the sphere was surprisingly warm, but she spared it little thought. She had to get out of there, had to go back. Those murderers had Philly, and she had failed to save him. Guilt and anguish surged through her.

After her eyes adjusted to the dark, she realized it wasn't actually a sphere.

It was a tunnel.

A very large one.

The darkness pulled at her navel and sucked her into its unending swirl. Brief flashes of pastels appeared, illuminating the passage into an enchanting black druse.

Then something odd happened. Throughout the blur of twinkling stars, flashes of Earth passed by. Spring melted into summer and fall froze into winter. The seasons changed so swiftly she lost count of the time passing by.

In between the fickle seasonal skies, people from around the world spun in and out of her vision. One moment Naila darted like an arrow past the canals and neo-Renaissance mansions of Amsterdam, and in the next, she weaved through the busy roads and skyscrapers of Dubai.

She tried to hold onto the wall, anything to stop its movement, but it wasn't a hard surface like she expected. In fact, when she touched a little starlight, static electricity buzzed through her, the light trying to tug her inside.

Naila withdrew her hand at once.

Her heart thumped so wildly, she was sure it would stop beating any moment from her fright. Around her, humanity grew as restless as she felt. Peaceful dining and smiling people turned into the crying and mourning of a full-blown war. Then another war started, and another, and another, and then there was light at the very end of the tunnel.

A clash was imminent, inevitable, and nothing she could do would stop it. She closed her eyes, tried to breathe away her panic. Far too soon, her journey ended.

Naila crashed onto a wintry landscape. The tunnel had spat her out and closed its gate. In its stead stood a pillar taller than a house. And snow. Quite a lot of snow. The familiar tribal spiral was chiseled near the top of the stone, its last tendrils of darkness fading into the snowy wind.

Naila's gaze darted around her, trying to make sense of her surroundings, but a thick cloud of mist obscured most of the setting. Her breathing grew shallow, hurried, erratic, leaving a lingering trail of frosty clouds. Wherever had those murderous monsters sent her?

Naila brushed away a curl that had fallen into her eyes, only to see her brown fingers turn ashen. The air was so cold it felt like swimming in a freezing ocean. The only thing that kept her from succumbing to the cold, was her unwelcome acquaintance—panic, that numbed her mind from coherent thoughts.

After minutes—or was it hours?—the mists slowly dissolved to reveal a breathtaking forest of giant trees rooted in the thick layer of snow. Naila glanced wildly about, but none made their presence known. Only she and that strange stone pillar. Through the snowy branches she caught a glimpse of the sky.

She gasped for air.

Waltzing between the twinkling stars in the night's sky, wasn't one, but two full moons.

She fell to her knees, her fingers curling around clumps of dead moss underneath the snow.

"Impossible."

Her fingers grew numb as she watched the twin moons with equal amounts of horror and fascination. Was she dreaming? She had to be... The snow-filled wind frosted the damp curls to her temples, as the bewitching scent of chrysanthemums and ice-covered pine needles hit her nostrils.

She pushed herself to her feet. With every beat of her racing heart, a familiar current leaped to her fingers. She opened and closed and opened and closed her fists. Anything to keep the gilded sparks from forming. Anything to keep the panic at bay.

She had to get a grip on herself. Had to find her friend.

"Philly?"

No answer.

Tentatively, she took her first steps in this strange new world.

The forest was unlike one she'd ever seen, not even in the countless photos of Philly's faraway ventures. The trees had trunks in the deepest cinnamons, reaching higher than even the Euromast. Naila squinted. Their branches bore flat, needlelike leaves, snuggling red cones underneath coats of ice.

The moons' rays swept over the wintry landscape, brightening the forest to the point she could make out everything as clear as if it were dawn.

She tried to rub the chill out of her quivering arms. *It's not real. It's not real. It's not real.* It just couldn't be real. This *had* to be a dream. She dug her nails into her forearm until they drew pain and blood.

The sight before her never changed.

"Philly? Please," she sniveled.

Naila edged around the pillar, her boots crunching in the snow. Her fingers grazed the massive coldness of the stone. Philly was trapped on the other side with Colios and Daena, and she had no clue how to get there. There was nothing she could do to save him.

She gnawed on her lip. Philly had spoken the truth: that her hallucinations were no lie, that is. A sliver of triumph elated her for a flicker of a moment. She had been right! Dr. Peeters and her mother had passed off an absurd reality as an illusion. But the cold soon brought her back to the present. To think she thought her life had ended with RIDA's rejection. How trivial it seemed but hours later.

What do I do now?

Naila sized up the pillar.

She couldn't climb the stone until she reached the spiral's carvings and didn't know how the gate worked. She wiggled her numb toes in her shoes. It was also far too cold to stay in the forest.

She glanced at the giant trees around her. There was no choice. She would have to find her way out of the woods. Look for something that could keep her warm.

The faintest hint of a sound hissed through the winds.

She froze in her tracks.

Between the rustling of leaves, snow crisped. Something headed her way. Every muscle in her body tensed. She let out a breath in relief when a fluffy white bunny inched its way out of a snow-covered bush. Naila smiled at the bunny as it cocked its head curiously. It was a tiny little thing with big lavender eyes.

The bunny's ears pricked up, and it leaped back into the bushes. The crunching of snow grew louder and louder. Far in the distance, a solitary figure appeared on a horse, with dozens of what seemed to be dogs following closely.

Naila jumped up and down, smiling widely, before swallowing back a cry for help. Relief warred with apprehension. She had thought herself to be alone in this world, but now that she wasn't, the question arose: who would she meet, friend or foe?

Her joy made way for dread as the figure neared. The person wore the same dark robes as Daena and Colios, and underneath the hood, she glimpsed that very same scarred grayish skin.

The horse was in even worse shape, with milky eyes burning with familiar flames and skin like leather drawn tight over the outline of its bones. Its hooves burned in the same ice-blue flames as its eyes.

Naila trotted backward until her back hit the cold of the pillar. Painful goosebumps covered every inch of her body as she took in the creatures following the stranger. They weren't dogs. Far from it. Bigger than wolves, with fur the color of snow, these canines had ruby eyes and large, saber-shaped fangs with lips too thin to cover their teeth.

The stranger murmured something incomprehensible. It was a woman, and she spoke in the same foreign tongue as Daena and Colios. One of the creatures howled, its cry a mixture of a wolf's deep yowl and a hyena's mocking whine.

Naila's forehead grew heated—a faint tingle in the two little marks. *Odd.* The flames usually pricked angrily at her fingers when they wanted out, never at her scars. The forest scent that hung in the air burned until a faint sweetness lingered. The scent of her flames, of her hallucinations. Or were they?

"You are Stormhold?" the woman tried again. The same language, and again, Naila understood every word.

"No, I'm not!"

Why did they keep mistaking her for this Stormhold person?

Naila shook her head. Whoever this person was, she was no doubt an ally of Daena and Colios. With her back pressed against the stone, she inched farther away from the stranger.

"Do not run or I'll send my ice-crawlers after you," the woman warned.

Slowly but surely, the moons revealed the woman's face until Naila's bright, brown gaze met the stranger's flaming one. A moment passed without either talking.

Then Naila dashed into the forest.

"*Ut ahsyl feylana*!" the woman screeched. *Get the girl.*

The ice-crawlers howled, their paws crunching in the snow, oh so close behind her. Naila's heart thundered. Every nerve in her body was on full alert. Her boots sank into the snow, slowing her flight through the ancient trees. She knew she could not outrun those creatures, but she would die trying.

Something stirred inside her, a familiar tingle she dreaded, yet for the first time welcomed. It burned through her fingers, ignited in her limbs, her ears, her eyes. Her vision turned twice as sharp, as if someone had pulled open a curtain. She could see it all. The fine lines in the bark of the trees, a curious silver owl hidden behind icy branches… and a city!

A city atop a mountain far in the distance.

Naila glanced back and realized the distance between her and the ice-crawlers widened. They snapped their jaws in anger, their crimson eyes glowing with ferocity. Their frothy gums emphasized their sharp fangs even more. She swung her head back to the hill ahead.

Maybe, just maybe, she could make it.

Her legs felt powerful. Somehow, even the uneven snowy ground could not obstruct her flight. She heard better, too, heard the nuances in the noises the ice-crawlers' paws made upon the snow. Could make out the difference in their sizes just by those sounds. Faster and faster, Naila went, but so did the canines.

An ice-crawler appeared through the trees to Naila's side. The beast jumped, his jaws foaming. It missed her by a hair's breadth. She had to change her course when yet another ice-crawler surprised her from the sky-high tree branches. The ice-crawlers knew these grounds like the back of their sharp-clawed paws.

Little beads of sweat formed on Naila's temples as the growling and snapping of the ice-crawlers' mandibles grew louder. To make matters worse, she could also hear the dampened clip-clops of hooves. They were cornering her, and there was nothing she could do about it.

"Halt," the woman said. "And I'll rein in my ice-crawlers. This is your last warning."

Last warning, *right*.

The top of the hill was so near Naila could almost smell it. She could already see the outline of a turquoise lake, its calm surface reflecting the ever-watching twin moons. A path of snow-tipped mountains led from the lake to the mountain with the city. If she could make it to the lake, she had a good chance of shaking her pursuers off. The possibility of freezing to death in the no doubt ice-cold water was a risk she'd just have to take.

Naila yelped as a sharp pain shot through her ankle.

She tried to tug her ankle back, but an ice-crawler clenched it in its jaw, its razor-sharp fangs sinking deeper into her flesh. Naila fell on the wintry forest floor. She scrabbled around her and threw snow at the ice-crawler. It did no good. In fact, the rest of the ice-crawlers would be there any moment. Fear seized her. She did not want to die.

Naila's hand stumbled upon a rock.

Determined to get away from the creature, she gave the flames free rein. Heat flooded her nerve ends, and her fingers... They burned with golden flames. Free, at last.

The stone sizzled in her hand, the flames licking at its surface. She felt its core of rock as if it were a part of her, willing it to mold to her liking. Needle-sharp spikes burst out of its surface. With a cry, Naila threw the stone at the ice-crawler.

It hit its mark with a deafening crack.

The ice-crawler whined before dropping dead. The heated needles had scorched half of its face away. Pieces of bloodied brain sullied the surrounding snow.

Naila tried to crawl upright, but the pain in her injured ankle was too great. "No," she groaned.

Her jumpsuit turned dark and wet with blood. Acid burned in her throat when she saw the ripped flesh of her ankle. Her eyes flicked to another ice-crawler in mid-air, ready to pounce. She held her breath as she looked death in its eyes. It was over for her.

The hit never came.

With a thud, the beast fell before her, the sight leaving its red eyes forever. Another ice-crawler followed suit. Embedded in the back of each of their heads was a single dagger with a black and crimson hilt. Tendrils of dark flames encased the daggers and evaporated in the icy wind.

Naila's head shot up in surprise.

Hidden between the thick tree trunks, far from the woman, was a great black stallion with eyes of the devil. A man sat upon the formidable animal, but Naila couldn't see his features, only his eyes that flashed darker than ebony. His dark, hooded cloak hid the rest of his face, but he was not like the woman, for his tan skin bore no scars.

The man unsheathed more daggers from beneath his cloak. Naila snapped out of her dreamlike reverie as she realized why. The other ice-crawlers were inches from throwing themselves upon her.

"*T'ilaa ni gloria*!" a feminine battle cry suddenly echoed behind her.

An arrow wrapped in teal flames swished through the air and entered an ice-crawler's skull between the eyes. The unknown woman landed on her boots between Naila and the dead ice-crawler. She was dressed in olive leathers, vines of black metal curling around her limbs and gloves. Her cloak floated in the freezing wind, obscuring her face from Naila's view.

Fast and graceful as a cat, the newcomer nocked another flaming arrow to her bow. One after another, she let arrows loose on the ice-crawlers, killing them swiftly and mercilessly. Her movements were precise, confident, unwavering. The ice-crawlers stood no chance.

The woman on the horse halted in the distance, taking shelter between the giant trees. Her features scrunched in fury as she watched the scene unfold.

When all the ice-crawlers lay dead around them, the girl, at last, pointed an arrow toward Naila's attacker. The woman on the horse, however, was long gone. Only a trail of melting hoofprints in the snow betrayed her earlier presence. Naila glanced toward the trees, but the man who saved her had disappeared too.

How strange.

The flames engulfing her savior's arrow extinguished into nothing. She turned around, the hood of her cloak slipping off in the process. Wild locks the color of burning whiskey were unleashed from the cloak, and a pair of fiery eyes stared straight at Naila.

Naila was too stunned for words, for she had never seen someone quite like the woman. Not that she was particularly beautiful, but the way she carried herself with the elegance of a queen and the sparkle in her onyx eyes hinted at a slyness a fox would envy. She couldn't place her background. Perhaps a unique mixture of East-Asian with some Caucasian, if any such races existed in this world.

Time crawled by without either uttering a word, until finally, the young woman broke the silence.

"Who are you, and why does a shadowreaper want you dead?"

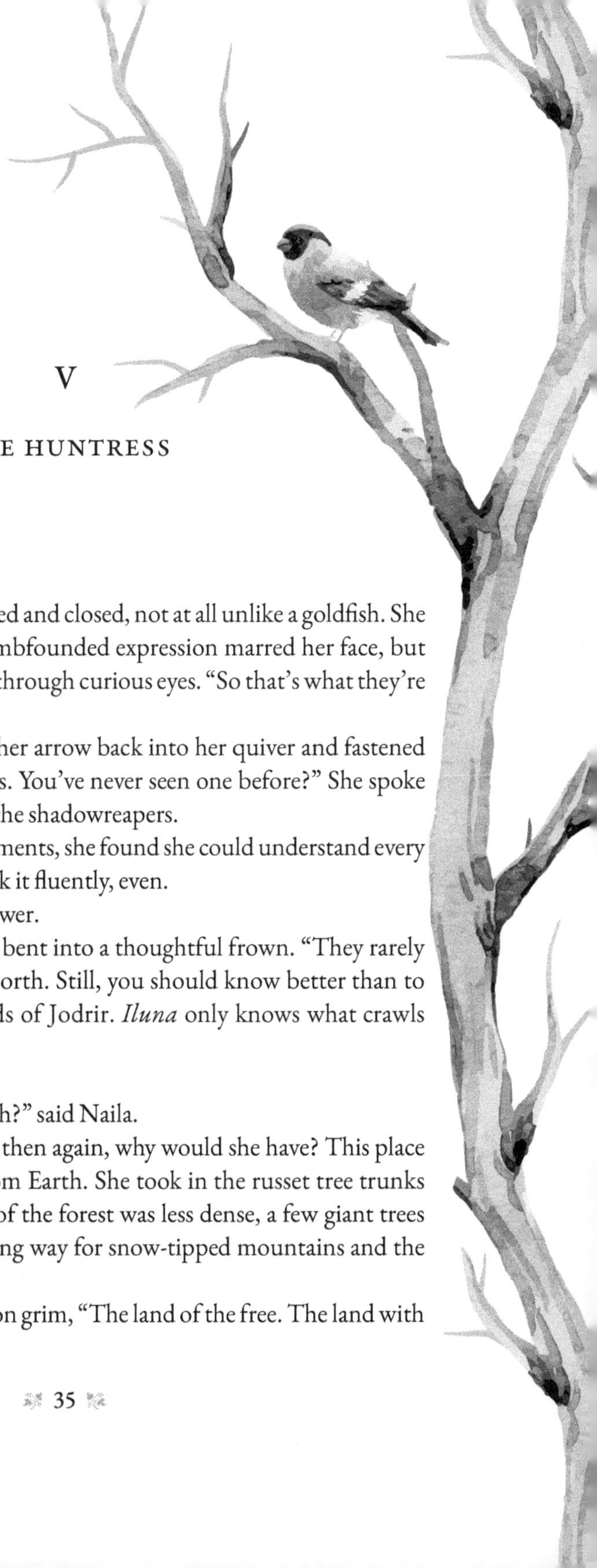

V

THE HUNTRESS

"S*HADOWREAPER*?"

Naila's mouth opened and closed, not at all unlike a goldfish. She was quite certain a dumbfounded expression marred her face, but the stranger only watched her through curious eyes. "So that's what they're called."

The young woman shoved her arrow back into her quiver and fastened her jade bow to her back. "Yus. You've never seen one before?" She spoke the same melodic language as the shadowreapers.

While it took her several moments, she found she could understand every musical word like before. Speak it fluently, even.

Naila shook her head in answer.

The girl's auburn eyebrows bent into a thoughtful frown. "They rarely show themselves so high up north. Still, you should know better than to wander through the redwoods of Jodrir. *Iluna* only knows what crawls within these woods."

Iluna... Two of moons.

"The redwoods of Jodrir, huh?" said Naila.

She'd never heard of it. But then again, why would she have? This place was likely worlds removed from Earth. She took in the russet tree trunks surrounding them. This part of the forest was less dense, a few giant trees scattered here and there, making way for snow-tipped mountains and the cerulean lake below.

The girl added, her expression grim, "The land of the free. The land with no laws."

Not what she wanted to hear.

"If it's so dangerous, why are you out here by yourself?"

The young woman narrowed her eyes ever so slightly as if trying to assess what she meant by those words. Finally, she shrugged. "Out hunting."

Naila attempted to push herself off the snowy ground, but an excruciating pain shot through her ankle. "Oh, fudge." The bloody patch on the leg of her jumpsuit grew larger. This couldn't be a hallucination. The pain was very much real.

The stranger glanced at Naila's bloodied leg. She opened her mouth as if to speak, but then her dark gaze rested upon Naila's forehead for the first time. "By the stars, you're a *nergayla*?"

"Nergayla? For heaven's sake, no," said Naila.

First, the jabbering about Stormhold, and now this talk of being a nergayla? Naila wanted no part of it. No, sir, she refused. Besides, she couldn't find it in herself to consider those allegations, not with the anguish of her leg and Philly's unknown state.

"Oh, wow," said the huntress. Her boots crunched into the snow as she inched closer to Naila. Her eyes glazed with something akin to wonder—or was it reverie?—and her hand reached out to Naila.

Unease knotted within Naila's stomach, whilst her heart rate sped up a few beats. Suddenly, she found herself afraid. She didn't know this person. For all she knew, this stranger was worse than Colios, Daena, and that other nasty woman.

"I thought nergaylas were only born every hundred winters," the huntress whispered. Then her hand dropped, and her eyebrows furrowed. "Where are you from? No šar nor hierodula priestess would let a nergayla roam a'free unchaperoned. Did you"—the huntress's eyes narrowed, as she stepped forward—"did you escape from the Ice Šar's claws?"

"Stay back," Naila warned.

"Calm down, I'm not going to hurt you."

"And I'm supposed to trust you?"

The huntress arched her brow. "Well, I did save your arse."

Touché.

"Thank you for that." Relief uncoiled the taut muscles of Naila's shoulders. "But look, I'm not who you think I am. I'm not this Stormhold or a nergayla or whatever fancy word suits your needs... There's been a mistake. A big one," said Naila, exasperation taking hold of her. "I'm not from here. Those shadowreapers hurt my friend and abducted me from another world! I need to get back, please."

"What do you mean by shadowreaper*s*? There are more roaming around?" The huntress glanced back to the trees; her fingers already wrapped around another arrow in her bronze quiver.

"Uh, yes. Two of them pushed me through some portal. Its gate is in that pillar over there." Naila pointed at the stone barely visible between the trees. A snowflake fluttered from the sky and landed on the tip of her brown button nose. Now that her flight had come to a stop, the cold crept up with a quick lashing. She rubbed her arms but nevertheless shivered.

The huntress threw her cloak at Naila. She herself wore an embroidered sheepskin tunic over olive leathers. A broad belt encased her waist. Naila offered her a grateful smile and quickly wrapped herself in the cloak's softness. It was surprisingly warm for its thickness but brought her little comfort. Her ankle ached and throbbed.

"You're lucky I was out hunting today. Very few dare to enter the redwoods." The huntress stuck out a gloved hand, the other hand resting on her hip, her eyes never leaving the markings on Naila's forehead. "That leg of yours does not look good. Why aren't you healing it?"

Naila didn't take the offered hand.

"And how am I supposed to do that?"

The eyes of the huntress widened in surprise. "You're a nergayla. It's what you do," she said in a disbelieving voice.

Naila sighed. "I already told you I'm not. My classmates would have a good laugh if they heard you talk."

The woman put her hands on her hips, her thick fiery locks fluttering in the frosty wind. "Then how did you get the mark of Ishtar?"

Naila blinked several times before comprehension dawned on her. She brushed a finger over the little diamond-and-crescent moon on her forehead. Her scars... The mark of Ishtar? So that's what had caught the attention of these strangers.

She waved the young woman's remark away. "They're just old scars from an accident." But even as she spoke, she doubted the truth of those words. How many sleepless nights had she anguished over the source of all her trouble? Those scars that had made her victim to the class's torment, that had marked her as the neighborhood's black sheep. A few times it had even gotten her mother into trouble when suspicious new teachers questioned the story behind their origin.

The woman pursed her lips. Naila could tell she didn't believe her words either, but to her relief, she dropped the subject.

"Well, if you can't heal yourself, then we have to get you to Havenmor, and fast. An ice-crawler's bite is venomous."

Venomous? Great. Just her luck.

The huntress stuck out her hand again, and this time, Naila took it. She squeezed her eyes shut when she got to her feet. Her ankle hurt so much, flickers of light splattered across her vision. Her ragged panting left small clouds in the air. Any moment now she would faint.

As if on cue, the young woman wrapped an arm around her, and she gratefully leaned against her petite, but strong form.

"Thanks," Naila said. The woman helped her climb down the hill to the lake. Step by step, ever so slowly. A little wooden boat was chained to the surface below. "I'm Naila, by the way."

"The name's Onyx."

Onyx, just like her eyes... A fitting name.

Before she could respond, snow crunched within the redwoods, followed by a parliament of snow owls hooting in alarm and taking flight from out of the snowy branches. The petrifying howls of ice-crawlers echoed anew in the distance, sending spikes of fear down Naila's spine.

"Suzano's balls," Onyx mumbled through clenched teeth as they hurried across the frosted path that led to the boat.

She did her best to keep up with Onyx's pace, but her aching leg made her stumble twice. When they finally reached the shore, one particular ice-crawler sounded so near she froze in fear. When she glanced over her shoulder and no ice-crawler was yet in sight, Naila let out a sob in relief. The echoing redwoods must have made them seem far nearer than they actually were.

The little boat drifting at the shore had a long yard mounted at an angle to its mast, and a wooden belly that ended in high curves. The tip of the mast was broken, and a thick layer of snow covered the inside of the vessel. Naila climbed into the boat. When she brushed some of the snow off the bottom, she found the wood was rotten.

She raised a brow at Onyx. "This is your boat?"

"*Lai*, we're borrowing it." Onyx winked as she cut the ropes around the sail to let it loose. "My boat is anchored somewhere else, but that's not an option now." She glanced at Naila's ankle with a meaningful look.

Naila did a quick prayer the little boat wouldn't sink. Winter swimming was not her forte.

The bone-chilling howls of the ice-crawlers crept closer and closer. She fumbled with the compass pendant between trembling fingers. How was the lake supposed to stop those beasts? Through the haze of her fear and her pain, she noticed too late that Onyx didn't climb into the boat. She turned to face the huntress but found her missing.

The clock ticked on, and still no sign of Onyx. Yet with every passing moment, the ice-crawlers drew closer. She heard it in their footsteps echoing in the snow, in the silencing of the forest... Felt it in the cold chilling her bones.

She inched to the edge of the boat when Onyx finally appeared at the top of the hill. She dragged behind her the carcass of a deer. An earlier catch, mayhap, from before she met with Naila.

Her eyes widened in disbelief. The huntress was mad. Who, in whatever world, thought about food when they were being chased by monsters?

Onyx dragged the deer down the hill, trails of blood painting a crimson road in the pristine snow. At last, the huntress threw her prey into the lake. The loud splash broke the silence between the ice-crawlers' howls. Onyx glided down the hill and waded back to their boat.

"What the—" Naila whisper-yelled.

"Hush," Onyx said, her eyebrows scrunched in concentration as she pushed the boat into the water.

A pack of ice-crawlers appeared at the top of the hill, rushing to where the deer floated in the water. Growls gurgled in their jaws as they scanned the lake with their crimson eyes.

Onyx climbed into the boat and set sail but moments before the beasts finally noticed them, a strong, wintry wind thrust the boat from the shore before the ice-crawlers reached it.

Five shadowreapers appeared atop the hill, their dark robes fluttering in the air, and their black, half-dead-looking horses whinnying. The woman from the redwoods was among them.

Naila's throat turned dry as the ice-crawlers let out angry snarls, their jaws snapping viciously. But neither shadowreapers nor ice-crawlers attempted to enter the lake.

Onyx steered the boat to the other side of the lake, where snow-covered pine trees grew at the feet of the mountains, and a narrow canal led to the faraway city. A drop of sweat dampened Onyx's temple. She realized Onyx was nervous.

Naila nibbled on the inside of her cheek and finally blurted out, "Why aren't they following us?"

"Shhh." Onyx glared and immediately turned back to her task. She didn't meet Naila's eyes when she whispered her next words. "There's an evil in these waters even shadowreapers fear."

For several moments, a pregnant silence reigned.

Without warning, the water splashed near the deer, and something—too quick for Naila to see—dragged the carcass into the depths of the lake. The ice-crawlers whined and hurried up the hills with their short tails between their legs.

The woman gave Naila a long, hard stare, and then she and the other shadowreapers also left the shore.

Naila tugged the cloak over her trembling frame. She didn't dare move, didn't dare speak. Her heart thudded painfully in her throat and all she could do was hope they would reach the mountain city quickly.

"Let's hope that deer is enough to satiate it," Onyx mumbled softly.

Naila didn't ask who, or what, Onyx referred to.

"Pity about the meat. It took me well over a bell to catch it."

Naila made no reply. Contrary to most Surinamese people, and much to her mother's surprise, she was a vegetarian; and proudly so, mind you. No *moksi meti*, meat-filled *pom* and *pastei* for her.

Onyx steered the boat gently, but it still etched a curtain of ripples upon the water's surface. In the distance, where the deer had been attacked, water bubbled. For a wrinkle in time, Naila thought those bubbles shifted in their direction. But then a wave brushed them away and no new bubbles appeared, leaving no hint of whatever lurked in the depths of the water.

It was only after they left the lake, through a narrow river between the mountains, that Naila dared let out a sigh in relief. The soft rays from Iluna, the twin moons, caressed the snow-tipped mountains until they shined like pearls. The cerulean water was a stark contrast to the dazzling white of the formidable peaks. They had long since left behind the redwoods. Now, pine trees dotted the slopes of the mountains.

Naila's ebony curls danced with the winds, blowing into her mouth and covering her eyes. She reached to the back of her head but came up empty. In all the hurry she had lost her precious hair clip. Pain skewered her heart. Her ma, ever the artist, had spent many a day to make the lush petals look like a real *fayalobi* flower.

The loss made Naila feel even farther from home.

"Greykeep mountains." Onyx interrupted her sorrowful thoughts. She gestured ahead.

On both sides of the waterway, colossal statues were carved into the mountains. Larger-than-life men draped in majestic lamellar armor over long-sleeved tunics and snug pantaloons, their garments reminiscent of a past long gone. Ornate conical helmets sat firmly above their grim-looking faces. The statues seemed to look straight at Naila, their eyes all-seeing, hands clutching menacingly around the hilts of their scimitars, the sharp tips resting securely between their boots.

"I've sailed this path many times, but every time I still get shivers like it's the first time." Onyx smiled; her eyes glazed with a faraway look.

"Who are they?" Naila shivered and tugged herself more tightly into Onyx's coat, although she didn't know whether her response was from the cold, the pain, or the sight before her.

"Suzano's twelve... The first šars of Lemuria."

Ah, emperors.

"They seem menacing." She, too, eyed them in wonder.

"Menacing? No, they're legends! Their descendants though..." Onyx pulled a face.

She eyed Onyx curiously. "You're not a fan of the current šars?"

"I suppose some are passable," Onyx said. "The lands are torn apart by their wars."

"Let me guess, for riches?"

"Riches? No, for something šars crave even more: immortality."

Naila sucked in a breath. "Is such a thing possible?"

"Not in the physical sense... well at least not for the people." The huntress shifted uneasily in her seat. "It's immortal fame they're after. To have your name carved in the sky, like the Legends." Onyx shot her a peculiar look. "You're really not from around here, are you? Exactly where is this home of yours?"

"Somewhere up there," Naila pointed to the sky with longing. Rigel, the brightest star in Orion, shined brightly. "A world far away, hidden somewhere between the stars."

"Another world, you say?" Onyx's eyes twinkled with a hint of curiosity. She adjusted the sail to catch more wind. "What's it like? Your home I mean."

Naila closed her eyes, the poignant visions of Rotterdam shaping on her retinas. "It's really the most un-Dutch city in Holland, the country I live in, but I think it has a charm few cities manage to achieve. Its center, which told tales of a medieval time long gone, got cut down like weeds in our Second World War. But, you know, out of those snipped branches a city blossomed, nostalgic of a future yet to come."

She reopened her eyes, ignoring the pain in her ankle. "Ma and I moved there from Suriname when I was an infant. I think Rotterdam is the kind of place where you can move from all over the world and still build a community as if you've lived there your whole life. You could easily call it home..."

"Yet you've never felt like you belonged," Onyx said knowingly.

Naila nuzzled on her lip but made no reply.

"Lotterdam," Onyx uttered the word with care, her mouth opening like a fish as if trying to test the word out.

Naila bit back a smile. It was funny how Onyx could be a fierce huntress one moment and a cinnamon bun the next.

"*R*otterdam."

"Never heard of it, and the scribes made me study every detail in the maps of Lemuria."

"Lemuria... You said that name before. Is that what your world is called?"

"*Yana*, we call our world the lands of Lemuria—"

"The lands of the everlasting sun," Naila finished. "It's a beautiful name."

Onyx smiled, pride filling her features. "It is. The world is enormous, but nothing of treasure exists outside the lands. The Seven Seas, the Wicked Oceans, even The Lost World are unlivable to us, Lemai. Only the most vicious beasts stroll around there." The wind blew Onyx's bushy auburn locks around her tan face. "If you're not from here," Onyx continued, her dark eyes focused on the waves ahead, "Then how come you speak our language, Tierratongo, fluently?"

"Something you and I both want to know."

Naila's eyes rested upon the huntress's petite but strong frame. So different she was. The unblemished leathers fit her like a glove. Around Onyx's limbs, black metal, the very same Naila had seen around Daena's fingers, curled into countless tribal flowers. Whoever Onyx was, she didn't live in poverty.

"Why did you save me?" Naila whispered as she thrust her chilly hands back into the cloak.

"Shadowreapers roam about, raiding villages to harvest slaves for the Shadow Šar. I thought you were a runaway."

The blood in Naila's veins froze. "What did you just say?"

"A slave. They don't have those in your world?"

Naila blinked but said no word. To which nightmare had these shadowreapers taken her?

"And you... And you just wander around the redwoods, saving slaves?"

For a while Onyx said nothing as they moved through the last of the mountain statues. "I'm looking for someone. In the land of the free, whispers go about without restraint." Her smile didn't reach her eyes. "But that's a tale for another day." Onyx's eyes shifted back to Naila's scars. "You know, in Havenmor, you'll find *some* will be very interested to meet you."

She shivered, but not from the cold. Her scars meant something to these people. When her ankle no longer hurt as much, she'd definitely have to find out more. "Well, I hope they'll at least help me with my ankle first."

They passed the rest of the trip in silence, each left to their own thoughts and conclusions.

Naila was certain her nose would fall off through frostbite by the time they, at last, stumbled upon a sign of life. In between the mountains, the city she had seen before rested atop a protruding hill. Thousands of lights from stone cottages gleamed like fireflies in an evening field of daisies. They spread from the foot of the mountain at the shore, entwining all around to the hilltop, where a grand silver ziggurat proudly stood.

"Welcome to Havenmor," Onyx said as she waved in the city's direction. "The seat of His Imperial Majesty Möndör Silvanus Eseliyon, the Lion of the North, protector of the Winterlands, and Silver Šar to the Empire of Skeldor."

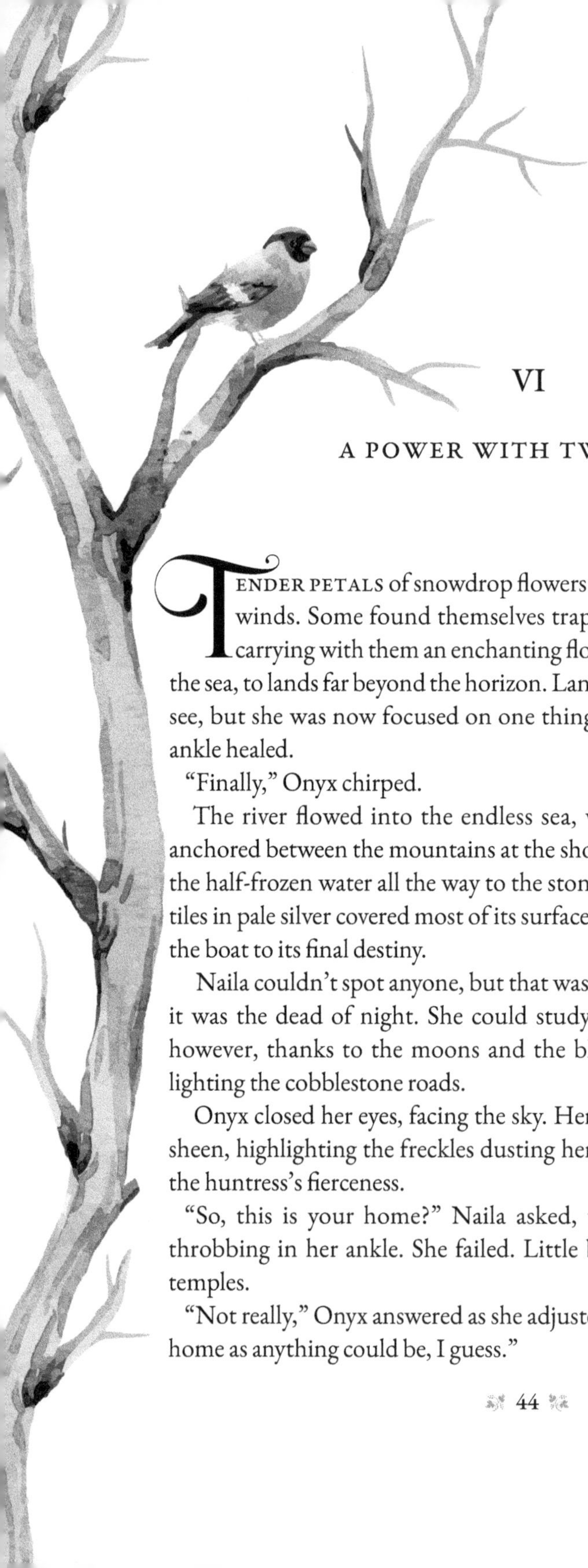

VI

A POWER WITH TWO FACES

TENDER PETALS of snowdrop flowers whisked through the midnight winds. Some found themselves trapped within Naila's sable curls, carrying with them an enchanting floral scent, whereas others fled to the sea, to lands far beyond the horizon. Lands she would normally yearn to see, but she was now focused on one thing, and one thing alone: get her ankle healed.

"Finally," Onyx chirped.

The river flowed into the endless sea, with Havenmor's vast harbor anchored between the mountains at the shore. *Iluna* illuminated a path in the half-frozen water all the way to the stones of the harbor, where mosaic tiles in pale silver covered most of its surface. Onyx's eyes lit up as she sailed the boat to its final destiny.

Naila couldn't spot anyone, but that wasn't exactly strange, considering it was the dead of night. She could study Havenmor without restraint, however, thanks to the moons and the bluish flames from the torches lighting the cobblestone roads.

Onyx closed her eyes, facing the sky. Her tanned skin glowed in Iluna's sheen, highlighting the freckles dusting her nose. It brought a softness to the huntress's fierceness.

"So, this is your home?" Naila asked, trying her best to ignore the throbbing in her ankle. She failed. Little beads of sweat formed on her temples.

"Not really," Onyx answered as she adjusted the sail, "but it's as close to a home as anything could be, I guess."

"Are you really just a huntress?"

"Why do you ask?"

"The way you killed those ice-crawlers... Your aim was flawless!"

Onyx chuckled. "The lands of Lemuria are as deadly as they are bedazzling. Learning to survive is not an option. It's a necessity."

"But you're so young."

Onyx clucked her tongue. "I'm nineteen winters old, I'm hardly the youngest, N. Besides," Onyx smiled, and a softness entered her eyes, "I had the best teacher."

N... The first time someone had given her a nickname. Well, aside from her mother. Naila wrapped her arms around herself. How she wished she'd left home on a better note. She couldn't imagine how worried her mother must be. And then there was Philippe...

"Well, I wouldn't be able to do what you did," said Naila.

"Maybe you're just selling yourself short," Onyx said thoughtfully. "Few meet an ice-crawler and live to tell their tale, yet dozens chased you and you live. I think you'll be a quick *learling*."

At once, everything came crashing back. RIDA. Shadowreapers. Ice-crawlers.

Your hallucinations are real, Naila. They. Are. Real.

Naila Stormhold.

Nergayla.

More to you than you think.

Naila clasped at her racing heart. She willed her nerves to calm, refused to allow the invisible claws of panic to get a hold of her. Not here. Not now. If only her mother or Philly were there. She recalled the words they had spoken to her many a time, that forced these anxious feelings to inevitably leave. *Breathe*. Slow and deep. In and out.

Tomorrow. She'd face this new reality tomorrow, not now; if it really proved to be real, that was... Thankfully, Onyx was oblivious to her inner struggle. How ashamed she felt over her panic attacks. They'd haunted her since the day Dr. Peeters had announced her diagnosis. But that was a lie, wasn't it? Unless *this* was a terrible dream.

When she trusted herself to speak, she whispered, "People... people believe I suffer from hallucinations. They say my flames aren't real. Am I dreaming?"

"What do *you* believe?"

A fair question.

What *did* she believe? Her whole life, she'd struggled against the label of psychosis. Struggled to accept Dr. Peeters' words that the flames she saw and felt in her fingers did not belong to the reality she lived in.

Nevertheless, something in her had always whispered those visions were true. But wasn't that what most in her position also thought? Wasn't it the very same thing others with psychosis struggled with? Naila brushed her fingers over the moonstone of her pendant. *What was the truth, and what was a lie?*

"I-I don't know."

Onyx pinched her.

"Ouch, what did you do that for?"

"If this is a dream, it wouldn't hurt, now, would it?"

Naila blinked.

"You know, you're an enigma. One moment you fight off ice-crawlers without a weapon, but then the next you're almost succumbing to a panic attack."

Her cheeks burned. So, Onyx had noticed.

Whatever.

Onyx didn't know her. Didn't know what she had suffered through.

They passed several ivory cottages with huge windows and snow-tipped cone roofs before they reached an immense gate. Positioned underneath an arched bridge, the gate stretched into the depths of the water. Its doors were covered in brass spikes and an ornate crest—a silver lion battling a snake. Strange silver symbols decorated the snowed-in bridge.

No, those weren't symbols… it was the written form of that language, Tierratongo. Written in cuneiform to be exact.

HAVENMOR

From the void we fell, to the stars we rise.

Strange.

She could read it as well as speak it. She didn't have time to linger on the oddness of the situation. Atop the bridge, several sentries watched them through narrowed eyes, the hilts of their scimitars clutched firmly. Cone helmets and lamellar armor rested atop their silver headscarves and tunics.

The suspicion melted off the sentries' faces the moment they noticed Onyx.

"Suzano's balls. We almost mistook ye for the Red Šar's whisperers," a dark-skinned sentry shouted from the bridge.

He shot Naila a pointed look.

She glanced at her jumpsuit. She supposed the dusty pink did look red in the night.

Onyx blinked then cupped her hands around her mouth and yelled back, "Why? No word from the Silver Šar? From Sil... Prince Silvanus?"

The sentry sighed and shoved his scimitar back into his scabbard.

"Well? Out with it!"

The looks on the sentries' faces were fit for a funeral.

"We lost the battle over Esyleron," another sentry said.

"No," Onyx hissed.

"The šargon barely managed to keep Daggedor from falling to that red devil too," the first sentry spat out.

"The šar... The šargon?"

The emperor... The crown prince?

"Alive."

Onyx smiled in relief.

"The šargon arrived just moments before you. We expect the rest of the imperial troops to arrive in the coming bells."

"Whatever is left of them," another sentry murmured, defeated.

The first sentry shifted toward Naila.

"Who's with ye, Onyx?"

Onyx shrugged. "Drowner."

The young man arched a brow. "Where's she from?"

"I—" Naila began.

"She lost her memory," Onyx interrupted her. "C'mon, Rezah, we're freezing over here."

The sentry waved and the giant doors cracked open, causing their little boat to bob up and down on the waves it created. Unfortunately, the movements also made the pain in Naila's ankle unbearable. It throbbed and throbbed. Her breathing became shallow as she puffed away the pain.

When dizziness overtook her, she clutched the edge of the boat until her fingers turned ashen. The world spun around her. She could see Onyx's lips moving, her face etched in worry, but her words seemed far away.

Naila retched into the water until her stomach conceded there was no more food to discard. Darkness seized her. The lights of her consciousness turned on and off.

"What is wrong with her?" A deep voice caressed her senses.

"An ice-crawler's bite." Onyx's voice.

Strong arms lifted her from the boat. A masculine, balsamic aroma not at all like Philly's.

"Well, I'll be. A nergayla!"

"I know, and I know."

Naila shifted in the stranger's protective hold.

"We must take her to the temple. She needs a nergayla's healing touch," Onyx said.

"Rezah, send for Zarqa."

"But, Your Highness, the night is late."

"Do as I say. Hurry."

The unknown man carried Naila to a place far and high. Curious whispers and Onyx's hurried murmurs trailed his steps. Her fevered dreams brought her back to a place, long ago, when Philly first taught her the map of the skies. Castor and Pollux had burned brightly that night. How they had marveled at the sight of the inseparable twins. One a man and one a god.

Her eyes fluttered open at the soft touch of hands around her ankle. An elderly woman with cloudy eyes stared back at her. Her wrinkled hands glowed with violet flames. Several other women clad in virginal caftans encircled her. Naila scanned her surroundings. She lay in a vast chamber with a high ceiling and marble walls, fortified with equally impressive pillars.

A metallic scent penetrated the chamber.

Blood. *Her* blood, to be specific.

Just the sight of it made her dizzy.

The woman inspected her ankle, her brow above her white eyebrows furrowed in concentration. The flames licked at Naila's skin, but it didn't burn. On the contrary, they were gentle and soothing. Sweat droplets trailed to her neck. Her hair, her clothes, everything was damp with blood and sweat.

"Can you help her, Zarqa?" Onyx whispered.

Naila's eyes took in the elder once more, finally seeing what, at first, she had missed. Located between Zarqa's brows was a lying crescent moon that shimmered like moonstone. Eerily similar to her very own markings.

"Hold her tight," Zarqa ordered, her voice gentle and final.

With an inferno of blue flames, she seared the torn skin of Naila's ankle. Naila's sight fractured into a thousand pieces. Her screams echoed through the chamber, reaching, no doubt, beyond the thick walls, before everything went black again.

EVER SO slowly, like ripples of sea waves kissing the beach at dawn, Naila regained consciousness. An antiseptic scent hung in the air, mingled with the crisp one of fresh linen. Naila stretched and yawned. She sniffed at the air, but it remained unchanged.

No sweet scent of Quaker Oats porridge or the minty notes of Marva-Moringa tea her mother always made her. In fact, no *kawina* song playing on her mother's vintage radio, either—the beloved Surinamese music that had found its origins when her enslaved ancestors had used songs to communicate with each other.

It took a moment before it dawned that her bed was softer than usual. Her eyes shot open. Sunbeams probed through a lancet window at the back of the chamber. She pushed herself up, every muscle in her back screaming in protest.

Several fur blankets covered her, something she was thankful for, because the room was chilly. She shrugged them off. Someone had dressed her in a linen caftan that reached her ankles. To her surprise, even her tresses were taken care of. They fell to her waist in silky coils and smelled faintly of vanilla.

She glanced around.

The chamber was small but cozy. Her bed consisted of a feather-stuffed mattress on a carved wooden frame, with a headrest in lieu of a pillow. An oil lamp was her only other companion.

A rooster cock-a-doodle-dooed outside.

She forced herself out of the bed and found a pair of sheepskin slippers awaiting her on the marble tiles.

What happened?

The memories hit her with the force of a storm. One moment shadowreapers had attacked her and Philly, and the next she got hurled out into the freezing redwoods. The icy coldness still gripped her bones. She lifted her foot and wiggled her toes. Her ankle didn't hurt anymore, nor did she have any scars.

The elderly woman had healed her with those flames. The same flames the shadowreapers and Onyx had used in their attacks. Naila spread her fingers and studied her palms. The very same flames *she* had summoned all her life...

It took her several attempts to stand firmly. Like a babe learning to walk, she staggered across the room. A little bird chirped just outside the window. She pulled it open, but immediately got hit by a cool breeze. The bird cocked its head. It was small and red-bellied.

"Well, hello, little fellow. I just had the most awful dream." Her fingers, growing stiff in the freezing wind, caressed her cold cheeks. "A dream that feels as real as my heartbeat."

She swallowed. Had she entered a full-blown psychosis? Was Dr. Peeters waiting on the other side of the door?

The bird chirped again.

"What did you say?" Naila pretended to understand. "I'm not dreaming? Why—"

Voices whispered from the other side. They were hushed, urgent, and solemn. *Onyx*?

She hesitated before tiptoeing to the door and reaching for the handle—a bronze lion with a ring in its jaws. Carved and wooden, the door was three times her five foot six inches height.

The voices grew softer. They were leaving.

Naila cracked the door open and crept into the hall.

To say it was immense was an understatement. Aside from the pillars, ivory rugs covered the marble tiles, and stone statues flanked the walls. A winged maiden with a diamond necklace, a hunter opposite a vicious scorpion, two identical crowned men... They were the Legends of the Sky. The stories she'd grown up with.

"Are you sure she's not a spy for *him*? That she's not pretending?" An elderly man murmured farther down the hall.

Naila quickly hid behind a statue.

"I saw it myself, Your Majesty," Onyx said. "Shadowreapers chased her through the redwoods."

"Shadowreapers, you say?" It was Zarqa's voice. The woman who had healed her. "That poor creature." A sunbeam speared the window, highlighting her wrinkly, ashen features that had no doubt been a luminous brown in her younger years.

Four shadows neared her statue.

"I think it's too much of a coincidence. Shadowreapers near Skeldor? Just as *he* declared war on us?" the elderly man said.

"Grandfather, for all *his* faults, I doubt he dabbles with shadowreapers. He loathes the lot," another man said. It was the same voice as that of the man who had carried her from the boat.

Onyx and Zarqa must be talking to the crown prince and his grandfather, the Silver Šar.

"Silvanus," said the šar. "Assumptions rarely lead to well thought-out roads."

"But—"

"You must think. Do not let passion cloud your vision."

"There's nothing wrong with my thinking. If it weren't for me, we would have lost Daggedor."

She peeked at them from behind the statue. Zarqa and Onyx, who had exchanged her hunting leathers for an embroidered top and loose pants that caught at her ankles, trailed behind an elderly man dressed in a silk caftan and a fur-lined robe, and what could only be the prince.

The šar's voice rose. "Your recklessness almost cost you your head. You should have reined in that foolishness."

The prince shook his head in disbelief.

Naila shifted her position to get a better view.

The prince was tall. Onyx was tall for a woman, but he towered well above her. The linen of his night-blue tunic tightened over his biceps, emphasizing his broad shoulders and narrow waist. He was surprisingly young, early twenties at most.

"Foolishness? Foolishness, you say? It's my job to protect Skeldor."

"No, that is *my* job. It is your job to stay alive and learn."

"So, you had rather we lost Daggedor to that sack of wine?"

The šar paused mid-step. "Think, *lugal*." *Think, boy*. He pressed his fingers into Silvanus's shoulders. Like with Onyx, she couldn't pinpoint the Silver Šar's background. His flaxen hair was streaked with silver, and his eyes were the color of the summer sky, but his features spoke of a mixed background. Mongolian with Russian or Scandinavian, perhaps. "If you were killed, then what would have happened? The moment I died, the empire would have gone to the Red Šar by default. *Then* we would have truly lost."

The prince shook his head. "We wouldn't be in this position in the first place if we went on the offense. He *needs* to learn he cannot bully us into submission—"

"Skeldor has and always will remain a neutral state. War must be avoided by all means."

Silas's jaw clenched. "Grandfather..."

Where the šar exuded calm authority, Silas crackled with youthful defiance. A budding flame flickering against the timeworn wind.

The šar sighed and patted the prince's cheek. "Go. See if the *feylana* is trustworthy. We must get to the bottom of her roots. What do you think, Zarqa?"

"I shall talk with the šaltana. She is a more skilled diviner than I am," said Zarqa. "But, I believe Ishtar may have blessed us. Three nergaylas in one empire..."

The šaltana. The princess. The prince's sister or, perhaps, his wife?

A faraway look entered the šar's eyes. "Let us hope you are right."

Naila trailed her markings with her fingertip. What was so special about the nergayla they thought her to be?

The prince and Onyx bowed to the šar, and he, in turn, left without another word, Zarqa following his steps.

"Well, that went well," Onyx mumbled.

But Silvanus chuckled. "You can come out now."

He turned around and stared straight at Naila. His chocolate hair reached just below his square jaw, and his eyes were the very same night-blue as his tunic. The prince was achingly beautiful. The type of man who could reach for the stars, whilst peasants like her were left behind in the shadows of his too-bright light.

She was immediately on her guard.

Onyx's eyes widened in surprise, as did Naila's.

She held in a little breath as she stepped away from the statue. She waved awkwardly and shot the two an apologetic smile.

"Uh, hi?"

"Good morning, little spy." A smirk formed on his lips.

Onyx dashed to Naila, Silvanus following at a leisurely pace. "How're you feeling?" Onyx rested the back of her hand on Naila's forehead. Her scarlet hair was a bushy mess. "You've been out of it for two nights."

Two days... No wonder her legs felt weak.

Naila peeked at the prince through her lashes. He must be a great actor because none of the feelings over the heated argument he'd had with his grandfather showed on his face.

He cleared his throat.

"Right," Onyx said. She beckoned to the prince. "Naila, this is His Imperial Highness, šargon Silvanus Cyrus Eseliyon, heir to the throne of Skeldor." To the prince she said, "This is Naila of Rotterdam."

"Well, Naila Wilhelmina Groenhart, actually." She had no idea how to address royalty, but to prevent her being rude, she mimicked what she'd seen on TV when Meghan Markle married Prince Harry, and bowed her head.

"Onyx, Onyx, why so formal?" Silvanus winked as he grasped Onyx's shoulder. "Just call me Silas."

Onyx arched a brow. Before she could say anymore, the prince took Naila's hand in his. He pressed his lips to her fingers, his eyes never leaving hers. His hair was deliciously messy as if he had run his hand through it many times.

Naila caught herself. Heat blossomed in her cheeks when she realized she was staring. It wasn't the first time she was thankful that her brown skin hid her blushes. What was she thinking? She knew men like Silas. Heard all about them in her classmates' stories. How their charming smiles disarmed your guards, and their smooth talk undid your clothes. Silas was the type of man her mother had warned her of. And she, Naila, was not the type of woman to fall into his trap.

She averted her eyes and stepped back.

Surprise *and* approval mingled upon Onyx's face, while an amused smile flickered across the prince's. He squeezed her hand lightly before letting go. "I'm glad you broke your fever, but I must say I'm confused. What did the shadowreapers want from you?"

This was her chance. She couldn't waste any more time.

"Your Highness, er, Silas, I need your help. Those shadowreapers attacked my friend and abducted me. Please, my friend could be lost in the redwoods this very moment."

Silas's face turned serious. "I already sent my men to the redwoods. There were no traces of your friend."

Her heart dropped. "The stone pillar..."

"The pillar disappeared," Onyx whispered.

Perhaps Philly was still back on Earth then. Maybe he had even managed to subdue the shadowreapers. Naila had to hold onto that. The alternative was an option she didn't want to entertain.

"If you tell us what the shadowreapers want from you, I may still be able to help," the prince urged gently.

Her fingers traced the etchings on her compass. "They called me Stormhold. I think they said some Shadow Šar wanted me."

The expressions on Silas's and Onyx's faces turned grim. To Naila's irritation, they locked eyes, holding an unsaid conversation she wasn't privy to. Then curiosity pricked her senses. What was the relationship between these two?

"Well, Stormhold is a common surname in Lemuria," Onyx contemplated.

"*What* are those shadowreapers?" Naila huffed in renewed annoyance. She refused to let these two go the way of untold secrets like her mother.

"Disrupters of peace. Elite hunter-killers who conquer in the name of the Shadow Šar, ruler over the Shadowlands." Silas spoke through gritted teeth.

"Are they... human?"

"Human?" Silas frowned.

Right. She forgot she wasn't on Earth. Despite the similar looks these people shared with humans, they didn't regard themselves as such.

"I mean like you. Er, Lemaian that is?"

"They are," Onyx said.

"Depends on your definition," said Silas. "Do you consider a blood traitor one of your own?"

He gave his arm to Naila, who, with an unexpected thrill, took it. She mentally scolded herself. Philly might still be in danger whilst she was fawning over a prince she just met, handsome though he may be.

Onyx flanked his other side, shooting him a warning look he ignored.

As he led her through the statue-filled hallway, Silas continued, "The Shadow Šar and his minions shackled their bodies to the power of the Unspokens. Now they're slaves to æther, its very existence both their elixir and their curse. They're always hungry for more, but forever tortured by less."

Naila stopped breathing, not wanting to miss a word.

"Æther?"

Both the prince and Onyx stared in surprise.

A victorious little grin crept on Onyx's face. "I told you she's not from here." She stuck her palm out and Silas grumpily handed her a crystal. To Naila she said, "Æther is the most coveted thing in all of Lemuria. A sacred fire that gifts its bearer power."

"Is that what you call those flames?" Naila whispered. Her heart thundered. She both feared and longed for an answer.

The prince unsheathed his scimitar in answer—why he carried the sword with him she didn't know, for who would want to attack him in his own empire? The hallway filled with a honeyed burn scent before Silas's blade ignited with cobalt flames. As the flames extinguished, Naila studied her own palms.

Æther. So, it had a name. The hallucinations that had haunted her... That had sparked in her fingers whenever she was upset. When she'd set that stone in the redwoods aflame to kill the ice-crawler, it had been æther. But... She'd also breathed life into flowers with those same flames.

"A power with two faces," she murmured in wonder.

Onyx and Silas locked eyes for the second time. A knowing look passed over their faces. The huntress said, "Most wielders of æther can only use it to enhance and destroy. But for a nergayla, N, æther also holds a power far nobler."

Before Onyx finished, Naila knew what she would say, and so she whispered the words herself. "The power of creation."

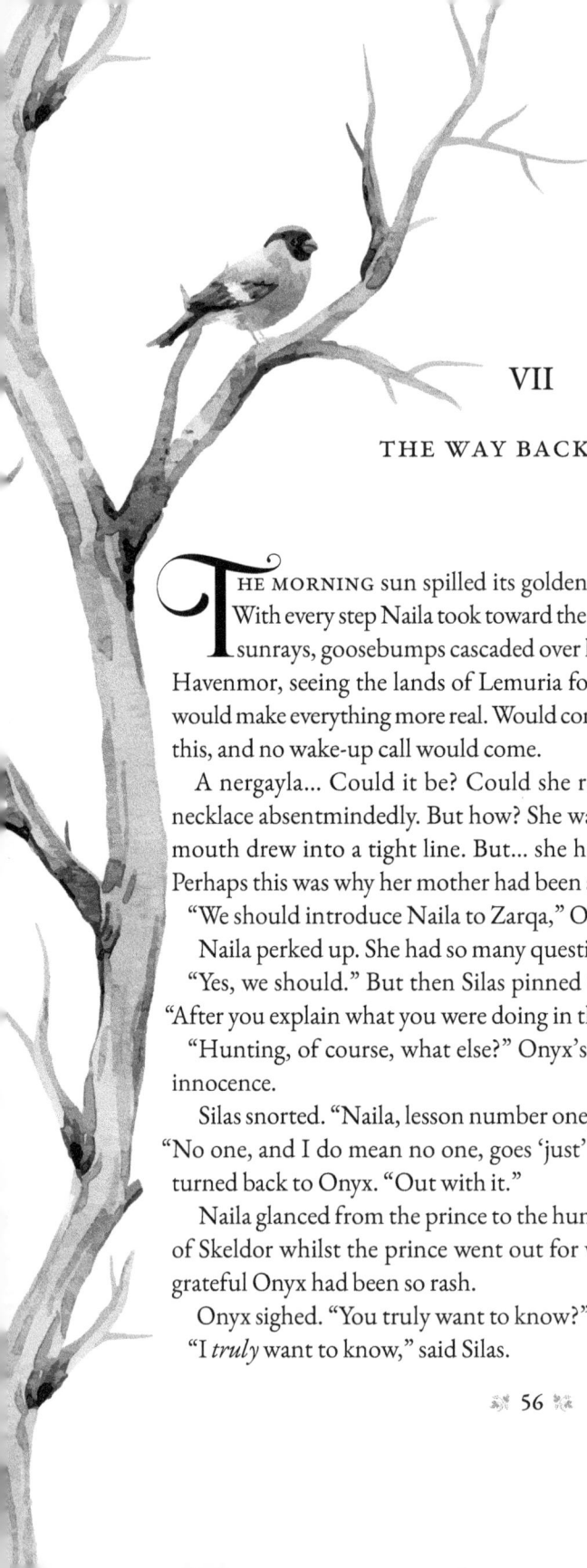

VII

THE WAY BACK HOME

The morning sun spilled its golden light into the temple's hallway. With every step Naila took toward the outside, and into the welcoming sunrays, goosebumps cascaded over her body. As if she sensed seeing Havenmor, seeing the lands of Lemuria for the first time in all their glory, would make everything more real. Would confirm she had really not dreamed this, and no wake-up call would come.

A nergayla… Could it be? Could she really be one? She fingered her necklace absentmindedly. But how? She wasn't even from this world. Her mouth drew into a tight line. But… she had no knowledge of her father. Perhaps this was why her mother had been so secretive.

"We should introduce Naila to Zarqa," Onyx chirped.

Naila perked up. She had so many questions for Zarqa.

"Yes, we should." But then Silas pinned Onyx with an unreadable look. "After you explain what you were doing in the redwoods."

"Hunting, of course, what else?" Onyx's face was the second coming of innocence.

Silas snorted. "Naila, lesson number one," he said to her conspiratorially. "No one, and I do mean no one, goes 'just' hunting in the redwoods." He turned back to Onyx. "Out with it."

Naila glanced from the prince to the huntress. So Onyx had sneaked out of Skeldor whilst the prince went out for war. She guessed she should be grateful Onyx had been so rash.

Onyx sighed. "You truly want to know?"

"I *truly* want to know," said Silas.

The young woman shrugged, not looking apologetic in the least. "All right, I went to *the Lawless* to find out where the shadowreapers sell their captives."

Naila shuddered. Just the word shadowreapers made her stomach clench in fear.

Silas froze on the spot. "You did *what*?"

"I told you, you didn't want to know."

He let out a choice of hefty swear words that shouldn't be anywhere near the vicinity of a temple. "What is wrong with you?"

Onyx's cheeks blazed as a fiery look gleamed in her eyes. "I am going to find her, Silas. No matter the price."

That pricked Naila's attention. Her tongue burned to ask just who Onyx was looking for, but Silas interrupted with a loud scoff. "No matter the price... No matter the price?!" He laughed humorlessly. "There doesn't have to be a bloody price. You could have let me find out. Why are you always so rash?"

"*I'm* being rash? You are one to talk!" Onyx put her hands on her hips. "And it's not as if you don't have enough family turmoil to keep you busy. I'm not going to wait until you sort everything out. Just so you know, as soon as I find out where they've taken her, I'll be going there. With or without your blessing!"

Silas scowled, a sharp retort obviously on the tip of his tongue.

Uncomfortable, Naila cleared her throat. "Er, guys? We have an audience."

A few young women, robed in linen caftans, eyed them disapprovingly as they passed by. They were dressed similarly to the women who had surrounded Zarqa during her healing.

Onyx took Naila's arm and guided her away, not sparing Silas another glance. At her questioning look, Onyx whispered, "We're in the temple of the Legend Ishtar. It's home to our nergaylas, priestesses like those hierodulas and their *learlings*. They are the ones who nursed you back to health."

Silas winked at the women. They pursed their lips, but a blush of pleasure crept up their cheeks. They immediately straightened at the whipping look from an elderly priestess. The elder stared at the prince with a derisive tilt to her lips.

Onyx tskd. "One day, Zarqa will ban you from the temple."

"Ah, but you will vouch for my innocence, no?" said Silas, their argument seemingly forgotten, although there was something in his gaze that told Naila this wouldn't be the end of it.

"I'll be at the frontline, helping her," Onyx said, sugary sweet.

"So, what are you two to each other?" Naila interrupted.

They blinked, looking momentarily confused. She hid a smile at the look on their faces.

"What do you—" Silas started.

Onyx shook her hands. "Oh, no, no, no."

"Red here is like my little sister." His lips curved into a teasing smirk. "So let's not get the wrong idea."

"We grew up together and believe me, no hearts have ever skipped a beat," Onyx added, and then to Silas, "Don't call me Red, you know I hate it."

Grew up together? Naila stared at Onyx. She was the only woman in the temple wearing pants, but her costume looked expensive. "So, are you, like, a princess?"

Silas frowned. "Well..."

"It's complicated." Onyx threw him a pointed look.

Naila shrugged, too distracted by the other questions inside her head to probe Onyx further. They paused in the vast doorway, atop stone stairs that led to an outer courtyard. The chilly wind that met her lost its sharp edge in the sun.

Beyond the garden was a valley where Havenmor's inner city burst with life. Nests of chalk-white cottages, adorned with winter flowers hanging from the balconies, rested between snowy roads. Cerulean waters and pristine mountains surrounded the fortified city for as far as Naila could see.

A little girl, likely one of the *learlings*, dashed over the mosaic garden floor toward them, with a basket in her hand. Her skin was a deep umber, and her eyes the azure of the seas.

Naila bent over to the girl. "Hi—"

Her breath caught in her throat. Etched between the girl's eyebrows was a faint, lying crescent moon. It wasn't a vibrant pearl color like Naila's, nor did it have the diamond on the top.

"Are you an angel?" the little girl asked.

"Oh heavens, no. What makes you think so?" said Naila.

"You're really beautiful."

She smiled shyly. "Thanks."

The girl cocked her head, her hair twists mimicking her movement. "Then are you a nergayla, like me? Zarqa said I was the first born in a hundred winters."

"I... well, um," said Naila, unsure herself of the answer.

"Oya, she hasn't eaten in days. Why don't you give her some of your barley bread?" A woman said softly.

Zarqa appeared with two hierodulas and an elderly man. Whilst the two women wore pleated caftans underneath their winter coats, Zarqa wore a caftan in a shade of gold so pale it almost looked silver. The lying crescent moon etched on her wrinkly forehead shimmered dimly in the same color as her dress.

The little girl pouted but broke off the bread. Naila eagerly accepted it.

"Zarqa," Silas said. "I don't believe you have been introduced to Naila yet."

"I haven't. Come closer, *yelud*," Zarqa said.

Yelud... child.

Her heart beat a little faster. So, this was a nergayla. She took in the woman's appearance. While Zarqa's light-brown skin had dulled and her eyes were ringed with cataracts, she emitted a vitality belying her age. Zarqa took her hands. Immediately, Naila's æther sprang to life within her, as if recognizing a kindred soul. It burned through her veins and sparked in her fingertips.

Zarqa's eyes fluttered to a close. "Such raw power..." she whispered.

But then Naila's flames transformed from curious to anxious. Her æther burned fiercely in her veins as if challenged. Her hands ignited in golden flames.

"Naila," Silas warned.

The hierodulas, the elderly man, and little Oya shifted nervously. Even Onyx looked uneasy.

But Zarqa shook her head, as if warning the prince to not interfere. The elderly nergayla's hands too, summoned flames. Violet flames battled Naila's gilded ones. She was no match for Zarqa. Her flames retreated, like a beginner realizing weightlifting one hundred and twenty kilograms was simply out of reach.

A peaceful calm soothed her senses, taking her far away, to an idyllic beach at sunrise, where gentle waves lapped rhythmically at the shore. Naila's eyes drifted to a close. She'd never known such serenity. When she opened her eyes again, she found her hands flameless, and Zarqa studying her. Unease knotted her stomach. She was both in awe of Zarqa's power and frightened that her flames had been lulled into sleep by someone else.

"You have great power, *yana*," said Zarqa, as if reading her mind. "But power means nothing if it doesn't accept you as its master." The nergayla smiled. "I was told shadowreapers brought you from a land beyond the borders of Lemuria."

A collective gasp shuddered through the two women who stood some feet behind their company. The hierodulas regarded Naila with wide eyes. "Could it be that she escaped from the Shadowlands?" one of them whispered.

"Don't be a fool. No one escapes from that accursed place. Mayhap a survivor from the ancient Lost World," her companion speculated.

"Silence," the elderly man hissed.

"Thoth. How nice of you to join us," said Silas, acknowledging the man's presence. "Thoth is our imperial scribe," he said to Naila.

Mr. Thoth cleared his throat. "Well, you did *summon* me, Your Highness." The elderly man turned to Naila. "You were telling us where you came from?"

Naila's eyes shifted over their expectant faces. Would they believe her, or would they brand her as psychotic as Dr. Peeters once did?

"Yes. I'm from Earth."

"Earth?" the old man said as he pushed his spectacles up his nose.

"Have you heard of it, Mr. Thoth?" Onyx regarded him with anticipation.

Naila held in her breath as she willed him to answer, and to do so quickly.

"Never in all my five and seventy winters."

Naila pouted in disappointment. "Like I said, it's not in your world."

"Whatever world would it be from then?" said Mr. Thoth. "I assure you, my dearest *feylana*, there are few in the lands of Lemuria who are as knowledgeable about the passings of the world as I am."

"Well, Earth is another world." At the bemused looks on everyone's faces, Naila pointed to the sky and added. "It's right up there, between the stars."

The little company of seven blinked but said no word.

"A sky traveler," chirped little Oya in wonder. "Just like—"

"Hush, kittling," said one of the hierodulas. "Those things only exist in fairy tales."

Naila fastened and unfastened her fists in the softness of her caftan. "I'm telling the truth."

"What Aisha says is no lie. There is no such thing as traveling through the stars." Mr. Thoth argued. "At least, not that we can prove..." The wiseman frowned as if deep in thought.

"I—"

"And surely there can't be another world with nergaylas? They are, to all means and purposes, Lemuria's heritage," Aisha said.

Naila braced herself to argue but thought the better of it. Regardless of her being a nergayla or not, they were right. As far as she knew, there was no one like her on Earth. No one else who could summon flames of æther. Not in the Netherlands and certainly not in South America's little Suriname where her origins lay. How could she explain something she didn't understand herself?

"The clothes she wore were definitely not from here." Onyx contemplated.

Naila's heart swelled.

At last, Silas squeezed her shoulder. "If Naila says she's from another world, then she is."

"B-but, Your Highness," said Mr. Thoth indignantly.

"And as the wisest man in Skeldor, I'm sure you can help us figure out what exactly happened." The prince raised a brow. "Can you not, Thoth?"

Mr. Thoth scratched his beardless chin. "The imperial library holds many secrets. I shall see what I can do."

Silas winked at Naila, and she answered with a grateful smile. *Thank goodness.* She didn't know what she would do if people in this new world were to write her words off as hallucinations too.

Zarqa offered Mr. Thoth a peacemaking smile. He shook his head but gave her his arm. "Let us talk no more of this." The nergayla patted his arm. "Naila of Earth, you are welcome to stay in the temple. It would honor our priestesses to see to your tutoring. I take it no one in your world has taught you the ways of æther?"

Stay? Train? Naila stared at her hands. This was the woman who could help her understand who she was exactly. But then an image of Philly in pain knocked the breath out of her. And her mother... she had to be worried sick.

"I'm sorry, Ms. Zarqa, but I can't stay here. I've got to go back to my mother and find my friend. He... He's in danger. I've got to help him."

"But how, N? None of us know of portals to other worlds," said Onyx.

Naila nuzzled on her bottom lip. "I'll think of something. I have to."

Silas leaned against a pillar and regarded Naila through watchful eyes. "Regardless of the world you are from, you have to realize you're in Lemuria now. There are less than two dozen nergaylas in all the lands of Lemuria. You can't go about wandering the lands with no direction. Every šar, every hunter-warrior, and every son of Belial will hunt you. Evidently, every shadowreaper will too. Not that I'm not up for an adventure..."

Naila shuddered. For a brief moment she had forgotten she was a wanted woman.

Onyx studied Naila with a calculating look. "We could help her..."

The prince raised his brow in amusement, whereas the others looked at her as if she had declared her undying love to Mr. Thoth.

Onyx shrugged. "Just a suggestion."

But the huntress's gaze told Naila the wheels in her mind were turning.

Naila sighed. "Then what am I supposed to do?"

Aisha stepped forward and took Naila's hands in hers, smiling warmly. "Stay with us, sister. Let Mr. Thoth see what he can discover while we teach you our ways."

Naila blinked away a tear, but finally nodded.

Silas clapped his hands together. "Well, then that's settled. Now we eat and we drink."

"Um, I want to go with you." Naila turned to Mr. Thoth. "When I'm not training in the temple, we can look together." No one had as much stake in getting her home than she herself. She would not put her fate in the hands of people she barely knew.

Mr. Thoth studied her with a little "Oh" of surprise. "Very well then."

She took a wobbly step toward the elderly scribe. Silas at once put a hand in the small of her back. "I think you'll faint of hunger before touching the first scroll."

"I can eat while searching."

"Stubborn." He shook his head but a little smile escaped his lips. "Fine, I'll order food for in the library."

"Your Highness—" Mr. Thoth began, exasperated. With one look from Silas he refrained from finishing his sentence.

A weight slid off Naila's shoulders.

She would find a way back home and to Philippe. But, in the meantime, she'd do everything she could to find the answers to the questions that had long haunted her. She wouldn't leave Lemuria without finding out who or *what* she was exactly.

This she promised herself.

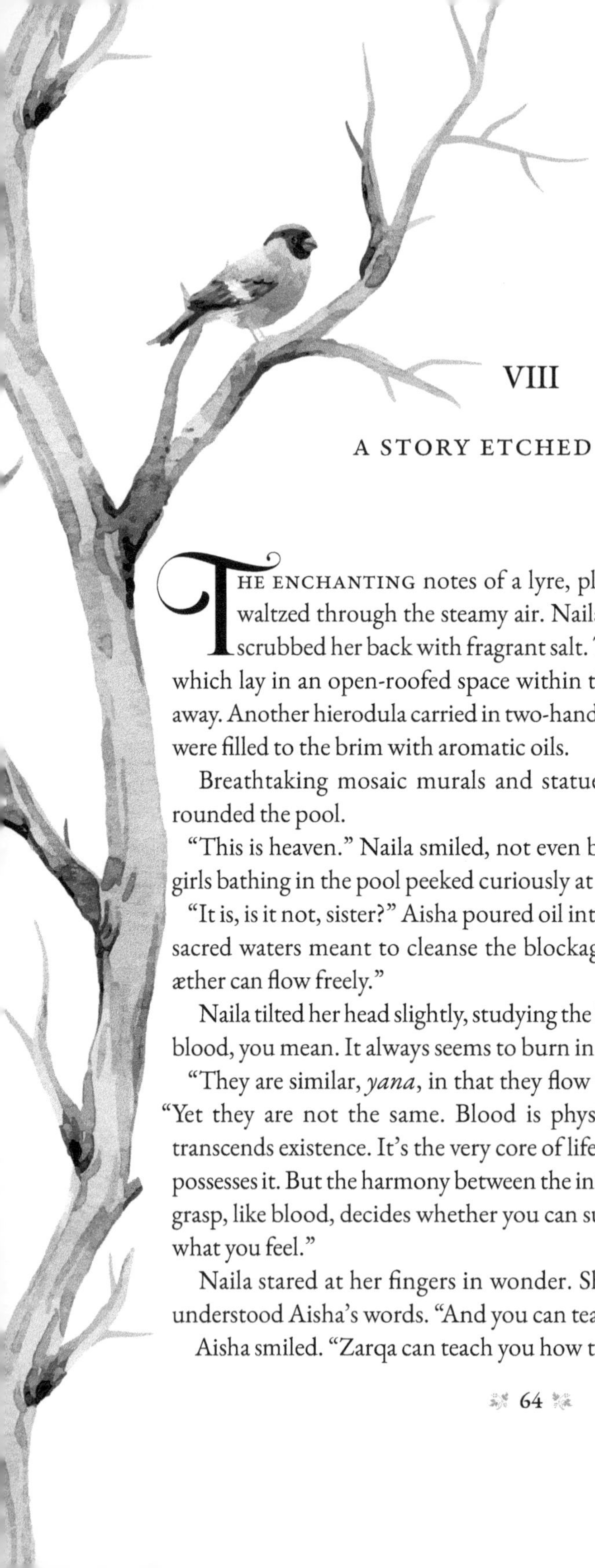

VIII

A STORY ETCHED IN SKIN

THE ENCHANTING notes of a lyre, played by one of the hierodulas, waltzed through the steamy air. Naila sighed with content as Aisha scrubbed her back with fragrant salt. The thermal spring's hot water, which lay in an open-roofed space within the temple, kissed all her aches away. Another hierodula carried in two-handled pottery amphorae. The jars were filled to the brim with aromatic oils.

Breathtaking mosaic murals and statues of the winged maiden surrounded the pool.

"This is heaven." Naila smiled, not even bothered by the fact that other girls bathing in the pool peeked curiously at her every now and then.

"It is, is it not, sister?" Aisha poured oil into Naila's long coils. "These are sacred waters meant to cleanse the blockages out of the body. That way, æther can flow freely."

Naila tilted her head slightly, studying the hierodula tending to her. "Like blood, you mean. It always seems to burn in my veins."

"They are similar, *yana*, in that they flow through the body," said Aisha. "Yet they are not the same. Blood is physical, matter. Æther, however, transcends existence. It's the very core of life and the afterlife. All of nature possesses it. But the harmony between the intangible and that which we can grasp, like blood, decides whether you can summon æther's flames. That is what you feel."

Naila stared at her fingers in wonder. She wasn't sure she completely understood Aisha's words. "And you can teach me how to use it?"

Aisha smiled. "Zarqa can teach you how to control *and* use it."

Control her flames... Just a few days ago, she'd never thought it possible. "When do we start?"

"We already started. The purification ritual is the first step. It's to prepare the mind and body for the intense path ahead."

Naila blinked. "But... Shouldn't we do exercises and stuff?"

Aisha chuckled at her pouting face. "There are several steps before you get to *that*."

"Do not look so disappointed, Naila of Earth." Zarqa appeared. Her steps were light as a cat's. The hierodulas immediately straightened. "What is time if not to make the fruits of our efforts meaningful?"

Naila sucked on her lip. "But I don't have time. I have to—"

"Then *make* time."

Naila slouched back into the water. She knew that look on Zarqa's face. It was the same one her mother had when she made up her mind.

"What's up next?"

Zarqa tutted her lips as if disapproving of Naila's speech, but she made no comment. "Hereafter, we must strengthen the mind. We will guide you to this through incantations from the celestial scrolls, and the breath of fire. Only after you have completed this step, will we shift our focus to bind the mind to the flesh. You will learn how to free your flames *at will* and how to lull them back to sleep."

The whole of Naila radiated with palpable joy. She couldn't wait to finally master her flames.

No more emotional outbursts.

The voice of guilt reminding her of Philly and her mother; she ignored. There was nothing more she could do right now. Her first search with Mr. Thoth the evening before had yielded nothing.

Zarqa and Aisha cast her soft smiles. "I see that pleases you," said the elder. "After Aisha has anointed you with our sacred elixir, you may join us in the Court of Echoes."

At Naila's confused look, Aisha whispered. "It's the temple courtyard dedicated to training."

After Zarqa left, Naila couldn't get out of the bath fast enough. Impatiently, she let Aisha rub every inch of her body with a herb-and-oil concoction that smelled faintly of myrrh. It tingled her skin the same way mint did. The other hierodula, Humaya, helped her put on a linen caftan.

She caught the gaze of one of the girls on the other side of the spring. The girl promptly looked away, cheeks burning.

"Don't mind those *learlings*, I shall remind them of their manners later." Aisha pursed her lips disapprovingly.

That piqued Naila's interest. "*Learlings*... Who else lives in the temple?"

"Well, there are several ranks in the temple. We have the high priestesses, the sêra, the senior priestesses, the heka, the junior priestesses, the hierodula, and of course there's the *learlings*. Then we have the diviners, the khaylūm. They are in a class of their own. But ruling over all are the ones blessed by Ishtar herself." Aisha looked at Naila with a hint of reverie.

"Nergayla?" Naila asked breathlessly.

Aisha nodded. "In Skeldor, we have Zarqa, who is a hundred and ten winters. Little Oya was born seven winters ago." She beamed. "And now we have you."

Naila fidgeted. She wasn't sure how to feel about this. On the one hand, she really needed to get back home. Her mother must be worried sick. On the other hand... her heart skipped a beat. She had been right. Dr. Peeters had been wrong. *Ha!* Her flames were no hallucination.

"Don't be too hard on them, Aisha," Humaya said timidly, as she knotted a golden sash around Naila's middle. "The *learlings* are taught at a young age about phæralei, but rarely see them in the flesh. Let alone phæralei as unique and vivid as Naila's."

Naila's eyes darted to Aisha and back to Humaya. "Phæralei?"

Both Aisha and Humaya froze, staring at her wide-eyed.

"We"—Humaya glanced uncertainly at Aisha—"We thought you knew. They're the marks on your forehead. The mark of a nergayla."

She peeked at their foreheads; the two women carried no markings. Naila brushed her fingers over her scars. *No*, phæralei. Her nerves sizzled with anticipation. They had her undivided attention.

"What are they for?"

Aisha frowned. "That, we wish we knew. Even the wisest of nergaylas in ages past have not unlocked its secrets. It's unfortunately a knowledge lost in the past. The only thing certain is that it brands one as a nergayla."

As a gilded headdress with a single lapis lazuli was woven into her raven braid, Philippe's words twirled through her mind. *The diamond of Virgo. Never forget...*

"The statues in the hall... why do they look like they represent the stars in the sky?" Naila whispered.

Aisha gave Humaya an encouraging nod, to which Humaya smiled shyly. "Because they are the Legends of the Sky, sister. The deities we serve. There are Marduk, Tiamat, and Sin and Shamash, to name a few. But in many empires, Ishtar is most beloved. This temple is dedicated to her."

"Ishtar... the winged maiden," Naila whispered, more to herself.

"*Yana*." Humaya nodded.

Virgo... Naila finished in her thoughts. A storm of chills swept over her skin. Whatever Philly had woven in his fairy tales, she hoped remained exactly that. A figment of his imagination.

THE COURT OF ECHOES was devoid of flora, except for silver barked trees with leaves as white as the snow fluttering through the sky. Little snow monkeys spluttered in the heated pond, and snow-tipped mountains filled the panoramic view. In the very middle stood an altar. Zarqa hummed over it, burning frankincense, whilst Naila sat cross-legged on a low bench.

"Kihaila Shanu.
Lumira Zura.
Ishtar Baylū."

Zarqa sang.

In echoes of silence, we bind these flames, with Ishtar's blessing, Naila translated in her mind. It was an old dialect of Tierratongo, but she couldn't begin to explain how she knew.

"Feel æther move through the feet that connect you to the ground. Clear your thoughts as it flows like a river through your limbs. Breathe as it ignites in the core of your body. The mind and the flesh become one once more," Zarqa instructed.

Naila pinched her brows in concentration, her eyes closed, but all she felt was the icy wind scratching her cheeks. All she heard were the winter jays chirping in the temple's courtyard.

"You focus too much on what is in the here." Zarqa tutted. "*Try* to focus more on what you want in the now."

What I want... what I want. She needed those flames to obey her for once, *for heaven's sake*. A whole week had already passed, and she had yet to complete this step in her training.

"Release the chains of the mind. Accept the impossible," Zarqa continued. She heard the nergayla's caftan shuffle as she circled Naila.

Philippe's words seized her anew. *In this infinite time with an infinite space, the impossible isn't only possible. It's also a certainty.* She could do this. Yes, she could. The flames had taken over so many times. This time, *she* would take over them. A numbness spread over her chest, beneath her compass pendant. Tingling and stinging battled the sensation until, slowly, but surely, a heat took her like an inferno. Smoldering in her heart. Burning in her lungs.

Her eyes flicked open. Without seeing, she knew gilded flames burned within them. To her utter astonishment, those flames also danced on every inch of her skin. In the past, it had just been her hands and sometimes her eyes when she got really upset.

"*Yana*, Naila of Earth, *yana*. That, my *learling,* is the breath of fire."

All of the courtyard flared in vivid colors, as if magnified by a master painter. As if every spark of æther in every presence of life burned to welcome her.

She tried to jump up, but the world spun around her.

"Easy there," said Zarqa, as she pressed her hand into the small of her back. "Those new to æther will find it draining."

She took a wobbly step. Her curled-toe boots met with warm, mosaic tiles, courtesy of the underground geyser. Zarqa urged her gently back into the temple with the press of her hand.

"Take a rest, dear. On the morrow, after you come back from the imperial library, we shall continue."

Naila climbed the stairs back into the temple, but Zarqa didn't follow. Naila curiously glanced back. A flaxen-haired woman entered the courtyard from a door previously hidden from sight. She was draped in a lavish fur-lined coat. Two guards stayed watch on the other side of the door. Could this be the princess she'd overheard Zarqa and the Silver Šar talk about? The... *diviner*?

Naila shifted her weight from one foot to another. Zarqa's sharp gaze, however, caught her eye. For a centenarian, she sure was perceptive as a cat.

Like a child scolded, Naila immediately turned and made for the hall, straight to her chamber, giving the passing hierodulas and *learlings* small nods in greeting.

"*Psst.*"

She glanced behind her, seeing nothing but colossal pillars, statues, and snow twirling outside the massive windows. She shrugged and continued.

"*Psssst.*"

Naila paused. Yes, she definitely heard something. Glancing about, but seeing no one in the vicinity, she stepped forward with curiosity. Someone left a window ajar and a few snowflakes swirled inside.

"BOO!"

A mass of fiery hair came into sight. Onyx stood on a ledge sticking out of the ziggurat's outer wall, using her arms to brace against the window frame. There were at least ten meters to the ground. Naila broke out in cold sweat at the thought of the height, but Onyx obviously didn't share her feelings.

"You gave me a fright."

Onyx giggled. The huntress stuck her head inside, stealing a look into the hall. "Where's Zarqa?"

"In one of the courtyards."

"Good." Onyx grinned, her freckles dancing vividly across her tan nose. "I thought she'd keep you chained inside forever."

Naila clapped her hands in excitement. "Oh, she didn't force me or anything. I've learned so much! Just now I managed to summon—"

"That's nice." Onyx yawned. Then her dark eyes glinted mischievously. "So, I heard about just the thing that might solve our, I mean, your problem."

She eyed Onyx warily. "And that would be...?"

"Don't look so suspicious. It's nothing bad, I promise." Onyx blinked innocently.

Naila rather thought she looked like Pinocchio.

"The Silent Hand is here in Havenmor," Onyx blurted.

"Er..."

Onyx lowered her voice. "Do not talk about it with anyone, you hear? They've been forbidden to enter Skeldor." She looked skittishly around before continuing. "The Silent Hand is the eldest thieving guild in the Winterlands."

Naila immediately straightened, but before she could respond, Onyx interrupted.

"Now don't get prissy on me before you hear what I have to say."

"What is there to say? They're thieves!"

Call her a goody-two-shoes, she didn't care. This part of peer pressure she'd never succumb to.

Onyx waved her words away. "If you want to know what is happening in the world, thieving guilds are the ones you should ask. No one else would dare spread any whispers that might anger the šars, you know."

Naila raised her brow, still skeptical. "How do we know the thieving guild doesn't spread misinformation?"

"We don't. It's up to us whether we think their words are worth following." Onyx shrugged. "So, are you coming?"

Naila fidgeted. The thought of hanging out with thieves, and possibly worse, went against her moral compass, but... What if they knew about a way back to Earth?

"I'll get my coat. Meet me at the gate."

"Take the gate at the back." Onyx climbed down then shot back up. "Oh, and make sure no one sees you leaving."

Moments later, Naila tiptoed out of the temple. Only a winter landscape of mountains and pine trees framed the back of the gold-capped ziggurat—a stepped pyramid. Onyx waved from between the trees. Naila scurried through the snow, tucking her head into the much-needed warmth of her coat. "So, what do you think they can tell us?" she whispered, though there was no one in the vicinity.

"Well, for one, what those shadowreapers are up to. They're the cause of your problems. I bet they're the solution too."

Her breath hitched. Onyx was probably right but she did not look forward to another confrontation with those dreaded folks.

Onyx pulled a sugary bun out of her coat and took a huge bite. It was shaped like a lemon and glazed with something yellowish. Onyx closed her eyes, sighing contentedly as she chewed. Naila had never seen her look so happy, although they had only known each other for a week or so.

Her fingers drummed rhythmically against her thigh as they trekked deeper and deeper into the pine forest. Finally, she threw out, "I think my father was from this place. Lemuria, I mean."

Onyx halted, swallowing the last of her bun. "What?"

Naila smiled wistfully, staring at the snowy sky. "I think I have a memory of him. I was very young, maybe even still a baby. We were in this huge room, the most beautiful I've ever seen. Turquoise and shimmering gold covered the walls, and the finest silk draped the windows. Someone sang to me, although I do not remember their face." She frowned. "And then *he* came in. Tall and powerful. Funny enough, I only remember his smile. Like a hearth in the middle of winter." Naila caressed her pendant, her eyes downcast. "But my ma told me this couldn't have happened."

Onyx squeezed her hand lightly.

"The shadowreapers called me Stormhold. I have a feeling that's his name."

"There are many Stormholds in Lemuria, N, but if he's here, I know you will find him."

Naila swallowed back a lump. Her eyes shifted to Onyx. "Why do *you* want to speak to the Silent Hand? I know it's not just about me."

Pain flashed across Onyx's face, but it was gone before she could blink. The crunching of their footsteps in the snow was the only sound echoing in the forest. At last, Onyx whispered. "I'm looking for my mother."

That was all she said, and Naila didn't dare ask more.

"There it is." Onyx pointed.

A small clearing lay between the trees. She almost missed the well in the middle, for a fallen tree trunk covered its opening. *No.* As Naila came nearer, she realized it wasn't a simple well. It was an inverted tower, lined with stairs spiraling deep underground. Moss and shadows clung to the stone wall.

Onyx adjusted the arrows in her quiver before descending the stairs. "They're holding a black market somewhere underground."

"How did you know about this place?" Naila hesitated before descending the stairs too. She cringed when her words echoed in the well's darkness.

"The Lawless told me back in the redwoods. I found them a couple of bells before you got dumped over there."

She glanced over the banister. Not the wisest choice. At the sight of the floor, many meters below, her heart hammered. Every instinct screamed at her to run back. She quickened her pace, forcing herself to follow Onyx. The cold bit into her skin and the stairs seemed endless.

Onyx peeked at her curiously. "You're scared of heights?"

She nodded, pressing herself as far as possible to the wall.

Onyx grabbed her hand. "Just close your eyes. I'll lead you."

Thankfully, she did exactly that, but it did little to lessen Naila's fear. After what seemed like ages, they finally reached the ground. She could have wept in relief.

A dark tunnel, dimly lit by torches, met them. Countless voices murmured in the distance. The Silent Hand was not so silent.

"Here." Onyx pushed a dagger into her hands.

Naila stared at it, dumbfounded. "What am I supposed to do with it?"

"Stab someone if they get too creepy, of course. What else?"

"I'm not killing someone, Onyx."

Onyx blinked, but then just shrugged. "People rarely know what they're capable of until they're confronted with a situation that challenges their morals."

"I'm not killing anyone," she repeated stubbornly.

"I think it's best to cover your phæralei up," was all Onyx said.

She quickly dragged the hood of her coat over her forehead. To her surprise, Onyx did the same. Then again, hair as bright-red as hers was bound to attract attention too.

She sucked in a deep breath. *Here goes nothing.*

Before she knew it, they reached the end of the tunnel, emerging into a vast underground space lit with oil lamps and filled with market tents. For a black market that wasn't supposed to exist, many Lemai seemed to have found it.

She slammed into someone's shoulder. "Oh, sorry."

The man, cloaked too, eyed her curiously.

Onyx pulled her away. "Come on."

The rich scent of forbidden spices entangled with aged leather and a hint of smoke. People, many with hooded cloaks like them, bartered with salesmen. There were ancient-looking artifacts, suspicious-looking elixirs, and preserved exotic animals she'd never seen in liquid-filled jars.

"Who are we looking for?" she whispered.

Onyx murmured. "He's called Riley Nine Lives. We have to look out for a symbol with two crossing scimitars."

Riley Nine Lives, huh?

Naila pursed her lips. Well, that sounded interesting.

"I think it's there," said Onyx.

Sure enough, two white scimitars were painted upon a pitch-black tent. Inside, a group of people ate and drank at a large floor table. Several shady-looking men surrounded them, seated upon cushions, and laughing and smoking midwakh pipes. The interior was lit with oil lamps and the faint scent of crystals and incense wafted through the air.

When she and Onyx neared, the group fell silent.

A broad-necked man stood up, sticking out his chest like a pompous cock. "State yer business."

Naila's eyes widened. He was inked in cuneiform characters from head to toe. She made to turn, no longer caring about any potential information, but Onyx gripped her arm. "Our business is with Riley Nine Lives and no one else." She held up a purse, jingling it so everyone could hear the many crystals it held. The man narrowed his eyes, but Onyx held his gaze without flinching.

A tiny woman, no older than forty winters, bellowed from the floor table. "Donathan, let our guests come in." Her voice was hoarse, as though she'd smoked for many winters.

Donathan beckoned with his head.

The people in the tent watched them with interest, their eyes mocking. Wordlessly, Naila followed Onyx, feeling increasingly uncomfortable with every step. They paused before the floor table. The woman took a long draw from her midwakh and blew a ring in the air. Two nose rings glinted in the dim light. Her eyes raked over Onyx and then Naila.

"The šars ain't fond of us." Her all-seeing eyes bored through them.

Naila's cheeks heated. How did she...?

"The šars have nothing to do with us," Onyx said smoothly. Naila almost believed her.

The woman chuckled, fine lines crinkling mockingly at the sides of her eyes. "Really? Cause ye sure smell like the palace and ye can see that one"—she beckoned to Naila—"is from the temple even from as far as Bulinya."

Smelled? Was she a dog?

"We're not here to cause trouble. We're looking for a man called Riley Nine Lives," Naila said hurriedly.

The woman smirked. "Yer looking right at *her,* girlie."

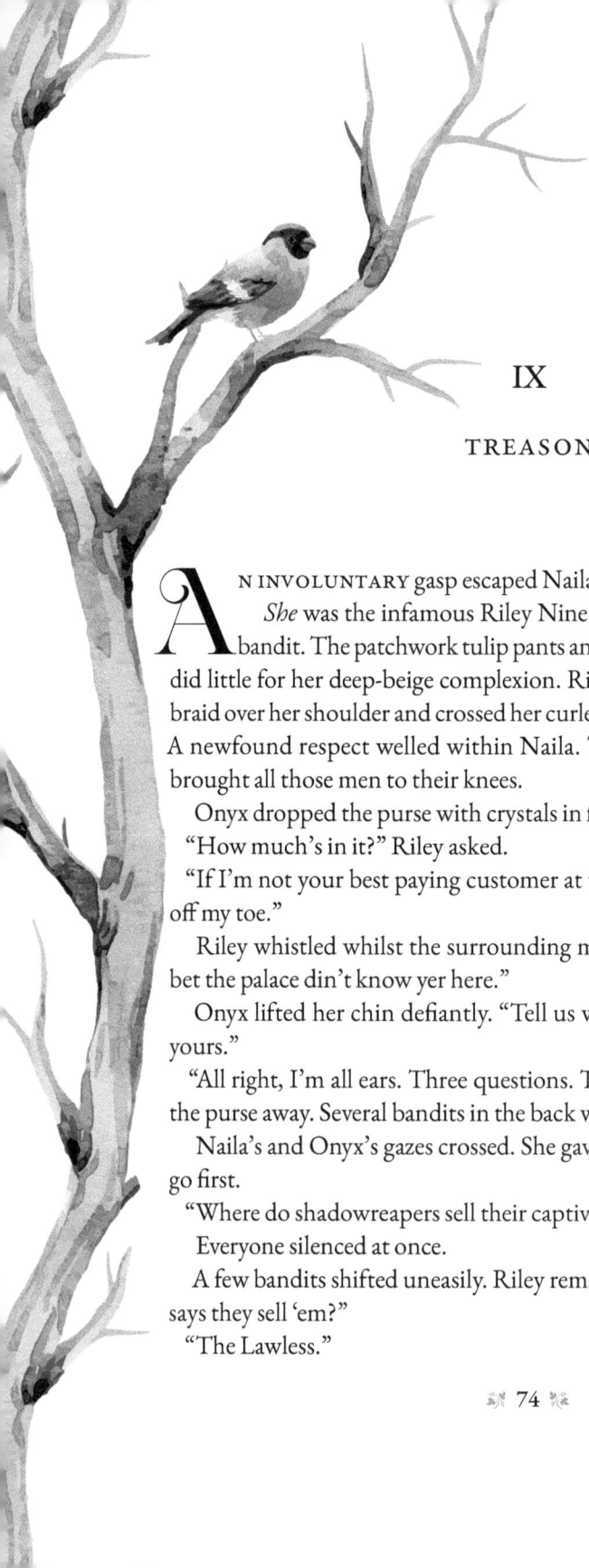

IX

TREASON

An involuntary gasp escaped Naila's lips.

She was the infamous Riley Nine Lives? Her eyes swept over the bandit. The patchwork tulip pants and much-too-large coat she wore did little for her deep-beige complexion. Riley Nine Lives swept her black braid over her shoulder and crossed her curled-toe boots atop the floor table. A newfound respect welled within Naila. To think this tiny woman had brought all those men to their knees.

Onyx dropped the purse with crystals in front of Riley's boots.

"How much's in it?" Riley asked.

"If I'm not your best paying customer at the end of the day, you can cut off my toe."

Riley whistled whilst the surrounding men chuckled appreciatively. "I bet the palace din't know yer here."

Onyx lifted her chin defiantly. "Tell us what we want, and the purse is yours."

"All right, I'm all ears. Three questions. Three answers." Riley snatched the purse away. Several bandits in the back watched it hungrily.

Naila's and Onyx's gazes crossed. She gave Onyx an encouraging nod to go first.

"Where do shadowreapers sell their captives?"

Everyone silenced at once.

A few bandits shifted uneasily. Riley remained unfazed, however. "Who says they sell 'em?"

"The Lawless."

Murmurs broke out. All eyes were on Onyx. While at first the thieves had been merely curious, they now definitely held their attention. There was something unsettling in their gazes, which set Naila on edge. They needed to leave as soon as they got their answers.

"Well, well. I see we ain't yer first rebellious act."

"Do you have the answers or not?"

A grin spread across Riley's face.

"Most of their captives become blood slaves in the Shadowlands."

Both she and Onyx flinched.

Whatever blood slaves were it did not sound good.

"Some, however, are sold on the black markets of Isolon. Whisperers say the shadowreapers 'been sniffing 'round Isolon a lot. The Black Šar's getting nervous." She blew out another ring of smoke. "I hope the one ye seek was sold there, girlie. No one returns from the Shadowlands, but y'already know that."

Onyx swallowed. Naila grasped her hand and squeezed it. The huntress's fingers were stone cold.

Naila scrambled all her bravery to ask, "We're also looking for a portal. One used by the shadowreapers. Do you know—"

A horn echoed in the market. Again and again. Louder and louder. At once, everyone snatched around them and made a run for it. A group of warriors clad in silver armor stormed into the marketplace. Their shields held Skeldor's unmistakable lion-and-snake crest. The Silver Šar's men. Complete and utter chaos broke out.

"Drat," Onyx said. "*Il-Ragab.* We have to get out now. They won't understand. They'll see this as treason."

Law enforcers?

"But—" Naila looked frantically around, but Riley Nine Lives was long gone with the purse and her answers. *Darn it!*

The rhythmic thud of boots on stone reverberated through the marketplace alongside cries of protest and the sound of breaking pottery. The Il-Ragab tore through stalls and upended crates, their eyes sharp and their faces stern. One by one, people were dragged out, their pleas falling on deaf ears.

"Onyx, they're blocking the only way out," she hissed.

"Not the only way." Onyx pointed at a dark tunnel on the other side of the underground market. The last of the thieves fled through its darkness. That was how they must have entered Skeldor unnoticed.

Naila eyed it skeptically. "We don't know where that leads to…" She wasn't sure whether the tunnel was more appealing than Il-Ragab.

"I guess we'll find out."

"You will not," a voice barked behind them.

Before they could say anything, an Il-Ragab officer snatched away Onyx's arrow-filled quiver, and another one grabbed them by the arms.

"By order of His Majesty, Möndör Silvanus Eseliyon, you are under arrest."

Onyx smacked him with her jade bow.

"*Ouch.* You little witch."

"Do you know who I am?" Onyx said haughtily.

Another officer plucked the bow out of her hand. "*Yana.* A traitor."

"You won't be so feisty once we throw you into the pit."

Onyx's face drained of color.

No, no, no. This wasn't happening… Tears welled in Naila's eyes. She was barely eighteen and already under arrest. What would her mother say? Her breath hitched, each inhale building a pressure upon her chest. The Il-Ragab dragged them out of the marketplace. The colors of the market swirled around her, voices fading into a muffled blur. She was so in shock, the height of the stairs hardly registered. Her fingers dug into her palm in an attempt to draw out pain and force herself out of her panic attack.

Onyx eyed her in alarm.

The icy wind whistled through the pine trees and slashed across her face. The officers pushed her and Onyx toward their chariots.

"Let us go, or I'll make you sorry," Onyx snapped.

"What is going on here?"

Silas appeared from the shadows of the trees, the reins of a silver stallion in his hand. The horse neighed, throwing back its moon-shade mane as if to underline its master's words. The tension in her body melted away at the sight of the prince, his presence like a lifeline pulling her back from the edge of panic. Perhaps they wouldn't be thrown in the pit after all. Whatever they meant by that.

"Prince Silvanus," the officer answered. "We caught them fraternizing with the Silent Hand."

"We did no such thing." Onyx huffed.

"We just asked some questions, I promise," Naila squeaked. He had to believe them. He *had* to.

Silas's night-blue eyes swept over them. His mouth twitched with the slightest disapproval, but he hid it promptly and said, "Let these two go."

"But... Your Highness," the Il-Ragab officer protested.

Silas pinned him with a look sharper than a dagger.

The man immediately let them go.

Naila sagged to her knees, not caring about the snow soaking her caftan. She could have wept in relief. Silas stomped toward them. Contrary to the first time she saw him, he wore a simple, dark, hooded cloak. Several days of growth dotted his jaw. It aged his appearance from early to late twenties. Not that she complained. His horse strutted behind him, carrying a travel bag across its back. Where had he been?

"Just great, Onyx," he spat. "Now you are dragging Naila into your foolery?"

"It wasn't her fault." Naila forced herself back to her feet. It wasn't, truly. After all, she had agreed to go.

Silas raised a brow, clearly not believing a word.

Onyx didn't seem to hear them. "Isolon," she mumbled, eyes glazed over. "They sell the captives in the black markets of Isolon."

The prince frowned. "What?"

The captives fortunate enough not to become blood slaves. But Naila swallowed back those words and her disappointment. Her eyes pricked anew with unshed tears. Riley had left her no answer. She was as far from home as ever. "Let's get somewhere warm, then we can explain what happened." Naila glanced about the pine forest, thinking. "We can go to the library. Mr. Thoth won't be there until later."

Moments later, they entered the regal warmth of the imperial library, a bronze-tipped ziggurat. Having spent half her week there, the library was as familiar to Naila as the temple. She led them to a private study room tucked away from the noisier corridors.

Onyx plumped down onto a seating cushion, causing a few sheets of parchment to flutter off the floor table. Silas, meanwhile, leaned against the tapestry-draped wall, his eyes obscured by the shadow of his hood. The normally tranquil room crackled with palpable tension. The prince was not amused.

Naila settled on another cushion and quickly summarized what had happened in the least inflammatory words she could find, more than aware of the increasingly darkening look upon the prince's face. She had no desire to listen to another bickering match between the two.

Silas rubbed his face with his hand. "The Silent Hand... Tell me I heard wrong."

Only silence met him.

Silas shook his head. "Now I'm glad Grandfather sent the Il-Ragab. If they hadn't interfered, those thieves would've kidnapped you two for a ransom, or worse. You know how much a nergayla is worth."

A shudder ran through Naila. Something told her Silas wasn't far from the truth. In hindsight, she should have thought things through... then again, she probably wouldn't have passed on the opportunity to find a way home.

Onyx pursed her lips. "We had it under control."

They had been nowhere near having anything under control, but for the sake of peace, Naila said soothingly, "At least Onyx has a starting point for her search, right?"

Onyx glanced at her guiltily. "I'm sorry you didn't get your information, N."

"I hope you don't think of sneaking to Isolon," Silas warned.

Onyx smiled sugary sweet. "Do tell where you sneaked off to these past few sunsets? Your grandfather isn't too happy with you right now."

That caught Naila's attention. Why was the prince sneaking about?

Silas patted the jeweled hilt of his ever-present scimitar. "That's of no concern to anyone." His lips curved into a teasing grin. "Besides, I can take care of myself."

Onyx scoffed. "Well, so can we."

He crossed his arms. "By doing first, and thinking last?"

"Oh, come off it, Silas. You're just bitter we didn't invite you."

Silas's grin faltered for the briefest moment. "Bitter?" He tapped the hilt of his scimitar. "Hardly." His voice cooled. "Just don't expect me to bail you out next time."

Naila blinked, surprised. She had thought the prince was being the responsible one, but clearly, she misread him. Onyx had hit the nail on the head. Against the law or no, he had wanted in on their dangerous little adventure.

Before Onyx could retort, she said, "Guys, I think Mr. Thoth is coming at any moment now. I'll see you tomorrow, okay?"

Silas eyed her curiously. "Did Thoth discover anything?"

She shook her head, fighting the sting of frustration.

Silas placed a gentle hand on her shoulder. His touch was warm, reassuring. "Cheer up. If there's anyone who can help, it's him. Of that I'm sure."

Her gaze met his, hoping against hope that he was right. His eyes, usually full of playful mischief, held a sincerity she didn't expect.

"Thank you," she said, her voice little more than a whisper.

His hand lingered on her shoulder, and though he withdrew it, the warmth remained. As soon as Onyx and Silas left the ziggurat, she went to search for Mr. Thoth, more determined than ever.

THERE WAS something magical about the library, Naila decided. Perhaps it lay in the scents of parchment and incense, or maybe it was the ambiance of dim oil lamps, lush rugs, and embroidered floor cushions. Ceiling-high shelves filled with scrolls covered the walls, whilst rows of tablets occupied the rest of the hall.

"There is nothing of use in this, master," said Mr. Thoth's *learling*, a boy of no more than twelve winters, from the end of the table in the cataloging room she'd found them in, as he made notes with his reed pen on another scroll.

Several rolled scrolls lay on their floor table, amidst a variety of root vegetables, goat cheese, and bread. As it had been for the past week or so.

"Yes, yes, much to our surprise." Mr. Thoth did his best to suppress a yawn. His eyes finally landed on her. "Ah, young Miss Naila. You have come to join us?"

She nodded. "So, no luck in finding anything?"

"I'm afraid not."

Naila bit her lip. There had to be something that could help her... Her fingers caressed the map of Lemuria, completely different in its forests and waters from Earth, but she found no clue. Her eyes shifted hungrily over the eleven crests from Lemuria's šars. *No*, ten. One was crossed out.

"Since the age of calanmos, over a thousand winters ago, Lemuria always had eleven empires, after the surviving members of Suzano's twelve," Mr. Thoth said behind her.

"Suzano died too?" Her eyes remained on the Shadow Šar's Shadowlands Empire.

"*Yana*. He died so we could be free." His voice carried a quiet respect.

Her fingers grazed the crests, tracing the texture of each carefully drawn line of ink. From the Shadow Šar's otherworldly pattern with a sun disk, the Silver Šar's lion coiled around a snake, to the Red Šar's serpentine dragon around a scepter... They at last landed upon the crossed-out crest of Ornesias and its former sovereign the Golden Šar.

As if reading her mind, Mr. Thoth continued. "The empires of Lemuria have always had their conflicts, but Ornesias and Crishire's rivalry eclipsed all. When the Golden Šar aided Skeldor against Crishire one too many times, six winters ago, Crishire's Red Šar was out for blood." His voice carried the weight of unspoken grief. "The late Red Šar and his eldest sons died in battle, including his šargon, Prince Reuben... or so some of the whispers go. His successor, the reigning Red Šar, annihilated the Golden Šar's court in revenge, annexing Ornesias to Crishire.

"It was a shock unlike any other, as you can imagine. What started in union with the great Suzano, is beginning to fall apart, land by land. I do not think Lemuria recovered from this unprecedented event. In fact, I fear the worst..." He adjusted his spectacles.

The dots connected in her mind. So, this was why there was enmity between the Silver and the Red Šar. *Great*. Another world with endless wars. Lemuria wasn't so different from Earth after all. Earth... The last words she'd spoken to her mother echoed. She hadn't even said goodbye. A sliver of despair twisted her stomach.

At first, she had thought this to be no more than a nightmare, but as the days darkened into nights and Iluna's light teased the temple bedroom's window without fail, it began to dawn her whole life had been a lie. How much had Philly known, and more important, her mother?

Æther pricked at Naila's fingertips, as if warning her she couldn't keep the flames at bay forever... Thank goodness for Zarqa's lessons.

The door flew open. Onyx and Silas sauntered inside, much to a scribe's displeasure. The woman tutted her lips. "Your Highness—"

Silas kissed her hand. "Ah, Mrs. Amat, so sweet the seasons treat you. I almost mistook you for your daughter." The dimple in his chin winked with mischief.

The woman's bronze cheeks flushed. "Oh, you flirt." A giggle left her throat.

Onyx rolled her eyes. She plopped down on the floor cushions and began to clean her jade bow. "And?"

What were they doing here? They had barely left a bell or two ago. Naila sighed. "Nothing." She perked up when she noticed the presence of Onyx's bow. "You've been back to the market? Did you find Riley?"

"*Yana,* but we've found nothing, I'm afraid," said Silas, serious now.

"Well, I did get my bow back," said Onyx.

Naila's shoulders drooped in disappointment.

Eying her, Silas took a sip from the wineskin he carried with him. "Well, if all else fails, we should go to the Shadow Šar, the source himself."

"The Shadow Šar will laugh in our faces. We'd have to force it out of him," said Onyx.

Silas smiled wickedly. "Exactly."

Naila's brows knitted. Contrary to reckless Onyx and thrill-seeking Silas, she would rather jump in the frozen sea than face the Shadow Šar and his shadowreapers, *but*, if that was what it took to get back home... She filed the idea away.

Onyx cast Silas a sidelong glance. "Are you serious?"

"Why wouldn't I be?" said the prince.

"And you call me reckless. There is no way your grandfather will let his precious heir out of his sight. Face it, Silas, you're stuck in Skeldor."

"Don't start with me, Red. I'm not saying we should storm into the Shadowlands like headless fools. But with a carefully thought-out plan..."

Naila's gaze shifted from Onyx to Silas. She took in the prince who was well on his way to emptying his wineskin. Their eyes met briefly and in the span of a heartbeat his eyes told a story of longing. The seduction of adventure gleamed in them, a hunger for the uncharted where rules were broken and limits ceased to exist. But his sense of responsibility seemed to pull him back. For the first time she realized what weight his duty must carry. He was bound to a life where decisions shaped an empire, not merely his own desires.

Silas sighed. "We'll have to wait for the right opportunity."

His gaze latched on her pendant. He frowned. His fingers curled around

His gaze latched on her pendant. He frowned. His fingers curled around the compass, his thumb stroking the etching of the broken diamond in a bed of stars. "Who gave you this?"

Mr. Thoth cleared his throat, glancing uneasily. His eyes, too, were fixed upon the compass.

Naila clicked open her compass pendant and told them the story, her voice hitching when she tasted Philly's name. To her surprise, the arrow had stopped turning around like it always did. It pointed to somewhere straight ahead. *Odd.*

"Hmm," was all Silas said.

"What?"

"For someone not from this world, you carry a lot from our history."

Her heart leaped. "Do you... know this emblem?"

"Ah, but do we know it," mumbled Mr. Thoth.

The atmosphere soured to that of a funeral.

"Who does it belong to?"

It was Silas who answered. "The Lemai's worst enemy."

She glanced from one to the other, waiting for them to explain. "Uh, what enemy?"

At once, they all seemed to have become tight-lipped, glancing at the prince as if awaiting further instructions. Silas adjusted his features and smiled as if nothing had happened. "There are... many enemies in Lemuria." His voice was too casual.

Mr. Thoth cleared his throat and nodded promptly.

Her pulse quickened, sensing the change in their mood, but no one dared to meet her gaze.

Silas dusted off his tunic and turned to the door. "Duty is calling. I hope you find what you are looking for, Naila."

As Silas and Onyx left the library and Mr. Thoth smoothly turned the conversation, an ominous thought chilled her to the bone.

The Lemai kept a secret.

X

A NAME UNSPOKEN

SUCH A wicked thing, the sun, shining without care, whilst Naila was yet again stuck in the library with Mr. Thoth.

She sighed.

At least her lessons with Zarqa were improving.

"And here we enter the hall dedicated to the battle at the Shores of the Blood Moons, which marked the end of the unspoken era," Mr. Thoth said, in the same monotonous tone Naila had listened to for the past two clock strikes. The imperial scribe hardly paid her a glance. Instead, he'd buried his gray head in a scroll, his small specs balancing on his long hook nose.

Naila did her best to keep her eyelids from falling while they strolled through the endless cases of scrolls. At first, she had gone *ooh* and *ahh* at the marble floors and pillars, the ornate wood cases filled with old scrolls, and the breathtaking frescos on the ceiling. That was, until she realized the imperial library was bigger than the Louvre. While she loved books and all they had to teach her, listening to Mr. Thoth could be such a chore. And that was an understatement.

She fumbled absentmindedly with her compass, whose arrow still pointed somewhere ahead.

The Lemai kept a secret.

Something they did not want her to know, or perhaps tried to forget themselves... Her fingers traced the outline of her compass's emblem. If she hadn't spent her days in the library, she would have interrogated some civilians until they spilled answers, for Silas and Onyx were as tight-lipped as Mr. Thoth.

"And this section here, holds scrolls mapping the lost cities of old." Mr. Thoth beckoned to a tiny hallway without looking up from his scroll.

The compass's arrow adjusted, pointing straight at that very hallway. Naila's stomach did a somersault.

"There's nothing to find there, I'm afraid. Most of these cities are no more than myths."

Naila perked up. *Mythical cities?* Perhaps those dismissed scrolls held information about Earth and old Mr. Thoth was oblivious to it. She clenched her compass, remembering Philly's words, *It will always point to home, here on Earth or far between the stars.* Could it really be? She had nothing to lose.

She tiptoed to the little hallway, peeking through her lashes to make sure Mr. Thoth didn't notice her leaving. She had nothing to worry about. The old man was quite content listening to his own voice.

The dusty hallway was divided into sections. Stone tablets resting below the cases identified the subjects, just like in the other hallways. Naila blew the dust off the tablets, row for row. The cuneiform scriptures indeed spoke of legendary cities; *Antilia: the lost empire in the jade sea* and *The Lost World: lands from an ancient time.* No Earth. And no Rotterdam, for that matter.

She sighed in disappointment and turned to leave when a sunbeam reflected on the moonstone of her pendant. The light hit a scroll. For one eerie moment, she was certain it ignited in crimson flames, but a blink of an eye further and the flames vanished into nothingness.

The stone tablet below the row read, *Nebiru: the fallen city of the Unspokens.*

The Unspokens... Where did she hear that before?

Naila hesitated but took a deep breath and reached for the scroll. She couldn't afford to lose any information that might bring her home. Naila blew the dust off the scroll and immediately had a sneezing fest. Hopefully, Mr. Thoth didn't catch on. With great care, she unfastened the gilded cord. Her heart thundered. The anguish of the unknown, of what it would reveal, held her in its grip.

Inch by inch, she opened the old scroll, for the faded papyrus must be hundreds of winters at the very least. At last, she succumbed to her anxiousness and tugged the whole thing open.

Huh?

There was nothing.

The scroll was wholly blank.

"N? What are you doing here?" Onyx frowned from the end of the corridor.

The prince and Mr. Thoth were with her. Onyx and Silas were only supposed to pick her up at midday... Was her time already up? After a lot of persuasion, Naila had reluctantly agreed to pause her search to go to a festival with them. Well to be honest, Zarqa expected her there and that woman did not take no for an answer.

Sure enough, both Onyx and Silas were dressed to impress; Onyx in olive-green with her signature tulip-shaped pantaloons, and Silas in silver armor, with an embellished tunic that depicted Skeldor's coat of arms.

"Well, I think Miss Groenhart must have gotten lost," said Mr. Thoth. "Come, come, my dear, I will show you the section of the great war's aftermath, but then we'll have to call it a day. The Akitu festival must excite you." Mr. Thoth winked at Silas and Onyx. "Oh, to be young again."

Naila opened her mouth to protest, but Mr. Thoth continued his monologue. She sighed and followed him. The blank scroll, however, she tucked underneath her cloak.

Onyx and Silas followed behind her at a leisurely pace, the latter not bothering to hide his yawns. To be fair, the only thing keeping her awake was the thought of missing something, anything, that would lead to home. Every moment awake, she had scrutinized all that came to mind, but neither she nor Mr. Thoth had come across clues these past two weeks.

"By the stars, can old Thoth be any more of a snooze fest?" Silas muttered.

"Hush." Onyx tried, and failed, to suppress a snicker. "He has ears you know."

"Mr. Thoth, sir." Naila tugged at the sleeve of his toga.

The scribe looked up in surprise. Apparently, he had forgotten all about them. "Naila, what is it, my child?" he said as he quickly recovered.

"It's just, there's a lot of scrolls here." She beckoned to the cases holding scrolls that no doubt described all major events of the lands of Lemuria in detail. "Can you narrow it down to those that describe the, um, Unspokens?"

"The Unspokens?" Mr. Thoth's jaw dropped, and so did his scroll. It rolled across the marble floor and stopped at the curled-toe shoes the hierodulas had gifted Naila, along with every piece of clothing she wore.

Silas and Onyx too, stared at her open-mouthed. So, she had hit a nerve. The Unspokens must be the secret enemy none dared to speak of. Her fingers gripped her pendant with anticipation.

"Goodness, child, we are dedicated to the celebration of the Lemai identity. We do not pay heed to those who revel in its destruction. The Unspokens and their worshippers have no place here."

"W-What is that supposed to mean?"

Silas hooked an arm around her shoulder, effortlessly pulling her closer with a teasing grin, his confidence as natural as the gleam in his eyes. "What it means is that some things are best left in silence. The Unspokens are exactly that: Not to be spoken of."

"But—"

His smile remained, but his tone grew firmer. "That is on an authority we cannot break."

Naila bit her lip, her frustration building like a storm ready to break.

Silas's eyes softened. "Rest assured. We wouldn't hide anything that could help you find your way back home. This I promise you."

She cast an unsure look at Mr. Thoth, who still looked stricken. She hoped she wouldn't be the cause of a heart attack. She gently eased herself out of Silas's grasp and picked up the fallen scroll. It looked ancient, like the scroll she had hidden within her cloak.

"Here you go." Naila handed it back. It relieved her to see a small smile forming on Mr. Thoth's thin lips. She tried a different approach. "Then... the city of Nebiru? I was wondering if you could tell me more. Surely a wise man such as you knows all there is to know about that place?"

Mr. Thoth's eyes sparkled, a pleased smile forming on his face. He rolled the scroll to a close.

"Ah, do I know of Nebiru? But I do, yes, I do. It's been my father's mission to uncover its secrets and that of his father and his father's father."

At Naila's questioning look, Mr. Thoth chuckled. "Legend says the lost city of Nebiru holds a treasure beyond our imagination. A city of black gold and crystals many say, but some say it is even more." Mr. Thoth frowned and whispered, "Some believe Nebiru can make sky travelers out of people. Sky travelers like you claim to be."

"Sky travelers?" Onyx repeated. She too, was entranced by the scribe's words.

"Come now, Thoth, we're too old for fairy tales. Everyone knows Nebiru doesn't exist," Silas drawled as he leaned against the door like he owned the place. Well, technically, as the crown prince, he would. His eyes, however, remained sharp and watchful.

But Naila's breaths quickened. Crazier things had happened; she would not dismiss it as nonsense. "What if Nebiru is real? What if it holds a portal?"

"My dear—" Mr. Thoth said.

Naila revealed the scroll she had hidden.

Mr. Thoth stared at it, confused.

"I found this in Nebiru's section. It..." She hesitated, but then straightened her shoulders. "It called to me."

Silas and Onyx peeked over Naila's shoulder.

"I doubt that'll help you. There's nothing on it," Onyx said skeptically.

Mr. Thoth seemed lost in thought. "Nothing on it *we* can see."

Silas frowned. "So, it holds a hidden message?"

He nodded. "We believe so. We call it the Hædur. An ancient language that only reveals itself to few."

"Well, then, we're wasting our time," said Silas.

"Perhaps it's a language that reveals itself to the Unspokens," Naila declared stubbornly.

The blood drained from their faces. Mr. Thoth stumbled backward. The prince reached for him to prevent the old man from falling.

Onyx tugged at the sleeve of Naila's old-rose caftan and mumbled behind her hand. "Let's not challenge Mr. Thoth too much."

Naila's cheeks heated. "I'm sorry."

When Mr. Thoth recollected himself, he pushed the blank scroll into Naila's hands, a wistful expression overcoming his face. His eyes briefly settled on the markings on her forehead.

"If... if it called to you, then you must keep it."

This was the last thing she expected him to say. Did Mr. Thoth finally believe her? If only just a little?

"Why?" Her voice broke with emotion.

"A feeling. Just a feeling, indeed. But ask no more, nergayla," Mr. Thoth begged. "Let the past stay where it is, buried deep inside its coffin."

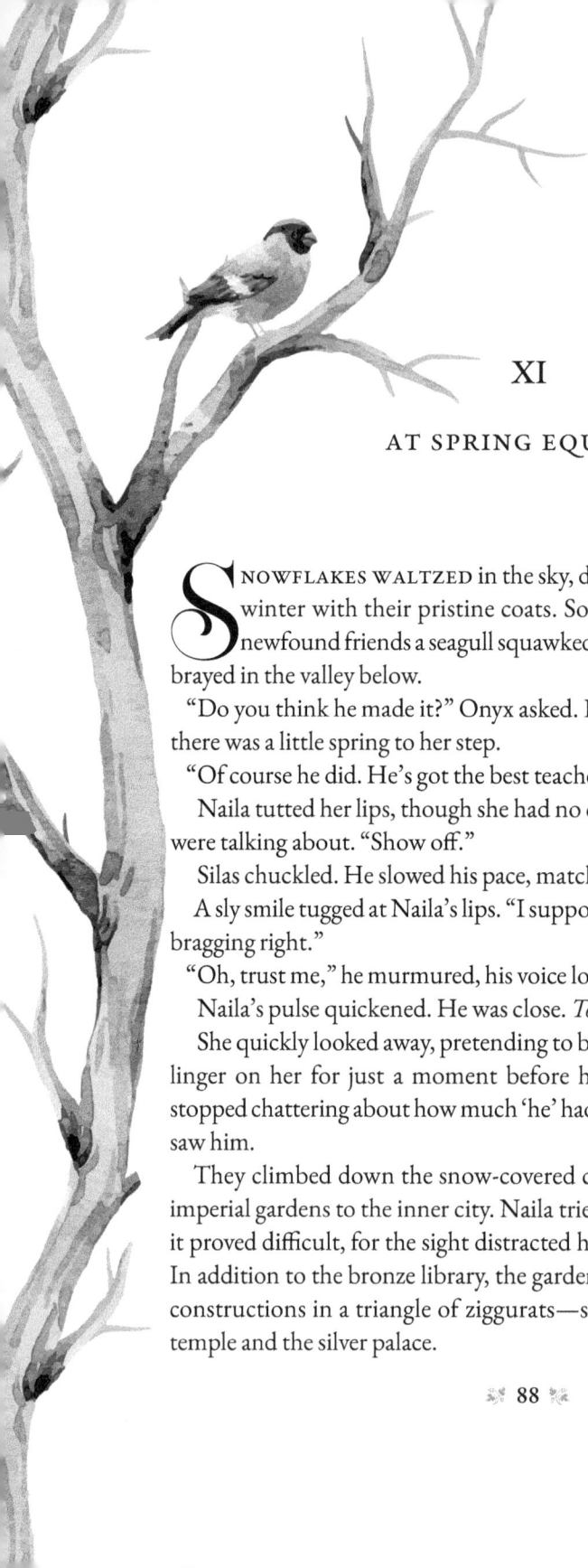

XI

AT SPRING EQUINOX

SNOWFLAKES WALTZED in the sky, draping Havenmor in the last of winter with their pristine coats. Somewhere above Naila and her newfound friends a seagull squawked curiously, and a donkey or two brayed in the valley below.

"Do you think he made it?" Onyx asked. Excitement laced her voice, and there was a little spring to her step.

"Of course he did. He's got the best teacher." Silas winked at them.

Naila tutted her lips, though she had no clue which friend of theirs they were talking about. "Show off."

Silas chuckled. He slowed his pace, matching hers.

A sly smile tugged at Naila's lips. "I suppose we'll see if you've earned that bragging right."

"Oh, trust me," he murmured, his voice low and teasing, "I always earn it."

Naila's pulse quickened. He was close. *Too* close.

She quickly looked away, pretending to be unimpressed. She felt his gaze linger on her for just a moment before he rejoined Onyx, who hadn't stopped chattering about how much 'he' had probably grown since last they saw him.

They climbed down the snow-covered cobblestones that led from the imperial gardens to the inner city. Naila tried to keep up with the two, but it proved difficult, for the sight distracted her. And what a sight to behold. In addition to the bronze library, the gardens held two further formidable constructions in a triangle of ziggurats—stepped pyramids—the golden temple and the silver palace.

Onyx turned to tug on Naila's hair, on which Aisha had spent a full bell in the early morn until it cascaded in glossy coils to her waist. The hierodula had finished the look with a crown of flowers that matched Naila's caftan. Flattered as she was, she didn't understand why she too, had to look her best. Aisha, however, wouldn't budge. This Akitu festival, where Lemuria celebrated the new year on the first day of spring, had everyone in a feverish trance.

"Thank the stars we got you out. I thought you'd be stuck reading dusty scrolls on Akitu of all days," said Onyx.

Silas chuckled. "If I didn't know better, I would've thought old Thoth had himself an admirer."

Naila hugged the scroll underneath her cloak. "There are so many scrolls there." She smiled dreamily. "Don't you find them interesting?" Even if she weren't obsessed with finding a way home, she would have found it a treat to spend her days in the breathtaking library. Well, when Mr. Thoth wasn't giving a monotonous monologue.

Silas stared at her, amused. "Ah, so we've got ourselves a little library mouse."

Onyx scoffed. "Almost every girl in town is a library mouse."

"But *they* only read to fulfill their naughty, naughty fantasies."

Heat crept up Naila's cheeks. She refrained from mentioning exactly what type of books filled her reading tablet back home. Every moment not spent dancing was filled with swooning over book boyfriends. Sure, she loved classics and literary fiction, but she also loved a good swoony book. *Sorry, well, not sorry.*

Onyx batted her eyelashes in mock innocence. "What say you, šargon? Here I thought *you* were the one that fulfilled those fantasies of theirs."

Silas flashed his teeth but made no reply.

They stepped past a group of boys, practicing in the snow, under the watchful eyes of armored men. They fought with scimitars in a warrior dance of some sort. She had never seen anything like it. Their movements were fluid, precise, elegant, and ended in flames of æther.

"What are they doing?"

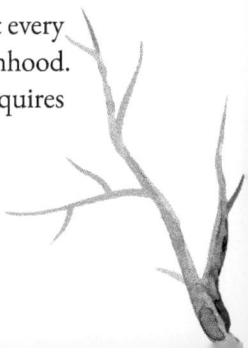

Silas followed her gaze. "Oh, that? The dance of flames. It's what every boy must master before he's eligible to enter the hunt—the rite to manhood. It's no easy feat." He glanced at the boys with pride in his eyes. "It requires full control over æther to complete, and one must have both stamina and patience. But our *lugals* are among the strongest and bravest in Lemuria."

Naila smiled. Of course, the prince would say that. They were his future soldiers after all. Even so, she couldn't help admiring the refined moves of the youths. It almost made her want to practice the dance of flames herself, and she was far from a warrior.

But Onyx stuck her nose up. "It's a men only thing. As if a woman cannot fight!"

"You got refused?" Naila asked, curious.

Onyx's cheeks burned. "I even cut my hair and pretended to be a boy. But the gatekeepers have senses like hawks."

As they reached the valley, the rhythmic waves of music hummed over the cobblestone roads. Stages, market tents, and a bonfire filled the inner city. Sky lanterns lit up the town in a dimmed ambiance, and civilians packed the snowy roads to the brim, all finely dressed in silver and pastels.

Naila felt giddy as a little girl in a candy shop as she followed Onyx and Silas to an open-roofed bazaar, adorned with pretty mosaic tiles.

"Pomegranates, pomegranates! Fresh out of Bulinya! Only one clear crystal per kilo!" a round-bellied man cried over the tittle-tattle.

The merchants sold everything from silks and cashmere to strange fruits and pottery. There were even several stalls dedicated to divination and smoking water pipes. They ambled past a stage where female dancers performed, the blue sparks of æther making masterpieces out of their flowing skirts.

Naila followed their movements with longing. Just two weeks ago that had been her dream. The knife of RIDA's rejection put an end to her wistfulness. With everything that had happened, there had been no time to think of its implications; she would face them when she got back home.

"A blessed Akitu, Your Highness." A plump girl pushed a box of syrupy pastries into the prince's hands, while her friends batted their eyelashes at him. Silas winked at the girls. They entered a giggling fit and Naila thought Pastry Girl would swoon for sure. The prince loved ladies and they in turn loved him. How unexpected. *Not.*

Onyx tugged at Naila's cloak. Grinning, she pointed at a stand looking deliciously close to a gingerbread house, with an overly long queue. "You can't visit Havenmor without trying our butter tea."

A puffy-hatted man walked about the line, disappointing several people with the announcement their favorite drinks were sold out. The moment he noticed Silas, however, he eagerly led them to the front of the row.

Ah, the perks of being royalty.

The sugary scents of chocolate and candy caught Naila in their delicious web, and she suddenly found herself thirsty.

Onyx ordered refreshments she had never heard of but sounded mouth-watering, nonetheless. If butter tea was anything like her beloved jasmine milk tea, she'd be in for a treat.

To the owner's delight, the prince paid with an abundance of crystals.

Onyx snuggled contentedly in her fur-lined cloak. For once, her boots did not carry the metal Naila had come to know as black gold. She took in Onyx's finely woven clothes. Come to think of it, she still didn't know what Onyx's relation to Silas was exactly. She was no princess. That Naila had already figured out.

"Where do you live?"

Onyx glanced up in surprise. "In the redwoods, of course."

Naila blinked, stunned for words.

"You didn't actually believe that did you?"

"Well..."

"I live in the palace."

"I thought only the imperial family lived there?" she answered, sensing an opportunity to get the information she wanted.

"*And* the šar's court, *and* other staff."

"So who are you then? Family, court, or staff?"

Onyx definitely wasn't Silas's servant. The young woman had too many freedoms for that.

Silas put his arm around Onyx's shoulders. "Onyx is family, of course."

Onyx raised a skeptical brow but didn't refute his words.

A cousin then, Naila mused. Silas and Onyx did embody a tight-knit family. She felt a pang of yearning. Growing up, she had no siblings or cousins to play with. And no friends, for that matter. Until Philippe entered her life.

"So you finally decided to show us interest, eh?" the prince teased.

Naila fidgeted with her sleeve, embarrassed. She'd been so preoccupied with her quest, she had spared the people who helped her little thought.

"Kidding." Silas tapped her nose. "*But,* I dare say you'll find us more pleasing than old Thoth."

Two young men approached them, dressed in silver uniforms almost as nice as the prince's.

"Prince Silvanus," said they.

Silas inclined his head. "Lord Angalim. Lord Dukar."

The twosome stared curiously at Naila, but Silas made no introductions.

As the prince conversed with the men and they waited for their drinks, Naila peeked at the chattering civilians walking about the snowy roads. A nearby girl had gray, curved eyes with a mass of brown curls and skin the same color as her hair.

Yes, more interesting than the city were Havenmor's inhabitants themselves. There was no majority ethnicity. In fact, she found it difficult to pinpoint most of their backgrounds.

From lily-white to regal cedar, with eye colors and hair structures in the rarest combinations, some even had eyes in shades she'd never seen before: violet, pitch-black, and pink, absent of other albinism features.

It was somewhat reminiscent of Suriname, a melting pot of ethnicities, where Amerindians, descendants of sub-Saharan Africa, India, China, and Indonesia, among others lived in relative peace. Where a mosque next to a synagogue was the most normal thing in the world.

"One silver beer, and two butter teas."

The puffy-hatted server arrived with their tray of drinks, and a few other bites as a bonus. Onyx immediately snatched the yellowish lemon bread and began chomping on it happily. The server openly stared at Naila, as if he noticed her for the first time, gazing from her frame to the planes of her face, to her eyes, and finally her forehead. Onyx cleared her throat mid-bite, at which the server's cheeks tinged pink. He skirted away.

Naila forced herself to not touch her forehead, knowing what had caught the man's attention. The pearly diamond atop a lying crescent moon. There was no make-up in this world that could hide the symbol from prying eyes.

"Don't mind him," Silas said between gulps of his silver beer—the same color as its namesake. The lords had carried on, "People don't know there's a new nergayla in Skeldor."

She shifted from one foot to another. She wanted to protest this stamp of nergayla they had given her, but all evidence suggested that she was exactly that. Nerves bit into her stomach. Was Zarqa planning to introduce her officially to the people? Was that why she had told her, in no few words, she expected her to be present at the festival?

"They shouldn't get too attached…" she murmured.

Silas stopped drinking, whilst Onyx stopped chewing.

"Because I'm not staying. I'm going home," she said, her voice firmer.

The prince seemed to choose his words carefully. "But until that time comes, you're here with us. We don't want you to feel like you don't belong, even if it's just for a whisper of time."

Her breath caught in her throat. "I…" The words refused to leave her mouth. An emotion welled up in her, too powerful to ignore. "For a whisper in time."

Why was it that in a world so different from her own, someone spoke the words she yearned to hear all her life? That she was seen. That she belonged.

He took her hand in his. His was big. Strong. Warm. "You might find this world has more to offer than you think."

The sunrays caught a few golden strands in his rich brown hair. The light reflected in his eyes, highlighting silver flecks drifting within a midnight ocean. Why hadn't she noticed them before?

Onyx cleared her throat.

At once she came back to her senses and pulled her hand back.

Onyx's gaze was sharp, a warning in it. Not to her, but to the prince, which *he* casually ignored.

Naila blew the hot vapor off the butter tea, eager to refocus the attention. "The shadowreapers… any word from them?"

Silas shook his head. "We sent word to the Ice Šar. Helped him comb through the redwoods even. Nothing."

"And they won't show themselves here?" She shuddered.

Silas gently squeezed her shoulder, his features softening. "Don't you worry. Havenmor is protected by more than just our sentries. You're safe here."

Naila took a sip from her butter tea and banished the shadowreapers from her mind. The creaminess spread around her mouth, tasting of honeysuckle, almonds, and a little shot of something liquorish. The drink set her entire skin aflame, but not in a bad way. She grinned at Onyx and the huntress grinned back.

"Told you it was good."

As they walked through the market tents, the cheerfulness of Havenmor's people infected her. She too, hummed to the melodies of the harps and the beat of the drums. It made her want to dance. From cheery pop to the sensual beats of the Caribbean's zouk—how she loved dancing.

Silas put out his hand.

She hesitated for less than a moment. It was just a dance.

He seized her by the waist and twirled her through the bazaar until they reached the very end. The stones thrummed underneath her boots as she tried to balance through the swirling festival around her, déjà vu to her lessons, only with a much taller and, dare she say, quite dashing partner. Laughing, they came to a stop, the people around them clapping and cheering.

"Silvanus!" Above them, the Silver Šar sat upon his throne on a balcony, surrounded by important-looking folks, an unmistakable frown marring his face. Naila stepped away from Silas at once.

"Naila!"

The hierodulas frolicked with baskets at the foot of the silver-draped stairs. She recognized Aisha, Humaya, and little Oya. Zarqa stood behind them, an unreadable look in her eyes. Oya hopped to Naila, her beaded twists swinging in the air. Her ivory attire complimented her glowing, dark-brown skin. "Naila! Naila! You're just in time. We're going to start the song."

"I don't—" Naila started, but Oya had already pushed a basket with dried flowers into her hands.

"Come, we must hurry."

Naila glanced helplessly at Onyx and Silas, but the treacherous two only nodded encouragingly. Oya shot her a joyous smile, the smile of a child who hadn't yet experienced the horrors of the world, and she couldn't find it in herself to deny Oya anything.

She desperately searched her mind for the lyrics the hierodulas had sung many times while she tried to escape unnoticed to the library. Oya pulled her to the row right before Aisha and Humaya, who smiled at Naila in surprise. A pang of guilt speared her.

Hand for hand, Naila, Oya, and the hierodulas threw dried flowers onto the snowy cobblestones and began their song to the admiring gazes of the people.

Death has come to an end,
The frost of winter finally bends,
The first light of spring thaws,
Frees Lemuria out of famine's claws.

We celebrate Akitu,
We celebrate rebirth,
We honor the coming,
Of the natural world.

Our boys with chins beardless,
Have grown to men fearless,
The fields barren and fruitless,
Grow fertile and again feed us.

We celebrate Akitu,
We celebrate rebirth,
We honor the coming,
Of the natural world.

Havenmor clapped and sang with them. A cozy warmth hung in the air, a spirit of solidarity, a sense of unity. For one slow heartbeat, a dangerous thought bloomed. *What if she stayed?* Her emotions pulled at every inch of her. *What if Lemuria was where she belonged?*

A heat within her skin sprouted to her phæralei, entwining around the tips of her fingers. Before she knew it, her fingers scorched with gilded flames. And the dried flowers... they bloomed like the first rosebuds of spring.

At the sight of the revived flowers, the chattering crowd broke into gasps of reverie. Some people wept.

Actually wept.

"Nergayla! Nergayla! Nergayla!" they cried.

Naila glanced around, at the people coming closer, touching her arms, grazing the blossoming flowers. Her heart skipped a beat or two, but the joyous smiles on their faces calmed her nerves. They weren't out to get her, such a contrast with her past. No mocking smiles. Only adoration.

Behind the crowd, a lone figure leaned against a tree, a man dressed in obsidian, the reins of a black stallion in his hand. A loose turban covered his hair and his face, unveiling only his gaze. Bright, brown eyes met eyes tinged darker than ebony. It was the man from the redwoods who had saved her!

"Come, Naila of Earth," Zarqa urged. "You excited the people, let us return before their anxiousness dictates their deeds."

She nodded but turned one last time. The man was gone. Zarqa led her through the madding crowd. Her heart thundered and her legs quivered. Was he one of Havenmor's civilians? Why didn't he make himself known?

"Nergayla! Nergayla!" The people kept on crying.

She gazed at them, confused. "Why are they acting like that?" She turned to Zarqa, only to see a stricken expression upon the elderly nergayla's face. Somehow, that unsettled her more than the craze of the crowd.

"More importantly, how did you do that?" Zarqa asked.

"Huh?" She bit her lip. "My emotions got the best of me. I'll try to remember your teachings."

Zarqa shook her head. "Not my teachings, no. To revive those flowers from death... Not even in the age of the Unspokens..." The nergayla mumbled more to herself than to Naila.

They were steps away from the Silver Šar's throne when Silas appeared before them, his expression wholly grave. Gone was any hint of flirting or teasing and an unspoken exchange passed between him and Zarqa. She huffed and tapped her foot impatiently. Why were these people so secretive? "Was there something you needed, *šargon*?"

Silas's gaze shifted back to her. This time she could read clear reverie within them. She didn't like it. Not him too.

"You had questions," he began. "But they are not my authority to answer."

"You already said that," she said, unsure where he was going.

"Not my authority," he repeated, somewhat lost in thought. Zarqa offered him a reassuring nod, bringing him back to the moment. "But I believe it's time you met someone who can. It's time to introduce you to the šaltana... my mother."

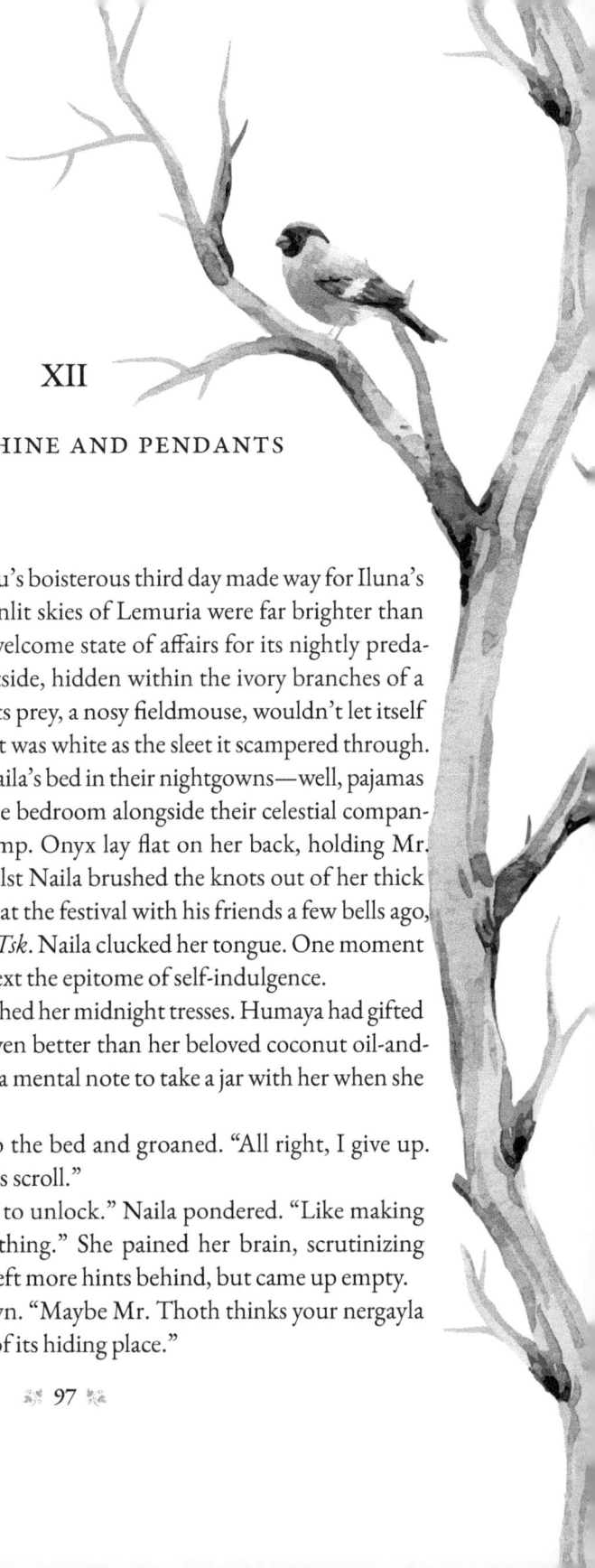

XII

OF MOONSHINE AND PENDANTS

THE FADING sun of Akitu's boisterous third day made way for Iluna's serene night. The moonlit skies of Lemuria were far brighter than those on Earth, an unwelcome state of affairs for its nightly predators. A snowy owl hooted outside, hidden within the ivory branches of a tree beside Naila's bedroom. Its prey, a nosy fieldmouse, wouldn't let itself be easily caught, however, for it was white as the sleet it scampered through.

Naila and Onyx sat upon Naila's bed in their nightgowns—well, pajamas for Onyx—as the moons lit the bedroom alongside their celestial companions and the chamber's oil lamp. Onyx lay flat on her back, holding Mr. Thoth's scroll to the light, whilst Naila brushed the knots out of her thick curls. They had left the prince at the festival with his friends a few bells ago, half-drunk and lost in revelry. *Tsk*. Naila clucked her tongue. One moment he was seriousness itself, the next the epitome of self-indulgence.

She hummed while she brushed her midnight tresses. Humaya had gifted her a hair balm that worked even better than her beloved coconut oil-and-shea butter routine. She made a mental note to take a jar with her when she went back home.

Onyx dropped the scroll to the bed and groaned. "All right, I give up. There's literally nothing on this scroll."

"I think it's a secret we have to unlock." Naila pondered. "Like making invisible ink visible, or something." She pained her brain, scrutinizing Philly's tales in the hope he'd left more hints behind, but came up empty.

Onyx stretched out in a yawn. "Maybe Mr. Thoth thinks your nergayla powers will force the text out of its hiding place."

Naila put her brush down. "You really believe that? About my flames, I mean?"

Onyx leaned her head against her hand. "I know you think you're from another world—" Naila started to protest but Onyx quickly went on. "And I believe you, I do. But, N, how do you explain your powers? What you did to those flowers is out of this world. Nergaylas can heal yes, but bringing back something to life? That is Legends of the Sky territory. *Ishtar* territory."

Naila stared at her hands unbelievingly and whispered more to herself than to Onyx, "This can't be real..."

"But it *is*. I saw it myself. The whole of Havenmor saw it. Those storytellers are already singing songs about you."

A power to create... It frightened her more than it pleased her. She didn't ask for this. Didn't want it. She stared at her hands, quivering with a barely perceptible tremor. "You know, I was the family's secret. The niece with hallucinations, the one nobody wanted around. No matter how hard I tried to fit in, no one wanted to be my friend. Just before I left, I was rejected by the academy I had been training for all my life. I felt like a failure in every direction."

She paused, the weight of her words hanging in the air. Earth and its bitter memories seemed like a lifetime ago. Even RIDA felt like a forgotten dream. She forced her lips into a smile. "Honestly, school and psychiatrists... they don't matter now. What I need is a way out of this mess. I just find it ironic I'm some super rare being in this world. My classmates would have a good laugh."

Onyx's gaze turned watchful, a sea of messages with the last things Naila wanted to see. Sorrow. Sadness. *Pity*.

"You know, my *māmān* always told me the road to success is paved with more setbacks than the number of times unsuccessful people ever try. One should never focus on the waves of existence, little bug, always on the destination, is what she said. It's not a failure to work hard to achieve something, N. Failure is not trying at all."

But she *had* tried.

Countless times. It wasn't just one rejection, Naila had been rejected all her life. No one had *really* seen her. She gazed at her melancholic reflection in the window's glass. In the moonlight, her phæralei gleamed like it belonged in the night's sky, just like her moonstone compass.

Kids had bullied her for those marks. Had called her a freak. In her desperation to cover them, she had caked them in layers of concealer the moment she entered high school, although it did little to hide them from prying eyes. It was strange to go bare-headed these days—*feylanas* only used lip stains and kohl for make-up.

Then something hit Naila.

"Will you... tell me what happened to your mother?"

For a while Onyx said nothing. At last, she let out a deep breath. "My *māmān*, Baosi, was sold as a fancy slave... we were both sold as fancy slaves."

Naila gasped. "W-What?"

Onyx fumbled with the empty scroll, the shadows of Iluna's light swaying over the edges of her face. "Shadowreapers raided my village on the night of my eighth winter. They stole our crystals, made labor slaves out of our men, and took them to the Shadowlands. They had no use for us women and children, so they sold us. *Māmān* and I got separated. I was blindfolded and scared so my memory of the auction location was shredded. Until Riley told us. Now, I can finally track down the auctioneers and find out who bought her. I just need to figure out how to get to Isolon."

"Oh, Onyx, that's horrible!" Naila squeezed her hand. "How did you get out?"

Onyx swallowed. "They sold me into Jericho the Cruel's harem as one of his slave concubines."

"Jericho the Cruel," Naila repeated in horror. Whoever that was, it didn't sound good.

She took in Onyx's wild locks. Even here in the lands of Lemuria, East-Asian features and ginger hair were likely considered a rare combination. An 'exotic' gem for a rich man's collection.

"Jericho was Crishire's late šar. It's there I met the šaltana and Silas. He was my only friend in that dreadful place. My protector in a time I was too weak to defend myself. When, uh, when the šaltana fled with Silas, they managed to smuggle me out too. I'll always be grateful for their sacrifice." Onyx tugged away one of her wild locks. "To 'abduct' one from a harem, is to directly insult a man's pride. And in Lemuria there's nothing more important to a man than his pride," she spat.

So that's how Onyx and the prince met. It explained their close friendship. The tension between the empires of Skeldor and Crishire made even more sense now too. This Jericho must be Silas's father. Crishire's new šar, the one who had conquered the Empire of Ornesias and had declared war on Skeldor, was likely a spiteful uncle.

"Your village... it was in Jodrir, wasn't it? That's why you're so at ease in the redwoods."

"*Yana.* I'm always on the search for word of my mother and though the Lawless are feared, I knew they could direct me in the right way. I—" Onyx's breath hitched. "I won't rest until I've freed her."

Naila squeezed her hand again. "Of course. And if there's anything I can do to help, I will do it."

Onyx rubbed her eyes. "I... There's dust in my eye."

Onyx wasn't fooling her. In the short time Naila had known Onyx she'd only ever seen her as fierce and carefree. This vulnerable side of hers melted away any apprehension Naila might've had. No one's life is only sunshine and rainbows. We all have our cross to weather through the storms.

"Do you know why those shadowreapers did this?"

Onyx shrugged.

"Nobody knows what's going on in the Shadowlands. I wouldn't be surprised if the Shadow Šar is building the Unspokens a shrine." Onyx scoffed. "He probably sent his shadowreapers to get the resources."

Naila perked up. "A shrine for the Unspokens, huh?"

Onyx's eyes widened, apparently just realizing what she had said.

"I remember... because they worship them. It's what Silas said that very first day."

Onyx winced.

"Please, tell me the truth. Who are they?"

"Were. Those bastards are dead, all of them. The great Suzano and the twelve made sure of that." Onyx crawled up to sit crossed-legged and stared out of the window. The moonbeams highlighted the folds of her glum face. "We don't know what they were, or where they came from. For all of Mr. Thoth's scrolls, the time before the age of the Unspokens is still a blank slate."

She folded her hands in her lap. "So, they're not Lemai, then?"

"I've already said too much. *Please*. You're meeting the šaltana on the morrow. I advise you to have this conversation with her."

The binary moons glittered again upon Naila's compass. Back home, it had never reacted to light the way it did in Lemuria.

"Look at that." Onyx pointed, seemingly happy for a distraction. "How weirdly beautiful."

Naila reached for the compass, tentatively, hesitantly. Her fingers brushed over its cool surface and her heart constricted with memories. It was during one of her father's ventures he'd found her compass; or so her mother had once told her. Hidden between lacquer works and wooden carvings, the moonstone compass called to him from a table at a Maroon market. Probably the same way it called to her now.

Ma... Philly...

Were they okay?

Naila clicked the compass open. The moonlight reflected on the inside.

Her mouth fell open.

The reflected light was simply stunning. Like a billion little stars in all colors of the rainbow.

"N." Onyx gasped from somewhere nearby, but she didn't listen. An untrained eye would miss it, but Naila recognized the constellations in the tiny glitters. There was Spica, Zavijava, and the binary star Porrima. A new moon in Virgo. A new beginning.

"N." Onyx tugged at the sleeve of her nightgown. "You really need to see this."

She followed Onyx's gaze to the open scroll. Everywhere the reflected light hit the scroll, crimson inscriptions appeared. It was strangely enchanting, like the beats of a lullaby a mother sang to her babe.

"What the—"

One stripe after another appeared. Her heart thundered wildly when she understood its contents. As if hypnotized, her fingertips trailed the engravings.

"It's a map," Onyx exclaimed.

Indeed it was.

One that led to the lost city of Nebiru.

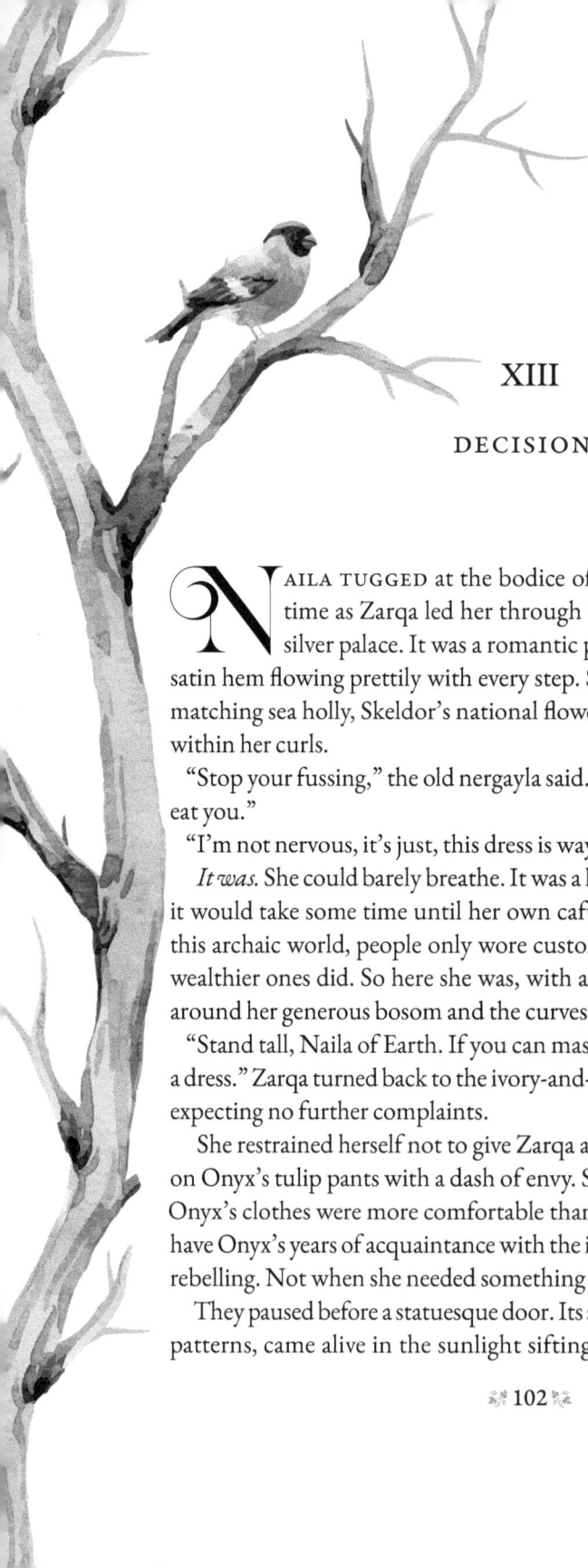

XIII

DECISIONS

NAILA TUGGED at the bodice of her caftan for the umpteenth time as Zarqa led her through the pillar-lined hallways of the silver palace. It was a romantic piece with flower appliques, the satin hem flowing prettily with every step. Sweet little Oya had given her a matching sea holly, Skeldor's national flower, which Humaya had braided within her curls.

"Stop your fussing," the old nergayla said. "Your Highness is not going to eat you."

"I'm not nervous, it's just, this dress is way too tight." She pouted.

It was. She could barely breathe. It was a hand-me-down from Zarqa, for it would take some time until her own caftans were sewn. Apparently, in this archaic world, people only wore custom-made attires. Or at least, the wealthier ones did. So here she was, with a dress that was a little too snug around her generous bosom and the curves of her hips.

"Stand tall, Naila of Earth. If you can master your flames, you can master a dress." Zarqa turned back to the ivory-and-silver tiles of the hallway, clearly expecting no further complaints.

She restrained herself not to give Zarqa a piece of her mind, reminiscing on Onyx's tulip pants with a dash of envy. She was more of a dress girl, but Onyx's clothes were more comfortable than *this*. Naila sighed. She did not have Onyx's years of acquaintance with the imperial family to get away with rebelling. Not when she needed something from them.

They paused before a statuesque door. Its surface, adorned with geometric patterns, came alive in the sunlight sifting through the windows' lattice screens. Two sentries stood guard, their silver uniforms mirroring the door's grandeur. Contrary to the other men she had seen in Skeldor, the sentries in this wing of the palace lacked facial hair, and their appearance had the hint of feminine traits.

She could feel the change in their expressions when their eyes landed on her phæralei. They nodded once to Zarqa and opened the door to the šaltana's quarters.

"Remember. You will be speaking to a princess, not to the local fishmonger." Zarqa put a firm hand on the small of her back, gently pressing her forward.

She fought the urge to roll her eyes. As if she didn't know that. Then her eyes took in the reception area. She blinked several times, momentarily awestruck by the lovely sight that met her. Never had she encountered such luxury. And the temple and library, she thought, had been luxury itself.

The room held immense arched windows, each a testament to fine craftsmanship. They were stained with floral patterns, bathing the room in a kaleidoscope of colors. The elegant plasterwork on the ceiling told a page in Ishtar's story. Velvet sofas and divans, sumptuous and inviting, were adorned with embroidered cushions. Exotic plants in exquisite pottery finished the picturesque room with a touch of lush greenery.

"Welcome, ladies." A voice as gentle as the lotus scent wafting through the room greeted them.

The šaltana sat upon a divan nestled within a bay window. She was draped in a lilac caftan, embroidered with silver thread. It made her already alabaster skin look a shade paler. Silas, dressed in his official uniform for the later festivities, stood next to his mother. His dark gaze roamed the curves of Naila's dress, a wicked little smile teasing his lips. Her cheeks heated.

Where the šaltana was fair, the prince was all sun-kissed skin; where he was tall and strapping, she was dainty and petite... However, when Naila looked more closely, she noticed the obvious resemblance between the two she had missed at first. They had the same night-blue eyes and the hint of a dimple on their chin. Despite her flaxen hair there was something decidedly East-Asian in the šaltana's features, however, reflecting her kinship with the Silver Šar.

"Zarqa." Silas inclined his head, though he couldn't seem to tear his gaze away from Naila. His voice took on a softer tone. "Naila. This is my mother.

Her Imperial Highness Sayana Line Eseliyon, a šaltana of Skeldor. Mother, this is Naila Groenhart."

"Thank you for receiving me." Naila bowed nervously. So much hinged on these next moments. She had to convince the imperial family to help her and Onyx get to Isolon. Her joy at finding the lost city's location had unfortunately been brief.

Mr. Thoth, and indeed Aisha and Humaya too, had wept when Naila showed them the moon markings on the scroll. It was unfortunately short-lived. The moment Mr. Thoth had put a map of Lemuria next to the scroll, the smiles had melted off everyone's faces.

"Dear, oh, dear," Mr. Thoth had mumbled as he shook his head in distress.

Onyx had let out a little gasp of surprise.

When Naila had asked what was the matter, Aisha had answered for them. "The lost city of Nebiru is in the middle of the Dark Forest of Isolon."

The Dark Forest... Naila stared at them blankly.

"Okay...?"

"*Okay*?" Onyx gaped. "N, Isolon is on a whole other continent. The only way to get there is through, one, Læriad, an empire torn by a civil war; two, Crishire, which would cost us our heads, mind you, or... or, three, through the Sea of Helath. Enough said. Why do you think I'm still here?"

The group shuddered, but Naila just blinked. Whatever got their undergarments in a twist? Yes, Crishire was written off. Even she knew the Red Šar and his lot did not look kindly upon Skeldorians. And, well, apparently, Læriad too. But the sea? They just had to arrange a ship.

"The Seven Seas and the Wicked Oceans, my dear, are not to be trifled with." Mr. Thoth adjusted his spectacles as if he read her mind. "Many *lugals* dare answer their call of dangerous adventures. Alas, but half of them receive pity and return alive."

"Not to mention, sister, whisperers say shadowreapers have been crawling around the Dark Forest as of late. It's a dangerous place," Humaya whispered softly.

Shadowreapers.

Every shimmer of hope, every tendril of joy, died a bleak death with those words. It appeared that she and Lemuria may yet be stuck with each other for some time to come. Unless she figured out something, and fast. Come to think of it, if shadowreapers were interested in the Dark Forest, it could well be because of Nebiru. Which made the chances even higher she could find a way home there!

She *had* to talk to the prince. Aside from Nebiru, she hadn't found anything that led to a way back. Life or death, she had to risk the journey. Preferably by ship, but if necessary, she would walk through Læriad or Crishire, no questions asked.

The šaltana beckoned Naila to come closer, breaking her chain of thought. She did as instructed, taking a seat on a floor cushion before the princess. The šaltana folded a finger underneath Naila's chin and lifted it until their eyes met. There was nothing between the princess's eyebrows. No mark that identified her as more than a regular Lemai. Yet she was a revered diviner.

"I have heard much about you from Zarqa and my son, Naila. They say you can bring dead flowers to bloom."

Her cheeks burned. "They're just flowers," she quickly said before thinking. Then she straightened her back and met the woman's gaze. No. They weren't *just* flowers. And she *needed* answers. "What is it you think I am?"

The šaltana took her hands in hers, pressing them lightly. "A nergayla, of course." She smiled gently. "Like the originals from the age of the Unspokens. I can see a halo blazing around your angelic frame. Warm and golden and pure like *Ishtar*. Æther flows strongly through your veins. But my dearest Zarqa has surely told you that already." The gaze she cast at the elderly nergayla was filled with tender fondness.

Naila shifted from one knee to another. Would she dare ask the šaltana? She studied the princess, who reached to brush her phæralei. The woman's eyes were filled with wonder.

"The Unspokens," Naila whispered, "tell me about them."

The šaltana pulled her hand back as if Naila had burned her. Silas and Zarqa exchanged uneasy glances.

"Please?" she said, refusing to give up. They promised her answers and she would not leave without them. "I need to know."

The šaltana shook her head, her eyes a war between fear and something else. Then she whispered, her voice strangled to a murmur. "It is such an irony you need to ask. You see, nergaylas are closest in blood to the Unspokens. More so than even shadowreapers are."

Naila whispered breathlessly, "Tell me more."

"They came from the sky... like Angels of Death announcing the apocalypse. Ethereal. Beautiful. *Ruthless*."

"What did they do?" she said, her voice soft, barely audible.

"They took everything from us. Our world, our cultures, our freedom, even our names... until the heights Lemaians once reached became nothing more than a myth."

A dark shadow bled upon Silas's face. She could see in all their gazes how difficult it was to talk about this. Even though they hadn't experienced the age of the Unspokens themselves, the pain of their ancestors had left lasting scars.

"So, they're not Lemai, then?"

"*Lai.* We do not think so. Some say they are fallen angels; others call them spirits; others swear they are from another time and place. I guess we will never find out."

"And those shadowreapers and nergaylas are their offspring? Is that why we, *they* wield æther so effortlessly?"

"No matter how hard people like to pretend otherwise, we *all* carry the blood of the Unspokens, Naila. What else would you expect after a thousand winters of slavery and rape? But the power to wield æther, it shows up in very few. The more blood of the Unspokens, the more powerful the æther."

Silas laughed humorlessly, finally breaking his silence. "It's funny how we loathe the Unspokens, yet the ones who have the highest amount of their blood are worshipped like deities and given the seats of power."

So, the Lemai had inherited æther from the Unspokens.

"I can see why it's painful to talk about them."

"It is," said the šaltana. "The Unspokens stripped every hint of decency from our ancestors, reduced them for ages to nothing more than a single instinct: the will to survive. We are still tending to the wounds of centuries of oppression, but the mere presence of æther will always leave a scar. It is both our greatest pride and our biggest shame."

Naila swallowed. She pulled out two scrolls, the original from the library and an inked copy. A look of disapproval veiled Zarqa's face. Aisha and Humaya were obviously terrible at keeping secrets.

Silas threw a look at the map and a frown creased his forehead. "Don't tell me Onyx put you up to this."

"She didn't." Naila cleared her throat and told them what had happened.

Silas's expression shifted. His face was a battlefield of astonishment and disbelief. The šaltana's, however, was one of wonder.

"What do you think, Zarqa?" said the princess.

Zarqa shook her head sadly. "I think Nebiru may well be real, but its existence bears no meaning if one cannot reach it alive."

Silas crossed his arms, an unreadable look on his face as he leaned against the wall.

The šaltana nodded, lost in thought. She glanced at Silas, reaching for him. At once, he took his mother's hand in his, pressing a featherlight kiss upon her palm. Naila warmed at the adoration he bestowed on his mother.

With a faraway look, the šaltana murmured, "I have long since known this day would come. Since the first day I knew I held the power of a diviner. On that dreadful day..." Her voice hitched.

"Mother," Silas said, his voice betraying worry.

The šaltana shook her head and continued, "I knew that one who bore the mark of Ishtar would be born, with phæralei complete and vivid, not just a hint of its former self as the ones the nergaylas of current days carry. Have I not told you this vision, Zarqa?"

"It is as you say." Zarqa took a seat next to the šaltana and took her other hand in hers as if to give the princess strength.

The šaltana looked straight at Naila. Her eyes were clear as the sky. "That person is you. *Ishtar's Chosen*."

A cold shiver washed over her. Her mouth opened and closed. How? When she was from Earth...?

"You see, this has been prophesied even by nergaylas of old, those in the age of the Unspokens, that is. We do not know the full extent of this prophecy, for it is only known to the Unspokens, but we know it has chased them to many worlds and ultimately led them to Lemuria. They were vile and evil, Naila. Their wanting Ishtar's Chosen could not mean any good."

Naila dare not let out a breath. She did not know where the princess was leading with this story, but she found it as enthralling as Philly's fairy tales. Reminiscent too.

Zarqa cleared her throat. "If this vision holds true, we must do everything to protect you, Naila of Earth. You must not go to the Dark Forest!"

Naila pinned her nose up stubbornly. "Then how am I supposed to get back home?"

The princess too, shook her head. "No, Zarqa, no. You must not let fear cloud your judgment. If the path to Nebiru revealed itself to Naila, then she must be meant to find it. It is, after all, called the City of Secrets."

Naila blinked. Admittedly she was looking for a way home, but mayhap Nebiru could answer the questions no one else could. Like who her father was and why a nergayla was born on Earth.

Silas watched the exchange, deep in thought, his arms still crossed.

"We do not know if Nebiru even exists, Sayana," Zarqa said.

Before Naila could protest Zarqa's words, Silas pushed himself off the wall. "We don't know if it exists, no, but if we don't try to find it, we'll never get our answers. Mother has never been wrong on account of both her visions and instincts. If she thinks Naila is meant to find Nebiru..."

Naila smiled at him with gratitude. His eyes bored into hers with an intensity she couldn't place. He seemed calm, almost resigned, as if he had expected this turn of events.

"So you'll help me?" she whispered whilst holding his gaze.

"Think about the journey, my prince." Zarqa shook her head. "It is too dangerous. Skeldor cannot lose its only prince."

Silas gave the old woman a crooked smile that made even Naila's heart race. "Well, that's why she has me."

Naila raised her brow, unable to resist. "Cocky, much?"

Leaning closer, his eyes gleamed with a playful spark. "Well, they do call me Skeldor's best swordsman."

The šaltana reached out and squeezed Silas's hand. She glanced at him lovingly. "You have a wild and restless heart, like the waves of the sea crashing against coastal rocks. Yet you've always restrained it when duty deemed it necessary. It's time to let go. I give you my blessing."

"Mother..." Silas's voice was low and raw.

"You know what you must do."

Silas swallowed hard. "Grandfather will be furious."

She patted his hand gently. "And yet you must not let others keep you from doing that which is right. Is that not what it means to be a šar?"

Zarqa folded her wrinkled hands in a prayer gesture. Her voice was soft yet unyielding. "My dearests, I pray you rethink. What good is following a path, adventurous though it may it be, if it leads you to a dangerous road with a price too high to pay? Again, we could lose both you and Naila."

Apparently, that was the wrong thing to tell the prince.

"I am no coward. And you can trust I'll keep Naila safe."

Zarqa shook her head in frustration. "Bravery is one thing. Foolhardiness is another."

Naila could see the war waging within him. The siren's song of adventure and the noose of duty. But the princess merely smiled dreamily. "Come now, Zarqa. You can be such a mother hen. But you cannot keep chicks from taking their first flight."

Zarqa sighed in quiet resignation.

Silas answered his mother's smile with a mischievous one of his own. "Grandfather will say I have a duty to my people here in Lemuria, not continents away."

"And what will you say?"

His dark eyes sparkled. "I shall say my people deserve a šar who is all that he can be, not less than he can be."

"Go, my son, and then return to us."

Naila's eyes shifted from the women to the prince, her heart pitter-pattering. Was this going the way she thought—hoped—it was?

The princess rose from the divan. She palmed her son's face, bringing it to hers until their foreheads touched. The sunlight shimmering through the windows cast a halo around their shadowed frames. Almost inaudibly, she said, "You look so much like your father. I-I wish he could have seen you."

Something told Naila those loving words weren't about Jericho the Cruel.

Silas squeezed his eyes shut, his chest rising and falling. When he opened them once more, she saw it—his resolve. His eyes gleamed, not with fear nor with worry, but with a fire of endless possibilities. One she recognized because it mirrored her own longing, to see where this wild journey would lead.

"Well then," he said, a roguish smile tugging at the corners of his lips. "I suppose we shouldn't waste any more time. Nebiru is waiting for us."

SCROLL II

A SONG WITHIN THE STORMS

So alluring its song, so enchanting its whisper,
The sea calls to the bird, it purrs to come hither,
As a siren, her waves hum tales of bewitching quests,
Eyeing the dreams beating within many a seaman's chest,
Watch out for the sea, watch out for her treachery,
For in her tendrils, those dreams will crumble and wither.

XIV

A BOY CALLED TRYTON

THERE WAS something lighter in the šargon's steps as they descended the flower-bordered steps of the imperial garden. The floral scent of sea holly combined with the sea-kissed breeze, and the morning sun reflected upon his silver armor. Naila peeked at him through her lashes carefully, so he wouldn't catch her staring. The lines on his face had loosened, and despite the shadow of stubble along his jaw, there was a boyish delight in the way he carried himself.

"We'll have to go across the sea," he said, unable to keep the excitement out of his voice. "Incognito. We cannot risk giving the other empires ammunition against Skeldor."

She nodded eagerly. "See, that's what I said, but Mr. Thoth and the others said the Sea of Helath was too dangerous."

They reached a narrow cobblestone path that led to the inner city, into the vibrant heart of the festival. Like a true prince, Silas stepped aside and gestured for her to go first. Unlike a true prince, his eyes slid naughtily over the curves of her figure. Her cheeks burned anew.

"Oh, the Sea of Helath is dangerous, make no mistake," he said. Yet the thought seemed to lure him more than deter him. Then a frown creased his face. "In fact, chances are, Naila, some may not survive this quest."

She sucked on her lip. Surely the prince was exaggerating.

He paused his step, his hand encircling her arm with a firm yet gentle grip that left tingles in its wake. She turned to face him, meeting his gaze. It was dark, serious. *Warning.*

"Do you understand?"

Again, she nodded, more to please him than herself. It was just a trip on a boat. What could be so dangerous about that?

"*You* don't seem scared," she noted, stubbornly.

His lips curved into a cocky grin. "Fear is not my style." His fingers traced the hilt of his ever-present scimitar. "Besides, I need to keep in shape. *Valkarian* here is rusting for lack of use." His eyes twinkled mischievously.

The sea crashed upon the rocks far below, as if hearing the prince's challenge. For a moment, the two of them stared in silence at the wild waves.

"It's been ten winters since last I left the Winterlands," he whispered as they continued their pace. His thoughts seemed to drift to a faraway place before his expression grew serious again. "Isolon's Dark Forest isn't far away from Crishire. Whatever happens, I have no desire to set foot in that place."

Curiously, she probed. "Because of the Red Šar? Your uncle."

His face darkened. "*Yana,* because of the Red Šar. My *brother.*"

She instinctively retracted her step, taken aback. "Brother? Your brother declared war on you?"

The prince shook his head, the lines around his mouth deepening. "It's complicated." There was something heavy in his voice like an unspoken pain. She had so many questions, but she sensed he wasn't in the mood to answer them.

The vibrant notes of music and laughter met them before the city came into sight. Onyx waved at them from near the Silver Šar's stage.

"I'll leave it to you to give her the news. I'll go talk to Grandfather," said Silas.

Nerves bubbled in her stomach. "I hope he agrees to help us."

Silas chuckled. "Trust me, he won't." At the look on her face, he winked. "Leave the worrying to me. I'd much rather see you smile..."

Moments later, Onyx beamed like a thousand sunrises when Naila told her what had occurred. The huntress didn't even notice a brave little bird stealing a bite from her lemon bread. "Silas agreed to go? He really did? Thank the stars the šaltana's plans align with ours."

Naila glanced at the decadent stage.

Oil-filled bowls lit with æther framed its marble edges. The šar sat on a grand silver throne in the middle, flanked by what seemed to be noble guests and an empty chair. The old man himself was draped in a lavish robe with an intricate turban beneath his crown. Despite hair the same color as his silver eyes, Naila could tell he too, had been handsome in his younger days. The šar shot a nasty glare at the empty chair beside him, as if the furniture had personally offended him.

"Lady Nehemia Onya vi Iliyas." A manservant bowed to Onyx.

Naila's eyes snapped to the redhead in surprise. *Lady what?* Onyx's cheeks darkened to a blotchy red, but she merely nodded, avoiding Naila's eyes in the process.

"Lady Naila of Earth," the servant inclined his head to Naila. His eyes paused briefly on her phæralei but lowered just as fast. "Follow me, please."

"Your name is Nehemia?" Naila whispered as soon as the man was out of earshot.

"No." Onyx's mouth twisted in discontent, "It's Onyx. Just Onyx."

Onyx fumbled with the ends of her wild locks and finally sighed. "I gave up trying to correct them. The Silver Šar is of the old stamp. He demands everyone be addressed by their official name, no matter how dreadful. And, well, officially, I still belong to Jericho's imperial harem, even if he's dead."

"I see..."

The balcony was lavish, as one would expect of royalty. Pale rugs, quite simply works of art, covered the marble tiles, and ornate floor tables were spread throughout the stage, oriental cushions circling them. The most beautiful thing, however, was the garden behind the bazaar. The walls were made of the finest crystal, so one could stare to their heart's desire at the snowy scenery.

"It's a polar bear," Naila gushed as she pointed to a bear that roamed in the snow.

It was twice as big as the polar bears she had seen at the zoo and as fierce as it was handsome. From its head to its limbs, the caniform's fur was an ombre of snow-white to silver to slate-gray. A unique snowflake, fitting perfectly in the picturesque garden.

"Polar bear? Whatever is that?" Onyx chomped on the remainder of her lemon bread.

They took a seat on their cushions at a table near the crystal wall.

"It's a cave bear from the Ice Caves," Onyx continued, "They're vicious creatures, the lot, but His Majesty loves them."

Without warning, the tantara of trumpets sounded through the inner city, followed by the civilians erupting in cheers. They had gone well and truly mad. Not at all unlike the swooning teenage girls Naila had once experienced at a concert of her favorite Korean Pop boyband.

"They're back," Onyx gushed.

Sure enough, a line of *lugals* sauntered toward the stage as the crowd cheered them on, just like they had done for Naila and the hierodulas days before. Many of the young men carried game with them, although some were empty-handed. At the front of the line was a lanky boy, no older than sixteen winters. Over his thin, yet strong shoulders, he carried a beast of an ice-crawler.

"Tryce. I knew it!" Onyx clapped with a grin from ear to ear.

The boy cast Onyx a cheeky grin. A pair of dimples formed in his bronze cheeks, and Naila immediately liked him. There was a boyish charm in his swarthy features.

Silas finally appeared on the balcony, met with a sigh from his grandfather, and nodded approvingly at the lads. He cleared his throat and started a speech whilst Onyx whispered explanations to Naila. "The Hunt is an initiation; the ultimate test a boy must pass to be a man."

"What do they have to do?"

"They need to catch a predator in the Frozen Forest. The bigger and more vicious the beast, the higher his esteem and rewards. It's important, you know, if he wants to have a chance at getting the girl of his dreams or enter the working spheres at a higher rank."

"And now, for the winner of the thousandth annual hunt: Tryton Barbaras, please step forward," the prince continued his speech.

The boy, Tryce, grinned and threw the ice-crawler's corpse with a heavy thud before his feet. The people cheered.

Onyx beamed. "That's my cousin!"

Naila, however, glanced skeptically at Tryce's youthful features. "Aren't some of them a little too young for this?"

"Age doesn't define adulthood in Lemuria, N. If you've mastered æther, then you're considered ready for the next phase in life."

Naila frowned.

"But what happens to those who don't have æther? I thought only a few people were born with it?"

"That's what crystals are for." Onyx threw a clear crystal in the air and caught it again. She squashed it in her gloved hand and when she reopened it, the crystal disappeared. In its stead, pale blue flames danced atop the intricate black gold covering her fingers.

Naila sucked in a breath.

"There are several Elysian Fields across the world. Fields rich in æther. With black gold"—Onyx wiggled her gloved fingers—"we can mold it into crystals. And with training, we can absorb the æther within these crystals. Even those born without the power."

"Oh, wow. Zarqa didn't tell me that."

"That's because nergaylas have no use for it."

After Silas's speech, the city burst into cheers anew and, unsurprisingly, the people started another feast. A female servant with a scarf-belt hung low upon her hips neared their table and supplied it with heated wine, cheese, roasted seafood, and vegetables. Naila glanced around the decadent stage and her heart skipped a beat. Silas sat at the very center. He was handsome as ever, with a roguish smile that could melt chastity belts off.

The šar fumbled with his seal ring. He was deep in thought as he listened to Silas. He didn't look menacing, but more like an aloof businessman in the attire of a Lemaian šar. Then again, Naila had been in Havenmor for less than a month. She knew nothing of the way of šars and empires.

"Who are these people?" said Naila as she filled her plate with food; vegetables and goat cheese only, of course.

"The Council of Elders, the nobility, some of the šar's consorts and concubines, and other relatives," Onyx said as she cut up her fish.

Naila paused her fork mid-air. "Consorts? Concubines? As in plural?"

"You look surprised," Onyx said. "Don't they have harems in your world?"

"Uh, not where I live. Tell me women at least have harems here too?"

Onyx laughed out loud, which earned her a disapproving frown from an elderly woman at a nearby table. "Dearling, they'd be beheaded before they could even think of getting one." She peeked over her shoulder and added in a whisper, "That isn't to say you can't have a lover on the side, provided you're discreet."

Naila's heart succumbed to a vice of sadness.

"Will Silas get a harem too?"

Onyx looked at her knowingly. "It's expected of šars. There's nothing more important than securing an heir. And by heir, I mean, a male one."

"So, people don't wed for love? How sad."

"Wed? Swear the bonding oath, you mean?" Onyx shrugged. "Rarely. Most *feylanas* over the age of sixteen winters get 'auctioned' at the summer solstice when we celebrate Firefalls. She rarely gets a say in the matter."

Naila scoffed. "What do her parents do with all those crystals?"

"Well, part of it goes to the šar's treasuries, of course. Someone has to pay for all those wars."

Wars... Of course.

Onyx turned serious. "A word of advice: Silas is as charming as he is handsome, but don't let it fool you. I'm afraid he carries too many scars to be emotionally available. Wherever he goes, broken hearts follow. *Always.*"

"I wasn't... I'm not interested," Naila stammered. 'Twas the truth. She admired him as she would a diamond she couldn't afford.

Onyx's eyebrow flicked upward.

Unfortunately, or fortunately, Naila was spared a reply.

The Silver Šar and his šargon walked past their table, deep in an argument. Naila pricked up her ears.

"You cannot be serious," the šar hissed. "We are talking about *the* Dark Forest, not a trip to the Greenfields. This is excessive, Silvanus, even for you."

"Mother is convinced something important lies in Nebiru. I cannot deny her wishes. Besides, I've been stuck all season listening to everyone's lectures. I deserve a break."

"Endangering yourself is not what I would call a break," the emperor whispered sternly as his eyes skimmed the stage. For eavesdroppers, mayhap. "You are the heir to Skeldor's throne. You *know* who will take over if you die."

Silas ran his fingers through his already tousled hair. "Really, Grandfather, this is not my first quest. How can I call myself heir to Skeldor's throne if I cower before every dangerous challenge?"

The šar tossed his napkin on a nearby table.

Naila didn't know where to look, so she settled on fumbling with her pendant. She hated conflicts... and she felt guilty. She knew the šar was right, but she could really use the help. Perhaps she was selfish, but she so yearned to get back home. Back to Ma, and Philly, and her grumpy cat.

She and Onyx stared at the two men, out of hearing distance now, as they finished their conversation. The Silver Šar closed his eyes and rubbed at his temples. Finally, with a sigh, he returned to his table. Silas, however, joined theirs.

"My lovely *feylanas.*" Silas grinned.

He flopped down on a cushion between them and snatched a piece of cheese off the board. Naila's cheeks heated when she realized they had the undivided attention of the Silver Šar and several attendants.

"Please thank your grandfather for inviting me," said Naila shyly as she pushed her food around her platter.

"Of course you're invited. You're the guest of honor."

"Huh?"

Silas chuckled. "You're one of two adult nergaylas in Skeldor. Grandfather is rather invested in you."

Naila chewed on her lip. She didn't like the sound of that at all. Apparently, Silas read the doubt on her face.

"Don't worry, he has no ill intentions." The prince chewed on his cheese and watched her intently. "He refuses to assist us in our little quest."

Naila frowned at the amusement in the prince's eyes.

"*But,* he also won't stop us. I bargained with him. He's given us two full moons to return before he sends his troops. He doesn't believe Nebiru exists, of course. Otherwise, he wouldn't have taken the deal."

Naila put down her cutlery at the same time Onyx narrowed her eyes.

"Silas..." Onyx said, not quite believing they were really about to leave on this quest.

"What are you saying?" Naila's mouth curved into a smile. Surely, he didn't mean what she thought he did. It was too good to be true.

Silas grinned even wider. "I'm saying, when do we leave?"

Naila's heart picked up a beat. For the first time in weeks, a sense of ease soothed her worried thoughts. There was also that nagging shimmer of fear, however. After everything that had happened, would she really take the risk of crossing the path of a shadowreaper? Even now, they still haunted her nightmares, and more often than not, she had woken up soaked in cold sweat.

When Naila collected herself, Onyx spoke again. "You two are forgetting one thing, though. Who in the seven hells would be crazy enough to take us across the Sea of Helath?"

Silas's lips curled into a lopsided grin and he glanced over at Tryton Barbaras, Onyx's younger cousin. "I know just the fellow for that."

XV

THE KING OF THE SEVEN SEAS

THE FIRST rays of the spring sun painted over the houses of Havenmor's quaint dock. A rooster cock-a-doodle-dooed, reminding the people a new day had come. Naila, Silas, Onyx, and Tryce, the newest addition to their little band of adventurers, strolled through the sleet, from tavern to tavern, looking for Silas's *fellow*. Vendors from a fish market behind the dock quarreled, and the smell of spices competed with that of salted frost water.

"Do we even know if he's here?" Onyx said as she shooed away a curious little monkey in a vest.

The chalky monkey bared its teeth and jumped to a barren tree, its eyes already fixed on other early morn trotters.

"He is," said Tryce from the back of the foursome.

He folded his arms behind his head and whistled jollily as if it wasn't much too early in the morning. Teens from Earth could learn a thing or two from him, Naila included.

With bronze skin and inky hair, Tryce hovered between boy and the brink of manhood. Despite being cousins, he and Onyx didn't look alike. His features were more similar to those of North India.

Naila eyed the boy and Onyx. "So, you're cousins?"

She may as well have proposed they hang out at a funeral. Both their faces dropped.

Tryce smiled awkwardly.

"Our mothers, er, were sisters." He left it at that.

Embarrassment prickled Naila's cheeks.

If she were to believe the hierodulas' nosy gossiping, Tryce descended from a notorious line of seamen, whose latest swashbuckling descendant had whisked his mother away. Unfortunately, the young woman had died a horrible death. She contracted the most fearful of all diseases, they whispered—*ut mortes nero*. Even its mention had made the hierodulas shudder.

"So, this fellow, er, the captain..." said Naila.

"Not just any captain. The king of the Seven Seas," Silas's eyes sparkled mischievously.

Onyx sucked in a breath. "Halfbeard Barbaras is in Havenmor?"

"Aye, who else did you think Tryce was leading us to?"

Onyx cornered Silas and Tryce in the middle of the pavement, her hands on her hips. "Why didn't you tell me?"

Tryce blinked with faux innocence, whereas Silas pinched Onyx's nose. "Because *you* would've blabbed to Grandfather, and then *we* would have to tell this quest goodbye."

Naila didn't like the sound of that. Onyx wouldn't snitch unless she had a good reason. "Uh, who is this Halfbeard?"

"*Baba* is the greatest cap'n in all the Seven Seas," said Tryce as he puffed his chest proudly. "Don't you worry, ma'am, he'll get you to Isolon before you can blink."

Silas rubbed his hands, a boyish glint sneaking up his eyes. "The king of the Seven Seas is an adventurer's dream. He's sailed across every sea in the world. Has been to every empire in Lemuria. Rumor has it he's even set foot on The Lost World."

"It's no rumor. He's been there. He's been there," added Tryce excitedly.

Silas ruffled the boy's dark, loose curls.

"He's a pirate," Onyx said flatly.

"What?" Naila paused mid-step.

"*Was*. Onyx, Onyx, why so dramatic?" Silas waved away her words.

Naila took a slight step back. "Guys... are you sure about this?"

Silas spoke before Onyx and Tryce could utter a word.

"Of course. Barbaras is as honest a man as any. Most šars, mind you, have pardoned him."

"Because he's paid them off with stolen crystals," Onyx muttered underneath her breath.

Silas and Tryce pretended they didn't hear her and, well, Naila was too eager to get back home to offer any further protests.

A man in a donkey carriage rushed onto the roadway, one hand on the ropes and the other curled around a flask. From the look of his rosy nose and glazed eyes, he was well past being drunk. The carriage nearly bumped into them before screeching to a halt before Naila's boots.

"Oi, loiter-sack. Watch where you're going, or I'll make sure this scrap of junk goes back to the dump," Silas growled.

Naila was quite certain the man was about to make a rude gesture, but he stopped dead in his tracks when he saw Silas's face. The prince had the ability to bring people to their knees with a simple, frosty glare. It made Naila wonder what other personas he kept carefully tucked away behind his usual cocksure smile.

Tryce patted the donkey's buttocks. "Move along."

The drunkard didn't have to be told twice. He hastily pulled the reins, steering the donkey for a U-turn, far away from their glowers.

Naila cleared her throat. "Guys." She pointed to the end of the road at a cozy-looking tavern, built in and around a thick tree. Its name was painted in Tierratongo above the iron-and-wooden door. "That's the Rusty Anchor."

It wasn't exactly hard to find. The night had long since said goodbye, but a small crowd was gathered around the infamous tavern. The cold air stank of ale, and drunken laughter filled the early morning. A lone horse neighed from the back of the pub, likely discontent with its owner's long absence.

"Are you sure that Halfbeard guy is honorable?" Naila eyed the tavern skeptically.

Onyx sighed, but the others guiltily ignored Naila's question.

"Silas..." Tryce said as he glanced meaningfully from Naila and Onyx to the crowd in front of the pub.

"Right. *Feylanas*, it's best you stay here. We'll be right back," Silas said, not waiting for an answer. He and Tryce marched to the Rusty Anchor.

Onyx rolled her eyes. "As if."

"There's no way you're going without us," said Naila.

The prince turned, not in the least surprised. "But—"

Onyx lifted a brow, to which Silas sighed but made no further comment.

When they arrived at the tree tavern, it became clear why it was so crowded. Two rugged men were locked in a fight.

"Aye, get 'em," a drunkard slurred.

"Perfect." Silas smiled, his gaze focused on the entrance. "This will help us get in unnoticed."

"What do you mean?" Naila glanced at the excited faces in the crowd. "Someone's following us?"

"In this part of town, there are eyes everywhere," Silas said, tightening the strap of his satchel. "Besides, it doesn't take a genius to figure out who you are." He looked pointedly at the pearly markings on her forehead. "Subtlety is not your strong point, sunshine."

"Excuse me?" said Naila. "Who's the one picking fights in the middle of the street?"

Silas chuckled while pushing her to the entrance, "Believe me, nobody would blink if I struck someone down in broad daylight."

Only a breath later, a nauseating snap sounded, followed by even louder cheers. To Naila's horror, one fighter had broken the other's arm. Acid filled her mouth.

"Barbarians," Onyx muttered.

"Keep. Moving," Tryce urged from beside Silas. His eyes were glued to the tavern, but it was clear he spoke to Naila. "Now is not the time to freak out, no disrespect, m'lady."

Naila swallowed back her emotions and let Silas push her through the door. Tryce ambled behind them as if he didn't have a care in the world. Knowing who his father was, the boy was probably used to this.

A sour stench of liquor, sweat, and something musty met them on the inside. The Rusty Anchor was filled to the brim, even though the day was young. Naila squinted to adjust to the dimness. Oil lamps and a chandelier made for the only light in a taproom framed by tree branches. Customers, mostly men, sat around floor tables, drinking and gambling, while others watched a buxom woman perform the seductive dance of the seven veils.

Naila tutted her lips.

Another world or no, sex would always sell. They squeezed between the tables. Some men openly leered at her and Onyx, but one glare from Silas had them looking the other way.

"Stay here," Silas whispered.

"Why? Where are you going?"

He didn't bother to answer but just strolled toward the bar.

The prince started a conversation, no, *flirted* with a pretty barista. She laughed at his words like he was Lemuria's funniest jester. Naila rolled her eyes when the woman leaned over the bar and her ample breasts almost burst out of her bodice.

"Once a rake..." Onyx yawned.

Tryce, however, whistled admiringly. "Will you look at that?"

"Be careful or you'll have drool dripping all over the floor," said Naila.

Tryce smiled sheepishly. "Don't you worry, m'lady. She ain't nothin' compared to you."

"Yeah, yeah." Naila rolled her eyes. "And stop calling me that. It's just Naila."

Moments later, Silas rejoined them with victory written all over his smug face.

"I got the key to the private room, and Halfbeard, my friends, is there just about now."

"I could have gotten you the key without all that hassle," said Tryce.

"*Yana*. But where's the fun in that?" Silas smirked.

Naila's irritation melted away. So that's why he randomly flirted with that woman. Still, she couldn't help but feel annoyed he had kept her in the dark. Last Naila checked; she was the center of this quest.

They followed the prince to a darkish room where more drunkards gambled. A lone hooded figure sat at the bar.

"*Baba*!" said Tryce, dashing to the back of the room. The hooded figure at the bar looked up curiously, but bent over his beer again before Naila could see his face.

"M'boy," a deep male voice grunted.

Tryce joined a table of several men. No one, not even Naila, would have mistaken them for anything less than pirates. A mousy man with golden teeth leered at her, from among other shady-looking figures. And then there was him.

Halfbeard indeed.

He wasn't as big as the treelike man beside him, nor exuded royalty like Silas, but Halfbeard oozed the aura of one who commanded respect. His skin was bronze like Tryce's and his thick, black beard ripped in half by three vicious claw marks on the side of his jaw. Whatever had attacked him was far bigger than an ice-crawler.

His dark eyes were cautious as they darted to Naila and her friends. "See yer got company, aye?"

Tryce scratched the back of his head. "Well..."

Halfbeard inclined his head. "Onyx."

The young woman scowled. There was no love lost between them, Naila noted. Perhaps because he had swept away her aunt like in a bodice-ripper book of old. Or maybe because he had dumped young Tryce upon her whenever he went sailing to another deadly quest.

"Well look who's come calling," Onyx said.

"I couldn't miss me boy b'coming a man."

"Reis *Halfbeard* Barbaras, it's nice to make your acquaintance," the prince hastily said before Onyx could give him a piece of her mind.

Halfbeard narrowed his eyes before taking a puff from his pipe. "Prince Silvanus, why color me surprised, aye? What brings ye here?"

The figure at the bar looked up once more, his face carefully hidden by the hood of his dark robes. Naila was suddenly aware of Silas's words: *There are ears all over this part of Havenmor.*

Silas put on a dazzling smile; the one that made women swoon and men good-spirited. "Let us eat and drink. Then we'll talk of business."

Halfbeard patted an empty cushion beside him, which Tryce took with eagerness. He snatched his father's beer and gulped it down. At Halfbeard's quirked eyebrow, he grinned cheekily. "Ain' I a man now?"

Three other cushions were arranged for Naila and her company before Halfbeard began the introductions. He thumbed at a sullen-looking fellow, whose beauty Naila had mistaken for that of a woman. "Me right hand and quartermaster Rē."

Rē grunted but said nothing.

The more Naila studied his olive features and long, shining hair, the more she realized Rē wasn't just beautiful. No, he was ethereal with the looks you would expect of the fair folk. But the perpetual frown on his face stained his beauty.

Halfbeard pointed at the greasy man who didn't attempt to hide his leering. "Jacobo, me boatswain. Right next to 'em"—Halfbeard beckoned to a dark, muscular man—"me master gunner Theodorus, but we call 'im Two-Toed Teddy." Everyone chuckled, including Two-Toed Teddy, whose smile was as inviting as that of a shark.

"And me," a rosy-cheeked, pot-bellied man burped. He smashed his mug down with a loud clunk. "I'm called Bubba. You'll find I'm the most important man on the whole of the Chimera." He winked.

Halfbeard chuckled. "That ye are. Bubba here is our cook."

Naila smiled at Bubba. He was the only non-intimidating one at the table.

"The rest of me crew is at the Chimera."

A barmaid refilled their mugs and put a platter of sheep cheese and barley bread on the table. Jacobo smacked the woman on the bottom. She glowered but said nothing.

Onyx glared at Jacobo and then at Halfbeard. "Oh, I just love the company you keep."

"Captain Barbaras, sir, uh, one of the reasons we're here is because of me," Naila said before Halfbeard or his men could retort.

It was best not to mention Onyx's mission, considering the enmity between her and the captain.

Silas shot Naila a warning glance. Naila didn't know if it was her imagination, but the room grew quieter. Several suspicious-looking folks from other tables glanced sneakily at them. Silas's warning, however, was not needed. Naila knew none were to be trusted. "You see, I need to visit a cousin of mine in Isolon."

Halfbeard blew a ring of smoke in the air. His eyes flickered to Naila's phæralei. He regarded her with unreadable eyes. "Isolon, ye say, aye? Then ye don't need me for it. The Black Šar's still out for me head. Why, it's better to travel by donkey carriage. Far safer too, *laí*?"

"I'm sure you're well aware the roads through Crishire and Læriad hold many dangers," the prince said.

"The Dragon Lord ain't an unreasonable man, hmm? Surely ye can work something out, what with being brothers and all?"

Tryce spat. "The Dragon Lord? Is that what they call the Red Šar now? Someone carrying that title should be noble and wise. He is cunning and vicious, a war-hungry snake, that's who 'e is!"

"Silence, boy. We don't mingle in the disputes of šars. You'd best not forget that," Halfbeard scolded.

Tryce sighed but said no more.

"Why does one of royal blood need to accompany you to your cousin?" Rē, the quartermaster, said. His face, which betrayed no emotion, was as flawless a canvas as his hair was black. If Naila were an artist, he would be a perfect muse.

"Our business is our own," said Naila.

Silas gifted her an approving nod.

"Be as it may, the Sea of Helath is the second, if not the most dangerous of the Seven Seas," said Halfbeard. "Yer asking this old man here to challenge the claws of danger."

Silas smirked knowingly. "What is the Sea of Helath to a crew of fine men who bested the Arctic waves and even the Ocean of Lost Souls."

The sailors puffed their chests proudly, their faces at war between fear and longing.

"No." Halfbeard blew out another ring.

"C'mon, *Baba,* ye promised me a quest when I became a man. Well, I'm a man now and this is what I want," Tryce said.

"Yer sixteen winters, boy."

Tryce shot his father an incredulous look. "*You* escaped the Iron Šar's pit at fourteen winters!"

"Tryton..." Halfbeard growled.

"Are ye a man of yer word or no?"

Father and son glared at each other, their stubborn jaws tilted upward, neither backing down.

"Yer the hunt's champion," Halfbeard hissed. "Ye could become anyone ye want. Tryton, ye don't *need* to do this. Don't follow yer pa."

"But this, *Baba*, is what I want. You promised." Tryce's voice held a hint of emotion.

Naila regarded them in silence. Somehow, she knew, this quest held something personal for Tryce. Back on Earth, she was desperate to find her place in the world too. How she had yearned for a sense of belonging. She knew how Tryce felt.

Halfbeard closed his eyes. "Say, *hypothetically*, I were to agree. What's in it for me, hmm? I ain' risking my men fer free."

Silas smacked a pouch of crystals on the table. They glittered prettily in the oil lamp's light; from rose to ivy to lavender. Halfbeard smirked darkly. "I got crystals enough, princeling."

Silas narrowed his eyes. "Say, *hypothetically*, you were to agree, then what would be your price?"

"Ye've got Two-Toed Teddy's brother in yer pit."

Teddy's eyes gleamed with excitement. He looked like a grizzly bear that caught a salmon.

Silas frowned. "Who?"

"Hanno Agmon," Teddy grunted. "Does it ring a bell?"

"That spying, murdering thief?" Silas hissed.

Teddy unsheathed his dagger; at the same time the prince drew his scimitar. Instantly, everyone at the table had drawn their weapon, Onyx aiming an arrow at Halfbeard with delight. They had the undivided attention of the rest of the tavern.

Naila cleared her throat. She pushed Silas's hand down, before doing the same to Onyx, trying to hide the nervousness from her smile. "Gentlemen. Lady. *Please*. We can discuss this with words. For goodness' sake, there's no need for violence."

Silas plopped down on his cushion. "Your price is high, Barbaras."

Halfbeard continued smoking his pipe. "One life for risking the lives of several. I'd say me price is low."

Guilt speared Naila. She didn't dare meet the prince's eyes, but her hand still rested upon his fist. Naila wouldn't blame Silas for declining, although a selfish part of her would be disappointed. For the first time, she understood the dishonorable things some agreed to, to save their own hide. She had no place to judge.

The prince's gaze grew dark. After what seemed like ages, he at last unclenched his fist. "Very well then." He shot a warning glance at Teddy. "You best tell your brother to watch his back. One foot in Skeldor and any deal is void. Got it? All *hypothetically* of course."

Teddy smirked. "Don't worry, prince. Ye ain' ever catching another Agmon brother."

Naila's heart pitter-pattered. Had the prince done this in the name of adventure or did he do it for her and Onyx? Her hand squeezed his. It was warm and so much bigger than her own. Calluses adorned his palm like trophies, reminding her there was far more to him than his rakish ways.

Finally, the corner of Halfbeard's mouth curved too. He ruffled Tryce's hair, before looking from one man to another. "Ye can keep the sea away from the man, but ye can't keep the man away from the sea. If this is what you want, boy..."

Tryce grinned, not with triumph, but with boyish excitement. "It is."

Relief washed over Naila. She couldn't have done this alone. Fate had put these people in her path. Surely this was a sign her journey home would be a success.

"Hanno in exchange for a safe passage to and fro. What say you?" said Silas.

Silas's offerings must have been more than the crew expected, for all the men grew jolly.

Halfbeard drank the remainder of his beer. "I say, when do we leave?"

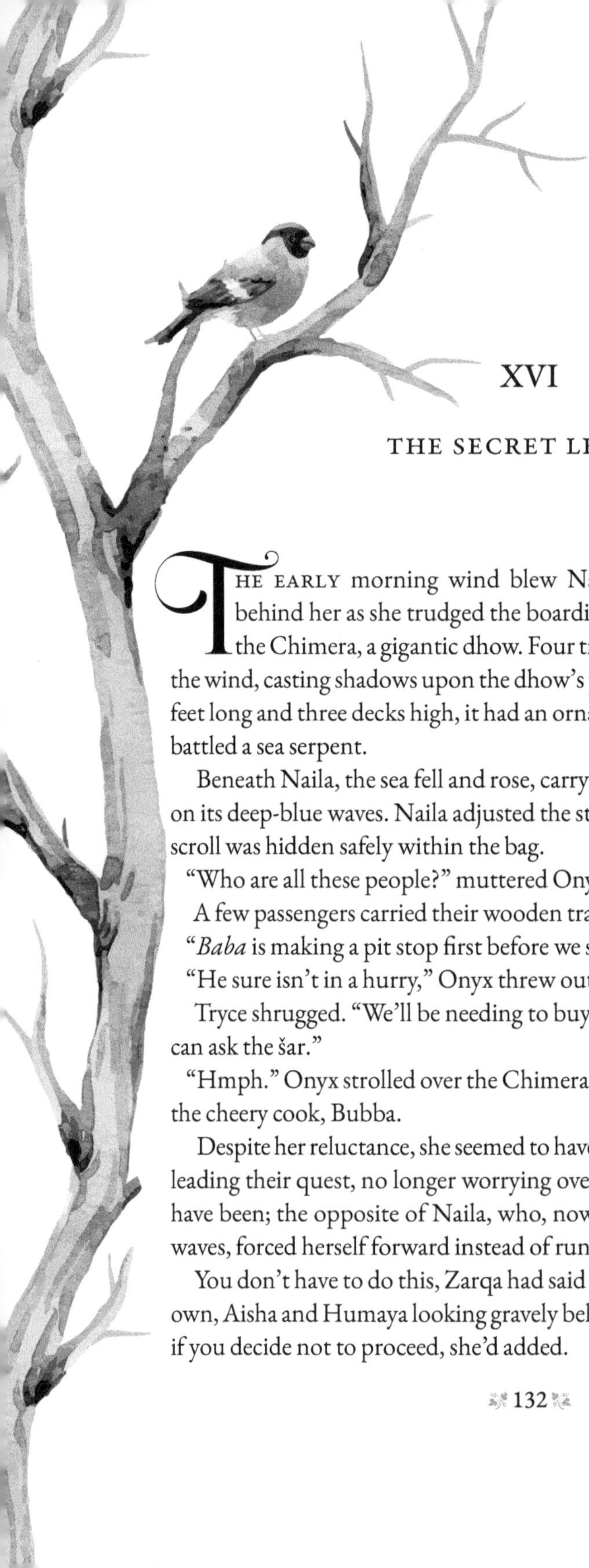

XVI

THE SECRET LETTER

THE EARLY morning wind blew Naila's curls in a midnight veil behind her as she trudged the boarding steps to her first ship ever—the Chimera, a gigantic dhow. Four triangular sails fluttered softly in the wind, casting shadows upon the dhow's powerful body. Over a hundred feet long and three decks high, it had an ornate stern upon which a chimera battled a sea serpent.

Beneath Naila, the sea fell and rose, carrying both a promise and a threat on its deep-blue waves. Naila adjusted the strap of her satchel. Mr. Thoth's scroll was hidden safely within the bag.

"Who are all these people?" muttered Onyx in the front.

A few passengers carried their wooden traveling cases over the main deck.

"*Baba* is making a pit stop first before we set sail for Isolon," said Tryce.

"He sure isn't in a hurry," Onyx threw out sarcastically.

Tryce shrugged. "We'll be needing to buy heavy weapons. It ain't like we can ask the šar."

"Hmph." Onyx strolled over the Chimera's vast deck alongside Tryce and the cheery cook, Bubba.

Despite her reluctance, she seemed to have come to terms with Halfbeard leading their quest, no longer worrying over what ought and ought not to have been; the opposite of Naila, who, now that she stood high above the waves, forced herself forward instead of running back to Ishtar's temple.

You don't have to do this, Zarqa had said as she took Naila's hands in her own, Aisha and Humaya looking gravely behind her. No one will mock you if you decide not to proceed, she'd added.

No, they would welcome her back with open arms. Little Oya would creep in her bed at night, begging Naila to tell her of Philly's fairy tales until she fell asleep. Naila sighed her wistfulness away. Havenmor and its lovely people had gotten to her. She adjusted the sea holly in her hair Oya had given her—still full in bloom because the girl had æshefied it; frozen its life force with æther, that is, as only a nergayla could.

Will you not let us complete your training in the ways of æther? Zarqa had whispered. It is as much a part of you as the heart beating in your chest or the feet that carry you to another journey.

Naila glanced at her fingertips. They didn't understand. Much as she yearned to discover the depths of her flames, the thought of being exposed back on Earth twisted her insides. If they discovered her powers to be true, she'd end up locked in a laboratory. Her heart clenched painfully. If only she had never lost her father. If only these flames weren't hers to bear. If only she hadn't been hurled into this world with its wars and its dangers. *If only... If only.* The icy air sliced through her, matching the cold dread knotting her chest. She glanced up, catching the determination on Onyx's face, the song of adventure on Silas's and Tryce's faces. The knot loosened. Fear was replaced by a strange elation.

An impatient horse grunted somewhere below, not far from where Silas conversed with Halfbeard, who was every bit the image of a ruthless pirate—and the nightmare of a dhow holding treasures. His turban, and the hair peeking above his half-buttoned blouse, were as raven as his beard. Well, the remaining half of it. Naila tried to guess Halfbeard's age, but his swarthy skin gave no clue.

Barbaras murmured something to Silas, then took a carefree inhale of his pipe. Even from afar, she could see the prince's shoulders tense.

"Come along now, birdy, the princeling ain' gon' run away." Jacobo, the boatswain, grinned at the top of the stairs.

His mousy brown mustache was a stark contrast with his golden teeth. He stuck out his hand, which, Naila couldn't help but notice, had dirty fingernails. Naila didn't need his help, but she still took it. She didn't want to offend the crew on the very first day when they still had a good six weeks' journey ahead of them.

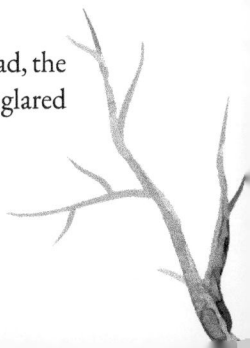

When she reached the deck, Jacobo didn't release her at once. Instead, the fingers of his other hand trailed the side of her hourglass figure. Naila glared at him, but he bared his golden teeth in a lecherous grin. Her fingers pricked with indignant flames begging to be unleashed.

"Everything all right here?" Rē said from behind Jacobo. His voice was smooth, but it held a threat that made her shiver.

Jacobo raised his hands in faux innocence.

Rē crossed his sculpted arms. The opal hilt of his scimitar swallowed every ray of light. The message was clear. It seemed all was not exactly well within Halfbeard's crew.

To Naila's relief Jacobo retreated. She smiled shyly at the quartermaster. "Thanks, Rē."

He grunted. His dark eyes shifted back to the ship's deck; Onyx and Tryce were strolling over to them. The moment he saw them, Rē made himself scarce.

Onyx arched a brow. "He's a grumpy fellow, that one."

Tryce stared after him with badly hidden admiration.

"He's scarce with words but ye ain't getting a better fighter. Saved Bubba from a giant squid, he did." He mimicked the battle with his hands. "Jumped into the waters, gutted the beast and pulled Bubba out of its tentacles, just like that."

Onyx blinked. "Did he now?"

"G-giant squid?" Naila breathed.

Tryce's expression turned grave.

"You best watch yer step, ma'am, else a tentacle might slip onto the deck unnoticed and BAM! Yer squid food."

Naila's stomach churned.

Tryce's mask broke into mischievous laughter. "You should see yer face."

Onyx flicked his head. "Don't tease Naila. Those beasts never come to the surface, N, don't worry."

"That one sure did." At Onyx's warning glance, Tryce changed the subject and beckoned to the deck. "Well, what d'ye think?"

The wind whistled faintly as it broke upon the magnificent sails. Tryce's smile was so full of pride Naila didn't have the heart to tell him she'd rather be anywhere else if the dhow wasn't her only way back home.

"Er, it's nice?"

Tryce puffed his chest. "It's the biggest ship in all of Lemuria."

Naila looked up curiously. "Really?"

"Yus!" His face took on a faraway look. "*Baba* built it for my ma. Said to her, Ain' no man can sink this dhow. As the Chimera weathers the storms, robust and fiery, so would his love for her sail until he was laid to rest."

Something softened in Onyx's expression.

Naila remembered the whispers in the halls, that Tryce's mother had died from *ut mortes nero*, that had taken lives as many diseases did: the very young, the very old, and those weak of body... Naila had been too young to remember her father's death, but Tryce had witnessed the loss of his mother at a tender age.

Naila took his arm.

"It's the loveliest ship I've ever seen, Tryce. It must have made your momma proud."

"Indeed, it must have." Onyx smiled too.

"Well," said Tryce, with a little shrug that didn't fool Naila. "Let me show ye yer hut."

He led them to the second deck, where the cabins were located. The hut was simple, but the bunk beds had straw mattresses and there was even a closet and a tiny drawer. Unfortunately, there was only one porthole, so most of the light came from oil lamps.

Naila started to empty her satchel, although there wasn't much to unpack. Two changes of clothes—tulip trousers with matching tops and cloaks—a jar of hair balm and a comb were all she had brought with her.

"Tryce is a nice kid."

Onyx nodded. "He's the only family I have left. I took him under my wing when Halfbeard first dumped him in Havenmor. He was as mischievous as he was snot-faced and skinny back then. Still is, to be honest." Then she added with a proud little smile. "Silas taught him how to fight, but I taught him how to hunt."

No wonder he had caught that big ice-crawler.

Naila took the scroll out of her satchel. To her surprise, a letter fell out of it. It was sealed with a winged woman upon silver wax—the emblem of Ishtar's priestesses.

She broke the seal.

The cuneiform characters were drawn in elegant calligraphy. It was a letter from the šaltana! She turned to Onyx, who was busy unpacking her bag, but then thought better of it.

Dearest Naila,

I urge you to read this letter by yourself and then put it to flames. I dare not even speak these words aloud and so I am compelled to write them to you. There is a part of the prophecy Zarqa and I have withheld from you.

We have uncovered only pieces of the scroll describing a powerful nergayla's birth so we do not fully understand its contents. Thus, there is a chance I am misleading you with this information, but in my heart I feel you have to know.

From the little we have managed to uncover, this prophecy spoke of Ishtar's Chosen and an antithesis. You see, what few know is that her weaver, Ishtar, was half of a greater whole, bearing resemblance to our beloved Iluna.

Ishtar is like the side of Iluna that shines brightly at night and makes the darkness bearable. But Iluna also has another side, the dark of the moons. The one hidden in the shadows... Together, these halves are believed to bring a balance to the worlds.

When I was in a dark place, suffering in Crishire's imperial harem and heavily pregnant with Silas, one thing kept me afoot. Nova, the most powerful living nergayla was gifted a rare foretelling: the child I carried would be Ishtar's Chosen's other half!

So, you see, your coming to us is because fate willed it so. It is because of these ancient words, kept a secret by nergaylas for ages past, that Father allowed this voyage. I spoke to him before my son did. I beg of you, do not mention any of this to Silas, for he does not know.

I am certain, you see, that my son has a spirit as fierce as it is unyielding. A fire that refuses to be contained. He will rebel against his destiny if revealed too soon. When the time is right, it will reveal itself to him.

All my love and stay safe,

S.

"What's that?" Onyx asked.

Naila squeezed the letter to her chest. "N-nothing... just a letter from the hierodulas."

Onyx smiled. "They weren't happy to see you leave, huh? I bet they dropped one last shocker on you to force you back."

Naila blinked but said nothing. If only Onyx knew. Was that what this was? A trap to stroke Naila's ego and lure her back to Skeldor? It wouldn't work. It wouldn't. She, someone from a high-stakes prophecy? It sounded so ridiculous. Like something out of a cheesy movie. Still, doubt took hold of Naila, for why else had the shadowreapers brought her to this place?

Naila folded the letter, making a mental note to destroy it when Onyx was out of sight. "Let's go back. I need some sunlight."

She left the letter behind in the hut. If only she could leave the sliver of doubt that had crept upon her behind as well. She would think of the letter on the morrow... *and* how she would respond to it. Until then, she would omit mention of it to either Silas or Onyx.

As they reached the main deck once again, Onyx climbed to sit on the dhow's taffrail. Silas and Halfbeard finally took to the stairs.

Naila's breath hitched ever so slightly, torn over gratitude for all the prince had done at no cost on her side, but at the same time over the šaltana's words ringing in her ears. Was she bound by fate to this man? A prince drunk on debauchery? And yet he was fiercely loyal with a high sense of benevolence. Perhaps she had judged him too soon.

Onyx's legs swung excitedly when Silas joined them.

"And?" Naila urged.

"Everything's arranged."

"Did you go over the route?" asked Onyx. "Where will we go ashore? Not Moonblight, I bet, what with the Black Šar having a hefty price on Halfbeard's head."

"No, he's dropping us off straight at the Dark Forest. He doesn't want to risk the Chimera being spotted. So, Nebiru is our first target and thereafter the black markets." Silas sighed. He ran his fingers through his dark-brown strands. "Halfbeard wants to do a pitstop at the Shores of the Blood Moons. Said some rich merchant joined at the last moment and he needs to drop him off." He shot the passengers a displeased look. "Apparently all these other people followed."

A pit stop?

Naila's stomach sank faster than a hippo in quicksand. So Tryce had been right. That would make the wait even longer. She glanced from Silas's solemn face to Onyx's stricken expression.

"The Shores of the Blood Moons?" Onyx repeated. "You know what rumors haunt that place. Barbaras can't mean for us to go ashore."

"Rumors? What rumors?" asked Naila.

Tryce appeared from behind Silas, his hands in the air, fingers wiggling as he did his best imitation of a creepy voice. "They say that place is cursed. That you should never take yer ship a'land or the Sea of Helath will haunt you itself."

"Nonsense. It's just a fairy tale," Silas waved Tryce's words away.

Naila couldn't help but wonder if the prince believed his own words. She wondered anew why they had to fraternize with pirates who had supposedly seen the light. She tugged her woolen shawl firmly into place. No, she did not like the sound of this at all.

"Are you forgetting it's mighty near Crishire too?" Onyx hissed.

"I know, and I can't do anything about it, all right? That merchant paid Halfbeard a small fortune."

An image of a hooded figure on a neighing stallion flared before Naila's eyes. The stranger at the bar. *Could it be?*

"Who is this merchant?" asked Naila.

"Who knows? Halfbeard promised not to stay too long. He can't be persuaded, so it's either this or no deal..." A muscle feathered along Silas's angular jaw.

"Do you think we'll be safe from, uh, your brother?" said Naila.

"We won't meet him, don't worry," Silas said simply.

Before Naila could ask more, his navy eyes rested upon her frame.

"Do you have everything? You didn't forget to copy the map?"

"Not only the copy. Mr. Thoth gave me the scroll itself."

Silas tugged at an ebony curl.

"You really have old Thoth wrapped around your pretty finger, huh? He wouldn't even trust me with his cheapest reed pen."

"I think he's just excited." Naila's cheeks flushed with warmth. She fiddled with her pendant. "There's a good chance the lost city of Nebiru is real and that we will actually find it."

"*If* we make it past the Sea of Helath, the Shores of the Blood Moons, *and* shadowreapers," Tryce chirped.

Onyx elbowed him. "Don't curse our quest."

Naila shuddered.

Well, then, there was that. Even the safest route to Nebiru was riddled with dangers.

Silas snorted. He unsheathed his scimitar. The razor-sharp edge blinked in the sunlight. "If *they* make it past *us*, you mean."

Tryce chuckled as he threw an arm around his cousin, their little band of aspiring adventurers complete. Halfbeard shook his head in the distance, likely still conflicted over having lost the battle with his son.

The lad's eyes danced with mischief. "You sound like yer looking forward to a clash."

"I'm dying for some action." Silas twirled his scimitar in his hand.

Naila, however, tried to suppress a panic attack at the thought of seeing another shadowreaper. She both desired and feared this journey. The only thing that kept her from abandoning it as a whole was her will to reach home, the wish to find Philly... and dare she say the companionship of her newfound friends who were fast on their way to becoming dear. Naila sighed. She would have to drag herself through this paralyzing anxiety. "I have this weird feeling you'll get exactly what you want."

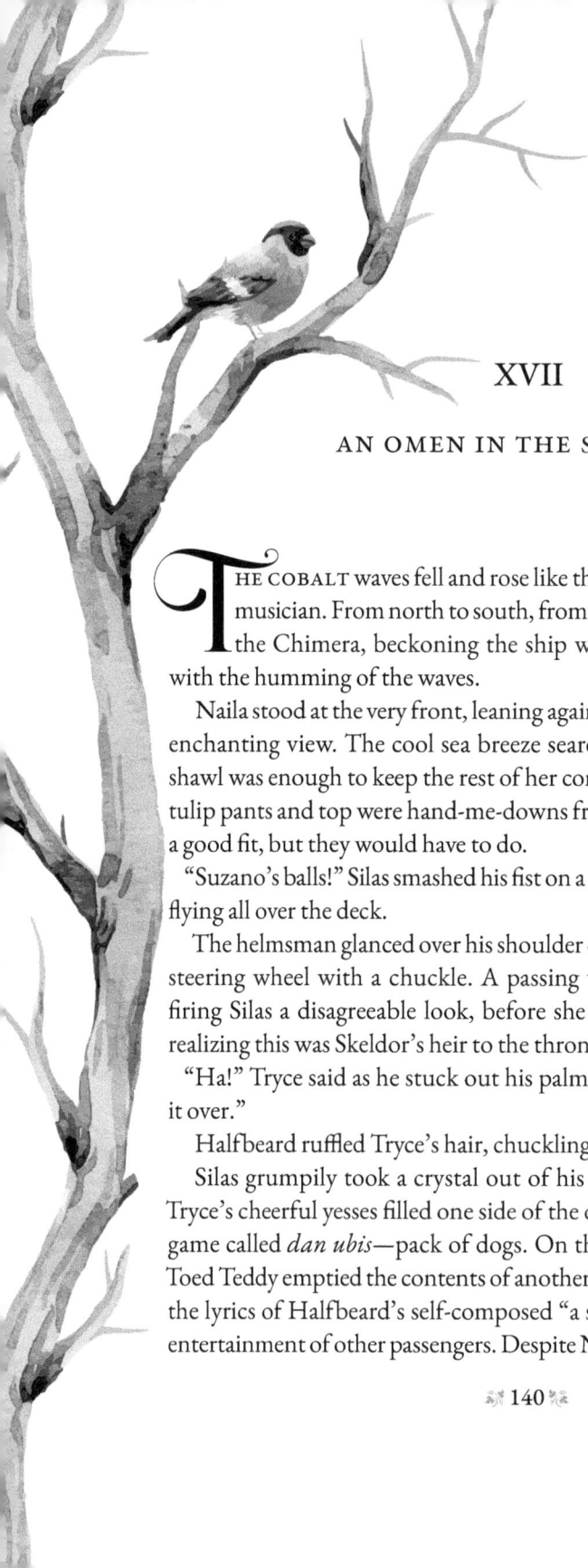

XVII

AN OMEN IN THE SHADOWS

THE COBALT waves fell and rose like the notes of a melody by a master musician. From north to south, from east to west, the sea surrounded the Chimera, beckoning the ship with tendrils of water, luring it with the humming of the waves.

Naila stood at the very front, leaning against the taffrail, as she took in the enchanting view. The cool sea breeze seared her cheeks, but her woolen shawl was enough to keep the rest of her comfortable. Like the caftans, her tulip pants and top were hand-me-downs from the hierodulas. Not exactly a good fit, but they would have to do.

"Suzano's balls!" Silas smashed his fist on a barrel, the pyramid-shaped dice flying all over the deck.

The helmsman glanced over his shoulder curiously, before turning to the steering wheel with a chuckle. A passing woman clutched her necklace, firing Silas a disagreeable look, before she urged her child onwards, not realizing this was Skeldor's heir to the throne.

"Ha!" Tryce said as he stuck out his palm, his face smug, "C'mon, hand it over."

Halfbeard ruffled Tryce's hair, chuckling. "'E's got ye there."

Silas grumpily took a crystal out of his pouch. His losing grunts and Tryce's cheerful yesses filled one side of the deck where they played a board game called *dan ubis*—pack of dogs. On the other side, Jacobo and Two-Toed Teddy emptied the contents of another barrel as they sang, and burped, the lyrics of Halfbeard's self-composed "a song within the storms" to the entertainment of other passengers. Despite Naila's foreboding, the first days at sea had started without a shadow in the sky, though they had yet to cross over to Helath. In fact, the Chimera was the only ship a'sail.

As the sky inched away from pastels to hues of midnight, the stench of liquor engulfed every corner of the ship. Naila spared little thought to the drunklings, leaning instead over the ornate taffrail, her own chaotic mind at peace for once. Schools of flying fish held her full attention; they were ocean blues and sea greens, and the tiniest ones were river browns.

"Eek," she squirmed as a fish flew so high it landed over the taffrail in front of her curled-toe slippers. The fish flapped its wing-fins in anguish, its eyes wide in fright. A fish out of the sea. Far from family, the very air around it a direct threat to its life. Naila knew exactly how the fish felt, but she would save it. She'd throw it back into the ocean, to its home.

"Aww, little one." Naila smiled as she bent over to pick up the fish. "Now why did you go and be so bold, huh? There's no water here, you know."

Squash.

Her hands froze mid-air as she watched in horror how Halfbeard's scimitar speared her little fish friend. A spark of æther on the blade's sharp edge disappeared as quickly as it had appeared. The fish spasmed one last time before its scaled corpse stilled. The captain lifted the fish, still speared by his scimitar, and threw it back into the sea.

Naila's skin tingled with discomfort and the bitter remnants of an old fear. "Why?"

Her eyes traveled over his massive frame until they rested on his scarred, bearded face. Halfbeard inhaled from his pipe and blew a ring into the air. A howling wind instantly swept the aroma of spices away. His head cocked to the side. He watched Naila in interest as if she was a treasury he wished to crack open. His coal eyes reminded her of little beads she wanted to prick.

He'd seen her trying to save the fish! What a bully.

"Yer not from around, aye... *nergayla*?"

Naila lifted her chin in defiance.

"Why did you kill it?"

Halfbeard rubbed his beard with his free hand. "It be poison. A single touch and ye'd be dead within a chime."

Naila blinked several times. Her cheeks heated with shame.

"I-it was so pretty. I'm sorry."

"Be careful who ye trust, devils be hidin' behind masks of angels."

Halfbeard took another inhale from his pipe and looked to the far distance. Graying clouds splattered across the burning shades of the setting sun.

"A storm is coming."

With those words he went back to the deck, where Bubba told stories of their bone-chilling voyages, complete with cozy lanterns and mulled wine. Tryce had all but stopped playing to listen, his eyes eager. Naila too, was tempted to join, although something in her warned not to get too attached to these people. She was going home, after all...

"For a first-timer, I'm surprised you're not emptying your stomach in the heads."

Naila spun around.

The salty wind combed through the prince's shoulder-length strands. Draped in blue-black, he looked as much a pirate as Halfbeard's crew. A *very* dazzling pirate.

"It's too beautiful out here for nausea," said Naila. "Mr. Thoth was wrong. The sea is no hell. It's heaven."

Silas's lips curved to a crooked smile, which, to Naila's annoyance, did a funny thing to her stomach. "Ah, but this is no Helath you're seeing. We're still sailing across the Enchanted Tides. In another few bells or so we'll cross Helath and then these passengers will finally be dropped off."

"So I better brace myself," Naila whispered.

Silas grasped a sail rope, balancing his weight. Inching dangerously close to her. She could smell his scent of amber and cedar, which reminded her of Philly's warmth. He brushed her cheek with his finger, leaving a path of tingles behind.

"Hmm?" He smiled lazily. "*Yana*. I suppose you best watch yourself."

She didn't know if he meant from the sea or himself.

Onyx's laughter broke their mesmer.

Onyx was locked in the dance of flames with another passenger. Pasha, Naila believed he was called. They had the undivided attention of crew and passengers alike.

"C'mon, O," Tryce burped, before continuing to slurp from a flagon. "Don' let a puny iceman beat yer arse."

Onyx swung a scimitar, but Pasha blocked it with a swift yet elegant move, æther sparks flying around them like fireworks. With another swing, Onyx's sword flew out of her hand. Pasha pointed his scimitar at her neck.

"Checkmate." He smirked, the bronze skin around his emerald eyes crinkling.

Onyx smiled sweetly. "Stalemate, you mean?"

A dagger in her other hand pointed at his abdomen.

The crowd erupted in cheers. "What's that, Pasha? Can't win from a dainty *feylana*?"

But Pasha too, grinned, his eyes gleaming as he took in Onyx as if for the first time. He whispered something Naila couldn't discern, resulting in Onyx's cheeks blossoming pink.

Silas beckoned Naila to join the rest, but the šaltana's letter was etched on her mind. How could she pretend to be jolly after what she had read? She needed time to think things through.

"Uh, I'm a little tired."

Naila retreated to her cabin, leaving her friends behind with the loud, drunken seamen. The mysterious rich merchant she hadn't seen at all. She supposed with a dhow that size one could easily keep to themselves.

The single oil lamp in her hut was just about enough to find her nightgown, but for once she welcomed the dark. Why did the šaltana send the letter now of all times? Although to be fair, when else would she have told her? The truth was, the past weeks had been chaotic. Naila didn't get a moment to herself between finding a way back home, training with Zarqa, and exploring Havenmor. Only at night did the shackles around her mind loosen, but by then she was so exhausted sleep crept up the moment she closed her eyes.

Naila gazed out of the porthole. The stars glittered like diamonds in a sapphire bed. A sight that had always calmed her restless heart. Was Philly looking at the sky now too? Is he even alive, a voice whispered. She gave it a mental slap and sat up straight. If Philly were dead, she would know it, she knew she would.

Her fingers found her moonstone pendant like they had a million times before. The compass which had revealed itself to be the key to an ancient mystery in a world far from Earth. Why had her father possessed such a thing?

To her surprise, the arrows didn't swirl aimlessly like they did back home. No, they pointed southeast. To Isolon, where the Chimera was headed... Just like in the library when they had pointed at the scroll.

"So now you start working, huh?"

Something dawned on her. It will point at your heart's desire, Philly had said. The compass pointing toward Isolon must be a sign! The šaltana was wrong. They would find another nergayla. Little Oya for example. She was exceptionally gifted, all the hierodulas said so. Oya could fulfill this prophecy of the šaltana's... Naila had other obligations. To her mother, to Philly.

A weight lifted off her shoulders. Feeling less guilty, she dipped her reed pen into a bottle of ink and began to write her answer. Long after, she resettled on the straw mattress, so different from the featherbed in the temple, and closed her eyes, instantly swept into the dark of her dreams.

She dashed across the hall on the second deck, the growls of ice-crawlers haunting her. There were no oil lamps, yet she could see every cobble on the floor. Passing a mirror she realized it was because there was *light. Her body burned bright, her phæralei as golden as the embers in her eyes. Even her pitch-black curls and golden-brown skin shimmered. She swayed and swayed even though her steps were steady, the rhythm turning more frantic as the moments passed.*

He had called to her.

Something older than time.

She couldn't resist his song. They were magnets, two sides of the same coin.

Ishtar, he whispered.

Ishtar, he called.

Her heart leaped into her throat. The growls of the ice-crawlers evaporated into nothingness. There, at the end of the hall lurked other eyes... No longer kept in the shadows, no longer covered in ebony, they were darker than the ocean but lighter than the night. Hauntingly beautiful, completely unexpected.

So reminiscent of the stranger in the redwoods.

She opened her mouth, willing her voice to answer. For she knew his name as well as her own. Stepping forward, she swayed so hard she—

Crashed.

Hard.

Right onto the wooden planks.

"Ouch."

Naila rubbed her elbow. She glanced about the dark room in confusion. The dhow rocked like never before. Outside, angry waves crashed against the walls, just as hard as she had crashed onto the floor.

Naila stumbled again, on her bottom. Every plank squeaked. The outside of the little porthole came dangerously close to reaching the sea's agitated surface. The dhow rotated, causing her to glide over the rough wooden flooring. She hastily grasped a bed pole to keep from smashing into the window. Fear clawed at her as the waves pulsed underneath the Chimera. The thin glass of the window was the only barrier between her and the merciless sea.

This is it, Naila thought, we're going to capsize.

Here at sea, only Mother Nature ruled. Time would tell whether she'd gift them mercy. Naila's heart sprinted like a cheetah on the hunt. The moment the ship rotated back, she crawled underneath the bed and clung to the poles. Thank goodness they were fastened to the floor. Hopefully, that would keep her safe.

"Naila!"

Silas.

"I'm here!"

Naila almost wept from relief, although she knew there was little Silas could do against a full-blown storm. It took Silas three attempts between the rocking of the dhow to reach her. Naila clutched his hands, and he pulled her from underneath the bed. Her legs trembled.

For all Silas's drinking, his eyes were clear and his clothes were still neatly pressed. He took her face in his palms.

"By the stars, are you all right?"

She nodded, staring at the planes of his too handsome face.

"What's going on?"

"A tides-induced hurricane, Helath's welcome gift." He grimaced. "Don't worry, Halfbeard will pull us through."

Naila jerked her head back in surprise. This was the third tide in less than half a day. The other two tides had brought about enormous waves, but none had caused a storm.

"Pull us through? We nearly capsized!"

Silas stroked the flyaway locks near her temples. It was weirdly calming.

"Halfbeard bears the gift of Enki, the water bearer. Worry not, he has it under control."

The water bearer... Like Ishtar he was one of the Legends of the Sky.

Naila was skeptical, but then the dhow swayed again, and she crashed into Silas. She buried her face in his hard chest. Out of the corners of her eyes, she could see the wood of the dhow burning with blue flames.

Halfbeard and his crew must be utilizing æther to protect the dhow from the vicious sea.

"We're going to die," she whispered.

"We won't. I promise."

Silas stuck out his pinky, and she hugged it with her own.

He led her back to the bed, and she snuggled into his arms, eyes squeezed shut, as they lay on the uncomfortable mattress. His scent was soothing, confident with a wink. Everything Silas embodied. She inhaled it deeply, and her fear subsided.

With every frightening wobble, Silas stroked her back soothingly, whispering words of reassurance. Naila tried to ignore the wrathful winds and pouncing waves, focusing instead on the melodic beats of Silas's heart. Despite his words, his pulse fluttered as fast as hers.

After a nerve-racking eternity, the waves finally calmed, and the ship sailed about as if nothing had happened. Silas was right. Naila did not doubt that few could do what Halfbeard had done.

"Is it hurricane season?"

Silas tugged the crown of her head underneath his chin.

"Well, if you call a whole year a season."

Her eyelids grew heavy, and it took everything to keep them from closing. The rising and falling of Silas's warm chest was a lullaby to her tired frame.

"It's because of *Iluna*," Silas explained as he ran his fingers through her long curls. "The moons influence the tides. Storms terrorize the Seven Seas and the Wicked Oceans nearly every week. It's why few sail them."

Great, just her luck. Naila stifled a yawn and asked him to tell her more about *Iluna*. Silas only shrugged and said, "Legend goes that Lemuria used to have only one moon."

"How did the second moon come to be?"

"Who knows? The only thing certain is that it's been there since the age of the Unspokens."

Naila wanted to ask more, but the dark of the dreamlands swept her away. This time there were no ice-crawlers, and the shadowed eyes were long gone too. There was only a pleasing, balsamic scent and Silas's calming voice.

XVIII

DEADLY WAVES

THE DHOW lolled steadily in its cradle of dark waves, as if the Sea of Helath had decided to play innocence itself.

Seated against the bulwark on the Chimera's deck, Naila studied the scroll in an attempt to memorize the map. Occasionally, she glanced at Silas, engrossed in a strategic discussion with Halfbeard at the bow. Pasha was charming Onyx at the stern, their laughter drifting across the deck. Silas shot them a troubled look.

Standing next to Naila, Tryce leaned over the railing and pointed out every sea creature. He was even worse than her insect-collecting uncle. "Naila, look!"

She sighed, not bothering to look up. "Yes?"

"It's a sea goat, it's a sea goat!"

Tryce's eyes lit up. He hoisted himself up the rails to get a closer look. The wind, that had lost its icy edge, pulled his loose curls in all directions.

"Watch out," she chastised. But the huge grin on his face made her look too. A shadow of a massive horned creature darted underneath the ship. She let out a little shriek. "W-What is that thing?"

"Is everything all right?"

She stole a glance behind her. Silas's curious gaze met hers, whilst Halfbeard stared, amused, from the bow.

Tryce dashed across the ship, going from one side to the other. "*Baba,* look! A sea goat."

"Well, I'll be," said Halfbeard, as he joined his son at the railing. "I believe yer be right."

"A *suyarmašu*?" Naila tested the Tierratongo word on her tongue.

Tryce beamed. "D'ye know how lucky you are? Sea goats usually hover 'round the Arctic waves. Not so far up north."

Naila joined him by the rails, attempting anew to spot the creature. Tryce's commotion prompted several other passengers to do the same. Regrettably, the creature was long gone.

"Suyarmašu's a mammal, but it lives in the sea." Tryce bounced on his feet. "It has flippers for limbs, and scales for fur. And it has these huge, huge horns on its head. Even *helicoprion* fears them." He stretched his arms wide as if to emphasize his words.

Helicoprion? The shark with a spiral-shaped jaw filled with rows upon rows of razer-sharp teeth? Or at least, that's what she'd seen in one of Mr. Thoth's scrolls. Naila shuddered. She failed to understand why Tryce was so excited. If it were up to her, she'd stay far away from those sea monsters.

Halfbeard chuckled. "Now let's not get 'head of ourselves, boy. That goat cain't beat helicoprion."

"It can, *Baba!*"

Tryce launched into a passionate monologue, listing all reasons why he was, indeed, correct. Halfbeard calmly lit his midwakh pipe, the smoke curling lazily as he listened with amusement.

Silas nudged her and whispered behind his hand, "Don't be shocked if Tryce invites a sea goat to dinner."

She stifled a giggle. "If Captain Barbaras doesn't turn it into the main course, you mean?"

Staring at Tryce with a frown, Onyx made her way to them. "What is all this noise about?"

For once, her locks were tamed into a sleek bun. Naila suppressed a smile. The huntress even applied a hint of color to her lips. Oh, she was interested in Pasha, all right.

Silas ruffled Onyx's hair, causing a few fiery strands to come loose from her bun. "Oh, just your cousin being *your* cousin."

"Ugh, you know I hate it when you do that." Onyx pushed his hand away.

Fast as an arrow, she clasped the hilt of Valkarian—Silas's sword. But Silas was faster. He snatched her wrist before she could draw the scimitar from its scabbard.

"Don't touch the sword, Red. I mean it," he said, his tone deadly serious.

Onyx met his gaze squarely and sing sang, "Don't touch the hair. And don't call me Red."

A sigh escaped Naila's lips. "Let's all just 'don't touch the' anything."

Onyx turned. "Pasha and the others are throwing a feast tonight. N, *you* are welcome to join." With a final flourish, she sashayed back to Pasha.

"A feast? Good. Just what I need," said Silas.

Naila threw him a look. "She didn't invite you."

His lips tilted into a naughty, crooked grin that did a funny thing to her stomach. "And you think that will stop me?"

She tucked herself into her shawl as if it would give her protection against the big bad wolf in the skin of a prince. The wool brushed her sensitive skin. Silas's eyes followed her every move, lingering on her womanly curves.

"Who is this Philippe to you?" he whispered.

Philly? Where did that come from?

"Just a friend," she said.

"Just a friend..."

Their eyes locked. The intensity in his caught her breath.

She swallowed. "So, you'll get a harem?" The words slipped out before she could stop herself.

He smirked knowingly. "You're quite direct, aren't you?" He leaned against the taffrail, playing with the jeweled hilt of his sword. "I'm not actually."

She released the breath she had been holding. Why did his words relieve her so?

Silas gazed into the distance. The sky, which was blue just a bell ago, had turned thick with mist and the sea's briny tang now held something faintly musty. "Mother was... mistreated in Jericho's harem. She was his form of revenge against my father."

So her suspicions held true.

Jericho wasn't Silas's sire.

A humorless smile appeared on Silas's face. "Concubines have little to no rights. Their existence is to please their patron's every whim. No one cares what happens in the harem. Who lives, who dies, who is abused. It's of no concern to the outside world." He closed his eyes as if the memory pained him, before opening them once more. "The imperial harem is a den of vipers. I watched it suck the life out of my mother." A faraway look entered his night-blue eyes. "I promised myself I'd never become such a man. I'd never make a *feylana* suffer like my mother."

Her heart swelled painfully.

The salty wind blew through Silas's deep-brown locks. With his black travel attire wrapped around his lithe, tan frame, he looked more pirate than prince. For all Philippe's and Rē's ethereal beauty, no man had ever looked as handsome as Silas.

She had... misjudged him at first. Yes, he was a charming skirt-chaser. But he was also so much more. A man with many layers—thrill-seeking warrior, political strategist, and a warm, just heart lurking underneath all.

Their eyes met... and held.

His hand reached out for hers and she allowed him to hold it. His thumb gently massaged the back, the roughness of his calloused touch kissing her sensitive skin.

"In Lemuria we consider nergaylas untouchable." His voice was but a whisper. "And, *yana,* you are so beautiful, it would be a sin not to admire you from anything but afar."

Naila held her breath as his fingers left her hand and traced the soft skin of her forearm.

"But I cannot fathom how any man can look at you and not want to feel if your skin is as soft as it looks." He clasped a dark curl between his fingers and brought it to his nose. "To confirm whether you smell as breathtaking as you look." His words caressed her every sense. Whether she wanted to or not, she couldn't stop herself from leaning closer and closer. Silas's eyes wandered to her lips. His voice was barely audible now. "To ascertain if you taste as my dreams tell me you do."

Oh, God, help me. But God was otherwise occupied.

Silas inched closer and closer. Was he going to kiss her? Was she going to let him? She took a deep breath. He smelled so good. Like the forest in spring.

A horn echoed, loud and clear. She at once pulled away from Silas. Woke up from a dream that couldn't be.

"All hands on deck!" Halfbeard bellowed. "An' all passengers to the main cabin!" His voice cut through the chaos like cannon fire. The captain moved swiftly, cutting a tangled rope with his knife. "Reef them sails, ye dogs! Secure the halyards!"

Just as she was about to turn around, the Chimera was hit hard by something crashing into it. Naila lost her footing. Silas, with ever sharp reflexes, caught her safely.

She couldn't see anything. The mist obscured all from her sight. No, this wasn't just mist. The air, thick and heavy, sparkled like a field of diamonds. *How peculiar.*

The dhow got hit by something once more.

Voices cried all around them, but she could only make out blurry silhouettes; couldn't discern their faces.

She glanced back at Silas, but he stared with a frown at what could only be Halfbeard's figure.

"Silas..." Pointing straight ahead, Naila let out a gasp.

Piercing the mist, all around the Chimera, were the skeletons of several dhows, black as the underworld they had lost their lives to. Some were near intact, whereas others were reduced to no more than rotting wood drifting angrily upon Helath's waves. Wood that crashed and crashed against the Chimera.

Tryce dashed before them, but Silas grabbed him by the shoulder. "Wha—"

"What's going on?" Silas demanded.

"It's the Dead Man's Waves." His eyes were wide, torn between fear and excitement. "They say Lamaštu haunts these waters, seducing seamen to their graves. She's still bitter she's not a Legend, y'know."

"I thought your father was going to avoid the Dead Man's Waves?" Silas snapped.

"It's not mapped. 'E didn't know the exact location." Tryce shrugged before unlocking himself from Silas's grip. "*Baba* wants all passengers in their huts."

Silas let out a storm of swear words.

Worriedly, his gaze swept over the mist-veiled ship. "We have to find Onyx."

They waded through the passengers who were rushing to follow the captain's orders.

Silas grabbed a red-headed woman by the shoulder, forcing her to turn. But it wasn't Onyx.

"Lamaštu!" a man cried. He was climbing the taffrail, talking to someone she couldn't see. "Lamaštu."

An icy cold seized Naila. "What is he doing?"

Silas followed her gaze. "Suzano's balls!"

Uttering "Lamaštu" one last time, the man hurled himself into Helath's waves.

"We have to save him!" Naila shrieked.

Silas seized her arm, shaking his head. "I'm sorry, but he's lost to us. Let's find Onyx."

Two-Toed Teddy grabbed hold of a woman with a baby just as she too, cried out "Lamaštu" and reached for the taffrail. Despite the chaos, he seemed unshakable. He barked something to Rē, pointing at the massive shard of a shipwreck—half a mast, splintered and jagged—looming out of the mist. It careened straight toward the Chimera's side.

Without hesitation, Rē lunged toward the mainmast, securing a coil of rope. "I've got this one!" He tied one end of the rope around his waist as he sprinted up the ratlines, racing to the height of the foremast. Perched high above, he swung out into the air, using the rope as leverage. Just as the mast was about to crash into the Chimera, he collided with it mid-air, slashing down with his scimitar and cutting through the rotted wood. A resounding crack echoed as the mast split, falling in harmless chunks into the sea.

An impressed smile lit upon Silas's face. "He's mad."

However, another piece of debris crashed with a boom against the dhow, shaking the Chimera so thoroughly she was sure they'd capsize. Naila tumbled toward the taffrail. Hard.

A wave of seawater soaked the deck. Followed by another one and another, as the drifting wood thumped against the dhow from everywhere. Complete chaos broke out on the ship. So many people screamed at once, Naila couldn't distinguish their voices.

She squeezed her eyes shut against the salt prickling her eyes.

Dazed, she pushed herself up.

"Silas?"

There was only the thick, shimmering mist and the shadows of the crew darting through it. The ship's steering wheel was unmanned, and they were on a collision course with another shipwreck! Where was Mr. Bones, the helmsman? She had to warn someone.

But then the world around her grew endlessly silent. The fog was so thick it obscured even the thoughts from her mind.

"*Nergayla*," a voice sweeter than nectar sang.

She glanced about her. Wha—

Her eyes grew wide. Her breathing increased to a featherlight fluttering, each heartbeat heralding the approach of another panic attack.

"L-Lamaštu?"

Long, sharp talons clasped the taffrail. The hands belonging to them were pale as a bloodless corpse. Climbing over the taffrail, a woman emerged from the depths of Helath. She was neither ugly nor beautiful. Completely bare as a newborn babe. A pair of sea snakes slithered around her limbs. Her eyes were bottomless, torturing pits.

"*Naila...*" Her long talons beckoned Naila. "*I see you, Naila.*" Her lips twisted into a grin. A snake crawled out of her mouth. *"You and I, we are not so different. The Legends have been so cruel to us. Let vengeance be ours. Let me—"*

A hand emerged from behind her and smothered her nose and mouth with a cloth. It was drenched in peppermint oil. Naila struggled to free herself.

"It's me," Silas said. "Trust me."

She blinked. Once. Twice.

The shimmering mist still danced around her, but Lamaštu had vanished.

"Are you all right?" Onyx cast her a worried look from next to Silas.

"I... Lamaštu..."

"It's the mist," said Silas. "It's so rich in æther it makes people see things that aren't there."

Her heartbeat slowed down. Lamaštu wasn't real. The words she spoke were nonexistent... She nuzzled her lip, then suddenly remembered something crucial. "The steering wheel!"

She made to move, but Halfbeard was already steering the ship through the wreckages with a cloth pressed to his nose.

"He was the first one I pulled out of the illusion. We were about to crash head-on into another ship, so he handled the steering wheel and I went to the rest of the crew," said Silas.

"How did you know it was an illusion?" Onyx asked.

"Lamaštu promised me something I knew was too good to be true."

"You're a hero!" Naila beamed.

Silas winked. "Didn't I say I was impossible to miss?"

Onyx snorted, but she too, couldn't suppress a relieved smile.

After what felt like ages, the Chimera finally emerged from the mist, leaving the ship graveyard behind. They sailed toward the sun once more. Naila stroked her arm. It wasn't real. Lamaštu and her words weren't real...

And so the days repeated themselves. At day, they would settle upon the deck, going about their way as if the Sea of Helath was a children's pool, all the while listening to Bubba's stories or Halfbeard's song within the storms. But at night, the waves would attack the dhow, and in several instances, a squall reared its vicious head. Every time Halfbeard pulled the Chimera to safety.

Naila wasn't the only blue person on board. Silas turned quieter with every passing day. He retreated to his hut even earlier than she did, and like her classmates always teased, she was the epitome of a goody-two-shoes. If Naila weren't sick to her bones, she would have talked to him, but she was too busy keeping her meals tucked inside her stomach with all the rocking of the dhow. The moment that had passed between them, right before the Dead Man's Waves, seemed like a long-lost dream, unmentioned by both.

After two weeks, Naila knew she would never set foot on a ship again.

"Me lucky charm! Where's that thing?" the helmsman cried around the mess where they ate breakfast: barley porridge flavored with wild onions and garlic.

"Now how is we s'pose ter know?" Jacobo yawned, scratching his buttock.

"I be need'n that seashell. The stars only know what Helath will do ter us!"

Tryce blinked innocently.

Naila pursed her lips in disapproval. The little rascal. He wasn't fooling her. Poor Mr. Bones.

Tryce winked at her conspiratorially.

"The stars only know what *I* will do if ye don' drag yer butt back to the steering wheel, Bones." Halfbeard grunted.

"But—"

Tryce stood up, his bowl half-finished; something very unlike him, considering he usually ate for two. "I can steer the ship, *Baba.*"

Ah, so that was his game.

Pasha snorted. "Are you sure about that, *yelud*? I'd like to leave this ship a whole."

"I ain' no kid."

Silas paused mid-bite, narrowing his eyes. There was no love lost between him and the merchant from Jodrir. He'd been watching him and Onyx like an overprotective brother. "Why are you still here?"

Onyx shot Silas a warning look, but Pasha let the barb slide. Before he could answer, Tryce pulled the attention toward himself again. "Can I, *Baba*? Can I? C'mon!"

Halfbeard scratched his beard. "Well, c'mon then, boy. S'pose now's as good as any to learn."

"Yess!"

Tryce dashed up the stairs, two at a time, Halfbeard trailing leisurely behind him.

Just as they finished breakfast, the watchman in the crow's nest bellowed, "Land ahoy!" Land ahoy!"

Naila ran up to the taffrails, cupping her eyes to reflect the sunbeams. A blue lagoon surrounded a volcanic island, which seemed to be the shape of two crescents facing each other. A monolith peeked from the sea-filled crater.

"The Shores of the Blood Moons," Captain Barbaras roared from the wheelhouse. "We dock here."

The Sea of Helath was eerily calm as the Chimera floated closer to the volcanic island. From up close, Naila could see the island was covered in a vibrant rainforest. Even from afar, she scented the sweet nectar of tropical flowers, drifting on the early afternoon's air like a hypnotizing hymn.

"With a name like the Shores of the Blood Moons, I would've thought it was some creepy island," Naila said as she bent over the rails to take in the enchanting blue lagoon.

The cerulean water was so clear she could see sea kelp dance underneath the waves, and a school of vibrant fish dashed away as the dhow sailed through their routes. Halfbeard chuckled behind her.

"Creepy? Nay, I wouldn' say so, even if that Red Šar's *nergayla* does 'er best to keep us seamen away with threats of a curse."

Rē shouted orders from the wheelhouse as Tryce, a huge smile on his face, steered the Chimera into a large beach cave under the watchful eyes of Mr. Bones. From the looks of it, they were going to the center of the volcano. The crater with its statue.

Naila turned to Halfbeard.

The long end of his loose turban floated in the winds, and in that moment, Naila could see why he was the king of the Seven Seas. He oozed confidence, demanded respect with his very presence.

"What curse?"

"Nova avowed the stars will call up'n any ship that anchors at the Shores of the Blood Moons. I s'pose none 'ave dared challenge 'er claim."

"But you and your crew did? And you proved her wrong, right?"

"Well." Halfbeard blew out a whisp of spicy smoke. "We didn' but after we leave, we'll see 'ow true them words hold."

Naila's jaw dropped. "What? Why would you endanger everyone just to prove this *nergayla* wrong?"

Halfbeard smirked. "Aye, so yer superstitious, I see."

"I'm not!"

Naila wasn't. She hadn't believed Philly's fairy tales of the stars nor her aunty's claim her lover's ex-wife had put a voodoo spell on her. What Naila did believe, however, was that the lands of Lemuria played by different rules. Rules she wouldn't dare to breach.

Halfbeard stowed away his pipe. "Our Crishirian merchant paid us well."

Naila arched a brow. "So, the price for possible peril is crystals? *Really*?"

"Those who revile crystals all fall under one denominator, *nergayla*." Halfbeard's mocking whisper tickled her ear. "They simply don' have 'em."

With a barked order to his men, the captain went back to business.

The beach cave led to a great lake embedded between the two halves of the volcano. Several wooden houses were scattered about the beaches. As the buildings grew bigger, nerves bubbled in the pit of Naila's stomach. It was the first land she'd seen in weeks. How she longed to feel the earth underneath her feet again.

The dhow bypassed the humongous monolith, which upon closer inspection was located on a smaller island in the middle of the lake. It was very similar to those of Greykeep mountains—a man with a scimitar and a shield. His features were similar to one of sub-Saharan African descent, just like Naila.

"Pack yer things and leave if ye must, but we leave within two bells and not a breath later," Halfbeard bellowed.

The Chimera had officially docked at the Shores of the Blood Moons.

XIX

OF DREAMS AND NIGHTMARES

THE SHORES of the Blood Moons was a place made of dreams, not of nightmares. It had the most peculiar forest, with trees of mint-green and rose and marigold. Fields of pastel flowers stretched between the feet of the trees, whilst colorful birds whistled the most beautiful songs. An island stuck in eternal spring.

Enchanted as she was by the view, Naila's mind was pinned on other things. This was her chance. She would sneak off the dhow and send the šaltana her letter. If she could distract the others, that was... Guilty as she felt, she wasn't ready to disclose the princess's secret. Not when she chose to ignore it.

Tryce stared as if dazed at a scroll next to her. The glint in his eyes told Naila the boy was up to no good.

"What are ye looking at, boy?" Jacobo demanded.

"I found a map in Pasha's satchel," Tryce whispered conspiratorially. "'t says it leads to a treasure here. S'pose that's why he came? Too bad it's in my hands now."

Naila gasped. "That's stealing!"

"It's borrowing if I give it back... *After* I found myself a treasure."

Jacobo snatched the map out of his hands. "Lemme see! The *nergayla* is right. I'll be giving it back to that scrote."

By the way Jacobo licked his lips Naila was certain he'd do anything but that. Unsurprisingly, the sailor scurried off the dhow, the opposite way of Pasha. *Ugh.* What a bunch of thieves!

Tryce burst into laughter.

Naila punched his arm. "You little devil."

A mischievous grin lit up his face. "It's fake."

That made Naila smile a little—she didn't like Jacobo much—but she did her best to keep a stern face. Her classmates had always teased her for being a goody-two-shoes, but what choice did she have with Tryce acting like a scoundrel?

"I suppose this is goodbye." Nearby, Pasha kissed Onyx's cheek.

He pressed a flower into her hands. His comrades already descended to the dock, whereas Silas and now Tryce too, offered him dark looks.

"I suppose it is."

Pasha unveiled his pearly teeth, winking. "Too bad your 'brother' and cousin shadowed us like guardian dogs."

Silas scoffed. "She is not getting dishonored on my watch."

Onyx shot him an incredulous look. "You are one to talk! Just how many *feylanas* did *you* dishonor?"

Naila agreed. Silas was a hypocrite, but she wasn't about to say so. This was her chance to sneak away. Her heart did squeeze ever so slightly. She hoped that hadn't been his intention toward her. Silas had gotten to her…

"Where are ye going?" Tryce glanced at her curiously. "We're not s'posed to leave the ship."

"*Shhh*. Are you coming or not?"

He grinned by way of answer.

They tiptoed over the boarding stairs, avoiding a foot here and an arm there, for the seamen had their hands full unloading cargo off the dhow. No sign of the mysterious rich merchant, however. Picturesque coral stone houses stretched out over the harbor as if they floated atop the sea. From baby-blue to soft-pinks, they would make the prettiest paintings.

Tryce pointed at a crowd in the distance. "There's a market! I bet we won't find any of their stuff in Havenmor."

Many of the locals were gathered around the edge of what had once been the volcano, where a large gate was carved within stone. Colorful market tents surrounded a giant tree on the town square before the gate. The air grew thick with the fragrance of spices.

"What stuff do you mean exactly?" Naila arched a brow.

Tryce grinned. "Snapperjack venom or the fangs of a thornclaw. And who knows, maybe even a blood crystal or two."

Naila froze, forcing Tryce to stop walking. "Venom? Fangs? *Blood crystals*?"

Tryce lifted his hands in innocence. "I'm joking. I'm joking."

"You'd better be."

"C'mon, let's go, before *Baba* drags us back."

Naila patted the pocket of her tulip pants to reassure herself she hadn't forgotten her letter. It pained her to reject the šaltana but what else was she to do? Believing the prophecy meant staying for its fulfillment. Naila couldn't abandon her mother and Philly for a prophecy that may or may not be true. The šaltana had to understand.

The merry notes of music hummed over the sand road that led to the marketplace. Men, women, and children were finely dressed in robes of muslins and silks. Many of them wore bronze wolf masks, too.

"What are they celebrating?" Naila asked.

Tryce beamed like a boy in a candy shop. "A *kaipura* festival, it has to be. Ye know, where they purify the land from evil spirits? Folks in the midlands love those. I ain't never been to one."

He dashed toward the feasting crowd. Naila had to run to keep up with him. Flame blowers used æther to create wolves of flames to the cheers of the people, whilst behind the giant tree, belly dancers entertained with dazzling smiles and flaming skirts.

Flags embroidered with Crishire's imperial emblem—a black serpentine dragon with a scepter clutched in its claw—fluttered softly in the sea wind.

"Looks like the Red Šar changed the emblem. It used to be a viper. His ego is bigger than an *elephaunt*," muttered Tryce.

"The Shores of the Blood Moons is part of Crishire?"

"Unofficially, aye."

No wonder Silas and Onyx had been on edge. Naila rubbed her arm uncomfortably. Maybe sneaking off the dhow hadn't been one of her brightest ideas.

"It's out of respect to his eldest brother, *lugal*," an old man cracked behind them. He waggled his shepherd's staff at Tryce as if to scold him for speaking ill of the Red Šar. "An ode to the late Prince Reuben II, who was the first to be called the Dragon Lord. An admirable thing to do, if you ask me, for the current šar was raised by his brother."

Tryce's brows flew up to his hairline. "Raised by his brother? Ain't imperial harems more vicious than a den of vipers?"

"*Yana*," said the shepherd. "Many a prince dies in fratricide before they come of age."

Naila frowned in confusion. "How many sons did the previous šar have exactly?"

"Šar Jericho vi Iliyas had no less than four and twenty strapping boys, *feylana*," said the old man whilst puffing out his chest, as if he had personally sired the princes. "But all of them are dead, except for two."

And Silas was believed to be one of them...

The old man's sight finally caught on Naila's phæralei. He gaped at her.

"All right, off we go." Tryce saluted the man and pushed Naila forward.

They strolled through the market streets but avoided lingering too long at any stand or talking with the locals. It proved hard to keep a low profile, however. People stared unabashedly at Naila, their eyes widening in wonder at the sight of her phæralei. Fortunately, Tryce's glowers kept their mouths shut and their hands to themselves. Naila wrapped her shawl over her head as a makeshift hood to cover up her marks.

When they reached the old, thick tree in the middle of the marketplace, Naila noticed it was plastered with linen rag pamphlets.

"What's that?"

"Hmm?" Tryce pulled his eyes from a group of vicious-looking canines locked in cages. Many men hovered around that particular market stand. His gaze followed Naila's. "Oh, the latest news."

Naila perked up. What kind of issues would these pamphlets talk about? Perhaps something about shadowreaper sightings. She pushed forward through the mass of people, avoiding pushy elbows and stepping feet as best she could. The pamphlets were inked in the elegant lines of Tierratongo's cuneiform characters.

> *"Following the battle over Esyleron in the Empire of Skeldor one moon ago, Skeldor's Silver Šar pronounced it an act of war. Whisperers say his imperial messenger notified the Red Šar yesterday morn, an official war would be the result should Crishire commence their attacks—"*

"Wow, I keep forgetting you're at the brink of a full-blown war." Naila glanced back, but Tryce was nowhere to be seen. "Tryce?"

Naila waded through the crowd but couldn't spot Tryce's head of floppy curls anywhere. He probably got caught up in one of his boyish excitements and forgot all about her. Naila shrugged. *Oh, well.* She'd best use her time wisely before she had to return to the dhow and continue the rest of their journey. She still had to find a postal office of some sort to send the šaltana her letter.

As she walked through the market, she found that some of the stands sold the loveliest things, with jewelry in every color and lip pigments in more than just blood red. There was also grilled seafood, fragrant spices, and luxurious items for which she didn't know the names. Some even sold exotic animals, to her horror. After half a bell or so, she finally found what she looked for. The cuneiform characters atop the wooden market stand read,

FESTUS' FLIGHT
Delivers to all of Lemuria within a sunset!

A flock of birds cawed from the back of the tent. Eagles, falcons, and hawks sat on a thick branch, waiting to take flight and deliver a letter.

"Uh, how much to send a letter to Skeldor?" asked Naila.

The vendor, a middle-aged man, regarded her through widened eyes.

"*Nergayla*," said he.

Naila sighed, but she didn't correct him. "Please?"

"For you at no cost at all. But a blessing would be appreciated."

A blessing? Whatever could her blessing do? Yes, she could rejuvenate flowers and affect objects with her flames of æther, but as far as she knew, it had no effect on people.

"Sir, I'm no miracle maker."

"No miracles, a blessing is all I ask. A blessing for my health."

The man stuck out his hands, palms up. His hands were discolored. Red spots covered the bronze of his skin. Not only there but also in his neck, now that she took a closer look. Naila's eyes softened. She took his hands in hers. For once she wished the man's words rang true. That her powers were indeed as he said. "May good health be with you, Sir Festus."

Her hands grew warm until a boiling sensation spread through her fingers. She knew sparks of æther ignited at the tips. A flow of precious warmth left her. With every breath she fell more and more into exhaustion. Her knees trembled. She struggled to stand. The cawing of the birds, the whispers of the winds, all of it grew silent. How she longed for a nap.

The man gasped. He pulled his hands out of hers. Naila got pulled violently out of her daze. The boils on his skin had completely retreated. She blinked once, twice, but the sight remained the same. The man kissed her hands. Tears filled his eyes.

"*Nergayla, nergayla*. You truly are Ishtar blessed."

"H-How could this be?" asked Naila.

Panic surged through her as she stared at the man's hands. The šaltana's words echoed in her ears.

You belong here.

Nergayla.

But she had even more pressing matters at the moment. The exchange had caught the attention of a few surrounding them. Naila grew uneasy. She hastily covered her phæralei with the hood of her shawl. She gave the man her letter and the silver palace's address and quickly left the stand. She only paused when she reached the other side of the market.

Naila put her hands to her heaving bosom. Her breaths came out raggedly. What was that? What *was* she? Hopefully Nebiru didn't only hold a portal but the answers the šaltana hinted at as well.

A vendor at a nearby stand waved at Naila.

"*Feylana*," she said.

It was a girl of no more than fourteen winters. Her skin was a beautiful dark cedar, but her eyes... her eyes were the azure of the sea. Her robes were that same azure color too. Etched between her brows was the hint of a scar: a lying crescent moon. Naila's heart skipped a beat. She looked eerily similar to little Oya. Was this girl a nergayla too?

The girl held up a flower hair clip of luminescent beads.

Naila's mood shifted like the remnants of a storm making way for a rainbow. It was a *fayalobi*. To think her favorite flower grew in the soils of Lemuria. Her fingers trailed the beads. It was so similar to the one she'd lost in the redwoods. The one her mother had made.

"Lovely, isn't it?" said the girl. "Black gold encased by soul-stones. All mined from the Elysian Fields. It is one of a kind, made by the Mehari, my tribe."

The Elysian Fields?

Those were the fields rich in æther Onyx had spoken of.

Naila stared at the flower, mesmerized. She loved jewelry but never had the money to buy something expensive. Her fingers continued caressing the hair clip. It spoke to her like no jewelry had ever done. Just like her compass. How she wished she could buy this gem. She didn't dare ask the price for something so precious.

The whinnying of a horse shocked Naila out of her thoughts and next she knew, a pouch of crystals fell onto the market table. The vendor's azure eyes grew wary but she accepted the pouch.

"Consider it paid..." a stranger spoke, in a confident masculine voice that reminded her of teasing shadows in the dark of the night.

The girl nodded. She hastily retreated to the back of the stand as if she were frightened.

Naila spun around. Behind her a great black stallion with devilish eyes neighed haughtily. A tall man leaned against the horse as if, like the stately animal, he owned the whole of the market. He wore dark hooded robes a shade darker than his steed. The male's loose turban hid the lower half of his face.

"For surely a piece so exquisite should be worn by a *feylana* who eclipses it in its beauty."

His words brought a shiver of goosebumps to her skin, as if they had personally caressed her inch for inch. But Naila couldn't let those honeyed words fool her.

"I can't accept such a gift."

"Oh, but I insist."

"No, it's okay. I wanted a red one anyway."

He pricked his finger to one of the leaves.

One by one the luminescent beads turned ruby as if a liquid form of the precious gemstone was trapped inside, testing the confines of the beads' crystal walls. Naila eyed them in wonder.

"Now it is. May I?" he said.

Naila reluctantly let him clasp the stunning piece in her curls, right above her ear. The man did not retract his hand at once. Instead, his calloused fingers caressed the softness of a curl, leaving in their wake an odd warmth that shot low to her belly. The marketplace was filled to the brim with people, yet it felt like she and he were the only ones existing in this time, this place. Her eyes shifted to the stranger. Wary. Apprehensive. The veils of his black turban uncovered only his eyes. Deep oceanic eyes so dark they looked made of shadows. Darker than ebony.

"What is the price? I know you didn't give it to me for free."

"Ah, but I did."

"I don't trust you."

The stallion grunted as if it dismayed him that Naila spoke in such a tone to his master. The stranger chuckled and stroked its mane. The animal was a fine creature. Tall, regal, and powerfully built. There was something about the animal that bothered Naila, however. It was eerily familiar...

"*You*," Naila gasped. She arched away from the man. "You are that guy from the redwoods."

"That I am." He arched a perfect brow. "The one who saved your life."

Naila swallowed back her fright. He was right; he had saved her. She owed him her life. Naila's eyes roamed over his shape. His black robes were made of the finest fabric, and his sun-kissed skin, the exposed part of it, was near flawless. Despite not seeing the whole of his face, she could tell he was handsome.

"Why did you disappear in the redwoods? And at the Akitu festival! I think I saw you again."

"The huntress had it under control. There was no reason for further interference on my part."

Naila blinked. Oh yes, Onyx.

Realization dawned. "You're also that wealthy merchant from Crishire."

The man didn't deny it, nor did he unveil his face.

"You overheard us talking at the Rusty Anchor, didn't you? Did you follow me?"

The stranger inched forward.

Naila had to raise her head to look up at him. He was as tall as Silas. He circled Naila. Slowly. Leisurely. Like a lion did its prey. His eyes felt like hands. They caressed her every inch. She felt the burn on her skin wherever they touched.

Naila straightened her back, but didn't turn to watch him. Instead, she focused on the monolith at the heart of the island, acting more at ease than she felt. For every nerve in her body screamed of danger.

"*Evening Star,*" said the stranger, "You appeared out of nowhere, a nergayla with no affiliation. Lemuria is ablaze with rumors the Shadow Šar is hunting you. It makes a man wonder..."

Evening Star... Ilaris in Tierratongo. A celestial body the Lemai associated with Ishtar. Its meaning translated to something close to kismet.

He paused before her, his fingers interlocked behind his back.

Naila's heart thundered in her throat. She'd been a fool to think her presence would go unnoticed.

"Your phæralei"—he continued as his eyes grazed her forehead—"are unlike any. They speak of an ancient legend. Of Ishtar."

Naila finally turned to glare at him. "I don't know what you're talking about."

He raised a brow skeptically but said no more.

She changed the subject, unwilling to learn more, for she was afraid of what she would discover.

"How do you plan to go to the mainland? There's no other dhow here but the Chimera."

Naila glanced around to be sure, but the Chimera was the only ship for miles and miles. The stranger fetched a pomegranate out of his saddlebag and fed it to the stallion. With one bite, the animal obliterated the fruit. The man petted the beast. Haughty or no, the horse was quite adorable when it ate. Naila wanted to stroke its mane, but kept her hands to herself.

"The Shores of the Blood Moons has an underground city connected to Crishire beneath the sea. What you see here is just its entrance."

"And you confess this freely to a foreigner like me?"

Amusement gleamed within his eyes. "Yes, I do. Even if you spread the word, what good would it do? Most wouldn't dare to anchor here and curse their ships. And even if they did, they are no match for Crishire's imperial troops. It's not for nothing they are called *ut Asanatæ.*"

The Immortals.

Naila rolled her eyes. Men and their pride. Her gaze shifted back to the monolith at the center of the island. It looked even more majestic from afar.

"I hear you are headed for the Dark Forest of Isolon."

"Who blabbed to you about that?" Naila asked.

"What are you seeking there?" he asked instead of answering.

"My business is my own."

The stranger's gaze promised her he would find out either way. "Very well then, but you must know there is a shorter road. One less time-consuming and far less deadly than the Sea of Helath."

Naila swung to the man in shock. "Really? Tell me." She added as an afterthought, "Please."

"The roads underneath this island don't lead to Crishire alone. They can also take you to Isolon."

Naila blinked several times, but then groaned. Silas and the others would never agree. "Thanks, but no thanks. My friends would rather not enter the Red Šar's lair."

"As you will," he said.

Is he..." Naila clenched her compass. "Is he really that bad? The Red Šar, I mean?"

The stranger's eyes were unreadable. "He is worse." And then he said, "Impressive, nay?"

"What?"

He tilted his head to the magnificent monolith.

"It is. Who is he? Another first šar?"

"*Lai*, he is much more. The scrolls say the day of his birth a thunderstorm overcame the lands of Lemuria, while cyclones raged over all the Seven Seas. And so they named him after a thunder god worshipped in ancient times. With his legendary scimitar Enlil, he led the Lemai to victory and the Unspokens to death."

"What was his name?"

"Suzano Stormhold."

Naila stopped breathing.

Stormhold... what?

Naila Stormhold is what the shadowreapers had called her.

Naila looked at the stranger. Cold sweat broke out in the palms of her hands. Then she finally noticed his eyes. Those dark, dark eyes. He wasn't only the man of the redwoods nor only the rich merchant from the ship. He was the one who haunted her dreams. The man of her nightmares. "I-I've dreamed of you."

For a heartbeat none of them spoke.

He reached for a curl and twirled it around his finger. "Did you, now?"

Naila didn't dare breathe.

"Naila!" Tryce called out from somewhere behind her. "Naila? C'mon. The Chimera is leaving."

The man already left her, tugging at the reins of his stallion.

"Your dhow awaits you," he said, before turning to take his leave.

"Wait," said Naila. "Please. Who are you?"

He paused, his back still toward her.

"When your ship leaves, we'll be no more than strangers, so names bear no meaning, *nergayla*. Should we meet again, introductions will be of better use."

The mysterious stranger left without glancing back, leaving Naila behind with a priceless gift and a heart full of questions.

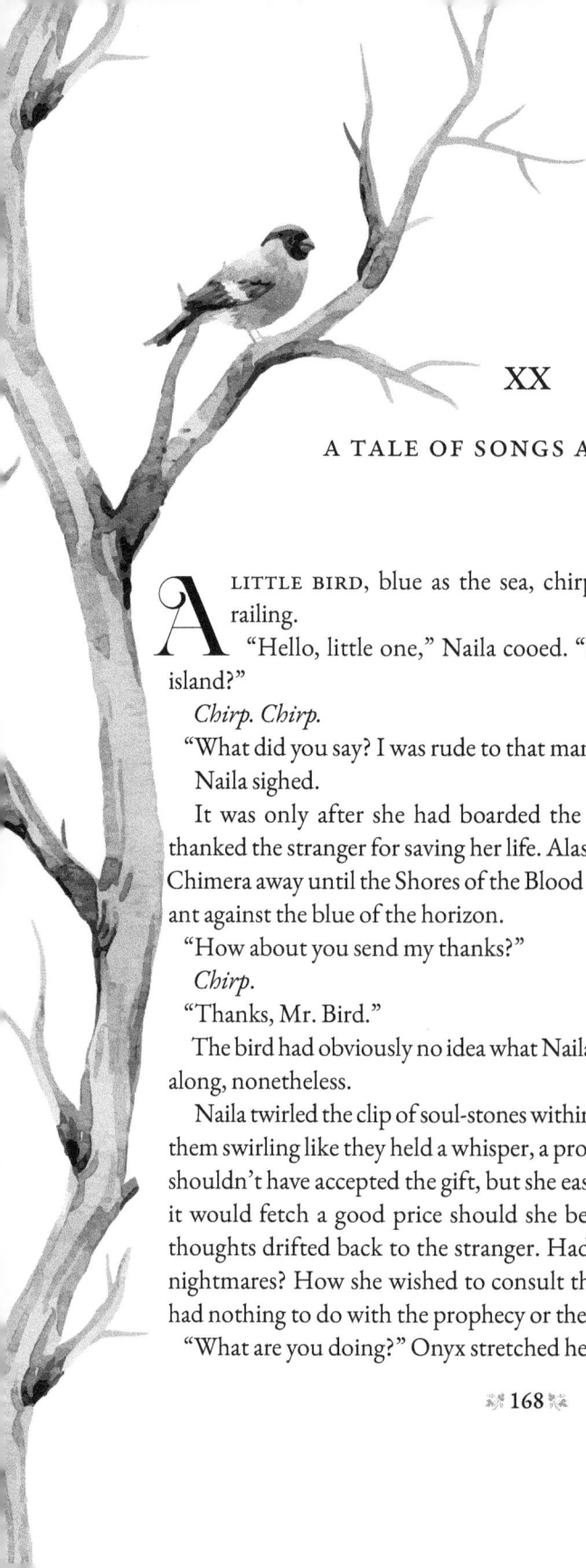

XX

A TALE OF SONGS AND SOULS

A LITTLE BIRD, blue as the sea, chirped happily upon the dhow's railing.

"Hello, little one," Naila cooed. "Shouldn't you be back on the island?"

Chirp. Chirp.

"What did you say? I was rude to that man?"

Naila sighed.

It was only after she had boarded the dhow she realized she hadn't thanked the stranger for saving her life. Alas, the Sea of Helath whisked the Chimera away until the Shores of the Blood Moons was no more than a wee ant against the blue of the horizon.

"How about you send my thanks?"

Chirp.

"Thanks, Mr. Bird."

The bird had obviously no idea what Naila mumbled about but it chirped along, nonetheless.

Naila twirled the clip of soul-stones within her palm, the ruby hues within them swirling like they held a whisper, a promise. *A warning*. She knew she shouldn't have accepted the gift, but she eased her conscience with the fact it would fetch a good price should she be in dire need of finances. Her thoughts drifted back to the stranger. Had he really been the man in her nightmares? How she wished to consult the šaltana. She surely hoped he had nothing to do with the prophecy or the Unspokens.

"What are you doing?" Onyx stretched her arms in a yawn.

The bird flew away. Naila tugged the hairclip into the safety of her shawl before Onyx's gaze fell upon it.

"N-Nothing. Just preparing for the last days at sea."

Onyx eyed her curiously as if she knew Naila hid something, but the huntress said no more. How quickly she had learned to read Naila's face. Almost as quickly as Naila had come to trust her, even with her life. A bout of raw emotion clawed at Naila. In less than two months, Lemuria had given her what she had longed for all her life. Acceptance. *Friends*. They had never judged her for her timidness or quirkiness. Had never thought less of her because of the color of her skin. For the first time, she'd felt truly accepted. Like she belonged. Yet she kept the secret of the hairclip to herself.

"Are you sad about Pasha?"

Onyx smiled conspiratorially. "He was... well, eventful, to say the least. But a big fat liar if ever I saw one. If he's a merchant, then I'm a bard."

Naila pained her brain but came up empty on what Onyx meant. Although to be fair, her thoughts had been much too occupied to truly see Pasha. "Well, at least he was handsome."

"I guess he was."

Naila peeked at the young woman. She didn't look too heartbroken over Pasha's departure, although she did make a point of casting Silas and Tryce a nasty glare every now and then.

Onyx sighed, throwing the petals of Pasha's flower into Helath's tumultuous waves. "He told me news about *māmān...*"

Naila jerked up. "What?"

Onyx continued her dissection of the poor flower. "Apparently, she was sold into a šar's harem."

Naila shuddered. Poor Baosi... forced to be some man's concubine.

"Did he know which šar?"

Onyx shook her head.

Naila covered Onyx's hand with her own. "Well this is a clue right? Now all we have to do is find out which šars's harem and get her out."

Onyx smiled sadly. "I keep forgetting you're not from here. A šar's harem is the single most protected entity in an empire. There is no such thing as sneaking in or out. But I'll find a way. I have to."

Naila's mood dropped. She wished to help, but her hands were tied. The moment she left Lemuria it would be up to Silas and Tryce to help Onyx concoct a plan. Somehow, this made her even sadder. As if she failed the woman who helped save her life.

"What do you know about soul-stones?" Naila asked some time later.

Behind them, Halfbeard bellowed orders to the sailors, at which the men adjusted the sails. A few passengers—rich ones from the island, who were all too happy with their first sailing trip—leaned against the taffrails on the other side, whilst others were huddled in their huts.

"Soul-stones?" Onyx's gaze turned puzzled. "Why are you asking?"

Naila shrugged. "Someone at the market mentioned them."

"You've been to the market?" Onyx hissed.

Naila blinked guiltily. "Only for a bit. Don't worry, Tryce was with me."

"My fool of a cousin! I will have a word with him."

"Nothing happened," Naila protested.

"Thank the stars." Onyx's eyes were wide with worry. "The Red Šars are the most vicious collectors of nergaylas. Someone could have kidnapped and sold you for a hefty price."

Naila pursed her lips. Surely Onyx exaggerated. Besides, she was an adult now, not a little girl to be looked after.

The huntress sighed. "And you shouldn't trust those folks. They always try to sell off mundane crystals as soul-stones. All of them fake."

"Why are they so precious?"

Onyx's gaze turned soft, as if Naila were a cute pet. "Soul-stones and black gold are what the Unspokens used to create their foul weapons and immoral rituals. One to bind and one to enhance."

Black gold was used to enhance, so that meant the soul-stones were used to...

"The binding. Of æther?"

"*Yana*, but let's talk no more of that. The price of soul-stones is so absurdly high that only the rich can afford them. Whatever you saw at the market was fake."

But Naila knew within her very being that the hairclip was real. Why had the stranger not kept it to himself?

A raindrop splashed atop her nose. Sure enough, the sky darkened in the distance. Another storm. A fresh bout of panic reared its head, surprising her, for her panic attacks had been few and far between of late. If only they could travel by land like the stranger had proposed instead of the dreaded sea. Her vision turned hazy with flickering spots, but the thought of Philly's and Ma's soothing words brought her comfort. She breathed in and out. She would be fine. Her friends were with her, after all.

"You all right?" said Onyx.

Naila nodded. She linked her arm with Onyx's. The two women joined the others in the main cabin, where the sailors drank and played games. Although it had a roof, it had but a single wall and no doors, so they could admire the sky to their heart's content. The room, unfortunately, already smelled of beer and mulled wine.

Silas and Tryce, as well as some of the crew, sat on a multitude of cushions and plaids surrounding a barrel. A thick candle atop the barrel illuminated the hut with flames of æther. Jacobo sipped at his flask, his eyes greedily roaming over the curves of Naila's figure. Thankfully, he made no leering comments. "Cap'n, sing us your song again, aye?" the boatswain burped.

Naila rolled her eyes. Jacobo was always drunk. She too took a seat on a cushion, far from him.

"Yes, if you will. I haven't heard this song of yours." Silas smirked.

She could tell the prince expected a lewd sailor's song. Ever since they left the island, Silas had cheered up considerably, to Naila's relief. She hated to see him unhappy. She wondered for the umpteenth time what could have put such a barrier between him and his brother and hoped that, in time, they would find a way back to each other.

"Can't, mate, someone's gotta work." Halfbeard smirked from behind the wheel.

Onyx shoved a flask toward Naila. "Here, that will scrap the frown off your face."

"Uh, what's in it?"

"Fire wine. It makes the heart merry."

Naila hesitated. She had never drunk before. Her mother had made sure of that. "I don't know if that's a good idea."

Onyx pushed the flask into her hands again. "To the seven hells with good ideas. One sip will not kill you."

Naila eyed the flask suspiciously but took a hesitant sip. Warmth flooded her body and softened the tense muscles of her shoulders. It felt... good.

One sip turned into two, and three turned into four, and then Naila was giggling and cheering with the rest.

"Look at all those fireflies," Onyx chirped from next to her as she pointed to the dim sky.

"Those are stars, dummy." Naila giggled.

"Those nosy constellations be always watching us," Bubba said, slapping his pot belly. "Can't even fart in peace."

"They're not nosy. They tell tales of the future." Naila drew an invisible line with her finger between Spica and Arcturus. "Virgo protects the diamond you see there." Naila pointed to the four-star constellation that connected Virgo to her neighbors. "It is a grave and noble burden, and so she is well protected by Hydra, Libra, and other constellations."

Naila eyed the stars with a wistful smile. How many times had she and Philly gazed at them?

"Virgo?" Tryce mouthed, looking jealously at the tipsy folks, for his father had denied him liquor.

"Yes, that is what she's called," said Naila.

Rē eyed Naila curiously. He too hadn't touched the wine, by his own choice. "What do you know of the diamond?"

"Oh, nothing much."

Bubba gnawed on sugarcane. "Tell us 'er story, *nergayla*. We ain' got nothing else to do, anyway."

"Well, many legends surround the celestial virgin, but my friend Philippe told me of one in particular." Naila sat up straight on her cushion and stroked the folds out of her tulip pants. The æther-lit candle flickered serenely in the shades of the coming night, bringing with it a cozy ambiance.

"Once upon a time, there was a goddess made of light. Wherever she walked, her light glowed upon the lands, and wherever she left, the lands cascaded into darkness. Her light brought with it fertility and love, and so the people grew fond of the goddess and named her the queen of songs and souls.

"There was one place, however, where her light never shone, for it was a place the gods that ruled the skies didn't dare enter: deep within the netherworlds, the throne of the king of shadows and darkness. And so, the netherworlds were barren and empty. The god of the netherworld, however, became enchanted by the light goddess. One day, he lured her through the seas of void that separated the world of the living from that of the dead."

Encouraged by the entertained looks of her companions, Naila continued, "A tragedy befell the people as the lands tumbled into gloom. For that was the result of a union of the two gods: it was neither light nor dark, neither fertile nor barren. A state of eternal twilight. The people ripped their clothes in two and cried out in sorrow and hopelessness.

"And so it remained until the other gods of the skies became exasperated. They crossed the seas of void to free their beacon of light out of the hands of the king of shadows and darkness. The goddess, however, did not want to leave, for the captive had fallen for her captor.

"To save the lands, but keep their heart's desire, the two gods created a diamond. In this diamond, she put her song, her soul, and her light; and he in turn put his shadows, his soul, and his darkness. So even as they stayed together, the day would never again have to miss its light and the night would never have to miss its darkness.

"This diamond became the very first star. After the diamond, they created many other crystals that filled the seas of void, giving birth to all the stars we admire in the night's sky."

Naila glanced at the rosy cheeks and watchful eyes of her companions. They hadn't interrupted her a single time. It seemed Philly's fairy tales had enchanted them as they had her. Finally, Jacobo let out a loud belch. Two-Toed Teddy blew out a smoky vapor from his pipe, while Silas snatched a flask from Onyx, turning it upside down above his mouth for the last drop of fire wine. Rē, however, kept eyeing her, an unreadable look molded on his beautiful face.

"Virgo, huh?" Silas glanced at the constellations with a renewed sense of wonder. "The Unspokens called her Ishtar."

"Yes," Rē said, his voice barely a whisper, "Ishtar, the first nergayla to live."

Ishtar?

A wave of unease washed over Naila. Philly's words rang in her ears, *The diamond of Virgo... Never forget.* He had put great emphasis on this fairy tale of his. There must be a hidden message. One Naila couldn't yet see. Could it be that the šaltana's prophecy rang true, after all? Did the Shadow Šar want her for what he expected her power to be?

The group continued on with tales of might and magic, unaware of the turmoil that raged within Naila, until Halfbeard joined them on the pillows. He had with him an oud—a little guitar-esque instrument—and began to play. Without saying a word, he finally gave in to their wishes and sang his song within the storms.

As Halfbeard's song neared its end, raindrops fell like petals from a wilted rose, wetting the deck, pitter-pattering on the roof of the cabin. Soon, the storm began. A faint cry whistled in the fitful winds, almost sounding like an angry wail.

"All the fates," Silas said, "Why can't this cursed sea stay silent for once?"

But Halfbeard and his crew didn't smile or curse. Their eyes were wide with something Naila didn't like at all.

Something close to fear.

"That's no storm." Jacobo stumbled over his own feet in his drunken stupor.

"Teddy," Halfbeard said, his tone low and quiet, tense with urgency. "Ring the bell. Now!"

Naila's nerves ran hot and cold. Silas, Tryce, and Onyx straightened at Halfbeard's words and swung to the spot the men were watching. Naila followed, but only saw the shroud of an approaching storm.

She was about to demand an explanation when something shifted within the fogs above the sea. Naila swallowed thickly, for a moment forgetting to exhale. A sudden chill crept up her spine, and her eyes widened in alarm. She made to step forward, but froze midway.

The wooden floor, the thick triangular sails… everything shuddered. High above the waves of the sea, so very near the Chimera, so very near her, something stirred.

Two-Toed Teddy rang the ship's bell.

"All alert. Men, take up your arms. Women to the main cabin. All alert. It's the nightmare of the sea!"

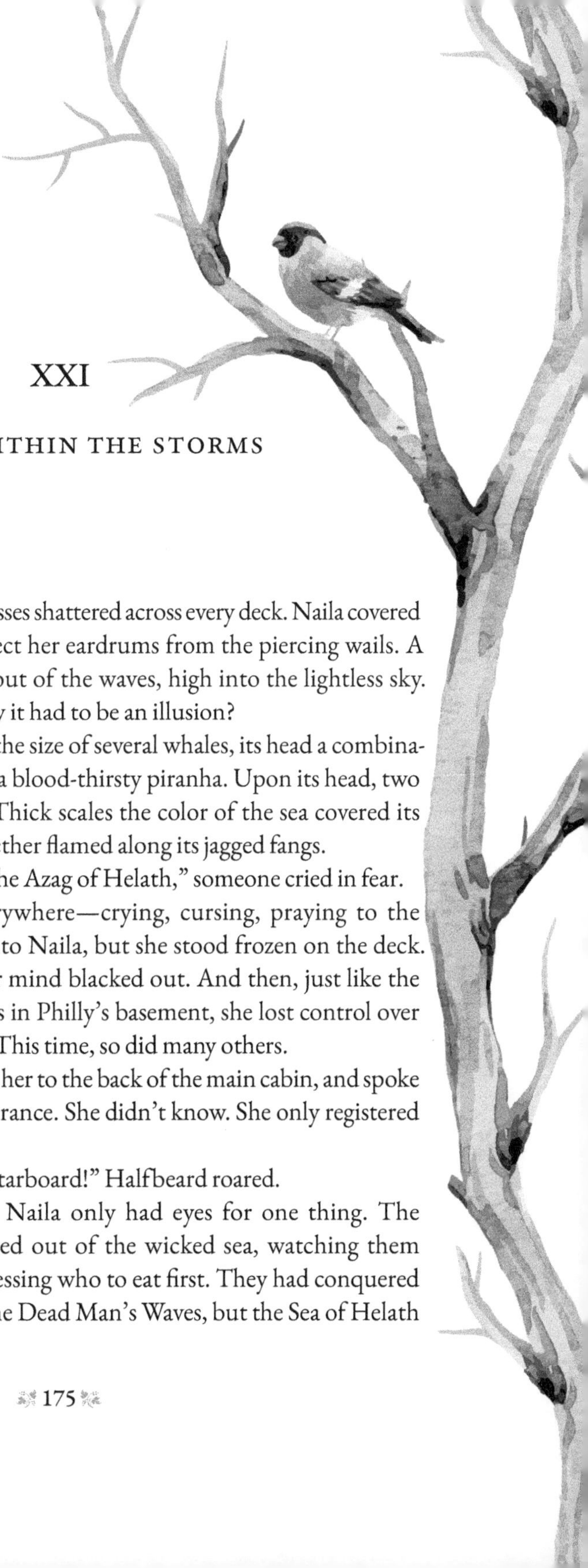

XXI

A SONG WITHIN THE STORMS

S*CRREEEKK.*

A hundred crystal glasses shattered across every deck. Naila covered her ears, trying to protect her eardrums from the piercing wails. A monstrous creature slithered out of the waves, high into the lightless sky. Did her eyes deceive her? Surely it had to be an illusion?

It was a mighty sea serpent, the size of several whales, its head a combination of a vicious crocodile and a blood-thirsty piranha. Upon its head, two powerful horns were rooted. Thick scales the color of the sea covered its serpent-body, whilst crimson æther flamed along its jagged fangs.

"The nightmare of the sea. The Azag of Helath," someone cried in fear.

At once everyone was everywhere—crying, cursing, praying to the Legends. Someone bumped into Naila, but she stood frozen on the deck. Her nerves short circuited, her mind blacked out. And then, just like the time Colios had slain the twins in Philly's basement, she lost control over her vocal cords. She screamed. This time, so did many others.

Silas took her by the arm, led her to the back of the main cabin, and spoke to her. Perhaps words of reassurance. She didn't know. She only registered his lips moving.

"All hands on deck! Hard-a-starboard!" Halfbeard roared.

The bell grew louder, but Naila only had eyes for one thing. The serpentine dragon that emerged out of the wicked sea, watching them through slit eyes, no doubt assessing who to eat first. They had conquered vicious tides, sea storms, and the Dead Man's Waves, but the Sea of Helath was far from done with them.

Tryce dashed across the deck, several passengers in night robes following him in fright.

"Is it the—" a man demanded, but his mouth opened and closed as if he did not dare finish his sentence. His hair was wet, as was the night robe that stuck to all the parts of his body Naila did not want to see.

"The Azag of Helath," Tryce confirmed, his voice cracking under the whips of horror and awe. He pointed at a pair of rocks in the distance. "*Baba*, we need to adjust by twenty degrees."

Halfbeard nodded and ordered Mr. Bones to do so, but the boy already rushed toward the helmsman, helping him pull at the steering wheel, trying against all odds to steer the dhow out of the rocky road and the sea serpent's jaws.

An ear-deafening screech thundered anew, followed by the shudder of the wooden planks. The creature struck out.

"Aarghhh!" the man in the wet night robe yelped, before the serpent's fangs ripped him apart.

The world seemed at once to slow, yet at the same time went by faster than Naila could keep up with.

"*T'ilaa ni gloria*!" The sailors cried in unison.

Naila didn't know how or when, but Halfbeard had gathered the men and armed them with spears and slings and arrows. Onyx and Silas, too, rushed to help. The sky lit with æsh-arrows, but they did nothing to slow the serpent down. It picked at the crowd like a hen picking worms, as the weapons burned on its shield of æther-coated scales.

"The sails!" Halfbeard barked.

Before Jacobo could answer, Tryce rushed to adjust the sails to catch more wind. "On it." Perhaps a good thing, for Jacobo stumbled like a drunken fool. The Chimera soared through the waves, but not fast enough.

As the sea serpent attacked again, Halfbeard's song within the storms echoed in Naila's ears.

Hear my words, it's an ode to the sea,

The sea serpent dove into waves that grew more restless as the storm reached its crescendo. For a few moments, Naila and others stared in anticipation, a fright response in a situation that demanded fight or flight.

The monster lunged out of the sea, splashing gallons of cold water over the Chimera's deck and drenching Naila's clothes.

Naila snapped out of her daze.

She patted her pockets in desperation. *The map!* It was in her satchel. She rushed down the stairs, ignoring the shocked protests.

"To the boats," Rē ordered from somewhere, his silky voice enviously calm and cool.

A flood of passengers buffeted Naila around as she went against the stream. There were too many people on the Chimera. How could this possibly end well?

She captured my heart, will it return to me,

"Eeek," a woman screeched from the deck.

Halfbeard's voice soared above the crowd, barking orders to his crew, but the serpent's shrieks soon drowned even that in a pool of frenzy.

"Where are you going?" a man roared in Naila's face. "We have to get out of here."

She didn't spare him any attention, pushing instead through the crowd. If she didn't get the map, everything would be meaningless. After far too long, she finally reached her hut. A loud snap shuddered through the dhow, unsettling even the air Naila breathed—the sound of wood fracturing into pieces.

Enchanting seamen with her ruthless lullaby,

The jolt threw Naila into the wall.

Close. She was so close.

"Naila!" Silas cried. "Naila, come back."

Naila finally reached the door to her cabin. She rushed inside and snatched her satchel.

Silas's footsteps filled the room. He yanked her by the arm and shifted her toward him. "By the seven hells, what has gotten into you?"

"The map," Naila said by way of explanation, "but I've got it now."

"Who cares about the damned scroll? We're about to become a sea snake's main course."

Silas pulled Naila by the hand, and this time, she complied. The scroll was safe in her hands, after all.

Nothing could prepare her for the sight that awaited them on the deck. Water and... blood underneath the shadows of the sea serpent, whom the sailors still attacked with arrows and spears. The beast bewitched her. Equal parts aesthetically pleasing and terrifying, æther hummed around its scaly body like the pumping of a heart. Naila felt it deep inside, pulsating in her phæralei. For a fraction of a moment, she thought she could even read its mind. Not in the language of words, but in colors of emotions. *Chainnedd. Releasseesh.*

She's fickle in her temper, like the autumn sky.

"Onyx!" Silas cried over the screeching winds.

Onyx waved frantically, relief flooding her face. Her gaze darted around the deck. "Where's Tryce?"

The deck was almost empty. Many survivors already sat in the safety boats as the sailors chopped at the ropes that bound them to the dhow, their eyes fearfully watching the serpent, who had now focused its attention on its attackers.

Finally, they located Tryce with his father at the wheel. They were arguing something fierce, but the raging winds swallowed their words.

A familiar face stomped toward them.

Rē grunted, "You have to leave. Captain's orders."

"I'm not leaving without my cousin," said Onyx.

Rē's eyes narrowed at the scene where Halfbeard urged Tryce to leave for the boats.

"Take the *feylanas* to the boat," said he. "I will get Tryce."

They stumbled over the creaking wood to a half-full dinghy. The dhow rocked harder than it did during a cyclone. The stench of burned flesh and the sweetness of æther darted through the winds. At the steering wheel Rē joined Halfbeard and Tryce's argument. At last, to Naila's shock, Rē knocked the boy unconscious, and dragged him to their dinghy.

But still, I return to her with every tide,

Silas lifted Naila into the boat. To her relief, Onyx was already by her side, next to a tear-stricken woman. Silas pulled out his dagger and started to cut the ropes that bound the little boat to the dhow.

A few æsh-spears flitted through the sky, one after the other. The smog evaporated... But the sapphire scales of the sea serpent, the ones not hidden behind the waves, were unscathed. Not even a minor scratch.

I'd sooner drown than tell her goodbye,

Rē climbed into the boat, with a groaning Tryce over his broad shoulders. As soon as they were tucked safely inside, Naila pulled a dagger out of someone's hand and helped Silas cut the ropes. If they survived this, she had to get herself a weapon.

"What about Halfbeard?" she said.

Rē's lips thinned into a grimace.

"He's sacrificing himself for us?" Onyx's face was stricken.

No one denied her words.

Cold horror seeped into Naila. She should have accepted the stranger's offer. They should have followed him, family drama or no!

My soul is hers, no strings attached,

The dinghy splashed into the sea, and for one bone-chilling moment, Naila thought it would capsize. But Rē infused their oars with æther from crystals to strengthen them. They, too, seemed to be gifted by the Legend, Enki. The boat kept as effortlessly afloat as Halfbeard had done countless times with the enormous dhow.

A rain of æsh-spears fired again, striking every scale on the Azag's body. The sea monster's eyes blazed furiously as it regarded the dhow through narrowed, slit eyes.

"*T'ilaa ni gloria*," the few remaining sailors shouted from the Chimera as they fired arrows and spears and stones until only mists and fumes remained.

Everyone cheered in victory, and even Onyx let out an excited chirp. She hugged Naila with a grin from ear to ear. "I can't believe they did it."

But Naila didn't smile.

Chainnned. Releasesh.

A fear unlike anything slithered its way up her spine. She felt... *knew* the beast was far from slain.

Screeeeeeeek.

Tryce groaned, and his eyes opened, dazed, before he shot up straight. "*Baba!*"

Everyone, be it in a boat or ship-bound, stared open-mouthed at the beast. A literal quiet before the raging of a storm. Naila held in her breath as the wind pulled apart the smoky whisps and unveiled the serpent in all its glory.

Then the creature struck back. Its shriek pierced the silence as it swung its barbed tail to the Chimera. Deep scratches marked the length of the sailing vessel.

"*Baba!*"

Agony ripped at Naila. "No," she rasped out, clutching her pendant, although she knew it would not bring safety. The serpent would slaughter the sailors.

It leaped at the dhow and bit off the front mast. A sea of æsh-arrows fired at it, but it only drove the serpent to a frenzy. The Chimera went full speed at the monster, forcing the raging storm out of her path. Halfbeard and his remaining crew were distracting the beast, sacrificing themselves, so they could give the others a chance to save themselves.

Their sacrifice could not be in vain.

Silas, Rē, and two other sailors took pairs of oars, rowing away from the Chimera, in the direction of the island they had left behind, whilst Onyx and Naila tried to calm Tryce whose cries pierced her again and again. Naila pulled the boy into her arms, her tears dripping upon his face, but his own eyes remained devoid of tears. From afar, Naila saw water already streaming into the dhow through the wide scratches. Even if the serpent retreated, the infamous ship was done for.

"By the Legends"—a seaman made a religious gesture—"We shouldn'a docked at the Shores of the Blood Moons. We shouldn'a challenged Nova's words of the curse."

With an ear-deafening screech, the Azag of Helath attacked the Chimera with its fangs and barbed tail. And then again. This time, it was final. The Chimera snapped into pieces. She had sailed across the Seven Seas and the Wicked Oceans, but this journey had been her very last. The serpent roared in victory and disappeared into the raging waves. The destruction of the ship had satisfied its hunger. For now.

Like the stars in the sky, we'll never unlatch.

Tears blurred Naila's vision as the Chimera sank to her death beneath Helath's waves. Captain Reis Halfbeard Barbaras fell to a seaman's grave. He died the way he lived: as a man who belonged to the enchanting but ruthless sea.

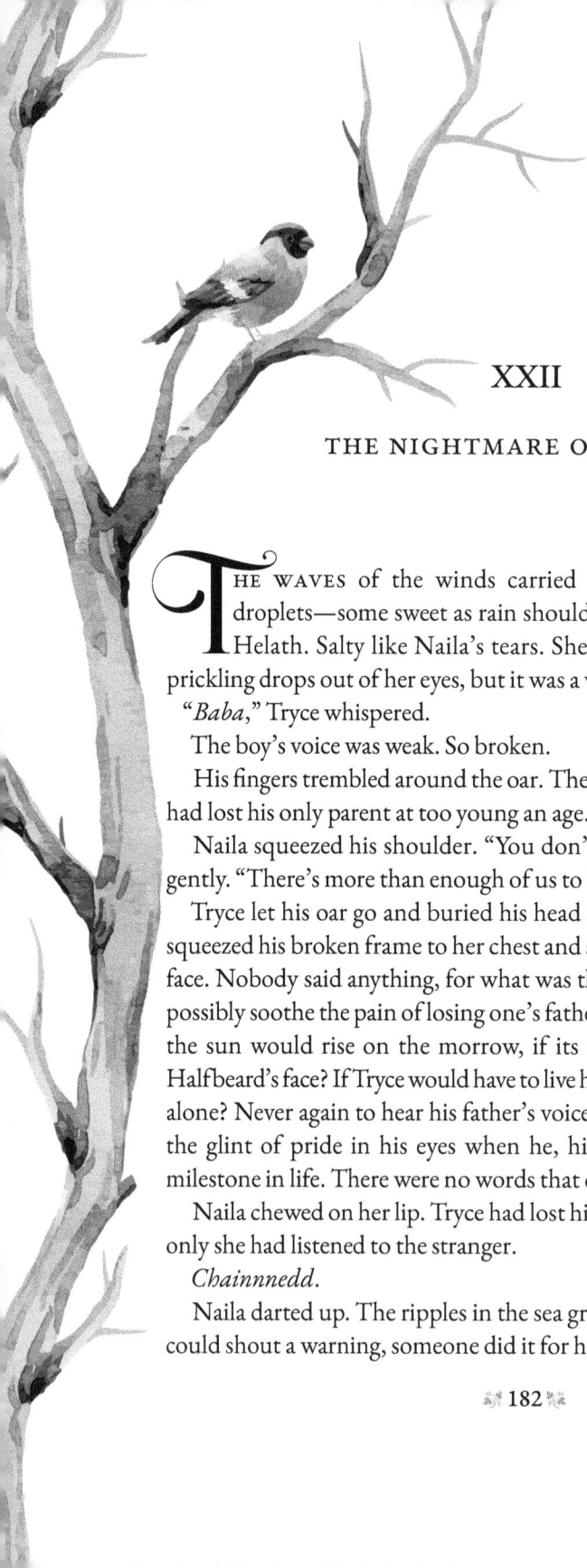

XXII

THE NIGHTMARE OF THE SEA

THE WAVES of the winds carried with them a shimmering of droplets—some sweet as rain should be, others salty like the Sea of Helath. Salty like Naila's tears. She batted her lashes to drive the prickling drops out of her eyes, but it was a wasted effort.

"*Baba*," Tryce whispered.

The boy's voice was weak. So broken.

His fingers trembled around the oar. The pain in his eyes told no lies. He had lost his only parent at too young an age. But still he did not weep.

Naila squeezed his shoulder. "You don't have to row, Tryce," she said gently. "There's more than enough of us to keep the boat going."

Tryce let his oar go and buried his head in his cousin's embrace. Onyx squeezed his broken frame to her chest and stroked the wet locks out of his face. Nobody said anything, for what was there to say? What words could possibly soothe the pain of losing one's father? How could anyone promise the sun would rise on the morrow, if its rays would never again caress Halfbeard's face? If Tryce would have to live his remaining life with memories alone? Never again to hear his father's voice or laughter, never again to see the glint of pride in his eyes when he, his son, would achieve another milestone in life. There were no words that could take the pain away.

Naila chewed on her lip. Tryce had lost his father because of *her* quest. If only she had listened to the stranger.

Chainnnedd.

Naila darted up. The ripples in the sea grew vast and restless. Before she could shout a warning, someone did it for her.

"Azag!" Jacobo cried from one of the other boats.

The sea serpent's monstrous head thrust out of the Sea of Helath, in the middle of the six boats that carried the Chimera's survivors. It splashed its barbed, finned tail around, causing large waves to crash against the dhow's sinking shipwreck as well as wash the little boats off their course. Silas blocked most of the water with his tall frame, but every layer of Naila's attire was drenched anew.

The monster's slit eyes searched from boat to boat until they snapped to Naila and her friends. It bared its fangs in a hiss. The wood underneath Naila's wet boots trembled to the vicious melody. Green liquid fell from the razor-sharp tips of the serpent's fangs into the water. The wicked sea met every drop with sizzling vapor. *Poison.*

No.

Naila shook her head.

This couldn't be.

Halfbeard's death could not be in vain. She refused to believe it.

"Azag! Azag!" people in the boats cried as they pointed at the nightmare of the sea.

Naila gaped at them in disbelief. *Fools.* All of them. They practically begged to be this savage hunter's prey.

Tryce, too, growled, hatred burning in the shadows of his face. He unlocked Onyx's arms and hissed at the Azag. "Monster."

Rē grabbed the neck of his blouse and forced Tryce back. "Hush, *lugal,* getting yourself killed will not bring your *baba* back."

Tryce started to argue, but Rē glared him down. Naila thought Silas could be intimidating, but the sullen quartermaster was a worthy opponent.

The sea serpent shifted its head to the ruckus. Fearful cries came from the boats as they frantically rowed to the Shores of the Blood Moons. The sailors in Naila's boat did much the same. The island's lights flickered like fireflies in the far distance, a beacon of safety and hope... But in the Sea of Helath, the Azag ruled supreme, and the waters bowed to its very will.

"No!" Naila cried as the serpent ducked back into the water. Somehow she knew what it would do.

Its æther-fueled body illuminated its trails underneath the sea's surface. It moved straight for the dinghies. With a piercing shriek, the serpent emerged out of the water and snatched a boat in its massive jaws.

It bit the wood into several pieces, the people within it joining the boat's unfortunate fate.

The serpent's head flicked to the other boats. It dove into the waters again, but almost instantly reappeared, attacking the other boats in a sequence of flashes. The empty darkness of the moonless night grew even darker with mournful cries. Even the stars didn't dare show their light, all covered by the gray, watchful clouds.

Naila bit back her vomit at the sight of bloodied limbs falling into the bottomless pit of Helath's sea. The monster's snakelike eyes finally fixed on the boat carrying Bubba, Jacobo, and Two-Toed Teddy, as it spat out the wood it found distasteful. Silas's hand found hers, but the warmth of it brought her no relief. Naila's stomach clenched in dread. Her eyes searched the waters. Only two boats remained. The rest had all perished within the serpent's jaws.

"Faster! Faster!" a sailor urged, as he rowed with wild abandon.

"What about Teddy and the others? We've got to save them," Naila squeaked. She would never forgive herself for the lives lost because of her quest.

"Hush, nergayla, we cannot take on the Azag. We should spare our energy for our own hides," someone hissed in the back.

Naila chewed on her lip. The thought of leaving her comrades behind made her sick. The sailor had a point, however, for what could they possibly do that did not involve all of them dying.

"It's distracted, so now is our chance to slip by," Rē stated.

Silas gnashed his teeth. "Naila is right. We can't leave them to their fates. But we need a plan. If we can find its weak point—"

"Rē, Tryce said you have experience with giant sea creatures," Naila said.

Rē squeezed his eyes shut. He sighed. "*Yana*, but *karuiles siunes* like the Azag are impossible to kill... *though*, legend has it, its eyes are its weak point."

The karuiles siunes. The great serpents.

"Well, then we have a chance," said Naila with more bravery than she felt. "Onyx is an excellent archer. Maybe...?"

Onyx's eyes shifted to Tryce's mournful face before meeting Naila's and Silas's gazes. She nodded, already reaching for her jade bow.

Without listening to anyone's objections, Silas beckoned the sailors to row into the sea serpent's territory.

"Are you mad?" a passenger cried. "That beast cannot be defeated! This will not end in one of your tales of glory. Those folks are all but dead already."

"Then we will die with them," Silas hissed. At once Naila saw the šar he was destined to be. There were no traces of his debauched self. This was a king ready for war. "If you want to live, you best prepare yourself to enter battle."

The prince had barely uttered the words when a deafening screech filled Naila's ears. The sailors on the other boat threw æsh-daggers aimlessly at the serpent. *Lord have mercy.* Didn't these hard-headed sailors see no æsh-weapon could breach its thick, æther-coated skin?

"Dimwits," Onyx hissed as her hands balled into fists over her bow.

Screeeeek. Naila's phæralei throbbed painfully. *Killl. Make mealss of themm.* An all-consuming rage shot through her nerves. Her sight flickered white with fury.

"Naila?" Onyx said, frowning. "Are you okay?"

Angry. She was so angry. It made little sense.

Then it clicked.

The rage she felt wasn't hers, but that of the sea serpent. Somehow, its feelings resonated within her, like they were her own.

Her heart pounded as the sea serpent readied itself to attack the other boat. If she could sense the serpent's feelings, maybe she could persuade it to let them go. Her breath quickened with the first sparks of anxiety. The edges of her sight turned black. *No, not right now. I can do this. I can do this.* The faces of her laughing classmates danced across her vision and all of a sudden she was a little girl again, alone in the play yard with no friends to play with.

Freak, freak. Naila is a freak. The children pointed at her and laughed.

Naila's breaths came out in shallow gasps.

She squeezed her eyes shut; tried to wipe those memories away.

"*Baba…*" Tryce's broken voice.

She couldn't hide. Not anymore. They were a hair's breadth removed from death, and Naila knew she could stop this. The time had come to stop hiding from the truth. To stop ignoring who she was. Æther prickled at her fingertips. She was not the names the bullies had called her. Gilded flames ignited in the palms of her hands. She was not the weakling she had convinced herself. Naila opened her eyes. She was Naila Groenhart. Strong and brave. She was enough. And she would put an end to this. The past was set in stone, but the future was *her* playground.

Naila focused her sight on the sea serpent, watching every whip of its tail and every howl leaving its jaws. Flames the color of spilled blood encased the serpent's scales like a web.

Naila's phæralei scorched her forehead, practically burning a hole through her skin. It wouldn't surprise her if it scarred, but she had to pull through. For everyone's sake.

Destroyyy. Squashhh themm.

Her eyes roamed over the beast's massive frame, but she only saw the web of æther. Then, ever so faintly, Naila saw a little red spot between its eyes. A spot that shimmered like a stone. A crimson soul-stone. A thin thread of crimson flames spilled out of the soul-stone and wove into the web of æther. *Those strongest in æther can bend minds to their will*, the hierodulas had said. Her suspicions had been true. Someone had shackled the serpent's mind, making it a slave to a sinister plot.

"This is not the Azag's doing," Naila whispered.

Silas and Onyx and the others looked at her, bemused.

"What?" Onyx said.

"It's not acting out of free will. Someone bound its mind with a soul-stone."

"How do you know that?" asked Silas.

Naila didn't explain. Her mind was focused on other things. Whoever had bound the sea serpent to his will had to be a master in wielding æther.

"Onyx, I need your help."

As if summoned, Onyx joined Naila at the edge, an arrow ready to fire. Naila didn't know how to throw a spear or fire an arrow, but subduing the beast wasn't about glory. It was about getting everyone to safety, and for that she needed teamwork.

Naila squeezed the hilt of Onyx's arrow, just like she had done to the stone in the redwoods. Golden flames licked at its surface and engulfed the arrow instantly.

"Aim at its forehead, right between the eyes," Naila said.

"But there's only thick scales there," said Onyx.

"Do you trust me?"

In answer, the huntress aimed at the sea serpent's forehead.

The serpent shifted its focus onto them, as if sensing their scheming. One chance. They only had one chance.

"Now!" Naila said.

Onyx let the gilded arrow loose. It swung through the air like a knife through butter, precise and effortless. The serpent followed it with its eyes, but didn't evade it. Almost like it wanted the arrow to hit its mark. With a crack, the golden flames obliterated the crimson soul-stone into a thousand pieces. The strings of crimson æther curled away from the golden flames, until they shriveled like leaves in a fire. The serpent stilled and stared at Naila.

Onyx whispered. "It's not dead."

"No, but it's free."

"What?" Tryce cried out. "Like that will do us any good."

Naila cast a quick prayer that the beast wasn't more vicious in freedom than it was under its previous master's control.

Youuu—the serpent's emotions filled Naila's mind. She could feel everything. Its emotions were as clear as words. Now that she had gotten a chance to get used to the serpent's language, she realized it didn't speak in Tierratongo. It spoke in the map's language. The Unspokens' language: the Hædur. *Youuu freed me. Howww?*

The boat swayed with the gust of an icy wind.

"It doesn't matter." Naila raised her chin. "All that matters is that I did, and now you're in my debt."

The serpent's eyes blazed with fury. *I ssseee, a new prissson in exchange for an old one, nay?*

"No, you mistook my words. All I want in exchange is for you to leave and never come back."

The serpent cocked its head.

"I-is she talking to the Azag?" someone said, flabbergasted. Out of the corner of her eyes she noticed everyone gaping at her with a mixture of fear and reverence. "Nergayla..." another whispered.

The serpent ignored them and continued, *Ifff I agree I am free of your debt?*

"You have my word, Azag."

The serpent slid closer to Naila's dinghy. Without æther, its slit eyes were a vibrant green.

Silas, Onyx, and the others ignited their weapons in æther, but Naila raised her hand to stop them.

"Naila?" Silas asked, unsure.

Naila squeezed his hand. "It's okay."

But she could see the doubtful expressions on their faces. The people's eyes shifted from Naila to the serpent, perhaps not sure who to fear more. A woman even arched her child away from Naila, as if she were a vengeful angel come to seek repentance for their sins.

Eyesss like the sun, hair like the night, and skin of the earth that bindsss them together. Who are you, nergayla? continued the serpent.

"Just a girl who wants to get back home," Naila murmured.

Ahh. the serpent's eyes glittered like mischievous emeralds. *And so, you are on your way to the legendary Nebiru, no?*

So, this serpent could read her mind, like Naila could read theirs?

What do you know about the fallen city of Nebiru? She answered in her mind. Spoke no words.

Mayhap it can give you the answer you seek. But what isss the worth of an answer if it cannot give you what you desire?

What do you mean? said Naila.

Nebiru houses the most powerful portal in the landsss of Lemuria, yes. But be warned, for Nebiru houses far more than that. Once you open a door, all othersss shall open as well.

I came here through another portal, but it no longer works... Is there an easier way than Nebiru? Can I create another portal instead?

Impossible. The Lemai simply do not have the power to create one. Even if they did, it would do you little good, for any portal isss only as strong as its creatorsss, said the serpent.

"Why are they staring at each other?" Tryce demanded. "I say we attack the beast!"

"Hush," said Naila. She continued to the serpent, *Who created the other portal, then?*

All portals have the same creator, be they in Nebiru or no.

The Unspokens... the Azag meant the Unspokens.

So the Unspokens created them?

The Unspokens? The Azag tilted its head in amusement. *Ah, like the Lemai you are frightened to speak their names aloud. The Ænunaki created the portals, yes. Mighty and powerful they are.*

The Ænunaki.

So that was the true name of the Unspokens... Naila played absentmindedly with her pendant as she regarded the beast. No, not a beast. Vicious it may be, but it was a sentient creature with a vault of knowledge. She'd be a fool not to make use of it.

Okay, so, seeing as you're so all-knowing, how do I create a portal if I had the power? Naila tested.

I do not know, for that is a secret buried many sun birthsss before my time.

How do I open an already existing one, then? For all Naila knew, even if they did find Nebiru, they might end up before a locked portal.

They who made Nebiru used the light of Iluna, for the moonsss increase æther's strength by two. However, to open a portal, Iluna's light by itself will not do.

Naila stared at the serpent in wonder.

One should sacrifice twins born on the first rays of a full moon. But be careful, for they need to be born at the very same time. One cannot be older than the other.

Naila's eyes widened in horror. This must have been how Colios and Daena opened the portal in Philly's basement.

"That's out of the question," she said.

"What did he say?" Silas demanded.

The dinghy rocked with the restless waves, but Naila's eyes never left the serpent.

She has a conscience, I see, said the creature. *I suppose there is another way—when the twin moonsss bleed red.*

Blood moons, you mean?

Yesss. The creature chuckled in its hissing voice.

But blood moons only come up once every hundred years!

Ah, as luck may have it, the blood moons will be birthed in two winters, when the maiden rulesss the sky.

But that's two years!

Then you best hurry and think up another solution, nergayla. Be quick before the tendrils of fate ensssnare you, for the brightest lights come with the darkest shadowsss.

Hmph, Naila answered in their dialogue of emotions, *Light always conquers darkness.* It was a universal truth, one that mankind clung to from the dawn of their existence.

The Azag of Helath bared its fangs in the faintest of smiles, as its scaly body retreated into the sea it called home. Its eyes glowed one last time.

Or ssso you have been led to believe...

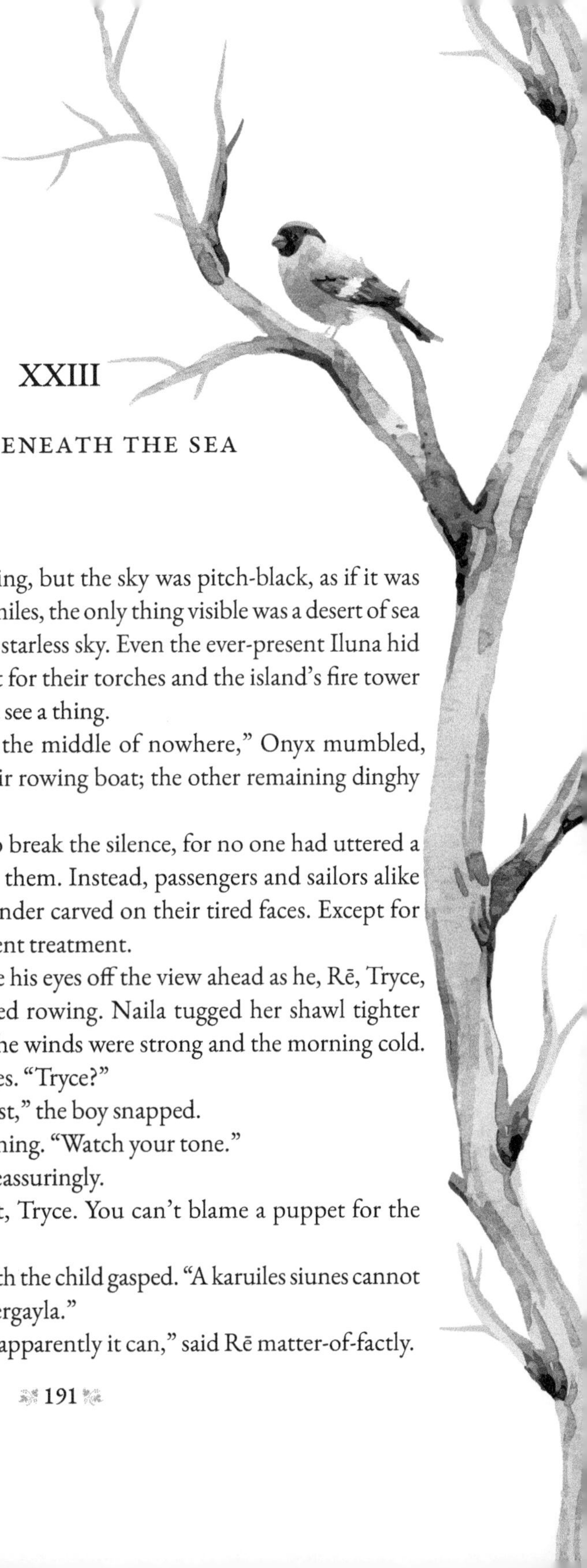

XXIII

A CITY BENEATH THE SEA

IT WAS early in the morning, but the sky was pitch-black, as if it was midnight. For miles and miles, the only thing visible was a desert of sea and mist underneath the starless sky. Even the ever-present Iluna hid behind the clouds. If it weren't for their torches and the island's fire tower in the distance, Naila wouldn't see a thing.

"It's like we're cast away to the middle of nowhere," Onyx mumbled, leaning against the edge of their rowing boat; the other remaining dinghy floated nearby.

The huntress was the first to break the silence, for no one had uttered a word since the sea serpent left them. Instead, passengers and sailors alike eyed Naila warily, fear and wonder carved on their tired faces. Except for Tryce. *He* was giving her the silent treatment.

Silas grunted but didn't take his eyes off the view ahead as he, Rē, Tryce, and the other sailors continued rowing. Naila tugged her shawl tighter around her trembling form. The winds were strong and the morning cold. She fidgeted with her wet sleeves. "Tryce?"

"We should've killed that beast," the boy snapped.

"Tryce," Silas growled in warning. "Watch your tone."

Naila squeezed Silas's arm reassuringly.

"Someone was controlling it, Tryce. You can't blame a puppet for the actions of its puppeteer."

"Controlled?" the woman with the child gasped. "A karuiles siunes cannot be controlled! Not even by a nergayla."

"Seeing what just happened, apparently it can," said Rē matter-of-factly.

"Then perhaps she is not a nergayla, but one of the Unspokens!" another passenger exclaimed.

Fearful murmurs broke out.

"Hush, you fools," Silas hissed. "The Unspokens have been dead for a thousand winters! She is no more one of them than you or I."

"It be true," spoke a sailor. "The Unspokens had wings. She could'na be one of those."

"You're right, she isn't," Onyx warned, her gaze daring them to utter another word.

At once they silenced, although some threw Naila a skeptical look. Still, they couldn't argue with spoken facts. Naila's heart broke a little. Was she to be an outcast in Lemuria as well? Why couldn't she be normal?

Tryce's eyes finally softened a little. He turned toward the fire tower. "Here, we live by the moral code, 'An eye for an eye, a tooth for a tooth, a hand for a hand—'"

"A foot for a foot, a burn for a burn, a wound for a wound, a bruise for a bruise," Naila finished, surprising Tryce, Silas, and Onyx.

Onyx blinked. "How do you know our oral tales?"

Naila didn't answer.

They weren't the Lemai's oral tales. They were words of the Old Testament, taken out of context. Although how they had found their way to a people who worshipped the Legends remained a mystery. Had portals between Lemuria and Earth perhaps carried tales back and forth?

"I respect your moral code, but surely it only applies to those who are proven guilty? The serpent had no say in its actions, Tryce. I know you're hurt, but your anger should be for the one who controlled its mind."

Tryce gnawed on his lip. While he made no reply, the anger on his face melted, to Naila's relief.

Squawk.

At first, Naila wasn't sure whether it was a sea breeze whispering in the dark or her imagination fooling her, but after a moment, she heard it clearly.

Squawk.

A majestic bird of prey, gold of color, flew toward them. A rolled-up letter was fastened to its leg. Naila straightened instantly. That bird had to be the šaltana's, and he no doubt carried with him the answer to Naila's letter.

Silas frowned. "It's Roc."

The raptor flapped its grand wings before settling onto the prince's shoulder. He, in turn, scratched the animal's head. "Why are you here, little fellow?"

The prince tugged at the letter, but before he could take hold of it, the bird jumped from Silas's shoulder onto Naila's. It nudged Naila's cheek with its feathery head, then looked at her with big doe-like eyes. Naila let out a giggle. *What a charmer.* She could always count on the gentleness of animals even when her own species failed to understand her.

"Careful," Silas warned. He threw her a leather glove. "His claws are made for hunting."

Naila put it on, even though it was much too large for her delicate hand. Her eyes softened as she stroked the bird's pretty feathers—they were ivory, tipped in a dozen shades of gold. The bird purred in contentment. "You're a pretty little thing, Ro-Ro."

"Roc," Silas corrected. "He's one of the great rukha, not some songbird."

"Ro-Ro," Naila repeated, her gaze challenging.

Silas shook his head. She was sure she heard him mutter *feylanas* underneath his breath. Naila ignored him and loosened the letter from Ro-Ro's leg. Sure enough, it was addressed to Naila Groenhart. She would read it later when she was alone.

Then Silas's eyes narrowed suspiciously.

"What is Roc doing here?"

Naila cast him an innocent smile. "Your mother is... mentoring me."

He arched a brow but, thankfully, said no more.

"The rukha?" Tryce thrust himself up, a sprinkle of wonder gleaming in his mournful eyes. "Where did ye get one of those?"

"A gift from grandfather to my mother," Silas said.

"A precious gift, indeed," said Rē.

"Why? What is so special about rukha birds?" asked Naila, not sure she really wanted to know.

"The rukha are bred and born in the Elysian Fields," said Onyx. "They can get over hundreds of years old and never stop growing. This here is a youngster."

"*Baba* once said he was chased by a rukha," Tryce whispered, his voice cracking over the first word. "Said it was so big it hunted full-grown *elephaunts* instead of squirrels."

"Aye, I remember that tale, m'boy. But Halfbeard, great as 'e was, tricked the bird into letting him go by rubbing himself with the juice of a corpse flower. I hear it stinks worse than a dozen corpses," said a sailor.

Everyone chuckled. Even Tryce smiled a little.

The sailor's eyes fixed on Naila. He said what everyone thought but none dared to say, "How did ye do it, nergayla? How did ye chase away a karuiles siunes with only a stare?"

"I didn't—" began Naila.

"Leave it will you?" Onyx snapped at the man.

As soon as the others had found themselves another subject to talk about, Onyx crawled closer to Naila. "There's no way you weren't involved, N. And you'd have to be immensely powerful for that." Onyx whispered. "Don't you see? Only the Unspokens had æther strong enough to see the mind of the great serpents. I'm beginning to understand why the Shadow Šar wants you so bad."

Silas, lost in thought and within hearing distance, murmured, "Ishtar..."

Naila studied her palms. *Ishtar's Chosen,* the šaltana had said. Yet she found that prophecy hard to believe. Wasn't Ishtar a Legend? A deity to these people? Naila was merely a mortal. Not the champion of a god. Besides, she didn't even believe in the Lemai's deities.

"Maybe, maybe there's something true to it. Although I don't know how that could be. I wasn't born in this place and my ma has no powers." What remained unspoken was the nagging fact she knew nothing about her father... Could he be a Stormhold? A descendant of the legendary Suzano who had defeated the Unspokens a thousand winters ago?

"Yet you know the myths of the Unspokens. The Legends of the Sky," said Rē.

She perked up. She hadn't realized he'd been listening too. And by Tryce's curious glances, it seemed he had been as well.

"What do you mean?" said Silas.

"That tale she told yesterday," Rē grumbled by way of explanation.

"I—" began Naila.

She thought about the shadowreapers who hunted her, about her powers of gilded flames. Of how the šaltana and the stranger of the redwoods had tethered her to Ishtar, and the shadowreapers had named her Naila Stormhold.

"I—" said Naila again, she locked eyes with Silas, but before the prince could stop her she told Onyx, Tryce and Rē everything she had learned from his mother. Well, almost everything. The contents of the letter she kept to herself.

"By the fates," said Onyx. She stared dumbfounded from Naila to Silas, hurt bleeding into her expression. "Why didn't you tell me any of this? We never should have left Skeldor. I was such a fool to propose this quest."

"No, you weren't. With or without your help, I would've left anyway. I *have* to get back home," said Naila, her voice a little louder now. This was the one thing she'd always been sure of. But now... now, doubt stained that goal. She shifted in her seat. She and Lemuria were more entwined than she had thought. Naila had to find out why.

"N, have you ever thought that this *Earth* is not your real home? That maybe Lemuria is?" Onyx said softly, not meeting Naila's eyes.

"I need to make sure my ma and Philly are okay."

Silas shook his head. "And then what? You will stay there and pretend none of this happened? If shadowreapers got to you before, they will do so again."

Naila stroked Ro-Ro's feathers gently. "What would you have me do? They're family. Would you abandon your mother?"

Silas and Onyx sighed simultaneously.

"She's right," Tryce whispered.

Naila glanced at Silas from underneath her lashes. She knew the šaltana would not like her next words, but the prince had a right to know. "There's more to this prophecy, Silas... The šaltana spoke of Ishtar's Chosen bringing a balance to the worlds... but not alone. She says this nergayla will do this with her other half. Her antithesis. She believes the prophecy speaks of you and me."

How she wished they would wave it off as a fairy tale. Silence overcame their little group. All gazes went back and forth between Naila and Silas. Onyx just frowned.

Then Silas laughed.

"The halls of the Red Palace hold many corners to hide a young *lugal*. Mother and Nova weren't as secretive as they thought. My brother and I used to eavesdrop all the time. These words come from Nova. And while I trust Mother's visions, I believe Nova has an agenda of her own."

Silas's denial didn't make her feel better. She knew then she *did* believe his mother.

Rē stared at Silas intently. "Crishire's imperial nergayla, Nova?"

"Ye don't believe that witch's words?" Tryce's mouth dropped in disbelief. "Look where *that* got us." He waved in the direction where the Chimera's wreck had been.

"Tryce," Naila scolded. "Nergaylas are not witches."

Tryce raised his hands, an innocent look etched on his face.

"Nova is wrong. I don't have special powers like Naila," said Silas, his eyes growing intense as he stared at her. Then he smiled. "And I sure hope I never become your *antithesis*."

"No, prince, Nova is never mistaken," said Rē.

He seemed so knowledgeable, Naila hoped he'd one day share his backstory.

The light of the island's tower inched closer and closer until, at last, it cascaded over the water before them. As they reached the harbor, only silence met them. The fire tower was the lone source of light on the crescent island. Not even the sand roads, where music had hummed the day before, were lit by torches. There was no sound to the wind, no laughter to be heard.

If they hadn't been there just a day before, Naila would have thought the Shores of the Blood Moons to be abandoned. Ro-Ro took to the air, circling high above the island. When Silas helped Naila out of the dinghy, she stumbled over her own feet and crashed against his lean chest. His arms enclosed her, steadying her. Her cheeks heated as she breathed in his masculine scent. Even after the wreckage at sea, he was still his dashing self.

"Are you okay?" he whispered, his lips feathering her temple.

She nodded, not trusting herself to speak. Why was her traitorous heart fluttering so?

"Where is everyone?" someone demanded.

"Where indeed?" Onyx answered, casting Naila and Silas a somewhat disapproving look.

At once Naila unlocked herself from Silas's embrace. He seemed somewhat disappointed.

Onyx hopped from their dinghy to the other and to the stone of the harbor. Even highly trained gymnasts would bleed with jealousy at her grace and finesse. Onyx's olive hood fell off her head, but for once her shock of auburn locks stayed tamed. Naila had plaited her own curls and Onyx's hair into pretty rope-braids earlier that night for lack of anything else to do. She was quite pleased with the results, if she said so herself. If they were stuck in unknown territory, they would be so in style.

"They're in Mort Nor below the ground," Tryce mumbled dispassionately. He pointed at the edge of what had been the volcano. It was the hill with the carved-out gate, an entrance to something below. "A man at the market told me it's where they stay at night."

Silas adjusted his scimitar, and to Naila's fright, the others did the same with their weapons.

She wished she too, had a weapon.

"What are they hiding from?" Jacobo sharpened his dagger.

He and the survivors from the other boat joined them on the harbor.

"Let's not find out. We go to the gate. Put off your lanterns and make no sound," said Silas.

Heart thudding and palms damp, Naila followed the others as they tiptoed through the abandoned hills of the town. The trees, so lovely in daylight, rustled ominously in the night. An owl hooted from somewhere in the forest. All the market stands were empty. Only crickets chirped softly in the dark.

After what seemed like ages, they finally reached the gate. The stone doors had intricate ornaments, complementing the climbing roses that framed the whole. Silas took hold of the bronze knocker and knocked twice. On the third time, the door cracked open.

An elderly man appeared. He held an oil lamp before him.

"By the stars, what brings ye strangers here at this time of day?"

"We got shipwrecked. Our dhow is lost to us. Will you give us shelter?" asked Silas.

"Shipwrecked ye say? And ye survived the Sea of Helath?" the man asked skeptically. His tanned skin was covered in wrinkles and age spots.

"It is as I say. Now will you give us shelter or not?"

"All right, all right. No need to be snappy. One can never be too careful."

Their party, all fourteen of them, followed the man through the doors and down long, steep stairs. It was a tedious descent to Mort Nor. Even though the inside of the hill was immense, the darkness of the rocky surface made it feel constrained. The dim light of torches, fastened to the walls, danced between the shadows of the rocks and cast just enough light to see the steps before them.

Ro-Ro, however, was not bothered by any of this. The bird of prey flew over the spiral steps until the dark swallowed all of his color. After what had to be at least half a bell, they reached the end of the steps.

"Suzano's balls," Jacobo moaned, "Can't these people shower? I can smell them from leagues away."

But it wasn't people they smelled. The volcano's scent of sulfur assaulted their olfactory glands, making it impossible for Naila to smell anything else.

At last, Mort Nor came into view. It was a city unlike one she'd seen before, with cottages completely carved out of coral stone. They had to be well under the sea, for some of the houses reached as high as the tower on the island outside, no doubt giving home to multiple families.

From the cracks of quaint curtains, light flickered over spring flowers that grew at the edges of the roads. It gave the stone of the city a sense of color.

Bubba the cook scratched his belly. "Who would've thought they'd be hiding all of this under Helath, hmm?"

"Ye've got to make us food, Bubba. I bet their food tastes as bad as the city smells," said Tryce.

The boy pinched his nose shut. He had spoken too soon, however, for as soon as they entered the city, the smell of sulfur evaporated in exchange for the sweet one of flowers and honey.

Naila couldn't stop a smile from breaking out. She took off her slippers and walked over to the soft grass. The villagers had made art out of rock, aromas out of odor, and created life where there was none. The inhabitants must love their island, with all its beauty above and all the flaws below.

"Come," said the old man, as he threw Jacobo and Tryce a nasty glare, "Let me find ye a caravansary."

THE CALMING scent of tea herbs reached Naila's nostrils at the same time light caressed her eyelids. *Was it morning already?* Naila couldn't find it in herself to care. The bed was too comforting to leave. She squeezed her eyes. It had been so long since she slept without being slurred into another dark dream. She yawned, stretching out as her hearing awakened to the thumps of woodwork.

"Wake up, sunshine," Silas drawled.

Naila's eyes flashed open. *Where was she?* Stone walls enclosed the room, whilst a flower-tiled floor spread underneath her bed. The chamber's multifoil window was wide open, letting in a soft, flowery breeze with the promise of spring... And the earthy fumes of ruins.

Ah, yes.

They were in Mort Nor after the sea serpent had rendered them shipwrecked.

Silas cleared his throat.

"Morning?" Naila said as the prince put a steaming mug of tea on her night table.

His dark hair fell in tousled waves over his eyes. The dark travel leathers, stretched over his lean muscles, perfected his rogue prince look. He looked... *delicious.*

"Are you done eying me?" Silas flashed her a lopsided grin.

Naila rolled her eyes, but her heart pitter-pattered. That smile of his was dangerous. She rose, leaning on her hands. Her skin puckered in the chilly air. The prince's gaze lowered to beneath her collarbone. Naila glanced down, her face heating when she realized her thin caftan stretched quite noticeably over the peaks of her ample breasts. Her skin wasn't the only thing puckering. She covered herself with her blanket, but contrary to that slimy Jacobo, she found she didn't mind Silas's attention.

"Who's eying who now?" Naila raised a brow.

Silas watched her through hooded eyes, but only sat down on the edge of the bed. He ran his fingers through his dark strands. His hair had gotten longer. It almost reached his shoulders. A frown marred his handsome face as he stared at the blues of the sky outside.

Mort Nor's ceiling was made out of æshefied crystal. A thin layer of the sea covered it from above, so they could stare at the colorful sea life to their heart's content. Naila took her mug and inhaled the herbal scent as she watched Silas stroke his forearm absentmindedly.

"Rē got us new travel equipment... It's time to leave," he said.

"How? We don't have the Chimera."

"The villagers have dhows. Nothing large, but big enough to carry a party of six. We can't stay here, Naila, Crishire is a den of snakes."

"Because of your brother..."

Silas's mouth tightened into a straight line. Naila wanted to ask him about the wedge between him and his brother, but she kept it to herself. She wanted Silas to trust her, to share his secrets of his own volition.

"Yes, because of the Red Šar. And because the Shadow Šar is after you. You know that."

Naila didn't miss the framing of his words. The Red Šar, not his brother.

Silas took her hand into his and rubbed it with his thumb. Her slim, brown hand looked so fragile in Silas's tan, roughened ones. The hands of a warrior, not of a pampered prince.

"Now that we know you're not just a nergayla, we have to be more careful. I don't know whether that prophecy holds true, but whatever the Shadow Šar is planning, it cannot be good."

Naila put down her half-empty mug. She sensed Silas had second thoughts about their quest to Nebiru.

"The Azag told me Nebiru really holds a portal. This quest isn't for nothing—"

He stopped caressing her hand and stood up so fast Naila almost tumbled back into her cushions. "Am I supposed to believe that viper? It's as dependable as the treacherous sea it calls home."

"It spoke the truth."

"Naila..."

"I know it did." Naila crossed her arms. "Look, I'm here, chased by shadowreapers in a no man's land, and they might've even killed my friend." Naila's breath hitched in her throat. Just the thought of Philly dying... "I can't afford to doubt the serpent's words, Silas, not when it means I might miss my only chance to get answers. To get back home."

His eyes softened. "I know."

"You have your duty, and so do I."

"Yes," he said, a glimmer of respect flickering in his eyes. "But tell me, Naila, would it really be so bad to stay?" His gaze turned watchful.

"I—"

Naila couldn't finish her sentence. *Yes*. Yes, it would be bad. For all of Earth's faults, it at least wasn't as dangerous as Lemuria. Even now, the carefreeness of not getting attacked at every corner, of not keeping a close watch over her shoulder all the time, faded into a distant memory. It shouldn't be that way.

The hopeful look melted off Silas's face at the no doubt visible answer on her own. He shook his head and went for the door. With his back to her, he said hoarsely, "Hurry and get dressed, we leave in a chime."

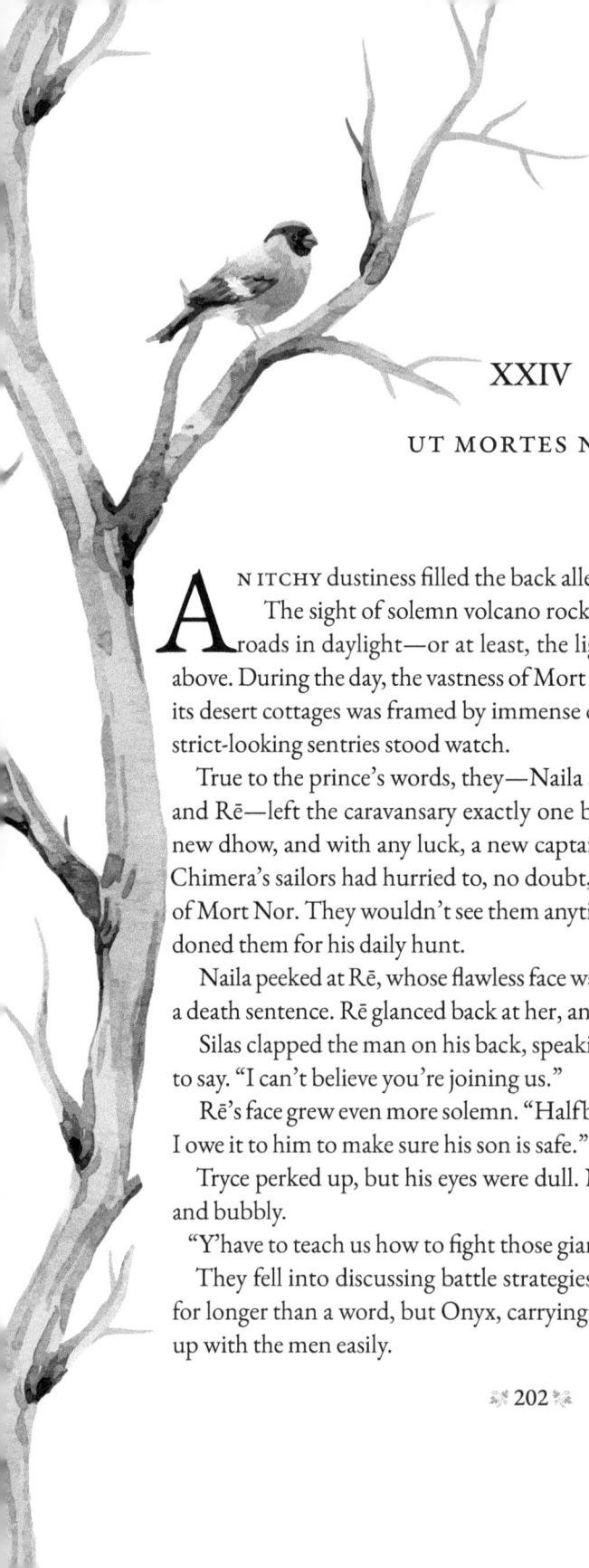

XXIV

UT MORTES NERO

An itchy dustiness filled the back alleys of Mort Nor.

The sight of solemn volcano rocks had melted to busy terracotta roads in daylight—or at least, the light that broke through the sea above. During the day, the vastness of Mort Nor felt palpable. The city with its desert cottages was framed by immense cave roads. Before each of them, strict-looking sentries stood watch.

True to the prince's words, they—Naila and her friends, as well as Tryce and Rē—left the caravansary exactly one bell later, on their way to find a new dhow, and with any luck, a new captain to join them. The rest of the Chimera's sailors had hurried to, no doubt, other more questionable parts of Mort Nor. They wouldn't see them anytime soon. Ro-Ro too, had abandoned them for his daily hunt.

Naila peeked at Rē, whose flawless face was solemn as a prisoner receiving a death sentence. Rē glanced back at her, and she quickly shifted her gaze.

Silas clapped the man on his back, speaking the words Naila was too shy to say. "I can't believe you're joining us."

Rē's face grew even more solemn. "Halfbeard gave my life purpose again. I owe it to him to make sure his son is safe."

Tryce perked up, but his eyes were dull. Not the old Tryce, mischievous and bubbly.

"Y'have to teach us how to fight those giant squids."

They fell into discussing battle strategies, too boring for Naila to listen for longer than a word, but Onyx, carrying a huge, wrapped package, kept up with the men easily.

Tryce had put on a brave face since his father's death, but he had nevertheless become as quiet as Rē. He had opted to be by himself just that morning, looking at the sea flowing above Mort Nor's crystal ceiling. He had only once shown the boyish smile she'd grown fond of when a sea goat darted by.

"What's that?" Tryce glanced at Onyx's package.

The huntress cleared her throat, before nudging the cloth-wrapped bundle into her cousin's hand. "I saw this on the market this morning and thought of you," she said softly, revealing a bronze battle-ax. "Māru—Dawnbreaker. For someone strong, like you." She smiled. "Remember when I first taught you to shoot? You were so frustrated, but you didn't quit. You never quit. You've always been that way. I'm here, Tryce." She beckoned to everyone. "*We* are here. No matter what or where, we'll face everything together."

Tryce swallowed hard, blinking as he fought to keep tears at bay. "Thanks... It's perfect."

Onyx threw her arm around the boy, pulling him into a side-hug, whilst Silas ruffled his hair. Naila's heart warmed. Tryce grinned widely, almost like his usual cheery self.

Even Rē smiled a little.

Naila adjusted her shawl over her phæralei as she studied the civilians. How different they were from the people of Havenmor. Still a melting pot of ethnic phenotypes, yes, but their tunics—knee length for the men and ankle length for the women—were beiges and browns instead of the pastel-colored caftans Naila had come to admire.

The day was young, but it nevertheless lacked the excited chattering of citizens going about their daily life, doing the laundry in tubs with lye and clay, bartering goat's cheese for barley bread or crystals for luxury goods. Instead, many a civilian huddled together in the narrow alleys between the coral stone cottages. Much like nosy gossipers back on Earth, rumors of the shipwrecked strangers had already spread through Mort Nor.

"...no doubt the Shadow Šar's doing," someone in the crowd whispered.

There was a halt to Silas's step.

Someone burst out in laughter. "Pray tell how he could've controlled the nightmare of the sea? It's a power unheard of since the age of the Unspokens, I'd say. Even Nova has no influence over the *karuiles siunes* and she's the strongest nergayla Lemuria has ever seen."

A toothless old man whispered, his voice conspiratorial, "Ah, but they say the dragon lords can seduce the great serpents to do their bidding with just the play of a flute. The Red Šar and his brother, the late prince Reuben, yes."

Naila glanced in question at Silas, but the prince just snorted and ignored the gossiping folks.

"Nonsense, old man," said another man.

"*Yana,* we are much too old for fairy tales," a woman carrying a tall straw basket on her head scolded.

Naila forced herself not to join the conversing people. Realization dawned on her. They all spoke as if the Azag was far from the only *karuiles siunes*. Her eyes drifted to Silas again, but he stared ahead, only the slight frown between his brows hinting that he heard the whispers of Mort Nor's inhabitants.

Naila turned to Onyx instead. "That thing in the lake near the redwoods... Was it a *karuiles siunes*?"

Onyx nodded. "They come in many guises. Usually, they don't bother with Lemaians, unless we breach the borders of their territory. If I knew you could talk to them, I wouldn't have offered my hard-earned deer."

"*Sengan* said he saw a shadowreaper yesterday," an adolescent boy chirped nearby, excited to join in on a conversation with the adults.

Naila stiffened. So did Onyx.

"Hush, *lugal*," his father chastised, "What did I say about spreading false rumors?"

Naila let out a breath in relief. Onyx, however, did not seem easily placated.

"Silas," Onyx warned, "Those rumors..."

He sighed. "I know. They've no doubt already reached the Shadow Šar. We need to get out of here and fast."

They hurried their steps until the gossiping folks fell out of hearing distance.

"Blood and bones, I hate this place," Tryce mumbled.

He swatted a huge fly as they reached the shadier side of Mort Nor.

Between the cottages stood a desolate desert market—the complete opposite of the vibrant one on the surface. Through the tan leather tents where merchants resided, Naila could make out several wooden huts scattered about.

Rē grunted. "Over there."

He pointed at the far end of the street to a shady-looking tavern, its name—the Bloody Buccaneer—etched in cuneiform characters above the round-top door. It wasn't exactly hard to find. The tavern was in the very center of what seemed to be cages... no, prisons, guarded by sentries. The front of those adjacent huts were lined with iron bars. Several beggars leaned against them in the dust of the road.

"Why do these captains always flock to questionable places?" Onyx eyed the tavern skeptically as she adjusted the arrows in her quiver; a question to which Naila would also like to receive an answer.

Before anyone could respond, a swarm of beggars stormed up to them, their palms held out.

"A crystal, please. Oh, if you could spare but a crystal."

The skin of the beggars was dangerously close to reaching a sickly gray, not unlike that of the shadowreapers. Yellow boils covered their limbs and faces.

Onyx gasped. "*Ut mortes nero.*"

Silas unsheathed his scimitar. "Stand back."

Rē swung his weapon around.

As one, the beggars retreated, crouching on the dusty road with their hands before their faces as if to defend themselves from inevitable blows. Dirty rags covered their ribs and too thin limbs. One in the front clutched his arm, blood seeping through his fingers.

The air smelled of dirt and litter and the metallic tang of blood.

Tryce and Onyx too, had uncovered their weapons, although they did not use them as Rē had done. Tryce looked stricken. His mother had died of ut mortes nero... A memory no doubt too painful when he just lost his father.

"Stop that," Naila cried out.

She grabbed Rē's arm. Halfbeard's quartermaster must be fond of gymnasiums. His muscles, though lean, were hard as steel. "You're hurting them, stop it."

"Do you not know what disease they carry?" he hissed.

Naila glared at him. "I don't care."

"Naila, if you get ut mortes nero, you die," Onyx said, not lowering her arrow. "You *always* die."

Naila loosened her grip on Rē's arm. She glanced at the emaciated beggars and then back at her friends. "Shame on you. On all of you. Is this how you treat the sick? You cast them aside like garbage? Treat them like feral dogs when they ask for basic needs?"

Onyx's eyes grew large, an unknown emotion flickering in them, but Rē's and Silas's expressions remained hardened. At last, the huntress cast her eyes down and lowered her arrow. Tryce soon followed.

"Naila... we can't help them," said Silas.

"We can give them crystals."

"It's no use. No one will take it from them. They'd rather chop off their own hand."

"Then we can give them food. Buy them shelter."

The prince sighed, but he, too, put his scimitar away. Rē's mouth tightened, and while he didn't put his weapon away, he also didn't proceed with his attack.

Naila left their circle, stepping toward the beggars. Her steps were sure, confident. She didn't hesitate. After all the death and destruction on the Chimera, she couldn't stand to watch helplessly. This injured man would *not* die.

"Naila..." Silas warned.

She ignored him. Ignored their protests as she squatted next to the injured man. The beggar arched away. His brown eyes were wide with fear. With distrust. Her heart broke. There was no question as to how he'd been treated in the past.

"Give me your arm," said Naila. She could heal him. Could do it again. Just like she'd done with the withering flowers and Sir Festus at the market above. Festus' disease hadn't infected her. For once she had no doubt that she truly was one of the nergayla.

Hesitantly, the beggar stuck out his shaking arm.

Silas groaned, but she paid him no heed. Her fingers trailed the beggar's grayish skin. Some of the boils oozed with yellow pus. For the first time, she hesitated. Ut mortes nero was completely different from the skin disease Sir Festus had carried. Naila exhaled and straightened her shoulders. She would start with the bleeding wound first.

Remembering Zarqa's tutoring, she willed the beggar her blessings within her mind, willed his arm to heal. Her fingers prickled with gilded flames of æther. A welcome sensation, for she knew they brought with them a gift, instead of the heartache of her childhood.

The man eyed her in wonder.

No one said a word.

A rush of warmth left her body. The man heaved and puffed and blew. Without looking she knew his wound began to heal. Her body grew weightless, however. Light as if floating on clouds. Before long, darkness blossomed at the edge of her vision.

Then there was nothing.

"NAILA."

Onyx's voice.

A cold, wet cloth rubbed over her face.

"Naila, wake up."

Her eyes fluttered open.

Onyx's hazy face came into sight. It took several blinks before her vision cleared. The young woman smiled, relief washing over her face. She pulled Naila into a hug.

"Thank the stars," Onyx whispered, squeezing her tight.

She clasped her arms over Onyx's lithe frame, carefully, for her arms felt shaky at best. Onyx's citrusy scent awakened her senses to the here and now. Her heart warmed. So, this was what it felt like to have friends. She glanced around.

They had laid her on a wooden bench close to the Bloody Buccaneer. Her friends surrounded her, each with relieved expressions.

"Told ye she would live," said Tryce as he shot Rē a pointed look.

The man humphed in answer.

"What happened?"

"What happened?" Silas arched his brow. He sat casually on the arm of the bench. "You almost killed yourself, that's what happened."

"Do *not* do it again," Rē clipped. "If we did not pull you away, you would have died trying to heal that man. And still you would have failed. There is no cure for ut mortes nero."

Naila's voice broke. "I only tried to heal his wound. I-I must've gone overboard."

"Nergaylas practice their whole lives to perfect the art of healing. It is best you steer clear of it, until you have done proper training," Rē said.

Naila nodded, defeated. For the first time since she started their journey she yearned for the further tutoring Zarqa had offered her. She had only learned the basics.

"Don't ye think it's amazing how Naila healed that beggar's wound? I thought it took winters of practicing to do that," Tryce said.

His eyes held childlike wonder. The others didn't share Tryce's sentiment. They looked on, faces folded with weary expressions, each of them lost in their own thoughts.

"What happened to the beggars?" Naila broke the silence.

The prince's gaze turned gentle.

"I've bought them food and a hut to stay in."

"Thank you, Silas."

The words felt inadequate for all he meant to her. When he'd held her during the sea storm, soothing her fears away with comforting words. How he opened up to see the views of others, despite not being what he'd been led to believe. Skeldor's prince was a man with many faces, and he, she had to admit, had gotten under her skin.

Naila squeezed his hand. He squeezed it back. The prince did not let go, but drew her palm to his mouth. He brushed his lips over the sensitive skin in a featherlight kiss. Silas closed his eyes and sighed. "Just when I think I've figured you out, you do something completely unexpected. Whatever will I do with you?"

A surge of heat blazed from where his lips had touched to the whole of her body.

Tryce made a gagging sound, snapping Naila out of her reverie.

She pulled her hand back. "Ut mortes nero... their skin looked like that of the shadowreapers'."

"They're both cursed. Cursed with an eternal hunger for æther, that is," said Silas.

"What?"

"No one knows why some get the disease and others don't, but all infected share the same fate: they're born without æther or little of it. Although they say shadowreapers can inflict it upon a person too," said Onyx.

"*Baba* said Iluna punishes them. They either die a slow and painful death or give their life to the Shadow Šar and become his shadowreapers," said Tryce.

"But how does the Shadow Šar save them?"

"Keep them alive, not save them," said Onyx. "We think he uses soulstones. Whisperers say he has ancient scrolls from the Unspokens to perform the necessary rituals."

"So, the shadowreapers had once been Lemaians... infected with ut mortes nero."

"*Yana.*"

"Well." Silas pushed himself off the bench's arm. "It's time to get going. We already lost two bells. Tryce, you stay here with Naila—"

"Huh? But I wanna come!" Tryce whined.

"We will be back in a few." Silas spoke as if he weren't interrupted.

Without further ado, Silas, Rē, and Onyx left for the Bloody Buccaneer. Naila pushed herself off the hard wood to sit up straight. Tryce kicked a pebble and muttered, "Always treat me like a kid."

A nearby sentry eyed them curiously. Naila covered her phæralei with her shawl before he could recognize her as a nergayla.

"Excuse me, what are you guarding?" said Naila.

"Thieves and murderers," grunted the sentry.

He stared ahead, pretending to ignore her and Tryce. He wore a broad leather belt around his waist, which separated the brown of his tunic from the geometric pattern below. Like many in Mort Nor, a shawl was draped over his clothing, the fabric carefully arranged so his sword arm was left free.

"Not a thief. Not a murderer," a voice hissed from the cage behind them.

Tryce sprang up. "What was that?"

"You keep that mouth of yours shut, tierkan," the sentry growled.

Tryce's eyes, however, gleamed with mischief.

"Tierkan?" The boy smirked.

Naila knew they should turn around and ignore it. Pretend they'd never heard what the sentry had said. She was about to do just that, determined not to let curiosity seduce her into another perilous disposition, but then the voice hissed, "Nergayla. I know what you are."

Two small hands, not much bigger than those of a five-year-old, grasped the iron bars. They were the color of scalded skin, but glazed with a lavender hue on its joints. Naila and Tryce glanced at each other. She read in his eyes what she knew was mirrored in hers, a curiosity that could not be contained.

They ambled toward the tierkan's cage.

"Careful," said the sentry.

"It's locked. We can't do anything wrong," said Tryce, his face schooled in innocence.

The sentry shrugged but said no more.

"Who are you?" Naila said.

The creature pressed his face to the bars, unveiling the whole of his body out of the shadows' tendrils. It was a tiny thing, no taller than Naila's waist. Its face was plump and its nose long. Rags the color of sandstone covered its stout body, with a matching pointed hat on its hairless head.

"Igigi, is what they call me," said he, his deep-set yellow eyes glistening with something close to pleasure. "I am one of the tierkans, yes."

Naila looked at Tryce in question.

The boy shrugged. "I never knew tierkans were real. Always thought they were ol' tales to send children off to sleep."

"Ah, we are real. Oh, are we real. Those accursed Ænunaki stole us from our homes, yes. They made us slaves in this too hot place."

"The Ænunaki?" asked Tryce.

"The true name of the Unspokens," Naila whispered.

Tryce stared without blinking. The sentry shifted in his position as if he were uneasy. It was as Naila suspected. The Lemaians hadn't uttered the word Ænunaki in many generations. With time they forgot the true name of their enemy.

"I know what you seek," Igigi continued. "The Dark Forest of Isolon."

Naila grabbed the cold, iron bars, and looked down at the tierkan. "How did you know?"

Igigi tilted his plump bluish head. His ears, round like that of a mouse, twitched. "What else could you be looking for, yes? Those dim-witted Lemaians cannot give you whatever it is you seek."

"Ho there," Tryce protested.

"I'm looking for answers... but I also want to go home."

"Hmm, and you think Nebiru can give you that?" The tierkan smiled.

"Won't it?"

"Mayhaps." Then he added, "I can help you get off this island, in exchange for my release, yes."

The sentry snorted. "You can dream, tierkan."

Naila eyed the tierkan.

It looked like a mischievous spirit from an Arabian fairy tale in the flesh. She didn't know if she could trust him. "Why are you locked up?"

"I did no more than those beggars you were so desperate to save, yes." He nodded.

Naila raised a brow. "Well, either way, we don't need your help. We're leaving this island in a dhow."

"A dhow?" said the tierkan. "Do not be foolish. No dhow leaves this island and remains in one piece. The Sea of Helath will swallow you whole, yes. Any captain who claims otherwise is a scammer, a liar, a cheat!"

The words of Nova. Naila's fingers trailed over her compass pendant.

"Then how do ye suggest we leave, munchkin?" said Tryce, his tone mocking, although doubt was laced through his features.

"Do not let my height fool you; we tierkans are as strong as we are smart. We work twice as fast with better precision than you, Lemaian. In the age of the Ænunaki, you were no more than third-rank slaves."

Tryce stepped forward, but Naila put her hand to his chest and pushed him back gently.

"Will you answer his question?"

The tierkan's glare turned into a sugary sweet smile. "There is a cave road that leads to Isolon."

Naila's hand squeezed Tryce's forearm. So, the stranger's words had been true.

The sentry struck the iron bars with his scimitar. The clash rang like a cracked bell, much too harsh and loud for Naila's ears.

"Do not listen to this creature. The cave roads are a maze. Once you get in, you never come out. There are none who know the way."

"Lies," said Igigi. "Mort Nor and all its cave roads were built by the tierkans, yes. I know the way." He pointed his blueish thumb to his chest.

"Naila? Tryce?" Silas called. "What are you doing over there? We found ourselves a captain. Come on."

Naila sighed. "I'm sorry, Igigi, I wish you the best."

The tierkan stuck out his hand and grasped the leg of her tulip pants. She halted her step and glanced at the curious creature.

"Do not forget my words, nergayla. When you are ready, I can take you and your friends through the cave roads. All I ask for is my freedom."

The tierkan retreated back into the shadows.

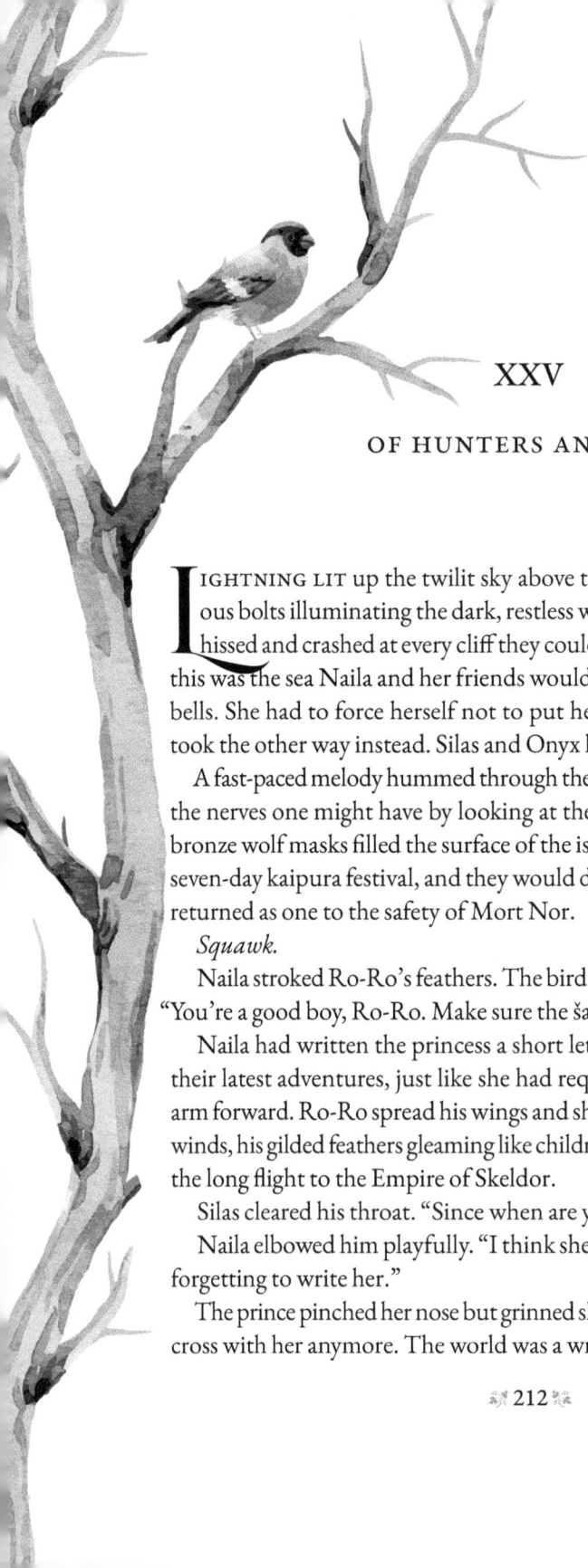

XXV

OF HUNTERS AND PREY

LIGHTNING LIT up the twilit sky above the crescent island, the thunderous bolts illuminating the dark, restless waves of the Sea of Helath. They hissed and crashed at every cliff they could put their tendrils on. To think this was the sea Naila and her friends would once more sail in less than two bells. She had to force herself not to put her foot down and demand they took the other way instead. Silas and Onyx knew what they were doing...

A fast-paced melody hummed through the winds, doing nothing to soothe the nerves one might have by looking at the vexed sea. A feasting crowd in bronze wolf masks filled the surface of the island. They still celebrated their seven-day kaipura festival, and they would do so until midnight, when they returned as one to the safety of Mort Nor.

Squawk.

Naila stroked Ro-Ro's feathers. The bird nudged her cheek with his head. "You're a good boy, Ro-Ro. Make sure the šaltana gets this letter safely."

Naila had written the princess a short letter to keep her up to date with their latest adventures, just like she had requested. Naila thrust her gloved arm forward. Ro-Ro spread his wings and shot into the air. He circled in the winds, his gilded feathers gleaming like children of the moons, before starting the long flight to the Empire of Skeldor.

Silas cleared his throat. "Since when are you and mother pen friends?"

Naila elbowed him playfully. "I think she misses you, and, well, you keep forgetting to write her."

The prince pinched her nose but grinned sheepishly. She was glad he wasn't cross with her anymore. The world was a wrong place without Silas's smile.

"C'mon," Onyx came out from the crowd and pulled them by the hands, "We might as well enjoy ourselves while we're still here." After failing to obtain more information about her mother in the tavern, Onyx seemed to want to drown in either feasting or planning ahead.

Silas ruffled Onyx's scarlet locks. "Who's the bacchanal now? I'd say you're worse than me."

The redhead scowled, swatting his hand away. "My dear *šargon*." She batted her lashes with false sweetness. "No one, and I do mean no one, is worse than you."

"I'll be back ere long," said Tryce.

Before anyone could stop him, he disappeared into the crowd.

"I will stay. Make sure to be back in time before that captain changes his mind." Rē shot the angry sky a meaningful look. Without waiting for an answer, he stomped toward a tree and leaned against it, arms crossed, expression solemn as per usual.

Silas saluted Rē. He followed Tryce, Naila and Onyx trailing behind. The crowd was dense and their voices loud. Exotic melodies of drums, lutes, and rebabs reached the heights of a crescendo. The people cheered with renewed energy. Naila tried to peek over their heads. The market stalls had made way for colorful tents, each with its own attraction.

"Look, *Māmān*, it's Fakyr the sword swallower!" A little bronze girl with two braids pointed at a tent behind Naila. The mass of people inched forward in excitement, forcing her and her friends to separate.

"Onyx? Silas?" Naila called over the cheers. She jumped up and down to look over the heads. The Fakyr person swallowed seven blades at once, and the people cried even louder. In their excitement, they pushed forward, which caused her to fall to her knees. Someone pulled her up. A cold, rough hand.

Silas?

Through the commotion, she couldn't see him clearly, but he dragged her out of the crowd. To safety.

No.

To a deserted sand road at the back of the tents.

The male's attire was russet linen instead of Silas's black leathers, and he was a good head shorter than the prince.

"*You,*" Naila exclaimed as she twisted her hand free from his grasp.

"Aye."

Jacobo grinned, his golden teeth gleaming in the light of a nearby torch. It was the only light in the narrow road, framed by the tents, the trees of the forest, and the rock of the volcano's edge. She sneaked a look around, but no one else was about. The people on the piazza were a good way out of hearing distance. Naila sidestepped Jacobo, but he blocked her way. His eyes were glazed, hungry. "Don't bother running away, birdy, it's only us here."

"Weren't you busy losing your crystals at a brothel?" Naila snapped.

"Aye, but ye can't turn lead into gold. There is no substitute for the real deal."

A chill crawled up her skin. He loosened the collar of his cloak and burped rather crudely.

"You're drunk," Naila stated as she tried to sidestep him again. There was no going past him. *Think, Naila, think.*

"Sober enough." Jacobo licked his chapped lips.

Naila stepped back, but with every step, he put one forward.

"What do you want, Jacobo?"

Jacobo scoffed and spat on the cobblestones. His eyes were dark as the moonless sky.

"Ishtar's Chosen, they call you, but is that so? Methinks yer a fraud."

Naila narrowed her eyes but refrained from answering, instead she glanced out of the corners of her eyes for any way out.

"I say you're one of them Shadow Šar's," Jacobo continued.

Naila stepped backward until her back hit the rocky wall of the volcano's edge. Her eyes skittered around, but the only way out was through Jacobo. She was trapped.

"Did he send you to kill the princeling?" Jacobo closed the gap until he was a hair's breadth removed from her. He stank of beer and too-sweet perfume. "Spellbind the princeling until he walks into yer trap of death. It'd explain why 'e entered this fool's quest with no troops, chariots, or them horses." He twirled one of Naila's wayward curls around his dirty finger. A glossy lock she failed to trap with braiding. "All for *you*."

Naila flinched when Jacobo's rough fingers trailed the outline of her throat until they reached the hem of her shawl. She shoved his hand, but he gripped her by the neck so tight she could hardly breathe. An overwhelming sense of dread numbed her from head to toe. This man was dangerous.

"Let. Me. Go," Naila gasped.

"I'd be doing Skeldor a favor, getting rid of you. But I ain' no unreasonable man, no. I'd be willing to negotiate the price of letting ye live." Jacobo licked her cheek, leaving a wet streak behind. She immediately turned her head to the other side. The pungent fumes of his alcoholic breath made her as nauseous as the sight of him did.

Hushed whispers came from the side road between two nearby tents. Jacobo stilled. A man and a woman giggled as they went to join the others at the town's square. She tried to scream, but Jacobo squeezed her throat so hard she couldn't breathe. He threw her to the sand.

Naila pushed herself back up. Her throat throbbed, a bruise no doubt forming around her neck. Who did Jacobo think he was to treat her like this? Anger flushed through her body, its heat running through her throbbing phæralei.

"Ain' no one gonna hear ye here," he sneered. "Best not make me angry."

He unbuckled the broad belt around his sailor's shirt, his eyes glazed with lust. When Jacobo pulled her back up, Naila stepped hard on his foot.

"Bitch," he snarled and backhanded her.

The iron of blood spread through Naila's mouth as Jacobo tore off her shawl. All thoughts froze in her body, which obeyed only one command. *Survive*. She had rarely been a flight or fright person, and now every nerve in her body itched to fight. Her veins pulsed visibly beneath her golden-brown skin.

Jacobo ripped her tunic open—an exquisite rose-colored piece embellished with golden flowers Aisha had given her—the mother-of-pearl buttons flying all over the sand and grass. His eyes grew dark as he trailed his fingers toward Naila's generous cleavage. Around his opened belt, the jeweled hilt of his golden dagger glittered in the single torch.

"No wonder you bewitched him so." His voice was hoarse, a whisper.

Lower and lower his fingers reached. Something snapped in Naila. Her hand flashed forward and within a blink of an eye, she grabbed Jacobo's curved dagger and pressed the tip below his Adam's apple. The heat of her anger gave birth to golden flames. They flared with a fury to match her own, engulfing the dagger and scorching Jacobo's throat where the weapon connected with his skin. A drop of blood trailed downward in the same way his fingers had trailed her throat.

Jacobo raised his hands and smiled, but there was no humor in his eyes. "Now, now, birdy. We both know ye ain' gonna kill me."

"Won't I?" Naila thrust the dagger forward until it completely breached his skin. Golden flames pulsed around it, in sync with her anger. The burning scent of flesh swamped the air. The roles had switched, she was now the hunter and he the prey.

"Argh!" Jacobo bellowed as his skin burned. "Stop, stop!"

"Swear never to lay a finger on me again," Naila ordered as she tipped her chin high in disgust, the skin around Jacobo's Adam's apple scorching black.

"I swear, I swear."

The crickets stopped chirping. The leaves of the trees stopped rustling in the wind. A sudden chill crept up her spine. Jacobo's face scrunched in confusion, but she paid him no heed. Then he too, froze on the spot.

The ground, the walls... everything shuddered. At first, she thought it was an earthquake. Or another one of the Sea of Helath's cyclones, come to terrorize her again, but this time by land.

The shrill whinnying of a dozen horses, like sharp nails scratching glass, interrupted the rhythms of the feast's music. It silenced the people, took over the plaza.

Then the screams started.

Fear stunned her body, freezing the golden flames on her skin into extinction. Naila clutched Jacobo's dagger tight, but her fingers trembled, leaving bloody scratches along the length of the sailor's throat. A mass of people scurried around the corner, some running into the little alley. Their faces were pale and bodies tense, a mocking contrast with their exquisite clothes. Chaos, fear, and panic spread like a wildfire. Naila's eyes were transfixed on the incoming mob, but she didn't really see them.

"Run!" someone cried.

"Quick, to the gate," another barked.

Jacobo slapped her hand away.

"See ye, sweetling." The boatswain saluted with a smug grin as he stumbled out of the alley like a cowardly dog, his pants dropping to his knees in his hurry. He'd left his golden dagger in her grasp. Before she could process what had happened, a warning bell chimed, followed by a sentry screaming,

"Shadowreapers!"

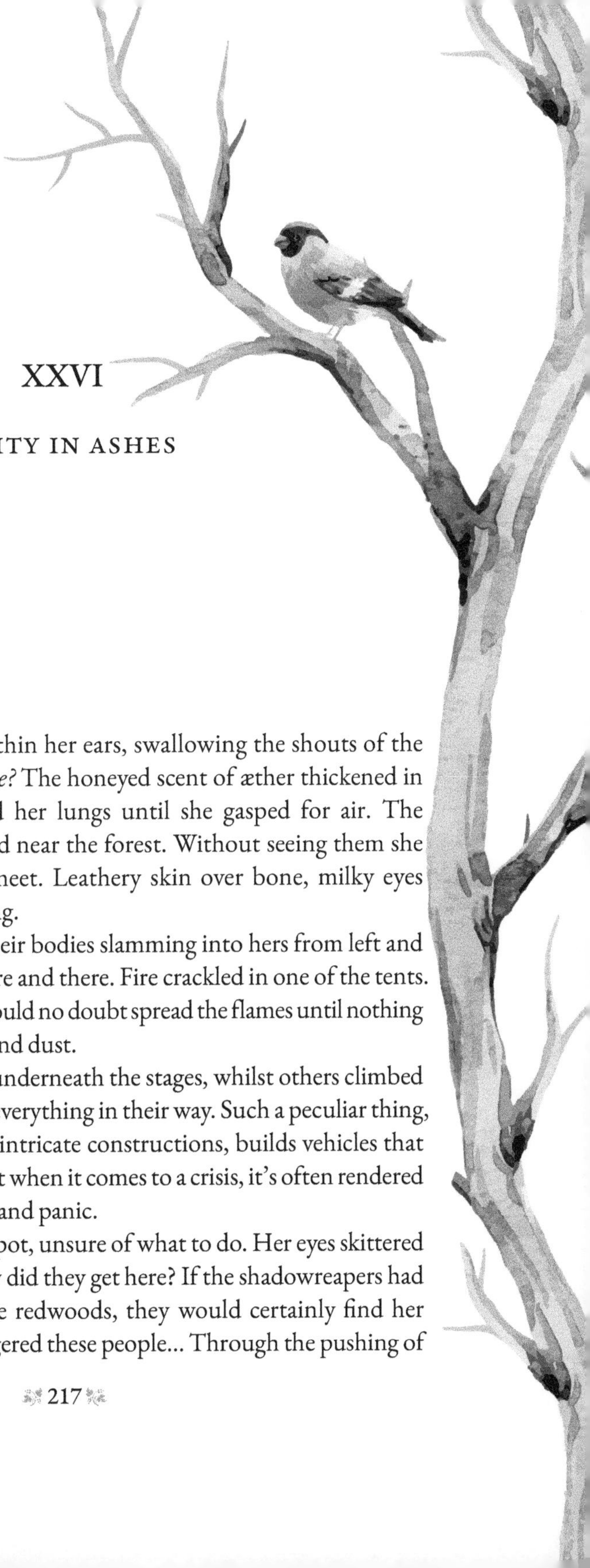

XXVI

A CITY IN ASHES

T*HUMP.*

They're here.

Thump.

They've come for me.

Thump.

Naila's heart drummed within her ears, swallowing the shouts of the civilians. *How did they find me?* The honeyed scent of æther thickened in the night's breeze. It burned her lungs until she gasped for air. The shadowreapers' horses neighed near the forest. Without seeing them she knew what her eyes would meet. Leathery skin over bone, milky eyes unseeing yet not missing a thing.

People darted past Naila, their bodies slamming into hers from left and right, a bronze mask falling here and there. Fire crackled in one of the tents. The winds from Helath's sea would no doubt spread the flames until nothing of the feast remained but ash and dust.

Yet some crawled foolishly underneath the stages, whilst others climbed into the trees, breaking down everything in their way. Such a peculiar thing, the mind. It invents the most intricate constructions, builds vehicles that travel to the stars and above, yet when it comes to a crisis, it's often rendered to no more than a slave to fear and panic.

Naila stayed rooted to the spot, unsure of what to do. Her eyes skittered over the frightened faces. How did they get here? If the shadowreapers had traced her seas away from the redwoods, they would certainly find her among this crowd. She endangered these people... Through the pushing of the crowd, a little girl stumbled into Naila's arms. She steadied her by the shoulders. It was the bronze girl she'd seen earlier. The girl smiled from ear to ear as if Naila was the answer to her prayers.

"You're a nergayla," she squealed. "Please chase those mean shadowreapers away."

"I—"

Naila opened and closed her mouth. What was she to say? She was the *very* reason they were here.

The girl's mother pulled her out of Naila's grasp.

"Foolish *feylana*," she cuffed her daughter at the side of her head. "If you want to pray to someone, pray to the Red Šar, but even he cannot send us *ut Asanatæ* in time."

The woman pushed her daughter toward Mort Nor's gate.

"May the Legends be with us," a man cried from somewhere.

"Quick *lugal*, find an aviary and send word to the Red Šar," a sentry bellowed to his *learling*. He and a group of other sentries rushed across the plaza. Their scimitars and shields were ablaze with the blues of æther.

"Naila!"

Naila's heart pounded against her ribcage.

"Onyx, I'm here."

It was a challenge to see her in the madding crowd. She didn't recognize her in any of the faces.

The villagers no longer had any patience left. They pushed Naila roughly to the side while they crammed their bodies along the small pathway, rushing to the gate. An unfortunate woman slipped and fell, but that didn't deter them from scurrying over her to... safety? Even in her shock Naila knew there was none.

"Naila," Silas called, this time much closer.

The world came into focus when Silas grabbed her by the arms. A soothing relief loosened her limbs. She didn't bother to swallow back a sob. She grasped the hem of his black blouse, leaning against the hard warmth of him, breathing in his welcome scent.

He rested his chin atop her curls, but only briefly. "We've been looking for you everywhere."

"N, thank the stars," Onyx said. She, Tryce, and Rē rushed toward them. The alley was empty, but the plaza was still a soup of chaos and madness.

Somewhere the clangs of scimitars sounded, as did the neighing of those dreadful horses. The shadowreapers were close. So close. *Too* close.

"Let's hurry to the dhow," Tryce urged.

"That coward of a captain already sailed away," Rē gritted his teeth. "We should go to Mort Nor. Find a hiding place."

Contrary to the civilians, his ethereal face remained stoic. Ever the rational one. Not one shadowy hair on his neatly combed head in disarray. If he were frightened, he did a mighty good job at hiding it.

"There is no hiding from hunter-killers," Silas said. He glanced from the gate to the plaza, to the forest. "We're trapped on this island, they know that. It's a matter of time before we have to face them."

Igigi's words came to Naila.

"No," she said. "There is a way. The tierkan in the cage... he said he could guide us through the cave roads."

"N, of all living things in Lemuria, tierkans are the last ones to trust. In fact, even if I and a tierkan were the last ones to live, I *still* wouldn't trust one," Onyx said.

"We have no choice. It's either we go with the tierkan or be at the mercy of shadowreapers." Naila held firm.

"There are dozens of shadowreapers." Rē's face was solemn, but there was something close to acknowledgment in the dark pools of his eyes. He seemed to understand Naila's line of thinking.

"Naila's right. I don't trust that stinkin' tierkan any more than you, but the shadowreapers are blocking the harbor. I don't know 'bout ye, but I'd rather be stabbed in the back by a tierkan than become the Shadow Šar's slave," said Tryce.

Silas's eyes met Onyx's, and the two held a wordless conversation. At last, she sighed and he inclined his head to the gate. "All right, then, we're wasting our time standing here."

Onyx thrust Naila's satchel into her hands. "Here you go."

"Thanks."

Naila stowed Jacobo's curved dagger inside her satchel. It was hers now. Jacobo no longer held a claim to it. They followed the remaining people on the path to the gate, close to the edge of the volcano, the last part of their path leading over the plaza. To her grief they found the glorious ancient tree cracked in half. Several sentries rushed past them, armed with æshefied swords, spears, and maces. The plaza was painted in the cedars, rubies, and opals of their attire.

At last, they reached the gate. Unlike before, there was no one to confirm their identity or grant them access. The civilians stormed down the stairs, not looking back to see who followed.

"We should close the gate," Silas said.

"How? We don't have the locks," said Onyx.

"We'll find a way. We have to stall them." To Naila and Tryce the prince said, "You go ahead and free that tierkan."

"What about you guys?" Naila began, panic arising.

"Go. We'll be with you before you know it. I promise."

Tryce took her hand. "Let's hurry."

She swallowed back a lump of emotion. She knew they were right. They had a role to play, as did she.

Somehow, through the chaos, Naila and Tryce managed to reach the prisoners' cages, although looking back, she couldn't begin to explain how. Everything went by in a blur.

Igigi pressed his chubby, purplish head to the bars. The moment he noticed them, a wicked smile curved his lips.

"So, you have changed your mind, yes?" said the tierkan.

"Your freedom in exchange for a way out of here," said Naila. "Give us your word."

The tierkan pressed his hand to his heart and bowed, a vision of innocence. "I give my word. Oh, do I give my word, yes. Now, make haste, nergayla. I can lead you through the cave roads but I cannot save you from a legion of shadowreapers."

Tryce unsheathed his ax. The moment it left his sheath it blazed with flames. The boy pointed the sword to the tierkan. "You better not try nothing funny or I'll have your head."

The tierkan waved dismissively. "Yes, yes, now hurry."

Tryce hacked at the lock.

The clangs of steel hitting iron echoed in the hollowness of Mort Nor, although much of the sound got lost in the chaos of the people. With the sixth swing, the lock gave way.

The tierkan pushed the door open, stepping outside with his hands in the air and his eyes big as saucers, as if he were a babe seeing the world for the first time. She wondered how long he had been held captive, but that was a tale for another time.

A loud thump thundered through Mort Nor, followed by the shuddering of the sands underneath their feet. Pained and frightened screams came from afar. Naila couldn't help but flinch. She hoped the little girl and her mother had found shelter elsewhere. That her friends were safe and would join them soon.

"There they are," said Tryce.

To her relief Onyx, Silas, and Rē, were among the mob of people dashing toward them.

"N," Onyx said, between heaving breaths. "I see you got him."

Naila nodded. "The shadowreapers..."

"We were too late." Silas shook his head, frustration bleeding on his face. He turned to Igigi. "It's up to you now, tierkan."

Igigi beckoned them to follow. His tiny body dashed through the crowd. They hurried after him, wrestling through the people who ran about with no purpose, except the wish to survive and the fear of losing their lives.

They nearly reached the outer ring of the undersea city when hooves clip-clopped far too near, sending tremors through stone. The cave road was close by. The immense opening, four stories high at least, beckoned them with tendrils of the void that lurked in its depth. So close yet so far. The shadowreapers were sure to reach them before they could hide in its darkness.

The tierkan threw several glances behind, his steps quickening. The sound of hooves grew louder. A figure appeared in the distance. A shadowreaper. There was nowhere to run. They simply weren't fast enough.

Silas halted. "Go, I will slow him down."

"What? No!" Onyx hissed.

Naila's eyes caressed the folds of Silas's solemn face. There was a look within his eyes that told her his mind was made up.

"Go, that's an order."

"Silas..." Onyx's voice broke. For the first time, tears wetted her eyes.

Rē, however, nodded. "Come, do not make it harder than it is. He has made his choice."

"It's suicide," Naila whispered.

"It's your only chance."

Rē dragged Onyx away, Tryce following suit. Her face was frozen in shock.

"I can't let you do this," Naila whispered.

No, no, no. Not Silas. He couldn't die!

"You don't have a choice. Now, go."

The tierkan tugged at her sleeve. "Do as he says, nergayla. A shadowreaper's claws you do not want to end up in."

Tears streamed over her cheeks. Silas's eyes were hard, determined. He was saying goodbye...

The tierkan pushed her to the cave.

This wasn't happening.

Silas pulled out his black-gold gloves, the enhancement for æther that would help him in battle. His eyes locked on Naila's. They were the clearest ocean blue. Held no secrets. Could he read in her eyes what she read in his? Those unspoken words. The regret of what could have been, of what slipped through their fingers like unopened letters into a fire.

"Wait," said Silas.

Naila unclasped Igigi's bony fingers and met the prince halfway. He linked his arm around her waist and pulled her flush to him. With trembling fingers, she stroked the hem of his shirt, of his leather coat. Her eyes caressed the sun-kissed skin of his face, the stubble that grew on his angular jaw, but most of all the emotion mirrored in his gaze.

His eyes lowered to her lips.

Her stomach did a somersault.

"You're a rake," she whispered.

"I know," he answered.

The prince drew her head to his. The moment his lips met hers, tingles ignited everywhere their skin touched. Her very first kiss. It was neither soft nor gentle, but feverish and spoke of want. Her lips parted and he took that moment to deepen their kiss. His tongue entered her mouth. The whole of him entered her very being. He was everywhere. Everywhere was him.

The tierkan cleared his throat, and like glass the moment shattered. Naila gasped for air. Her knees quaked beneath her.

"We. Must. Go," said Igigi, but then his eyes grew wide.

Ice-blue æther reflected in the shimmering sand, outlining the shadow of a nearing figure.

The æther of a scimitar.

Fear scratched at Naila's throat, her stomach, her limbs.

The æther of *Colios's* scimitar.

"Go," Silas hissed.

Igigi tried to force her forward again, but she stood frozen.

There in the flesh, Colios strode toward them, his dark cloak floating in a howling wind that escaped from the cave roads, his gloved hand clenched around his sizzling scimitar. He was alone. There was no sight of Daena or the woman of the redwoods, nor of the other shadowreapers that had joined him in his hunt.

"Naila Stormhold," Colios said, his eyes aflame with æther. There was no humor in his tone, no sarcasm either.

He looked as frightening as he did in her memory. The sickly gray of his skin, the row of black-gold teeth etched in the leather that covered his jaw, the flames of æther that burned in the void of his eyes. The latter a sign she'd come to know was usually only present when æther was enhanced by black gold.

Silas angled his body before hers. The blood vessels underneath his skin pulsed with æther. His gloves ignited, the embers blasted to full-blown flames around his sword and within his eyes. With his dark hair stuck to the rugged angles of his face, he again looked more pirate than prince.

The sweet burn of æther made it difficult for Naila to breathe. Just like the thick smoke of fireworks on New Year's Eve.

"There's no need to run, no need to hide. We are not the enemy," Colios continued.

No.

"What did you do to Philippe, you murderer?"

"The same thing I do to everyone standing in my way, so it would be wise to call your guard dog back or he will share your Philippe's fate."

His eyes glinted with promise, emphasized even more by the dullness of his skin. Naila recognized him for what he was. Colios had suffered from *ut mortes nero.* Had he feared death so much he'd rather spend his remaining life shackled to the Shadow Šar?

It took several moments before Colios's implications fully registered. Naila covered her mouth, as agony ripped at her. "No." She didn't want to believe Colios killed Philly, but the look on his face crumbled her hopes to dust.

"Enough," Silas growled.

Thunder rumbled from a storm on the surface, high above the city. The heavens cried, in sync with Naila's own screaming soul. So much death. So much pain.

"I don't believe we've met," Silas continued.

"Silvanus the Brave." Colios twirled his sword. "Yes, I know you. Skeldor's beloved prince, so ruled by his impulsivity, old Möndör Softsword is frightened to die, lest his cocky heir drive the empire into destruction. And destruction it shall get if you stand in the Shadow Šar's way."

Silas flinched, but immediately straightened into a relaxed pose. "Your tongue will cost you your head, shadowreaper."

Colios mirrored Silas's pose. They were like two predators facing each other, waiting for the first one to pounce. Colios beckoned to Mort Nor's increasing ruins. "Is that so? Setting foot in your twin brother's empire. He'll be even more eager than I to kill you, you know. After all, you are all that stands between him and Skeldor's throne. At least I will give you a painless death."

Naila's hands tightened around Igigi's thin arm. Twins... Silas and the Red Šar were *twins*? His family relations grew messier with every passing moment.

To her surprise, not a hint of annoyance etched Silas's face. He was all unadulterated confidence.

Silas pointed his blazing sword at Colios.

"Leave my brother to me, shadowreaper. And Naila is coming with me. You'd better give up on this pursuit of yours."

"That I cannot do."

Silas and Colios leaped to each other. The radiative blows of their æshefied swords created sparks of fireworks.

"They say you are Skeldor's best swordsman." Colios bared his teeth between blows. "I must say I find you lacking."

Silas slashed Colios's leg and the shadowreaper grunted in pain. Blood wetted the shadowreaper's pants. Silas's lips curved into a devilish grin. "Less talking, more fighting."

Colios unsheathed his second scimitar but the prince blocked his blows. They were caught in a dance of flames. If Naila wasn't frightened to her core perhaps she could have admired the elegance of their twists and blocks, the expert wielding of their swords, the rain of color birthed out of the clash of their weapons.

But Naila was afraid for Silas's life.

They were so consumed by the dance of flames, it took her a moment to notice the nearing crew of three. It took every ounce of strength to hide her smile of relief. Onyx, Tryce, and Rē were on their way back, blazing weapons in hand. Except for Rē. While he didn't have æther, Naila knew he was as strong as any who did. Stronger even. Shadowreaper or no, Colios was no match for four highly skilled warriors.

"Poor Möndör Softsword," Colios mocked. "How cruel are the fates to have his enemy's spawn inherit his throne. Be it you or your twin."

Silas's body grew rigid, decisiveness oozing from him, but for all the jabs at his impulsivity, he didn't give in to Colios's provocations. Colios struck again, but the prince evaded him with expert precision. The shadowreaper on the other hand, blocked Silas's attacks with equal finesse.

Rē threw himself upon Colios, but the shadowreaper pushed him off without breaking a sweat. The fight turned to classless fists as Silas tried to overpower the shadowreaper. Naila dashed to Rē, who'd been thrown several meters away by Colios. Her fingers already pricked with æther, ready to heal her friend, but fortunately, and much to her surprise, Rē didn't have so much as a bruise.

"*T'ilaa ni gloria,*" Onyx shrieked.

She and Tryce had come to join them again! Rē rushed back to the struggle and before they knew it, it was four against one. Naila unsheathed her dagger, following Rē. Without thinking, golden flames already licked its sharp surface. Breathing in, she forced her fear away. She had never fought in her life, but there was a first time for everything.

Colios's sword blazed brighter than any sword she'd seen before. He ignored the others, his eyes only pinned on Silas with a clinical precision. "You may be blessed with Sin and Shamash's strength, but I, my prince, have Sariel's gifts running through my veins."

Colios's eyes widened before he fell to the sands.

Behind him stood Igigi, his fist sheathed in venomous green flames. "You forget, shadowreaper, while the Ænunaki and the tierkans received the finest meals of æther, you Lemaians only got the crumbs that fell off the table."

Silas pinned Colios to the sand, but it was unnecessary. The shadowreaper was completely paralyzed.

"Guys, hurry," said Naila. "More are coming."

At least five riders galloped toward them, tiny flickers of darkness before the fire that consumed Mort Nor.

Igigi bounced from one foot to the other. "Hurry, we must hurry to the cave roads. He will not be paralyzed longer than a chime. We will shake them off within its maze."

Naila took off her shawl and dashed toward the struggling three. "Here, take this and bind his feet and hands so he can't follow us."

"We should kill him," said Tryce.

"Cut off his head, yes," agreed Igigi.

Tryce kicked Colios's shin for good measure.

Even more death... When would it end? It was one thing to cheer from a distance as an enemy got its due, but a whole other thing to contribute to his murder. And murder this was, regardless of his deeds. She would never be able to look at herself again.

Naila said, "No! Bind him and let's leave."

"Naila," Onyx began.

"Enough blood has been spilled because of me..."

Her chin lifted in defiance. She glanced at her friends one by one, not buckling beneath their doubtful stares. This was one thing she wouldn't budge on.

Silas sighed, but his eyes softened. "Let's go."

"Foolish nergayla," Igigi muttered, but Rē did as Naila said.

Colios said nothing as they tied him up, his thoughts locked behind unreadable eyes, together with the rest of his secrets.

The scent of fire and ashes filled Mort Nor. The cries of the people afar did not silence. There was nothing they could do against the swarm of shadowreapers. Nothing they could do to help the people who had given them shelter. All they could do was run and save their own hides.

A tear rolled down Naila's cheek.

"Come, nergayla, there is nothing we can do for them," said Igigi.

With one last look at the burning city, Naila followed the tierkan into the cave roads.

XXVII

OUT OF THE DARKNESS, INTO THE COLD

Out of the flaming night, into the dark of the cave roads they went.

Coward.

She was a coward.

Failure.

She had failed.

Murderer...

Naila bent over in pain. How many lives were lost because of her? What had become of the rest of Halfbeard's crew? Of Two-Toed Teddy and the ever-cheery Bubba? She stumbled against Rē's back. Or was it Tryce? There was no light along the cave roads. No way to know the path they walked except for Igigi's occasional grunts.

A familiar fist tightened around her chest until she saw flickers of white. *Air*. She needed air. Her feet felt like they held the weight of her past, her future. Onyx ripped her cloak and wrapped it around an arrow. She ignited her torch with æther. A group of bats rustled on the rocky ceiling, their tiny bodies huddled together. One of them flapped the thin membrane of its wings. Watching her. Judging her. She gasped for air. No matter how deep her breaths, she couldn't get enough.

Ma... Philly... She needed them.

Why was life never straightforward? Why were the sacrifices she had to make to get things right, ones that chipped at her soul?

"N... You all right?"

Onyx squeezed her arm gently. She barely saw Onyx's face in the dark of the cave, but she knew Onyx didn't have to see *her*. Her gasps said enough.

"Come. Sit."

The huntress led her to a stone. As soon as her bottom met with the flatness of the rock, she lowered her face between her knees. Hoping, wishing, the rush of blood to her brain would rein in her breathlessness.

"What's going on?" asked Silas.

"Give us a moment," said Onyx.

Onyx stroked her back. All Naila heard was the dripping of water alongside the stones and the echoing steps of the others. The smell of the cave, damp and earthy with a hint of mold, made her head spin even more.

"This isn't your fault, you know," Onyx whispered.

"Isn't it? If I didn't want to find Nebiru, no one would have died. Half-beard wouldn't have died."

"You're shouldering a burden that's not yours to bear. One could go about their life and still be kidnapped for just the color of their hair. Would you see that person as a victim or the one at fault?"

Naila sucked in her lower lip. "Of course the victim. Always the victim."

"You see? Your actions are your own. Let the actions of the shadowreapers be theirs to face. Whether in this life or the next, justice will demand its price."

Her breathing slowed.

Agony still clawed at her heart, but the pain became bearable. There was a truth in Onyx's words. She pushed herself up. The plains of Onyx's unique face became visible.

"So, you don't blame me?"

Onyx smiled. "Of course not. I see you."

Onyx squeezed her hand reassuringly. Relief washed over Naila. After the sailors' reactions when she'd subdued the sea serpent, she had been so frightened she would be alone again. An outcast. *A freak.*

"The shadowreapers... They won't stop," Naila whispered.

"Then we will force them to," said Silas.

The prince dropped next to her and pulled her into a gentle embrace. His soft, warm lips brushed her forehead. Naila's eyes fluttered to a close, tension leaving her body. For a moment there was only his soothing scent.

"Aargh, you cannot stop them, foolish Lemaian." Igigi broke the spell.

He sat cross-legged on a stone opposite Naila, his pointed shoes pressed together. "Even now they have no doubt dragged those *ut mortes nero* infected beggars with them, turning them into another legion of shadowreapers, yes."

"How? No ship of men can leave the Shores of the Blood Moons. That's what Nova's prophecy said, didn't it?" demanded Tryce.

"Ah, but shadowreapers are no longer men, now, are they?" said Igigi.

Tryce kicked at a pebble. It bounced on the rocks, leaving a trail of echoes behind. "Still think it's weird. That Azag who hunted us... The shadowreapers who found us 'cross Helath of all things."

In the shadows, she saw Rē lock eyes with Igigi. His face fell into solemness. Did he know something they didn't? Naila found herself not wanting to know. The day had been eventful enough.

A *kree* echoed through the cave. Igigi's round ears twitched underneath his pointed hat. "Come, we must go. The screechers are awakening."

"Screechers?" Tryce said, his brows furrowed in confusion.

For once, Naila wasn't the only one who felt that way.

"There is a reason none wander through the cave roads," said Igigi. "Did you know the Ænunaki"—Everyone but Naila flinched—"let us built the cave roads to connect all the lands of Lemuria? Underneath sea, underneath mountains the cave roads lie. Few recognize their entrance for what it is. Those who dare roam about find themselves lost in an endless maze or eaten by the dreaded screechers, yes."

Igigi's eyes glinted with delight. "Deadly vermiform creatures they are. Long as a dhow and thick as a cottage, their scales the color of blood. They kill in gruesome ways, with venom that eats away your flesh, and fangs that strike your bones like lightning. Your only chance against a screecher is to run, and fast, yes... If you see them in time, that is. They can sniff you from miles away and move about soundlessly to sneak on their prey. Even now, I'm certain they know we're here, yes."

"I'll smash them to pieces!" Tryce swung his ax around.

It seemed his sadness had made way for anger.

Igigi jumped off his stone and pushed his finger into Tryce's chest. "You will do no such thing, smashy-smashy. We will be out of here before they corner us. Come, come."

They followed the light-footed tierkan through the darkness. In their hurry, they did not bring any candles or oil lamps. Onyx's makeshift torch would have to do.

"Igigi. You aren't the only one who knows these roads," Naila whispered.

"What do you mean?" Silas said.

"At the market, I met that rich merchant from the Chimera. He told me about these cave roads. He traveled them to get to Crishire."

There. She said it. It felt like confessing her sins. The man whose eyes had haunted her dreams was no longer a secret. She could feel their frowns. Naila fumbled with her compass, opening it, seeking for the warmth its sight would bring like a long-lost friend. The arrow pointed southeast, the opposite of where they were going. Silly thing. It had to be broken, again.

"Impossible," Rē said. "If the city had not been under attack, the sentries would have stopped us from entering, as they no doubt did him. Do not believe anyone so lightly."

"No, she is right. Nomadic tribes sometimes use the caves, yes, and smugglers too," Igigi said quietly.

"I don't think he belonged to one of those tribes. He was alone."

"Then a smuggler he was," was all Igigi said.

"What did he want from you?" said Silas.

Naila hesitated. "He saved me… in the redwoods. Before you got to me, Onyx."

"Huh?" said Onyx, while Silas demanded simultaneously, "He followed you?"

"Maybe he's the one who tipped off the shadowreapers!" Tryce said.

Naila suddenly felt defensive although the stranger was as much a mystery to her. "No, you're wrong. He was nice, really. He even bought me a gift."

"What gift?" said Silas, his voice razor-sharp.

Somewhere during their conversation everyone had stopped walking. They circled Naila—Silas and Tryce with their arms crossed, Onyx with her hands on her hips, Rē his usual stoic self. Even Igigi cocked his head in curiosity.

Naila fumbled in her satchel. The scroll rolled open and fell to the ground, but Igigi caught it just in time.

"Thanks," she said.

Igigi stared at the scroll like a squirrel at the last acorns of fall. "So, this is your map to the fallen city of Nebiru, hmm? How long it has been since my eyes have seen the written language of the Hædur, yes. Did you know there is power in its spoken words?"

Naila shrugged and put it back in her bag. She pulled out her flower hair clip for all to see. Igigi, in turn, stuck his hand out. For the first time she noticed black gold was carved within the creases of his palm. Soft emerald flames of æther followed the vines of metal until they flickered in his palm like an oil lamp's flame. Green æther... Hers was golden, the Lemaians' were blue, and now she found the tierkans' were green. She made a mental note to ask its meaning. *Later.*

In the light of the flames, the flower's soul-stones came alive, their color twisting like sheets of silken red.

"By the stars," said Onyx. "So that's why you asked about soul-stones."

Silas's brows furrowed, the look on his face one of confusion. "He gave you this?"

Naila shrugged. "I was admiring it."

"Do you know what it's worth?" said Rē. He looked as confused as Silas.

"I think he was too rich to care."

But her friends looked doubtful.

Igigi, however, smirked. "A courting gift. You have yourself an admirer, yes."

"Don't be silly. Some people don't need a reason to be nice, you know," said Naila.

She clipped the *fayalobi* flower in her curls for good measure.

"Well, whoever he was, he's long gone," said Silas. He stroked his arm absentmindedly.

There were no lies in the prince's words, yet even now she felt the presence of the stranger's blue-black eyes, looming in the shadows, promising that they would meet again.

Fortunately, it was the last they said on the subject.

"NAILA, NAILA, wake up."

Tryce shook her by the shoulders.

Naila rubbed the sleep out of her eyes. The last flames crackled in their dying campfire. The first they had dared to make in four days. Remnants of roasted mushrooms and cave fish were still skewered above the embers. The urgent whispers of the others echoed somewhere in the cave. Her hand searched the ground for her satchel, but it came up empty.

She jerked up, glancing around. Her bag was nowhere to be seen.

"Tryce?" she whispered, a sense of horror slithering up her spine. "Where's my bag?"

Tryce's mouth tightened. "That nasty little dwarf stole it. He left us here to die!"

Naila's hand clasped her mouth. "The map... It was in my bag."

Tryce rubbed the back of his neck and glanced away. Anger trickled from his face the same way devastation no doubt did from hers.

Kreeeee. The cry came from somewhere far too close.

Great. Just great, Naila thought.

"What in Suzano's balls was that?" Tryce hissed.

His hand was already on the hilt of his ax.

"I think... I think it's one of those screechers."

Naila rushed to gather their belongings. Tryce threw the contents of his flask onto the campfire until the cave was yet again a road of endless dark.

"When I get my hands on him, he'll wish he stayed in that prison," Tryce spat.

"There's nothing we can do about it now. Let's find the others."

Her words were far calmer than the emotions that raged inside. That scroll had been her way back home... How was she to find Nebiru now? Igigi had played them for fools.

"N? Tryce?" Onyx's voice.

"We're here," said Naila. "But we have to get out of here, there's a screecher nearby."

"Things just keep getting better." Onyx sighed.

"Did ye find 'im?" Tryce demanded.

"He is gone. Left no trail. That tierkan knows what he is doing," Rē grunted.

"Sack of wine," Tryce hissed through his teeth.

"He stole my bag," said Naila.

Her vision blurred with tears. The enormity of what had happened slapped her across the face. Hard. Igigi hadn't stolen her precious hair clip, nor her compass pendant. No, he had only cared for the map. Had wanted it from the moment he'd laid his beady eyes on the scroll.

"The scroll..." Horror crossed the plains of Onyx's face. "There is no scribe or šar who will not pay a hefty price for such a thing."

"He didn't steal anything else. I doubt he's after crystals."

"No. Tierkans are hoarders. They do not care for crystals," agreed Rē.

Footsteps echoed across the stone.

Silas came into sight. "That tierkan may have abandoned us, but at least he did it near the exit of the cave road."

"Thank goodness," said Naila.

Despair made place for relief. Igigi, at least, wasn't *that* evil. They followed Silas, and at last, after almost a week, rays of sunlight broke through the darkness of the cave until finally, they were outside.

All around them were dunes of terracotta. Palm trees and some olive trees were scattered about, inching toward the searing sun.

"Remind me never to complain about the heat again," said Onyx, unfastening her cloak.

Tryce threw himself on the cinnamon sand, making a sand angel with his limbs.

"Stop doing that. You're getting sand all over the place," Naila scolded.

The boy grinned, dimples forming in his bronze cheeks, his onyx eyes glinting with mischief. Naila couldn't find it in her to stay annoyed, it was the first genuine smile he'd shown them in a week. Tryce had that boyish charm about him that could wrap one around his finger. How dangerous he would be when the boy became a man. Dangerous to the hearts of Lemuria's *feylanas*, that was.

Rē cupped his hands over his eyes, squinting into the distance. His face was as happy as one who just ate Brussel sprouts. It seemed like nothing ever put him at ease. "It's a desert."

"You don't say." Silas took out his flask, eying a nearby well. "At least there's water." He inched toward Naila, his eyes softening. "Don't worry about the scroll. We'll find Nebiru, one way or the other."

She nodded, but her happiness deflated. Silas wouldn't go back on his words, she knew that. He and Onyx had stayed loyal to her even when the quest had proven to be impossible over and over again. *But,* Nebiru had been lost to the Lemai for a thousand winters. How were they to find it without the scroll?

"Hey." He tilted her chin until her bright brown eyes met his cobalt ones. Why was it they turned more breathtaking every time she looked at them? "I promise."

"Isolon has no deserts," Rē interrupted.

They finally took in what bothered Rē. From her memory of the map, she knew Isolon was mostly covered in mountains and forest.

This was *not* Isolon.

THE SUN's fire dimmed to Iluna's beams and reclaimed its throne on the early morn. *Lost, they were lost.*

All because Naila had trusted Igigi! How many sunsets had passed? She didn't know. All she knew was they were left with two options: go forward into the unknown desert or back to the screecher-filled cave road. She lay against the well, the only reprieve in the smothering desert, twirling her pendant with her fingers.

"Lift your arm higher, like this." Onyx corrected Tryce's pose. She was teaching Tryce how to hunt with his shining new ax. "Stand a little straighter."

The boy threw his ax at a scrabbling desert fowl. The bird jerked upright. Before Tryce's ax hit true, it dashed away, faster than a roadrunner.

"You're too loud," Onyx scolded.

"I wasn't s'much as breathing," Tryce protested.

"There's enough cacti to last for days," said Naila, not bothering to lift her head.

Tryce groaned. "Can y'even call that food?"

Silas chuckled. "You will if you keep aiming like a granny."

He returned to sharpening his scimitar, tan skin wrapped over a lean physique peeking from underneath his collar and sleeves. Was there anyone more handsome? His eyes met Naila's staring ones. She quickly averted her gaze, her cheeks burning. There hadn't been any opportunity to discuss *that* kiss.

Silas cleared his throat. "We can't keep loitering here." He ran his fingers through his hair. "We have to make a decision. We can't go back into the cave, so we might as well try the desert."

Onyx shot him an incredulous look. "There are only five deserts this could be, and our chances are slim to none to find our way through any of them." She frowned a little. "Although I suppose I'd rather die of thirst than be eaten by a slimy worm."

"Don't you have a compass?" asked Rē from beneath the shade of a curved palm tree. Despite the rough week, his ethereal looks glowed even brighter in the desert sun. "We can use either that or the stars as navigation."

It struck her then. "My compass!"

Naila pulled the pendant open. Its needle still pointed southeast, like it had done in the cave. It hadn't been broken. Igigi had led them on the wrong path, and she, foolish she, had trusted the tierkan instead of the one thing Philly had promised would always point back home.

"Yer a genius," Tryce clapped his back.

Rē frowned at the compass. "I do not think it is pointing north."

Naila grinned. "No, I think it points to Isolon. It somehow reads where I want to go."

"That's... peculiar." The prince rubbed his forearm.

"A magical compass, huh?" said Onyx, as she joined them to glance at the pendant too.

"There is no such thing as magic. From the look of it, that compass is made of soul-stones. Someone must have bonded you to it," Rē grunted.

Soul-stones... So not moonstone.

"You mean the way nergaylas bind empires to soul-stones to create shields?" asked Onyx.

"*Yana.*"

"But a single nergayla cannot do it, can they? I thought they built on the power left by their forebears."

"It is as you say. This Philippe of Naila's must have kept a lot of secrets."

Naila stroked her pendant sadly. *Who were you, Philly?*

"Well, there's our answer. Isolon is back on schedule. You are by far the luckiest girl to have walked these lands, N." Onyx tugged at Naila's curl. "I'd like to know where we are, though."

"How do you know so much, Rē?" asked Naila.

Rē's expression became closed off. He stared at the mirage of the horizon. "I was a blood slave once." He bared his right shoulder, unveiling the remnants of a branding mark. The group grew silent. "A captive to the Iron Šar in the War of Iron before blood slavery was abolished in the Empire of Gudea. They drained my æther, until I was no more than skin and bones."

"How did y'escape?" asked Tryce, his eyes wide, but admiring. Naila knew Rē was something of an idol to him.

Rē tapped his head. "After I lost my æther, they assigned me as the imperial scribe's valet. I learned everything I could from him with more eagerness than his best *learling*. He gifted me with education. I worked my way up from there. After serving in the Iron Šar's *keshig* for ten winters I paid for my freedom."

Even Onyx stared at Rē with admiration. "Never give up, huh?"

Was she thinking of her quest to save her own mother?

"Never give up," Rē agreed.

A group of animals bleated; perhaps desert-dwelling goats come to quench their thirst at the well.

Naila jumped up, "A nomadic tribe!"

The others followed her gaze.

A tribe of azure-robed people riding upon camel-like animals neared the well, together with their herd. One of the girls strolled curiously toward them, a large bucket of water balancing on her head as if she had done it many a time before. It was the girl from the market. The one who had sold her the flower of soul-stones. Naila glanced at the girl's tribe. They were all dark-skinned like the girl, with eyes the same color as their blue attire.

"*Feylana*." The girl smiled, somewhat bemused. "We met at the market."

"So, you remember me. Can you tell us where we are? My friends and I are lost."

"Of course," said the girl, but she frowned a little. "You're in the shifting sands of the Red Desert."

The group grew silent once more. Only the song of the desert wind and the bleating of the animals broke the silence. The girl's words were like a shadow that had taken away the sun's promise of hope. The prince stood rigid, his mouth slightly open, as if he couldn't believe what he just heard.

"Do you know where that is?" said Naila.

"When we find that tierkan, I'll skewer him," Silas gritted through his teeth.

Onyx's face too, was ashen.

"Where are we?" Naila repeated, confused at her friends' reactions.

The tribal girl said in their stead, "Welcome to the Empire of Crishire."

SCROLL III

BOUND BY BLOOD

She soars, she flies, she basks in the light,
The winds of fate glide through her feathers,
Makes bearable her plight,
Beware, beware,
There is no light without shadows,
No moon without the night,
Ever watching, ever scheming, the dark looms out of sight,
Waiting to capture and take away the bird's flight.

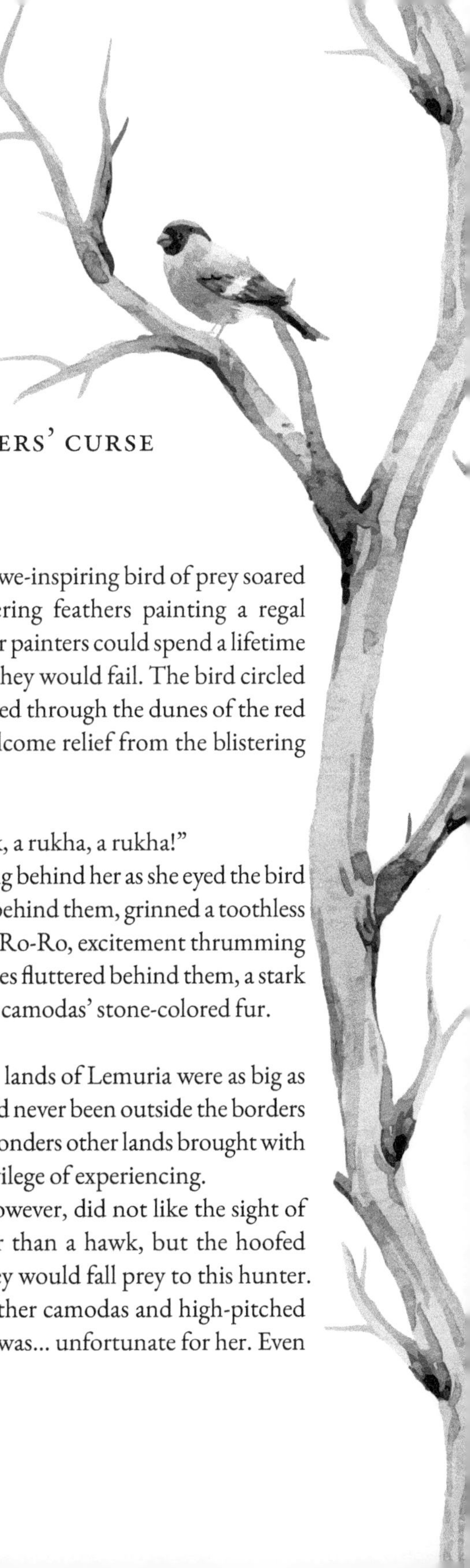

XXVIII

THE SHADOWREAPERS' CURSE

GILDED AS the afternoon sun, an awe-inspiring bird of prey soared through the winds, its shimmering feathers painting a regal picture against the sky; one master painters could spend a lifetime trying to capture on their canvas, and still they would fail. The bird circled above the caravan of camodas, which trekked through the dunes of the red desert. Its shadow poured over them a welcome relief from the blistering sun.

"Ro-Ro is back," Naila squealed.

The girl, Sephanya, pointed. "*Baba,* look, a rukha, a rukha!"

The Mehari girl's jumbo box braids swung behind her as she eyed the bird in innocent wonder. Her father, who rode behind them, grinned a toothless smile. Several other Mehari also pointed at Ro-Ro, excitement thrumming through the nomadic tribe. Their azure robes fluttered behind them, a stark contrast with the cinnamon dunes and the camodas' stone-colored fur.

Naila suppressed a smile.

It was in these moments she realized the lands of Lemuria were as big as the continents of Earth. Many Lemaians had never been outside the borders of their empire. Had never seen the exotic wonders other lands brought with them. The ones she, ironically, had the privilege of experiencing.

She beckoned Ro-Ro. The camodas, however, did not like the sight of the nearing raptor. Ro-Ro was no bigger than a hawk, but the hoofed mammals seemed to sense that one day they would fall prey to this hunter. Naila's mount grunted in answer to the other camodas and high-pitched bleating of the other herd animals. Which was... unfortunate for her. Even without opening its thick lips, the animal already smelled of compost on the scorching desert day.

Naila shifted in her saddle, between the humps of the camoda's back. She'd never rode a horse before, let alone a camoda that was twice its size and waddled like an overdue pregnant woman. The animal waddled again, and all was for naught. It simply refused to move. *Ugh.* Naila threw the reins to her lap. It was hot; she was hungry, and the animal wasn't cooperating. Ro-Ro nudged her cheek with his feathery head, as if the bird sensed her discomfort.

The rukha made a point of ignoring the camodas' growling by clicking haughtily. *He* was there to stay, the šaltana's letter beneath his clawed foot. Naila hid the letter in her shawl. Her compass fell open in the process, revealing that they were still on the right path. She would read the letter at night... When the others were asleep.

Onyx chirped happily next to her. She rode her camoda like she was born on its back. If there was anything Onyx couldn't do, Naila had yet to discover it. "Don't worry," Onyx stroked the animal's long fur. "They take a little time to get used to, but they're faster in the desert than your average chariot. We'll be in Isolon before you can blink."

"Here." Sephanya took a leafy branch out of her saddlebag and handed it to her. "Camodas take great pleasure in acacia."

"Thank you." Naila smiled shyly.

The Mehari, the nomadic group who had been kind enough to help her and her friends get to the border of Isolon, were unlike any Lemaians Naila had ever seen. She peeked at the girl from underneath her lashes. Such a beauty was she, her skin only a shade or two removed from ebony, with eyes the color of the clearest lagoon. Etched between her brows was a faint scar, like the hint of phæralei that hadn't fully bloomed. In fact, all the Mehari had those markings...

Naila wiggled the branch before the camoda's muzzle. It immediately snatched it, humming contently. The camoda wiggled until it had Naila's favored position. She scratched its hairy head with a little smile.

"*T'alfera ana emaya*," the Mehari girl whispered, beckoning to the beast. *You have brought me joy.* The Mehari's way of showing gratitude.

Naila thought it curious for someone other than her to say something like that to an animal, but then she remembered the Azag. She had thought it a monster, but it *had* been sentient. Naila followed the girl's lead and spoke the words to the camoda, "*T'alfera ana emaya.*"

The camoda grunted, spraying phlegm over the heated sand. To her delight, it shifted into a position even more comfortable.

"The Mehari have a special relationship with camodas." Sephanya patted her camoda with a hint of approval in her eyes. "One bound by æther."

Naila glanced over the train of camodas, but she couldn't see any telltale signs of the mysterious flames she had come to know intimately.

"I don't think they're using it now," Onyx whispered.

"What does a bond like that mean?"

"It means the Mehari can use both theirs and the camodas' bodies to generate æther. It makes them not only twice as powerful but also allows them to use the heightened senses of the animal."

A vision of the shadowreapers at the redwoods bled before Naila's eyes. Of their horses with eyes and hooves burning with flames.

"The shadowreapers! They can do it as well," she stated.

"It seems like the bad guys always draw the longer end of the stick, huh?" Onyx flicked a scarlet lock over her shoulder. "Maybe I should switch sides."

Naila grinned. They both knew Onyx would rather cut her hand off than betray her friends. And she, well, she'd never been one for power, but she wouldn't mind learning a trick or two.

"And we?"

"*Lai.*" Onyx hesitated, as if she were debating something internally, but then shook her head. "It's a ritual straight from the Unspokens, punishable by death."

Naila perked up in her saddle. "Why?"

What did it matter if the ritual came from the Unspokens, or no? The people already used æther, they might as well make their lives easier using this ritualistic bond.

"It gives you power over an animal's mind. And if people start there, who's saying they'll stop at animals? The šars fear these bonds, despite few having such a power. We do use it in a modified ritual, though. When consorts are bonded through the blood oath." Onyx peeked at Sephanya. When she saw the girl was occupied with throwing dried insects to Ro-Ro, she lowered her voice. "That's why you never become a concubine. At least as a consort, you can force your man to keep his appendage in his pants."

"I thought šars had harems," Naila whispered back.

"Šars, of course." Onyx waved dismissively. "But you can bend a lower-ranked suitor to your will."

Naila pursed her lips. It was not the answer she sought. All she could see was Silas and the harem his grandfather was bound to force on him. "Well, if you can't use it on animals, then why are the Mehari walking free?"

"Æther runs so strong in our bloodlines, my people bore many nergaylas since the age of the Unspokens," Sephanya answered in Onyx's stead. The girl had apparently eavesdropped the whole of their conversation.

Onyx batted her eyes innocently, but Sephanya just stared at the tangerine stains of the setting sun, her expression tranquil like the sight before her, as she tossed Ro-Ro the last contents of her insect-filled pouch. "Hundreds of summers ago, our *gavana* made a pact with Crishire's fourth Red Šar, Dayamon the Conqueror. To escape the lion pit, we had to hand over any nergayla born to us to the Red Šars. And so it has been ever since."

Naila tensed. She stared at Onyx, and then at Sephanya, unable to so much as blink. "They sacrificed children for power?"

"Don't judge my forebears too harshly, nergayla. It was a deal in name only and the Mehari knew it. It was either voluntarily giving up a child every four generations and safety for the rest of the tribe, or the Mehari got annihilated, our people sold off to the highest bidder, and we'd *still* have to sacrifice our nergaylas. Permission to perform the rite was just Dayamon patting us on the back."

"But it's just *wrong*."

"I know, but the curse of a leader is to make painful sacrifices for the good of their people."

The girl steered her camoda to walk closer to Naila's. Her lips pursed to a tight line. "I heard you mentioned them… Those worshippers of the Unspokens."

"You mean shadowreapers?" Naila frowned.

"You must not call their name so easily. There is power in a word."

"But the Mehari are so strong in æther. Even if they attacked us, what match would they be for dozens of you?" said Naila.

"Make no mistake. Even we cannot survive a shadowreaper's blade."

Unease reared inside Naila until it ensnared her like a merciless snake. "How so?"

"Their blades are poisoned. It takes but a scratch to enter your veins, feeding on æther until the infected dies. Like a curse come to life."

Naila clenched her fists around the reins of her camoda—Ro-Ro, swallowing the last of his snack, cocked his head in alarm—but she said no more. Not during the rest of the short day, when they trekked through mostly flat desert land with dunes scattered here and there; nor when they stumbled upon a ziggurat, made from rock and gold like Ishtar's temple. An empty circle locked with a colored one was carved above its entrance, instead of the diamond upon a crescent moon.

"Is that Sin and Shamash's temple?" Onyx gasped.

"It is," Silas said. He pulled the reins of his camoda, forcing the animal to slow its pace so he could ride next to them.

"Sin and Shamash?" asked Naila.

Silas tapped her nose. "Ever the girl with the questions." His eyes lingered on her lips, and she felt her heart pitter-pattering.

Sephanya inquired. "You do not know? They are the Legends of the divine twins, like Ishtar is to the stars of the maiden. Here in Crishire, the people crave their blessing even more than they covet the healing touch of a nergayla."

Silas murmured. "Naila is not from here."

He stared at the ziggurat with a faraway look, a smile tugging at the corner of his lips, as if he were absorbed in a long-lost memory. No matter how much he despised the reigning Red Šar, his brother, his *twin,* it didn't change the fact that Crishire was his fatherland. The one where he grew up from infant to boy, from boy to the cusp of manhood.

"Are they like Ishtar? As in, do they have powers too?" asked Naila, breathless. She forgot Ishtar wasn't the only Legend with a following among the Lemai. The hierodulas had mentioned a few, and Halfbeard and the sailors had mentioned the Legend Enki.

"Sin and Shamash have a different set of powers." Silas explained. "Mastering their gift of æther increases physical prowess, agility, speed. It breeds the perfect warrior. My paternal ancestors are gifted by the divine twins. Not like you, mind you, but strong in their own right."

It explained how Silas had held his own against a dreaded shadowreaper.

His jaw locked as the wistfulness left his eyes. Naila knew this didn't sit well with him. His twin had made Skeldor Crishire's sworn enemy, after all.

How ironic, considering the same blood flowed in their veins. Instead of reigning over the world as powerful allies, theirs was a fate of endless wars as bitter rivals.

Silas kneaded his arm absentmindedly. He winced before rearranging his features into the cocky smile that always ignited a kaleidoscope of butterflies in her stomach. "Let's not waste time on a history lesson. The view is much too beautiful for that," he said, eying her meaningfully.

He stuck out his hand for Naila to grasp, and she embraced the roughness of his palm against the softness of her own. His eyes darkened with unspoken words, but what was there to say? No matter how they felt about each other, their relationship had no future. The moment he was crowned Silver Šar, he'd be given a choice of the most beautiful women—all better suited than her. Surely he would forget her? Moreover, she would go back to Earth long before, to never again see the teasing glint in his eyes, never his smile, nor the dimple it carved on his chin...

"We will set up our tents at the temple," an elderly man at the front of the caravan bellowed.

He was all wrinkles and bent bones, but from the way the Mehari followed his lead, there was no doubt he was the one in charge. *Gavana*, Sephanya had called him. Naila barely heard him, however, or maybe she just didn't care, for worry ate away all her wonder and only one thought was on her mind.... .

Several bells later, when the sun had said its goodbye, and Iluna made her entrance, their woolen tents stood proudly between the terracotta dunes near the temple, as nests between the branches of a tree. Naila, Silas, Onyx, and Tryce shared a tent between the four of them, whereas Rē had opted to stay in a smaller tent on his own. He likely avoided Tryce's snores.

"I'll have you know plenty of *feylanas* fall for my charms," said Tryce, puffing his chest like a rooster trying to impress the hens. "On the Chimera, that *feylana*, Gispa, even begged to spend the night with me."

Onyx giggled, tears streaming down her face, as she rolled over the colorful rug. Tryce's face flushed into shades of red and purple. He spluttered indignantly over Onyx's outburst.

Onyx made a shooting gesture in the air, like firing an arrow at Tryce's heart. "That *feylana*, whose name is *Gizella*, spent many a night with your *baba*, little charmer."

Tryce's mouth dropped. "Always such a spoilsport."

Onyx stuck out her tongue. "Sorry, virgin."

"I-I ain' no virgin!"

Onyx arched a brow. "Uh, yes you are."

Tryce crossed his arms and pouted like a petulant child. "You don't know how many *feylanas* swooned before my, um, trembling... staff!"

Silas snorted. He threw a branch at Tryce's head. "Your talk needs work, virgin."

Tryce balled his hands to fists, but before he could speak, Naila interrupted, rolling her eyes. "There's nothing wrong with being a virgin. Absolutely no shame in being one." She tutted her mouth disapprovingly at Onyx and Silas, who shrugged in mock innocence.

Tryce scratched the back of his neck, embarrassment still tinting his cheeks.

Silas threw a stick on the little fire he'd made to roast a desert hare, while Naila watched his every move with hawk-eyes. His grip lacked its usual strength, and his normally tan skin was worrisomely pale. Scarabs buzzed and squawked outside, their tiny bodies hidden by the dark of the star-filled night, but still there was this agonizing silence. The silence of someone keeping secrets.

"All right, I know I'm a looker, but you've had several moons to get used to that."

Naila didn't laugh.

"How's your arm?"

Silas's brows shot up. He obviously wasn't expecting that question. Onyx and Tryce glanced at him with curiosity.

"You're hurt?" Onyx frowned.

"I'm not."

Naila pushed herself up from the embroidered rug the Mehari had gifted her. She crawled over to Silas and pushed up the sleeve of his left forearm.

"Hey!"

She gasped... Or was it the others? A black gash scarred Silas's forearm. Around it, the skin was a festering sickly green.

"How did that happen?" Onyx demanded, her posture rigid and alert.

But Silas didn't answer. Naila did.

"A shadowreaper's blade."

XXIX

AN OASIS OF MYSTERIES

THE DAYS in the desert passed like time in an hourglass, an endless stream of sand. The Mehari's caravan of camodas trudged through never-ending dunes, with majestic ziggurats, olive trees, and peyote cacti sprinkled here and there. Naila anticipated every sunrise, for it brought them that much closer to Isolon... and because of the growls of nocturnal animals that rendered her sleepless every night, even behind the safety of the Mehari's æther-coated tents.

Still, they were not moving fast enough.

Silas coughed.

Whilst the prince carried on as if no word was spoken about shadowreapers' blades, even he could not hide the pallor that seeped through his skin. He caught Naila's worried stare and shot her his most cocksure smile.

"Don't worry your pretty little head. I'm fine. Really."

She caught Onyx's gaze who also couldn't hide her worries.

Naila had tried to heal Silas ad nauseum, but all her attempts proved fruitless. If only she had had the time to complete Zarqa's tutoring.

"Maybe we should go back. To Skeldor, I mean," said Onyx.

Naila nodded. "There must be something your mother and Zarqa can think of."

Silas stared at them, hard. She knew what went through his mind. Going back meant she would miss her chance to get to Nebiru, but she couldn't let Silas die. She just couldn't.

"Though I suppose it will take weeks to get back to Havenmor..." Onyx sighed.

And by then Silas would be dead; Naila finished the sentence in her thoughts. "Well, there must be something we can do?"

"Naila, it's all right, really. I'm not that easy to kill." The prince cracked another smile. It was as believable as a red-handed thief pleading innocence. "When we get to Isolon, we'll find a nergayla. Besides, mother said I was chosen to help you for all that balance in the world nonsense, right? I can't do that if I'm dead."

Naila sighed, stroking her skittish camoda absentmindedly. "But the Mehari say they don't know a cure and they know a lot about nergaylas."

Silas groaned. "The Mehari aren't all-knowing."

Naila could tell that even he didn't believe his own words, but for his sake, for everyone's sake, she'd indulge him.

Onyx gnawed on her lip. "We could ask for Nova..."

Silas snorted, but Onyx continued hurriedly. "Levias may help if—"

"Levias would finish me off himself before waiting for the poison to do its job, and you know it, Red."

Onyx sucked in her slightly trembling lip. The fact that she didn't protest her much-disliked nickname was a testimony to how worried she was. "Maybe..." the huntress sighed and said no more. For once she held an unspoken conversation with Naila. The message was clear. If there was no nergayla in Isolon then they would search for Nova, whether Silas wanted it or not.

"*Gavana*, look, an oasis," a Mehari man cried.

Sure enough, in the distance, a group of palm trees stood proudly at the base of a small volcano. Behind them was the pale green of grassland and the rocks of a waterfall, fed by a narrow river. Mist alluded to the presence of a hot spring someplace in the middle. A sense of giddiness washed over Naila. She could finally have a normal bath after almost two weeks.

Tryce waved from the front of the caravan and rode toward them. Rē remained there, murmuring something to the chieftain. When the lad reached them, his eyes raked over Silas's frame. "Rē asked *gavana* to stop here. Don't ye die on us, *šargon*."

He stuck out his arm. Silas clasped it in return, in some sort of masculine comradely gesture, a weakish smile on his face.

The wind whistled gently, sending fine grains of sand brushing against their tent. Inside, the flame of an oil lamp cast the tent in dim light. Shadows danced across the canvas with the flame's every movement as though the night itself was restless.

Kneeling next to Silas, Naila wrung out a damp cloth in a bowl of cool water. The heat of his fever radiated like the desert sun, yet his eyes were oddly clear.

"You should drink more water," she said.

But he just stared at the ceiling, seemingly not hearing her words. "I was born in Crishire, but I never thought I'd die here too."

She swallowed.

So, he was finally past deluding others. She remembered the words in the šaltana's letter she had read earlier that night.

By the stars, the princess had written, *although I knew the day would come for my son to return to Crishire. If not by the call of his birth land, then surely by the call of his twin... or his late father's grave. My dearest Elijah.*

We were bound by blood, I being his only consort. He never visited the chambers of his concubines, Naila, despite everyone's objections. He loved me, as I loved him. I suspect we might have been star-fated: eternal soulmates blessed by the stars.

For your quest's sake, I hope you will not meet Silas's brother. Levias detests us, and it pains me to say his feelings toward me are justified. I have wronged him, kittling. I have done what no mother should ever be forced to do. I pray every day to the stars that he will find it in his heart to forgive me.

"Did... do you yearn for peace with your brother?"

Silas chuckled, squeezing his eyes shut. He shook his head before reopening his eyes. "We are well past diplomatic solutions."

"What happened?"

"Levias and I are twins... but we have different sires."

She sucked in a breath, didn't dare make a sound.

"My father, Elijah, was the love of my mother's heart. Theirs was a love so deep, grandfather couldn't but agree to give mother away as father's consort. It was a good match besides. Father was to be Crishire's Red Šar, you know. For he was the eldest, older than his twin Jericho."

Naila dabbed the droplets on his forehead but nodded encouragingly for him to continue.

"But my uncle Jericho had always been cunning, a snake who coveted status and treasures, and all things out of his reach. On his father's deathbed, before father could be crowned Red Šar, he murdered him. His own identical twin."

Silas squeezed his eyes shut as if in pain. "With the blood of my father still dripping off his fingers, he forced mother to be his concubine. Forced himself on her. That day she conceived twins: the son of the man she loved, and the son of the man she hated."

"Oh, Silas," Naila murmured.

"Mother was traumatized. She couldn't look at Levias, couldn't see him without seeing the man who had raped her and killed the man she loved. Her contempt for Jericho colored her actions... And while I will never condemn her for the actions she did out of suffering, my brother, too, was a victim. I still see his face, whenever she accepted my gifts with a warm smile and his with a cold shoulder..."

Silas smiled sadly, shaking his head. "I don't know why I'm remembering all of this."

She said no word. Only dabbed his forehead tenderly as he fell into a long deep sleep.

It was well past midnight when Onyx and Tryce returned, and even later when their breathing slowed to a deep rhythm. While Silas and Onyx did not make a sound, Tryce groaned as if in pain between his snores. At one particular moment, she could make out the word, '*baba.*' He put on a tough front, but she knew he wasn't anywhere near processing Halfbeard's death.

For her part, she couldn't sleep. Thoughts of Silas dying and shadowed eyes haunted her dreams, interlaced with a strange humming. A lure that whispered sweet, seductive words. Begging her to go outside, urging her to follow the lights.

She waited for another bell or so to make sure her friends were asleep. *Follow the lights.* She draped her shawl over her caftan and tiptoed out of the tent, finally giving in to the tugging sensation. The crescent moons glowed delicately in the star-adorned night, but palm tree leaves barred most of their light.

Le sigh.

She mentally berated herself for not bringing an oil lamp. Although, to be fair, it would attract critters of the night... Creatures, she'd rather not see.

She stiffened for a heartbeat when the crisp night breeze carried with it the sounds of the camodas, goats, and sheep in a nearby stable-tent and the whinnying of a horse somewhere in the distance. Naila let out a relieved breath. A wild horse seeking water, perhaps.

Dazed, she bypassed the Mehari tents and extinguished campfires until she reached a grass trail lit up by fireflies. *Follow the lights.* She figured it led to the oasis' hot spring. Leaving without the others was a dangerous idea, but Naila couldn't resist the tugging even if she wanted to.

Where would it lead?

Besides, dust stuck to every crevice of her skin. She was desperate for fresh, sandless air. The past weeks had been an upheaval of emotions. Halfbeard dying, being hunted by shadowreapers, and now Silas at death's door... And then the šaltana's story!

Poor, poor šaltana. To think that sweet woman had suffered such a tragedy. Naila needed to calm her restless mind. Soothe her throbbing heart. Dear heavens, did she need that well-deserved bath. Palm trees and desert rose bushes circled the meadow, alongside an almond tree in full bloom. All the while she followed the lights of the fireflies. Monkeys gibbered high in the trees and Naila spotted one of their curious rose faces in a fluffy shower of golden pelt.

"Why, hello there," she cooed.

The animal shrieked and jumped to a higher tree branch.

They're more frightened of me than I am of them.

It didn't take her long to spot the vapors of the geyser. A basket of white sand enclosed the rocky spring. Pale stones underneath the water ignited a scenic light under the ever-watching Iluna and her sister stars.

A perfect bath for a cool desert night.

She couldn't see the whole of the hot spring, however. Protruding rocks obscured half of it. After making sure the coast was clear, Naila disrobed and tiptoed into the inviting water. She sighed when her sore muscles found relief in the heat. Almond blossom petals floated on the surface, producing their familiar sweet, seductive scent. Even misery had a piece of heaven.

She unbraided her plait and ran her fingers through her midnight curls, which had grown over an inch since she came to the lands of Lemuria. It almost reached her waist. A cloud slid away slowly, unveiling the constellations written in the pages of the night. They lit the sky like diamonds sprinkled over opals. Naila lived for this moment. Its beauty reached so deep within her, it owned every hidden corner, every solemn place. Her fingers traced the outline of *Bellatrix* and *Alnitak* and the whole of *Orion*. Within no time, she located a hint of her own constellation Virgo—the star *Elgafar*.

She smiled. Elgafar... a perfect name for her new dagger.

Between the crickets and the monkey chatters, a bird whistled its distinctive song. It didn't need to be the loudest to rule the night with its powerful melody. The nocturnal sounds were a lullaby to her ears. She knew she had to get back, but this place was an Elysium. Just for a little while, she'd close her eyes and forget...

Those shadowed eyes beckoned her, and the fates mocked her anew. More than anyone, she knew what was at stake. Since long before history, they had made that sacrifice for the greater good. The end of all things should not come to fruition, or else everything had been for naught. But the song of her soul disagreed profusely. It scratched and screamed at her to answer the call. Together, they were strongest.

Together, they would conquer.

With a start, Naila roused to the burbling of water. A sense of peril struck her like lightning. Her heart hammered in alarm.

"Here I thought no one but me knew of this place," a deep, velvety voice echoed.

A handsome man emerged from the shadows. He sat but a rock away in the geyser. Not Mehari, not shadowreaper, but a stranger. How could she have missed his presence? Naila ducked into the water until it covered her to her chin.

The stranger smirked and Naila forgot how to breathe. His face was all angles, with a proud mouth, and thick, golden hair that reached his broad sun-kissed shoulders. But it was his eyes that demanded full attention—shades of the ocean at midnight. They lured her into endless depths of promise... Of peril. Although a smile wreathed his face, everything about him oozed danger.

The water rippled as the man inched closer until the rock no longer separated them. It belatedly dawned that, like her, he was fully naked. Naila didn't dare let her gaze travel the skin the water left bare. The stranger's arms stretched sideways over the rocks as if he owned her little hot spring.

"How long have you been here?" She hated how hoarse her voice sounded.

"A while."

"It's not nice to join a lady in a bath you weren't invited to."

"I never claimed to be a gentleman." His dark, calculating eyes took in her face. "And it would do you well to remember more dangers lurk in the dark than desert lions."

"Is that a threat?" Naila scowled.

He reached for one of her wet inky tendrils and twirled it around his finger, studying it with a hint of possessiveness in his eyes. As if like the hot spring, he now owned Naila too. A flush rose from the tips of her toes to the very roots of her hair, leaving a field of goosebumps in its wake, even though she was well submerged in the steaming water. She tried to pull away, but he didn't let go. His gaze was firm and intense. *Too intense.*

After a few breathless moments, she broke off their eye contact.

"Nergayla… You appeared out of nothing mere weeks ago and already the lands of Lemuria are filled with tales of your beauty." His deep, husky voice lowered several tones. "I must say, for once, the rumors hold true."

"You did your homework, huh?"

"The world doesn't belong to the weak." He let go of her hair and ignored her glare. She scurried away. "Nor to the strong. It belongs to those with knowledge."

"To those who intimidate and manipulate, you mean."

"Effective tools, I admit. But in time, both are worthless in the hands of a fool."

There was something achingly familiar about him, even though she'd never seen him before. Naila narrowed her eyes at the nearby bushes. Behind them, an equally familiar black stallion grazed contently, neatly folded traveling leathers fastened to his saddle.

"You! You're that guy from the redwoods."

And the man of her visions. The nightmare she had just awakened from…

"And so we meet again."

"Who are you? You promised me your name," she demanded while watching his face with hawk-eyes for any sign of a lie.

"I go by Reuben."

Reuben… like the deceased Dragon Lord who had been Silas's oldest brother. Well, cousin, considering Jericho the Cruel had been Silas's uncle, not his father.

"I'm Naila."

"I know."

"Well, Reuben, it's time for me to leave."

Naila waited for him to turn so she could get out of the water and get dressed, but he made no effort to do so.

She huffed in annoyance. "Close your eyes now."

Reuben shot her a lopsided grin.

"What for? I've been sitting here"—he pointed a long ring-clad finger to the surrounding spring—"for well over a bell before you woke. I assure you there's nothing left to hide."

Naila's cheeks flamed in indignation. *How dare he.* Against her better judgment, not caring that he was taller and stronger than her, that he was no doubt a man few would dare to cross, she had to put him in his place. "Didn't your mother teach you any manners? I'm sure she'd be ashamed of you spying on innocent naked girls."

Reuben's face was unreadable, but she saw a hint of danger behind his dark eyes.

"It's a good thing, then, that I have no mother." He tilted his head sideways and regarded her as if she were a fascinating painting from a brilliant artist. "But it wouldn't have made a difference if I did. People are in the business of pleasing me, not the other way around."

"Arrogant, much?"

Naked or not, she made to leave.

He grasped her arm in a soft but firm grip. "Sit down," he ordered as if he were a warlord and she his soldier. His tone left no room to argue.

Naila's pulse fluttered like the wings of a caged hummingbird. Why had she thought it a good idea to leave the safety of her tent for a senseless bath? Now here she was, at the mercy of this stranger.

Reuben let go of her and rested his head on his hand, his elbow leaning on the rock behind him. His eyes grazed the *fayalobi* clipped in her hair with approval, which made her wish she had sold it. Then they lowered.

"That compass... Where did you get it?"

Naila glanced at Philly's little moonstone compass resting atop her heaving chest. "It was a gift."

"A precious gift it was."

Curiosity warred with fear within Naila.

"Do you..." she hesitated, "Do you know more about it?"

"The insignia of the opening clip"—Naila's eyes trailed the small infinity sign Reuben mentioned—"is the royal crest of the Unspokens."

She remembered Silas had hinted at it being from the Unspokens, but a royal crest?

"W-What?" Naila grasped his steely bicep, completely forgetting they were indecent. She noticed faint markings on his left arm, but the steam made it difficult to see.

He arched a brow in amusement.

Heat crept up her cheeks; she let his arm go at once.

She settled back against the rocky wall, her fingers brushing her compass pendant. Her father had possessed an heirloom from the Unspokens. The Ænunaki. He never found it at a Maroon market... That raised the question: Where *did* he get it from?

Reuben narrowed his eyes. "It seems you are telling the truth."

He let the words linger, but Naila paid them no heed. She clicked her compass open and closed. The needle still pointed to the southeast, where Isolon stood. "Why would I lie?"

"You wouldn't be the first scavenger to plunder the Unspokens' ruins, and try to sell their artifacts for blood crystals."

Naila chewed on her lip. This stranger seemed to know a lot... Maybe he knew something that could help Silas.

"Hey, do you know something about shadowreaper blades?"

"A rather random question, but, *yana*, I do know a thing or two." His eyes twinkled. "However, everything comes at a price, including information."

Naila pursed her lips. She wasn't sure she'd like what he would say. "What price?"

"Simple. I answer your question, and you answer mine."

That was it? Naila nodded hesitantly—she had nothing to hide, after all. She worded her question clearly and carefully.

"Is there an antidote to the poison of a shadowreaper's blade?"

"There is."

Naila couldn't keep herself from breaking out in a smile. So there was a cure. Silas would be safe. "What is it? Tell me."

"No."

Reuben shook his finger. "It is my turn now. Which land are you from?"

"I'm from Earth," she answered without batting her eyes.

Let him fester on where that was. His expression, however, didn't reveal any of his thoughts. If the information surprised him, he was quite good at hiding it. *Never mind that.* Naila had to word her following question precisely, so she could cut their conversation short and go back to her friends.

"How can I get the cure?"

Reuben clasped his hands behind his head and studied her through hooded eyes.

"You really want that cure, I see... But *you* are not hurt. One of your friends then."

Naila lowered her eyes. This man was highly perceptive.

"Your answer."

"It is called *iscias*, the most precious of antidotes, for it takes two winters to brew and the æther of a nergayla who has fully come into her power... It takes *all* of the nergayla's power. A blood crystal, you see."

Naila sucked in a gasp. Her vision blurred with tears of terror, of hopelessness. So close, yet so far.

"So, there is no hope then..." she mumbled to herself as a tear trailed down her cheek to drop into the steaming water.

Reuben's finger curled under her chin and he lifted her face to meet his oceanic gaze. He brushed his calloused thumb over the sensitive skin of her cheek and caught another tear. An unfamiliar flush of warmth smoldered low in her body.

"Every self-respecting šar has iscias, so what you need to do is bargain with one."

"The Silver Šar would never have a remedy such as that!"

Reuben scoffed. "That weak old man is a fool. When shadowreapers infiltrate Skeldor and poison it to the core, he shall realize his mistake."

"He's not a fool." Naila frowned and pushed his hand away. "He's just... And I fully understand why he'd not make such a foul elixir. It's wrong. At least the Silver Šar's heart is filled with love."

"Love you say?" His face lit up with mock amusement. "Of all things, love is the most powerful curse. It makes us yearn for that which we cannot have, torments us with visions of our loved one's death, and tears us apart when it inevitably happens. Love kills more than any poison."

"And still, I'd choose it a thousand times over the atrocity of a sacrifice."

"So you say, but will you leave your friend to die?"

A lump caught in her throat. Just the thought of Silas dying haunted her day and night. How precious he had become in such a short period. As much as she despised iscias, could she really reject it if it kept Silas from certain death?

"If not the Silver Šar, then who can I go to?" Naila questioned. Even as she said those words, she already knew the answer, and she didn't like it. Not at all. "The Red Šar, he has iscias, doesn't he?"

Reuben kept his silence as if waiting for her to continue.

"He won't help me."

"It depends..." He pushed his lip to the side with his thumb while thinking. "But it will come at a steep price. Now for my last question. How far are you willing to go to save your friend?"

Naila stared at him, wide-eyed. She knew something as rare and coveted as iscias would have to be paid off with something worth just as much. If iscias was worth a nergayla's life... Still, no matter her words, she knew to the marrow of her bones she would do anything to save Silas.

Understanding dawned on the planes of Reuben's face. He knew her answer. She didn't have to speak it out loud.

Reuben rose out of the pool, not attempting to cover his nudity. He was magnificent, his virile beauty a piece of art—like God had spent extra time carving him out of flesh and bone, not stopping until he was perfect. With his back half toward her, she, at last, saw the markings inked on his left arm. A black serpentine dragon. Its scaly body curled around his arm, while its horned head opened its menacing jaws on his muscled chest.

"Whisperers say the Red Šar left Irkalla to visit his summer palace in Lethos. The Mehari will show you the way," said Reuben.

The Mehari? So he had spied on them, and they had never so much as seen him or his stallion.

"Why should I trust you?"

He glanced back one last time and, in a flash, his eyes reminded her who she spoke to... That shadowed gaze from her dreams held one clear message: stay away.

A hint of a smile tugged at the corner of Reuben's mouth.

"You shouldn't."

XXX

BLEEDING SCARS

A SOFT, FEATHERED head rubbed against the apple of Naila's cheek, easing her out of a dream filled with skulls, flames, and a pair of shadowed eyes. She massaged her temples, seeking to soothe the pounding behind her eyes before her sight came into focus. It was Ro-Ro. He shuffled his wings, drawing her attention to a silver-edged letter bound to his foot.

"You're back." Naila scratched the bird behind its head.

He picked at her finger, demanding a snack.

Naila reached for her pouch of dried scarabs she kept just for him. "Such a good boy, flying through a cold desert night just to get to me," she cooed, praising the bird.

Ro-Ro puffed his feathered chest and nudged her gently.

"Another letter from Mother? What do you two keep gossiping about?" Silas rubbed the sleep out of his eyes, his face impossibly pale.

"Obviously you." Tryce yawned.

The look on Silas's face told her he did not like that idea at all.

He beckoned the bird with a slight tremble to his fingers. With a swift movement, Ro-Ro went to the prince's side, but not before Naila snatched the letter away.

"Do not tell mother I'm sick," Silas warned.

Naila shifted in her seat, not meeting his eyes. *Too late.*

"Naila..." His voice grew impossibly low.

She jumped up, collecting her satchel. "I think I smell food. Let's not make the others wait."

Before Silas could utter another word, she scurried out of the tent into the heat of the morning sun.

As they resumed their odyssey through the red desert—Naila rode with Tryce and Rē in an attempt to avoid Silas's prying—she pondered over Reuben's words. The Red Šar possessed iscias. Now she had the impossible task of convincing Silas to swallow his pride and request the rare concoction of the brother he so despised. *Cunning and vicious, a war-hungry snake,* is what Tryce had called this twin of Silas's. Would he kill them then and there if ever he saw them? But the alternative was Silas dying...

"Say, how far is Lethos?" Naila asked nonchalantly, as if talking about the weather.

"Lethos? What's that, a tavern?" yawned Tryce.

Rē cuffed the boy's head.

"Ho!" Tryce protested, almost falling off his camoda.

"It is the city of scholars, you fool. The birthplace of philosophers like Kalam Amar-Sin who wrote *The Debate Between the Stars and the Legends* and the poet Hamaru who gifted us the verses we sing at Firefalls."

"Oh, *that* Lethos." Tryce grinned sheepishly. He frowned and turned to Naila. "Why're ye asking?"

She shrugged. "Just wondering."

Tryce did not look convinced.

"There is no way to know for sure, although it cannot be too far from Isolon's border," said Rē. "Šars keep the detailed maps of their empires close to their chest. The less your enemy knows, the higher your element of surprise. Make no mistake, we would die in this desert if we did not have the Mehari."

"Wow, y'sure know a lot."

"I just pay attention."

"Do you think the Mehari know where it is?" asked Naila.

Tryce's gaze turned sharp. "We should try to evade the Red Šar's notice, not dance in front of him with a sign that screams 'we're here'."

"Right," said Naila, conflict burning on her face.

"Here." Rē held out a chunk of manna bread to her. A sweet gesture, which might have made her smile, if his ethereal face wasn't so stoic as usual. Did he bottle up all his emotions? A remnant from his vicious slavery days, perhaps.

"It's okay." Naila shook her head. She had lost all feelings of hunger.

Sometime later the chieftain said in his wavering voice, "You are silent, *feylana*."

Naila shot up in her saddle. The sun glowed ginger on the horizon. She'd been so lost in thought, playing with her compass, she hadn't noticed the elderly man riding next to her at all. Draped in deep-blue robes, countless wrinkles folded his ebony skin, and the rings of cataracts paled his azure eyes.

"Huh, oh, I-I just didn't sleep very well."

"The red desert is dangerous if you do not know its dwellers, but we Mehari know these regions since the age of the Unspokens. Rest assured, you are safe from the creatures of the night... and tonight we shall have even more shelter."

Naila wasn't too worried about the nocturnal beasts. While she had heard their sounds aplenty, peculiarly, none had come across her path the night before. The chieftain's words, however, piqued her interest.

"Why is that? Are we close to Isolon?"

He pointed at the distance. Naila followed the direction with her eyes. The sight had completely bypassed her: a vast plain of mountains painted against the twilit sky, their peaks hidden by tufts of mist. Smoky mists drifted aside, revealing a ziggurat embedded in their midst.

"We will stay overnight at Gomorra in the smoky mountains."

"Gomorra?"

She could swear excitement lit up his eyes. "It is an ancient ruin from the age of the Unspokens. A temple dedicated to Marduk, Legend to the stars of the divine scales."

Libra... Philly's favorite Legend of the Sky.

By the time they reached Gomorra, the sky had dipped in darkness, the bright stars of Virgo their only guiding lights.

"*Gavana*." A young man sped to them, his camoda grunting all the way. "*Gavana*," he repeated, "Our scout detected *doran* horses a half day's ride from here."

The chieftain's hunched back straightened a little. "Make haste," he ordered. "I want everyone sheltered in Gomorra in one bell's time."

Naila's stomach fell. She didn't like the sound of it at all.

"What's going on?" she asked.

Tryce's mouth thinned. "Shadowreapers," he spat.

How? *How* did they keep finding them?

As they rushed toward the ancient ruins of Gomorra, its gate at the foot of a rocky mountain came into sight. The corners of the ziggurat stretched into the adjoining mountains and the top high above into the sky. Naila froze at the sight that met her. Two immense statues framed the gate, as if guarding it. Her eyes wandered over the muscles of their calves, the lean lines of their thighs and abdomens.

Their bodies spoke of tales when the world was young, and the very essence of masculinity took its first breath. Broad-shouldered and toned to perfection, they embodied the perfect warrior. Out of their backs sprouted powerful wings, whilst their hands carried strange weapons akin to long triple-edged swords. Naila knew without a doubt, no soldier alive or dead came close to the power these statues possessed.

Peculiarly, their faces were hidden by helmets of horror, which reminded her of the tengus she had seen in mangas: half man, half bird.

"Impressive, nay?" said Rē, as he observed her through unreadable eyes.

"Are they supposed to be Marduk?"

"*Lai*. They, Naila, are the Unspokens."

For a moment, Naila forgot to breathe.

To finally see the Ænunaki, even if not in the flesh... Her heart thumped in her throat. How could there be such beauty in such cruelty? Her mind wandered to the faces behind the masks. Would they look human, like the Lemai? Like *her*?

Onyx and Silas trudged toward them, while the Mehari gathered around the gate. Watching. Waiting. There was no handle to open the stone doors, no slit they could squeeze through.

"Okay, what now?" Onyx frowned.

Sephanya appeared as if called. "Watch."

The chieftain slashed his palms open with a blade of black gold and pressed his bloodied hands on the gate. Æther sprang from his fingers and spread like a wildfire over the intricate carvings. For a few moments, nothing else happened. Then the clouds drifted away to unveil Iluna. Her soft beams caressed the flames. They flared almost as bright as the sun itself. With a heavy groan, the stone doors opened, exposing an infinite hall of darkness.

"That's why he's *gavana*, the Mehari's strongest," Sephanya whispered. "His strength in æther is second only to that of the nergaylas."

The chieftain entered the hall with several of his men. Sephanya strolled after them, leaving Naila and her friends staring. They lit up a torch at the entrance and, like domino stones, a row of torches ignited in the hall. No, not exactly a hall, but stone stairs that led below the mountain.

"Come," Rē said.

After everyone entered Gomorra, the chieftain closed the gate the same way he had opened it. And so, they started their way around the ancient ruins that had once belonged to the Unspokens. *The Ænunaki.* It was utterly silent, aside from the camodas' grunts, the bleating of sheep and goats, and Ro-Ro's occasional squawks. The stairs, fortunately, were flat enough for the camodas to descend with little difficulty.

"Look at that," Naila whispered.

She held a tallow candle to the walls. They were painted with ancient symbols and beautiful winged maidens with phæralei like Naila's. Chokers with gilded stones decorated their delicate necks. Onyx, too, pushed a candle to the ceiling to examine the murals. Dozens of people were drawn in a circle. In the middle was a painted stone split in two—half golden and half shadowed. The gilded half was the same stone the maidens wore.

"Oh, wow." Onyx beamed.

They were like little girls in a shop filled with sweets.

The stairs went on and on. Naila's feet ached after what seemed like a week, although she knew it couldn't be more than a bell. She felt a blister or two form at her ankles. Silas's breathing grew heavier and heavier.

Rē offered Silas to lean on him.

Silas, obviously in denial of his worsening state, snapped, "I can walk by myself."

Rē shrugged. "Suit yourself."

Naila said a quick prayer that they'd arrive at their shelter soon. Silas was deteriorating faster than she had expected. After what seemed like ages, the stairs finally ended, making way for a hall filled with more murals and sculptures.

"This place is filled with statues of the Unspokens," Naila said.

Clad in intricate armor, with majestic, feathered wings, they looked as imposing as the ones at the gate.

"Seems like it," Onyx mumbled.

"So, they had wings?"

"They're always shown like that," Tryce mumbled behind them. "But *Baba* found some of their skeletons in the Ice Caves and those were wingless. They looked exactly like Lemaians, is what 'e said. Well, maybe a 'lil taller."

"How did he know those skeletons weren't just Lemaians?" Onyx asked, skeptical.

"He just know... *knew* those things."

Naila hit her foot against a gilded chest. "Ouch."

"What is it?" Onyx dashed toward her, an arrow already drawn into her fingers.

As if this abandoned temple held any threats... Naila shuddered. Dear heaven, she sure hoped it didn't.

"Just an empty chest."

"Weird."

"People make a good crystal scavenging the Unspokens' ruins. They even found rituals to enhance æther; Irkalla's walls were built that way. That's why they're unbreachable... Not even a hurricane can put a dent in them," said Silas, rubbing his injured arm absentmindedly. He was impossibly pale.

"Wow," Naila said.

She was even more impressed that Suzano Stormhold had led the Lemaians to victory against these powerful Unspokens. If hurricanes couldn't hurt them, then what could?

A Mehari man urged, "We cannot delay."

They trudged through several halls before they stumbled upon another massive hall with a door they could lock. Or at least, the chieftain could. There was a small opening in the ceiling that led to the night's view outside. Large enough for birds, but too small for anything else.

"We rest here," the chieftain said.

Tryce and Onyx set up the rugs and cushions. "Ugh, that rukha pooped on my rug," the former complained while Naila tended to Silas, his head resting in her lap. His fingers reached up, caressing her cheek, sending little shivers through the whole of her body.

"I miss your smile," he whispered.

"You'll see it when you get better," she said.

Silas tried to crack a smile, but the effort pushed him into a coughing fit. She gently wiped the sweat off his forehead with a cloth. Her heart squeezed painfully when she noticed the sickly green from his left arm had spread to his neck. Climbing the stairs had claimed a lot of his energy... *His æther.* They had no choice. Ruthless or no, they would have to see the Red Šar.

She plucked up all her courage to broach the subject.

"Guys, I think I have an idea how to heal Silas."

Silas's eyes fluttered open. He ignored Naila's protests to push himself up. "What?"

Naila's hopes of convincing her friends crumbled to dust when she told them about her nighttime endeavor.

"Didn't that rat Jacobo teach ye not to wander on yer own?" Tryce scolded.

"You could've been kidnapped or raped, N." Onyx threw her hands up.

"And we wouldn't have been there to help you," Silas finished. "How do you think that would make us feel?"

Naila winced. Yes, they were right. In hindsight, she knew it. She couldn't explain why, but there was nothing that could have stopped her from going to that hot spring, danger or no. And... it worked out for the best. There was a solution for Silas if only she could make her friends see it. To her surprise, it was Rē who came to her rescue.

"What is done is done," he clipped. "Let's hear what she has to say."

In one breath, Naila told them about Reuben—Silas turned even paler—and about iscias and the fact the Red Šar had it.

"Reuben?" Silas frowned.

"Yes, that was your eldest cousin's name, wasn't it?" she mumbled.

"The one who died in war," Rē stated.

Surprised he knew about this too, Naila waited for Rē to continue. The rest of his communication was in pure silence, however, via a surly look on his flawless face. She was a bit of an introvert herself, but at the very least she tried to strike up a conversation when people were around. Grumpy Rē, though, couldn't be bothered when he didn't feel like it. Not now, and certainly not in the past few weeks.

"Crishire and Ornesias were at war for over a hundred seasons until six winters ago, when Jericho the Cruel, his heir Reuben, and his other sons met the Golden Šar in battle. Crishire conquered Ornesias, but Levias was the only one of his family to mysteriously survive. They crowned him Red Šar then and there, at the mere age of seventeen," Onyx said in Rē's stead, "It was a victory that named him Levias the Magnificent."

"You think he killed his father and brothers?"

"No one ever found their bodies. But it wouldn't surprise me if Levias did. There's nothing he wouldn't do to get what he wants. You're naïve to think he would help me. If I die, Skeldor is his by default, as we're the only male heirs to grandfather's throne," said Silas.

This was a different version from what Mr. Thoth had told her, although he had warned her of many rumors. The thought of facing Silas's brother frightened her more than ever. What a ruthless colonizer. Something dawned on her. "What if Reuben is still alive? And he *was* that guy from yesterday?"

Silas scoffed. "If Reuben was alive, he wouldn't send me to Levias for iscias. He is, *was* the most noble of my cousins."

"Wait a minute. You don't seem surprised at all about this," Naila said as she regarded Silas's calm expression. "You knew about *iscias*. You knew, and you didn't tell us."

"We all knew, N," Onyx whispered, not meeting her eyes.

"But as you said," continued Silas, "It's a remedy that sacrificed a nergayla. One life for another. The chances of getting iscias are slim to none. Our best chance is to get to Isolon and ask the Black Šar for help. He, at least, isn't Skeldor's adversary."

Onyx chewed on her lip.

Naila knew she wouldn't need much convincing, not if it meant saving Silas's life, but she was too angry with Onyx's deception. "When were you going to tell me?" she squeaked. She held up her hand when Silas opened his mouth. "No, *were* you ever going to tell me?"

The silence that followed told her all she needed to know.

"I can't believe this. I thought we were in this together."

Silas ran his fingers through his damp hair, a telltale sign he was frustrated. "You were already so depressed with recent events, you would've only blamed yourself and what use would that have been?"

Naila tutted.

"Don't give me that look, you know I'm right."

"I'm not a baby," she said.

Silas grasped her hand, but she shook it off.

"Maybe we should sleep this off. Give Naila's suggestion some thought," Onyx said, shooting Silas a shrewd look.

"No. I'd rather die than go to Levias," Silas gritted.

Onyx's cheeks flamed with irritation. "Don't be rash, Silas, Skeldor needs you."

Naila narrowed her eyes. "You of all people know how guilt eats away at you. Don't make me stay behind like that. Don't make me the cause of your death. Don't. Be. A. Coward."

Tryce sucked in a breath at the same time Onyx exclaimed, "Naila, watch your tone. Silas is heir to the throne of Skeldor!"

Silas squeezed Onyx's hand to silence her.

"Say I reach out to Levias... there are worse things than death. He could use me to blackmail Grandfather into doing his bidding."

Naila hadn't thought about that.

"But he's also your twin," Naila whispered, her tear-stained eyes not leaving Silas's gaze. "If there's anyone who can get through him, it should be you."

Silas shook his head, sadness shadowing his face.

"Levias is in a dark place where I can no longer reach him."

Naila took his hands into hers. They were big still, and strong, but devoid of color and so, so cold.

"What happened? Help me understand."

She shivered at the flash of anguish she saw in the depths of his indigo eyes. Ro-Ro humped onto Silas's shoulder, bumping his cheek in affection, as if he could sense the prince's sadness.

"You know my uncle forced Mother to be his concubine. She turned into a shell of her former self, withering away like a dying flower with every passing day in the hands of that tyrant. Grandfather waged war with Crishire, spared no effort to get her back, but ultimately failed. Irkalla's walls are simply unbreachable and *ut Asanatæ,* perhaps the strongest legions in the lands of Lemuria."

Silas swallowed.

Naila stroked his hands in hopes she could ease his pain, but he only grimaced.

"Nova had her vision when mother was pregnant with me and Levias, the one where she claimed one of our fates was entangled with Ishtar's Chosen. But the vision also revealed something else: that person would either be her redemption or her curse."

Silas chuckled humorlessly.

"My mother, innocent as she's gullible, believed Nova. She thought it to be me. In her desperation to save this chosen one from Jericho's influence, she convinced Nova to help us escape. Nova arranged to smuggle us out. I guess she believed her own nonsense. But the Red Palace's walls have many ears, and someone betrayed us. Jericho caught us just as we were about to board a wagon to Skeldor."

Naila stopped stroking his hands as horror overwhelmed her.

"Jericho said he'd indulge Mother and accept her leaving, but she could only take one son with her. Either that or keep us both and stay. I think he thought she'd choose the latter, but Nova's prophecy drove Mother's actions. She would do anything to prevent me from becoming Ishtar's curse, so that meant keeping me out of Jericho's claws, no matter the price."

"Oh, Silas." Naila covered her mouth as a tear trailed down the apple of her cheek.

"She did what no mother should ever be forced to do. She chose me and left my twin behind... That night grows vague with time, but one memory will always stay with me: the moment Mother made her choice and I saw something break inside Levias. The moment his eyes died... We used to be close, Lev and I."

Silas's eyes became empty pools of devastation. Naila could see him swallow back his emotions. More tears dripped down her cheeks as she did what he couldn't do—express his sorrow. For the šaltana, for him, and for his poor brother, who had been abandoned by his mother into the hands of his sadistic father.

"Jericho never allowed us to write to him. By the time we could, Levias already started to antagonize Skeldor. Jericho brainwashed him. Mother still sends Lev letters, but I don't know why she tries. Not after all he's done... Is *still* doing.

"There won't be a happy ever after. It's too late for that," Silas concluded with a tone of finality.

Naila frowned. It was clear Silas still held affection for his brother, even if grudgingly. Surely Levias must feel the same way?

She made to reply, but Onyx shook her head in alarm. Tomorrow, Onyx mouthed, perhaps sensing that a good night's sleep might make Silas more susceptible to Naila's plan.

It took a long time for Naila to fall asleep. A tremble in the stones, however, dragged her out of her shadowed dreams. She pushed herself up, rubbing the sleep out of her eyes. The hall was filled with whispers and the nervous bleating of the camodas and the herd. Several torches were already alight, and everyone was wide awake. Sure enough, the vibrations of stones grinding together echoed through Gomorra again. Dirt from the stone ceiling rained on their faces.

A Mehari scout dashed into the hall, his eyes wide with fear.

"Shadowreapers," he spat. "Dozens of them."

XXXI

THE MISTS OF GOMORRA

TRAPPED, THEY were trapped.

Naila paced around the rugs, waiting for word from Rē and Onyx, who were drawn into a heavy conversation with the chieftain, while she was left behind, watching over a pale, sleeping Silas. Most of the Mehari were also crowded near the chieftain on the other side of the chamber. Ro-Ro squawked, spreading his wings for yet another flight. The bird was as restless as she. As anxious as all of them.

"How could they open Gomorra's gate?" someone whispered in an urgent tone.

"Isn't it obvious? They brought a nergayla with them," Sephanya's father answered.

A nergayla . . ?

A clang thrummed through the stale air of Gomorra's hallways, followed by a forbidding silence. The shadowreapers drew closer. It was simply a matter of time before they found Naila and her allies... and there was nowhere to flee. Naila dove for Silas, clutching his sleeping body into her arms. He groaned weakly. His eyes fluttered open and she knew then and there he would not make it past that week.

Silas rubbed the sleep out of his eyes. "What's going on?"

"Shadowreapers," she whispered.

At once he straightened, his eyes filled with alarm. He reached for his scimitar, even though he was in no position to fight.

Like seawater lashing against the doors of a sinking ship, indigo flames seeped through the cracks of the hall's door. A gasp. More cries. The flames simmered over the carvings of the stones, sparing only the stain-free wall behind Naila. Not to destroy, but to seek… someone.

For some reason, those petrifying flames made her think of the woman in the redwoods.

"Morgana," Tryce snarled as he cocked his head to the dissipating embers.

Her head shot up. The youth leaned against a nearby wall. Naila hadn't seen him approach. He apparently had learned from Rē, his idol, how to be silent as a stormless wind.

"Shadowreapers snatched her as a babe from under Jericho's nose." Tryce made a grabbing movement. "Bards still sing the tale of her abduction, y'know."

"How do you know it's her?" asked Naila doubtfully.

"The hue of her æther. A nergayla's is usually close to purple," Silas mumbled.

He pushed himself up but failed to hide his wince.

Naila cringed at the sight but refrained from drawing him into another argument.

Her mind wandered to a curious fact. The æther she had used, had been golden, not blue.

"So, æther always comes in shades of blue, never in another color?" Naila said hesitantly, not sure she wanted to know. Knowledge only made things more complicated. And she, well, let's just say, she felt a certain kinship with ostriches sticking their heads in sand. All she wanted was to save Silas and find Nebiru. If she could do that, everything would go back to normal again. She reached for Silas's cold hand. If she said this often enough, a lie may just become the truth.

"*Yana*, although the scrolls do say the Unspokens had æther like blood. Take that as ye will. I bet it's false, just like those wings of theirs," said Tryce.

"Never mind that," said Silas, impatiently. "Tell me what's been going on."

As they filled him in, his face turned grim. "Does *gavana* know a way out?"

Tryce shrugged. "If there's anyone who does, I bet it's him."

Silas went to join Onyx and Rē.

Ro-Ro settled on Tryce's shoulder, his noble head taking in the walls. Just the thought of being stuck inside this hall, vast or no, made Naila claustrophobic too. Naila's eyes wandered back to Silas's sickly frame. If they came to blows with the shadowreapers, there was no way they could avoid every poisonous blade. So many would die...

She met Tryce's gaze. He too frowned over Silas's state.

"D'ye really think the Red Šar will help?"

In truth, she didn't know, but Reuben seemed to think she stood a chance. Every fiber in her being knew not to trust the stranger, but this, she knew, was no lie on his part.

She nodded.

Tryce pushed himself off the wall, much to Ro-Ro's hooting displeasure. The bird seemed quite fascinated with the wall, as if it was the most impressive thing it had ever seen. Tryce sighed as if resigned. "Then we need to get to Lethos... if we can escape this place, that is."

Naila couldn't help a smile. At last *someone* was coming around.

Ro-Ro fluttered to Naila. She stroked its head. "What's up, Ro-Ro? Why are you acting so weird, huh?"

The bird cocked its head at the blank stones of the wall and squawked.

"Yes, it's a wall. There's nothing of use for us there, little one."

Ro-Ro, however, didn't agree with her disinterest and flew excitedly to the wall, his hooked beak tipping at the blank stones. When Naila made no move, he fluttered back and forth, cackling impatiently.

Tryce made a circling gesture with his finger. "That bird is cuckoo."

Naila sighed. With another hoot from Ro-Ro, she finally joined the raptor at the wall and put her hands on her hips. "Okay, I'm here. What now?"

She'd barely uttered the words when a faint indentation in the wall gleamed in the dim lights of the chamber. It was so narrow one could easily miss it if not looking closely. Naila followed the indentation, her heart fluttering as she realized what it was.

"Is that...?" Tryce's words lingered in the air.

A hidden door. Perhaps one that led out of Gomorra.

"Guys..." Naila called. "I think we found something."

Mere moments later, all, including the chieftain, assembled around Ro-Ro and the wall.

"It's a secret passage," *gavana* said in astonishment as his wrinkled hands caressed the chalky rock. From the breach in the ceiling, a thin shaft of moonlight illuminated the uncarved stones. "But where does it lead, I wonder?"

Silas knocked on the door. An echoing sound answered, confirming a hollow space behind it. "Do you think it leads to outside?"

The chieftain's lips thinned. "Possibly. Gomorra is full of hidden passages created by its owners; the mists of Gomorra, my grandfather's father, used to call them. Yet I have never encountered a hidden passage here in all my seventy winters."

The chieftain's mouth opened in awe as he stared at the hidden gateway as if he couldn't quite believe his eyes.

"If there's any chance it can lead outside, then we need to risk it," Naila said. Ro-Ro squawked as if in agreement.

"There's no lock, though," said Onyx. "Do you think we can break it open? Maybe with scimitars—"

"Not so fast, *feylanas*." The chieftain held up his hand. His eyes were wary. "With the Unspokens, things are never easy. We do not know what hides within the dark of these mountains. Legend claims the hidden paths of Gomorra are infested with the Unspokens' divine guardians. Vicious creatures who protect their masters' secrets and will shred everything on their path to pieces. I am not sure which one would be worse—them or the shadowreapers. At least with the latter, we know what we are up against."

"So, we won't try?"

Silas gently squeezed Naila's shoulder. "Naila, they can't risk it. There are women and children here."

Naila nuzzled on her lip. "Then what about the shadowreapers?"

"We have a plan. No one knows Gomorra as well as *gavana* does. Not even the shadowreapers," said Sephanya.

"We will play the game of the tortoise and the hare," the chieftain elaborated. "We will lure them through the maze of Gomorra until they cannot stay here any longer."

Naila huffed. "You think that will work?"

"It will," Silas mumbled. "It's quite genius, in fact. Shadowreapers are slaves to æther. They can't survive without its most powerful enhancer: *Iluna*."

Tryce blinked. "So, sooner or later they have to give up, and we can sneak out."

"We don't have all the time in the world. You're dying," Naila hissed, her voice growing louder with every word.

Silas winced. "Naila..."

"Please gather your belongings, we leave within a bell," the chieftain said, finishing the conversation.

An aura of finality surrounded him. Any further arguments would be a waste of breath. She shook her head in disbelief. Anger pulsed through her, sparking gilded flames in the tips of her fingers. She squeezed her hands into fists to quash them and pivoted back to Silas. But the moment Naila turned to him, she knew something was wrong.

Silas coughed, blood seeping through his fingers.

Onyx rushed to him. "Silas," she squeaked, and for once, her voice broke. "We need to get to your brother. Naila is right..."

"I'm not going to Levias," he hissed stubbornly. "I'd rather die than beg him for iscias."

Onyx huffed in frustration, her face turning scarlet. "If not Levias than the Black Šar, all right? But either way we don't have time to sit this out."

The Mehari already started gathering their belongings, unleashing their camodas and cattle as *gavana's* second-in-command ordered them around. There was no time to waste. Soon the shadowreapers would be upon them. It was either saving the tribe or helping, and likely still failing, to save the prince. Naila drew in a calming breath and straightened her back. She knew what to do.

"*I* will go to the Red Šar."

"How do you plan to do that?" Rē grunted at the same time Silas barked, "No."

"I think I know how to open this door. If it leads to an exit, then I may just reach Lethos in time. I can bargain with the Red Šar," she continued, ignoring Silas's protests, "I know I can. If I can convince him to give Silas iscias, I may also convince him to send help."

"Naila..." Silas began.

"And if your plan fails?" Onyx demanded.

"If it fails, then Silas and I will die, but staying here for too long will kill Silas too, you know that."

Onyx's eyes filled with fear, doubt, and unshed tears as she eyed the prince; as if Naila's words unlocked a secret garden filled with emotions she'd never dared face before.

Naila's tone softened. "Trust me, as I did you."

Silas stared at her with a blazing look. It seemed to dawn on him that Naila would not be persuaded to let go of her plan. He shook his head but chuckled softly. "Always so stubborn."

"If we don't do this, we'll lose ye for sure, Silas," Tryce urged.

Onyx's dark eyes first locked with Silas's resigned ones, and then finally with Naila's golden-brown orbs. "*Yana*, Naila. We will do this, but we will go with you."

"Thank you." Naila's voice was thick with emotion.

She threw her arms around Silas, Onyx, and Tryce, and even Rē. The latter shifted uncomfortably but accepted her hug with an awkward pat on the back. For a breath of a moment, a sliver in time, they sat there hugging—five individuals leaving the cusp of adulthood, each with their own dreams, paths, and demons to battle. The storm of unrest inside Naila calmed to ripples on a lake. She didn't know whether they would get through this, but for the first time in weeks, a shimmer of hope sparked within her.

Rē informed the Mehari of their decision, to which *gavana* said, "So here is where our paths diverge. A brave and noble decision, I must say. We will try to keep the shadowreapers off your path, but know they are not easily deceived."

Naila pulled Sephanya into a hug. "Stay safe. If we make it to Lethos, we'll ask them to help you."

A hesitance crept into Sephanya's posture. The girl locked eyes with Naila, and not for the first time she wondered whether the gift of foresight affected more of the Mehari than Nova who they'd been forced to give up to the Red Šars.

"Let our paths cross again, nergayla," said the girl. "Beware the mists of Gomorra, but above all, beware the Red Šar."

She turned without another word or glance. As soon as they said the last of their goodbyes, they turned to the hidden gate.

"So," Rē said, eyeing the stones skeptically, "How will you open it?"

"Well, here's to nothing," Naila said.

She pressed the insignia of her compass to open it.

Onyx's eyes widened in understanding. "Like Mr. Thoth's scroll."

"You little genius," Silas smiled proudly.

Naila's cheeks heated a little. She waited for the moons to cast their glow through the crack in the ceiling then stuck out her compass, capturing

Iluna's light with it. She angled it to reflect the moonlight onto the hidden doorway. It took several moments before her fingers held it in the right position. She held her breath and she knew her friends did the same. The dark hall was as soundless as it was empty. Even Ro-Ro and the camodas *gavana* had gifted them did not so much as make a murmur.

Like water in crevices, an intricate pattern of symbols surrounding a winged man illuminated on the stone surface.

"By the stars," Onyx whispered.

The gate snapped open, and a swish of clouds filled the hall in a blink of an eye. It stank of sulfur and something rotten. The camodas groaned, shifting restlessly in their spot. Tryce pulled at their reins, preventing them from running away.

"The mists of Gomorra," Rē stated. Even he seemed to be in awe.

"I can't see a thing," Silas said as he tried to waft the mists away.

"Patience," Rē said.

Rē was right. As quick as the mists appeared, they also vanished, leaving a creepy dark tunnel beyond.

"Er, are we really getting in there?" Tryce said, unsure.

Onyx's camoda nudged Tryce's forward. "Yes, and you can go first," she said teasingly.

As soon as they'd entered the hidden hallway, the gate closed behind them.

"Oh, no," Naila whispered. She pressed the scarf of her shawl to her nose to suppress the surrounding stench.

"What does this mean?" Tryce asked nervously. "We're not trapped, right? Right?"

"I guess we have no choice but to move on," Silas said with a sigh.

At first glance, the hallway was similar to Gomorra's other hallways, with murals and symbols etched on its pale stones. The only difference was the wisps of mist that shrouded the floor. Ro-Ro stayed rooted on her shoulder, completely silent but for his eyes caressing every rock and pebble. Naila shivered as she took in her surroundings. Scattered all around them in the mists were skeletons and stray bones... Their torches didn't allow for much light, and she had the unshakable feeling they were not alone. "Creepy, huh?" she whispered as she handed the bird a scarab from her pouch.

Without warning, something shot through the air, followed by a bone-chilling roar and the groans of a camoda. It had flown too fast for Naila to see it clearly, but it was far larger than even a camoda. The camodas shuffled and growled. She almost fell off her saddle. When the chaos subsided, they found their pack camoda missing.

"What happened?" Naila said at the same time Onyx æshified an arrow, Tryce raised his ax, and Silas and Rē unsheathed their razor-sharp scimitars.

Out of nowhere, torches on the walls ignited with crimson flames, all the way up ahead to a circular space with a gilded lectern. The lectern carried a breathtaking black-gold gauntlet, which in turn held a key atop its palm. A river of liquid silver streamed around the circle. Naila didn't know if it was her imagination but the silver waves seemed to reach higher and higher and higher...

She snatched Elgafar, her own dagger, out of her satchel. Fear gripped her throat as she felt the nauseous warning in her stomach that they were being watched. *Being hunted.* The creature flashed through the air and landed in the dark mists before them. The severed, bloodied leg of the camoda fell next to it.

Slowly, like the petals of a perished rose falling one by one, the light revealed what had been hidden before... and Naila saw one of the most frightening sights she'd ever seen in her eighteen years of life.

That of a monster.

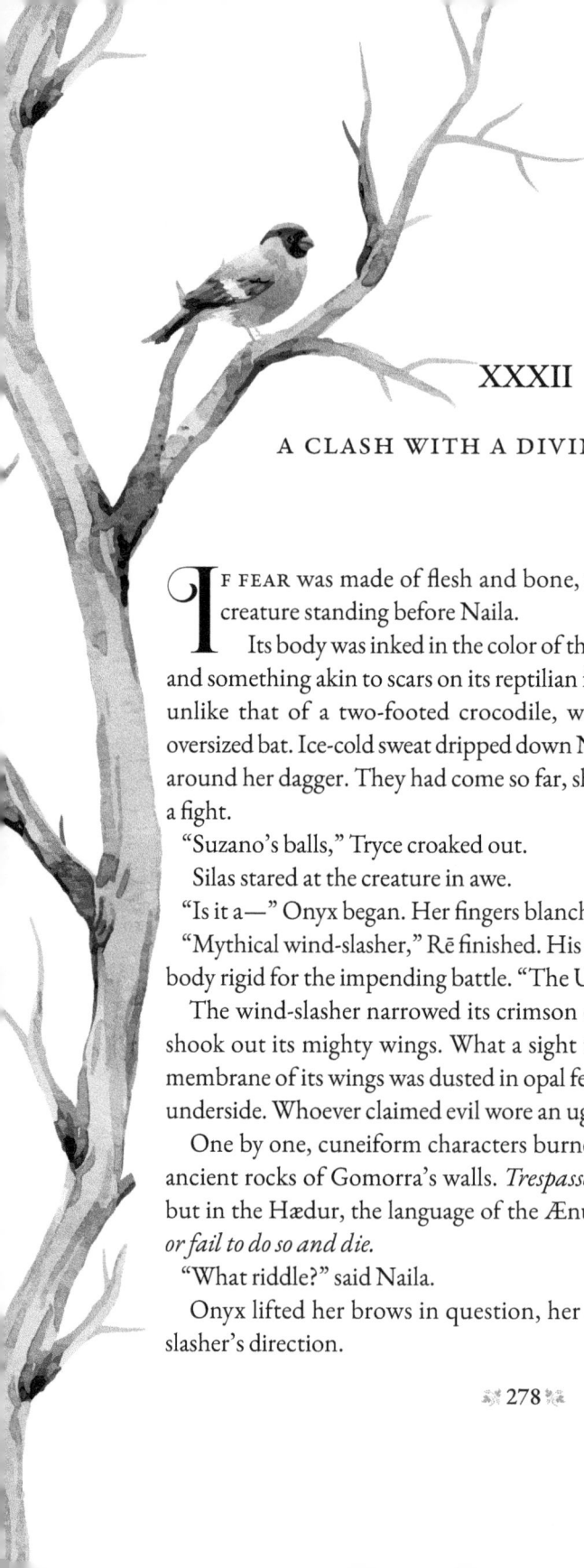

XXXII

A CLASH WITH A DIVINE GUARDIAN

IF FEAR was made of flesh and bone, it would bear the name of the creature standing before Naila.

Its body was inked in the color of the night, with slashes of crimson, and something akin to scars on its reptilian face. Its feathered body was not unlike that of a two-footed crocodile, with the wrinkled wings of an oversized bat. Ice-cold sweat dripped down Naila's neck. Her hand clenched around her dagger. They had come so far, she would not go down without a fight.

"Suzano's balls," Tryce croaked out.

Silas stared at the creature in awe.

"Is it a—" Onyx began. Her fingers blanched around an æsh-arrow.

"Mythical wind-slasher," Rē finished. His scimitar twirled in his hand, his body rigid for the impending battle. "The Unspokens' divine guardians."

The wind-slasher narrowed its crimson eyes on their mortal frames. It shook out its mighty wings. What a sight they were to behold. The thin membrane of its wings was dusted in opal feathers with a scarlet hue on the underside. Whoever claimed evil wore an ugly mask?

One by one, cuneiform characters burned in crimson flames upon the ancient rocks of Gomorra's walls. *Trespassers*, it read, not in Tierratongo, but in the Hædur, the language of the Ænunaki. *Solve my riddle and live, or fail to do so and die.*

"What riddle?" said Naila.

Onyx lifted her brows in question, her arrow never leaving the wind-slasher's direction.

"What are ye talking about?" Tryce gaped at Naila, as if not quite sure she was still sound of mind.

Silas followed her gaze. "That must be the Hædur."

Of course. The others could not read the old tongue...

Far behind the wind-slasher, the gauntlet sparkled like black diamonds, shedding some of its light on the circular canal of silver water. It was no doubt the treasure the creature protected.

"Guys, the water is rising," Naila said in alarm.

Waves of liquid silver spilled over the stone tiles, ever so slowly filling the hallway. It was not her imagination.

"Not water, mercury," mumbled Rē. "Highly toxic."

"All right," Onyx breathed out, her eyes shifting from the creature to the rising level of mercury. "So, what's the plan? Kill the beast or run for our lives?"

Tryce threw out, "We'll kill that beast, of course."

Silas nodded. "Running will lead to our death. Tryce is right, we have no choice but to kill it."

More characters appeared on the walls.

It has a head but never weeps and has a bed but never sleeps,
It mirrors the ever-pregnant ones and that which sets when the day is done.

"What does it say, N?" asked Onyx.

Naila's eyes shifted from the walls to the wind-slasher and back. "It's the riddle." She translated the words to her friends. "I think this guardian will let us go if we solve it."

Solving the riddle had not been their first trial, she realized. The first one was to actually *read* the riddle... and somehow Naila had passed. A thousand thoughts spun through her mind, none fit for this place or time. Mercury streamed toward them like an unspoken threat. The wind-slasher bared its vicious teeth but, peculiarly, made no move.

Tryce gaped at her. "How are we supposed to barf out an answer just like that?"

Onyx eyed the creature with a calculating gaze. "That which sets when the day is done... sounds like the sun to me."

"Yes!" Naila grinned. "And the pregnant ones must be *Iluna.*"

"But what mirrors them?" Rē pondered.

The flaming words flickered to darkness.

Time was up.

With a chilling roar, the wind-slasher leaped toward them, leaving crater after crater in the stones in its wake, whilst its powerful wings clashed against the ceiling. Rocks crashed down, missing them by a hair's breadth.

Ro-Ro squawked, flying around Naila's head in panic. As if she could understand the language of birds. The camodas too, bleated restlessly. Naila pulled at the reins to keep herself from falling.

"Seven hells," Onyx hissed.

Fortunately, the girl had the reflexes of a seasoned warrior. Onyx fired an æsh-arrow at the wind-slasher but the creature was lightning fast. With a furious screech it tore Onyx's camoda's head off with a snap of its jaws.

Fear gutted Naila. "Onyx!"

A vision of elegance and grace, the girl did a backward somersault and landed on her curled-toe slippers with little to no sound. She drew another arrow and fired at the beast, to no avail.

They had to solve the riddle. *Now,* before it slaughtered them.

Rē, however, had another idea. He jumped off his camoda and dashed toward the lectern. As expected, the winged terror followed him. He stopped mid-stride, right before the bubbling mercury stream, and threw his scimitar at the creature. Naila wasn't quite sure why it surprised her, but his aim was perfect. It hit the wind-slasher's skull with a deafening crack. Relief calmed her fluttering heart.

It was over.

Thank goodness.

"What—" Tryce started.

No.

The sword fell with a powerful thump to the stone. The wind-slasher? Unharmed. It cracked its head from side to side and bared its rows of fangs. A growl left its jaws as its eyes sharpened on Rē's frame.

"Quick," Silas barked, "Naila make a run for it. We'll try to distract this thing before it makes Rē the next dish on its menu."

"Make a run for it?" Her eyes widened in disbelief. "There's nowhere to run, you said it yourself. We either solve this riddle or die."

Silas didn't listen. He dashed toward the wind-slasher, who in turn pounced toward Rē.

"Wait for me," Tryce said, his ax reigniting with flames.

Onyx whistled on her fingers just as the creature reached Rē. "Over here!"

Great. Just great.

Elgafar gleamed in Naila's grip. Would she join them in battle? Contrary to the others, she wasn't trained in the dance of flames or the arts of war. This was not a movie where she suddenly had the skills to fight like a black-belted ninja. This was real. And she was just Naila, a demure social outcast who wouldn't hurt a fly. Any bad choices would stain her life with their consequences. No, today was not the day to test her physical prowess.

There was more to strength than fighting, however. To whom belonged victory? Was it the emperor with the order and the crystals, the general who came up with the strategy, or the legions who actually fought in the war? Mayhaps it was all.

Naila had a riddle to solve.

She took hold of the camodas' reins and steered the skittish animals back into the mists. She'd bring them to safety and then return, hopefully, with an answer.

Head... weeps... bed... sleeps.

What could possibly mirror *Iluna* and the sun?

She brought her camoda to a run with a squeeze of her legs. The grunts and snarls farther down made her nervous. If anything happened to them... Naila cursed out loud when the hallway came to a dead-end far too soon. Her camoda grumbled anxiously. It crushed a stray skull underneath its two-toed foot.

Maybe, just maybe, she could reopen the door without moonlight...

Something flashed above her. The stones underneath her slippers shuddered and the dim fires of the torches flickered. Ro-Ro stopped mid-flight, squawking. The hairs on her arms bristled. Step for step, with no hurry, the wind-slasher left the shadows. It surveyed her leisurely, keenly, with a calculated coldness.

Her camoda pushed itself up on his hind legs.

"Easy, easy."

The terrified animal had no ear for her pleas; it threw her from the saddle. Her vision doubled from the impact, as pain burned a path through her back. With a final grunt, Naila's camoda galloped back to the dark of the hall, the other camodas following on its heels.

It was just her and the wind-slasher.

There was nowhere to escape. The wind-slasher charged toward her. By instinct, a nonexistent one for the preceding eighteen years that finally showed its face, Naila narrowly escaped its sharp claws. The stone next to her wasn't as fortunate. It fractured into pieces. Ro-Ro screeched angrily and attacked the wind-slasher with its claws.

"Ro-Ro, no!"

With a fierce smack of its claw, the wind-slasher ripped Ro-Ro's chest open. The beautiful bird of prey fell to the ground in a pool of blood.

"Ro-Ro..."

Pain cut her open. She pinned the predator with a look of horror. Vertical pupils in a pool of crimson stared back at her, like a river of doom with no beginning or end. Her ragged gasps and the sound of stone crunching underneath the wind-slasher's claws filled the utter silence of the hallway.

"Naila," Onyx and Silas called from somewhere behind at the same time the creature raised its claw.

Onyx's æsh-arrows rained on the wind-slasher, to no avail. This was really happening. She would die. All alone in a place without Ma and Philly. In this moment, as she stared at death's cruel, beautiful face, she finally realized the acceptance of her classmates meant nothing in the grand scheme of things. She was enough. She had always been enough.

A scorching determination filled her.

Mirror... Bed... Head...

The wind-slasher's claws ripped through the flesh of her shoulder, leaving angry marks. It attacked her again, but this time Naila grabbed its claw. A warmth in her fingers melted to a river of golden heat, pouring into an avalanche of flames. She had never felt so awake, so empowered... *so alive.*

The fires in her veins burst forth, scorching the feathers on the creature's claw. It howled in pain. For the first time, fear entered its crimson eyes. What had been a formidable apex predator, that had no doubt slaughtered many men and destroyed sturdy buildings, regarded her, Naila Groenhart, as if she were a threat.

"River," she whispered.

The wind-slasher's eyes widened at her single word.

Naila released its claw, all the while keeping its gaze locked. "River," she repeated, "the answer to the riddle is a river."

XXXIII

THE GRIP OF LEGENDS

YOU CANNOT domesticate a monster.

You can, however, beat it at its own game. The wind-slasher backed away. It eyed Naila warily, almost curiously, before fading into the shadows.

Ro-Ro whimpered. Blood sullied his gilded wings. Naila reached for the brave raptor, stroking his quivering feathers. She squeezed her eyes to a close. *Not Ro-Ro. Please.* A tear rolled down her cheek. She vaguely registered that æther once more pulsed through her fingers.

Something pecked at her hand.

Not to harm, but in a caress. The love song of a soundless bird.

Squawk.

Naila reopened her eyes.

"Ro-Ro," she squealed.

She tugged the bird to her chest.

Ro-Ro croaked again. His mangled body was healed scarlessly. *Had she done that?* It didn't matter. The only important thing was her sweet messenger bird was alive. Tears of relief streamed down to her neck as the bird nudged her cheek affectionately.

"Naila, are you okay?"

Onyx and Tryce came to a stop next to her, scanning the area with wild eyes. "What happened? Where is that beast?" Tryce demanded. "That mercury retreated all a'sudden."

He darted to the dim corners of the corridor, his æshefied ax in hand, but the wind-slasher was long gone.

"I solved the riddle... It left."

The two gaped at her.

"W-What?"

Naila told them what had taken place, at which Onyx pulled her into a tight hug. She whispered, "I'm sorry... Remind me to never underestimate you again."

Naila smiled weakly, trying to evade Tryce's hand ruffling her already tangled mass of curls. "I will."

Footsteps echoed in the hall. But the moment Naila turned, she knew something was wrong. Rē strode toward them, carrying Silas's limp body in his arms.

They rushed toward him.

"Silas." Onyx shook the prince. Her voice broke. Silas mumbled something incoherent, but he didn't give any indication he'd heard them. "Come on. Please, *please* open your eyes."

Naila grabbed at her heart in despair. It couldn't be too late. It simply couldn't be. She stared at the prince's pale face, as he drifted off like a haunted sleeping beauty. "How far is Lethos?"

"*Gavana* mentioned a full day's ride without rest." Rē's face was grim. "*If* we manage to shake off the shadowreapers *and* don't get lost."

She could see he thought it a lost cause, but she wouldn't give up. "Th-then, let's hurry."

Onyx rubbed the tears from her eyes.

Tryce patted his cousin's back. "That's right, Onyx. We'll save him. So, let's hurry."

Sizzling flames of Hædur characters blazed anew on the wall.

My learling, Gomorra, sets you a-free,
Take the Grip of Legends and return it, completed, to me.

Tryce elbowed Naila. "Well? Is it letting us go?"

Naila nodded. She spelled out the new words. "Return it to who?"

"Some dead Unspoken, I imagine," Onyx said.

Rē's eyes gleamed with something untranslatable. "Perhaps that gauntlet on the lectern..."

Naila frowned. "Should we... take it?"

Tryce's eyes twinkled. "Of course, we should! It's a relic from the Unspokens. It will make us a fortune."

"I don't know, Tryce." Onyx sounded as doubtful as Naila felt.

He scoffed. "We suffered through that wind-slasher and an impending river of mercury. We deserve to get paid for our efforts."

A camoda licked his cheek. Apparently, the animal agreed.

"Ugh." Tryce shoved the camoda's face away. "Nasty beast."

Rē shrugged. "He has a point. If all else fails, we can use it as payment for iscias." He strode toward the lectern, not leaving Naila and the others any choice but to follow. There was no hesitance in his posture. He plucked the black-gold gauntlet from the lectern and that was that. For a flicker of a moment, a wrinkle in time, Naila thought the gauntlet shimmered like rubies. It must have been her imagination.

At once, the floor shuddered.

"What—"

The stones groaned until a door, previously hidden from their sight, slid open. All, even Naila, drew their weapons.

A waterfall of pale yellow cascaded over the dark, wet stones.

"Sunlight! It leads to outside!" said Tryce.

For the first time in an era, the sun shed its light upon the halls of Gomorra. A warm breeze swirled into the hallway, scenting the air with the rich, earthy aroma of the red desert.

"I'll take Silas." Rē grunted as he mounted his camoda, not wasting any time.

"This one's mine," Tryce chirped.

Naila shrugged and took a seat behind Onyx on the remaining camoda. Her arm still ached, so she didn't mind her friend taking the lead. She rolled her shoulder, testing. The deep wounds of the wind-slasher's claws must have healed when she cured Ro-Ro.

Onyx sighed, serenity washing over her tan face. "I never knew how much I hungered for the sun until this moment."

"We must have been inside for longer than one night," Rē stated.

Time lost on the prince's health...

"We can't linger. We need to get Silas to Lethos and fast," said Naila.

"Right, but how do we get there again?" said Tryce. "Without getting lost and turning into a desert lion's feast, I mean."

Naila pressed her compass open. As expected, the needle pointed to a new direction: northeast. Her little compass remained in tune with her desire. It illuminated the road to whatever her heart craved.

A longing look spread over Onyx's face. "I need to get me one of those."

Grunts of relief left the animals as they paced to the door, and finally onto the heated desert sand. Naila glanced one last time to Gomorra, but the door groaned to a close, leaving the ziggurat behind to its exquisite majesty.

"Hiya," Onyx bellowed.

She didn't have to repeat it. The camoda galloped through the dunes, relieved, Naila imagined, to leave Gomorra behind. Naila held onto Onyx. The sky was cloudless, a perfect pastel blue wiped clean of any remnants of a storm.

"We've been inside for only a few days, but the whole world already changed." Naila observed in awe as she took in the metamorphosed desert land.

The terracotta dunes were still there, and so were the palm trees and peyote cacti. Accompanying them, however, were delicate fields of the palest greens sprinkled here and there. They bore magenta peonies and other desert flowers in all hues of the rainbow; like a Monet painting, come to life.

"*Yana*." Onyx beamed. "Even barren deserts can blossom into fields more beautiful than the rarest butterfly. Although I suspect it's the influence of a nearby Elysian field."

Naila's smile shriveled under the weight of worry. "I guess now comes the hard part."

Onyx nodded. "Let's hope you're right and Silas sharing his blood still has some meaning to Levias, or we'll have a big problem leaving a meeting with him. Alive."

Alas, even the brightest skies could not diminish the darkest clouds.

"We have company," Rē growled.

Naila's stomach plummeted. Far on the blue horizon was a single stroke of black. Shadowreapers.

Tryce gaped at the sight behind him. He uttered a few vulgar words.

"How?" Onyx hissed.

She urged the camoda to a faster pace with her knees.

"The camodas are the fastest creatures in the desert," Naila said, although she wasn't sure if it was to calm the others or to reassure herself. "They won't catch us, right?"

The following silence told all.

"Fast as camodas might be in a desert, doran horses are bred for speed and endurance," Rē murmured.

Still, Naila wasn't completely wrong. For several bells, the shadowreapers remained in the far distance. They didn't pause, didn't dare linger. It surprised Naila that the camodas kept up for so long. When night came, however, the animals paced slower and slower.

"We have to rest," Rē barked. "The camodas are no use to us in this state."

Onyx shook her head. "They'll catch up with us. We can't afford it."

They kept their pace throughout the dark of the night, under the watchful gaze of the ever-shining stars. The rustling of bushes and howls beyond the dunes made the presence known of the creatures of the night, but none approached them. Perhaps they sensed the shadowreapers.

Naila's eyes burned with exhaustion. Her muscles ached from sitting upon the jiggling camoda, blisters no doubt forming on the softness of her skin, but she didn't dare complain. It's peculiar how much one can endure with death on one's heels.

Dawn broke at last. In the distance glistened the first ray of hope.

"Is that—"

"Lethos," Onyx cheered.

Between the red dunes stood a grand volcano amid an even grander oasis—enclosed by a high, imposing fort. Colossal statues of two warriors framed the vast gate of Lethos. Unlike Gomorra, these statues were Lemaian. A city spiraled around the volcano all the way to the very top, its many domes shimmering like mother-of-pearl in the morning sun.

Close, too close, a doran horse whinnied. Naila didn't dare look, but she knew Rē was right. The camodas' tiredness had delayed their flight considerably. Soon the shadowreapers would be upon them.

"Come on." Onyx urged their camoda with another squeeze of her ankles. "Hurry. So close."

"We can make it," Tryce said, "If the sentries let us in."

The thump of hooves in soft desert sand spiraled Naila into a state of alarm. "Hurry, Onyx!"

"I'm trying!"

The camodas groaned as the river Naranil came into sight; it led straight to Lethos, only to curve around the fortified city.

"*Lai*," Onyx pulled the reins, "Only a little further."

Desert riders or no, the animals were thirsty and hungry. It was a testament to their riders' prowess that they kept the camodas from defying them for a sweet drop from Naranil.

"*Ut ahsyl feylana*," a voice snarled.

Daena.

Naila grew cold. Out of the corners of her eyes, she saw the dreaded dark robes of several shadowreapers and the heaving jaws of their undead looking horses... It wasn't only Daena. Colios was there too, and no doubt the woman they called Morgana.

Fear gripped her by the throat until she gasped for air. But even that wasn't enough to soothe her lungs, to calm her nerves.

Rē drew out a dagger and swirled it into the distance. Naila was about to scold him for wasting a precious weapon like that, but then she saw where it was headed. It cut through the air and hammered against a flame beacon. A warning station for Lethos.

Cling. The bell rang loud and true. There was no chance Lethos's sentries could miss it. Rē was a genius.

A shadowreaper tugged hard on Naila's shawl, but she tightened her arms around Onyx.

"You cannot escape us," Daena hissed.

Her doran horse whinnied, flames of æther burning in its milky eyes. Unlike the camodas, it showed no sign of weakening.

Ro-Ro shot to the shadowreaper, scratching her face with his claws.

"Cursed bird," Daena screeched.

In her raging attempt to fend off the bird, the distance grew between the shadowreaper and Naila. It was a short-lived victory, however, for the other shadowreapers neared.

They wouldn't reach Lethos in time.

All of a sudden, æsh-arrows rained from the sky. Sure enough, dozens upon dozens of sentries swarmed the impenetrable walls of Lethos, bow and arrow in hand.

With an agonized whinny, a doran horse fell dead to the sand, taking its rider with it. More arrows burned through the sky, piercing another shadowreaper, and scorching the desert sand with their flames. The sentries' aims were close to flawless. No arrow hit Naila or her friends.

More sentries appeared on the fort and even more arrows followed in the air.

"We retreat," Colios hissed to the other shadowreapers.

Naila rested her head against the back of Onyx's petite frame in relief. They made it. They were safe.

The shadowreapers left, but not before Naila heard Daena's warning loud and clear.

"Soon, Stormhold. You cannot evade us forever. There is no escaping destiny."

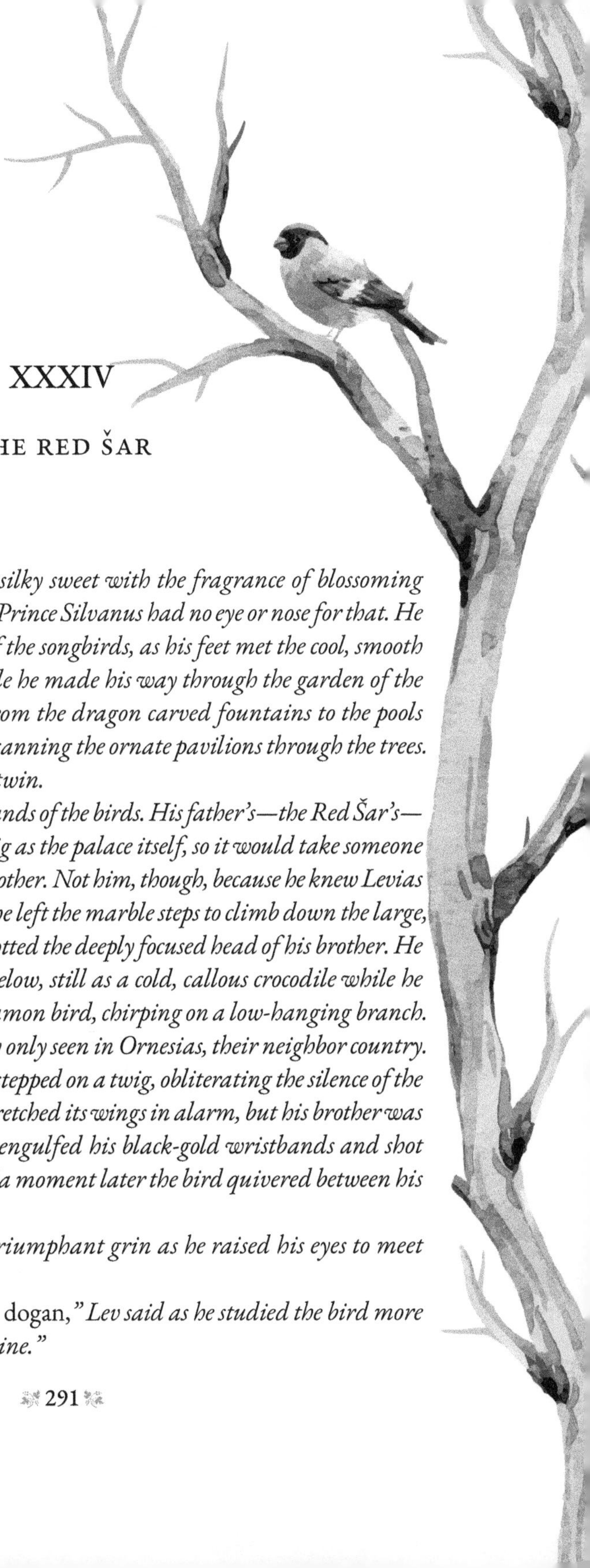

XXXIV

THE RED ŠAR

THE MORNING air was silky sweet with the fragrance of blossoming almond trees, but young Prince Silvanus had no eye or nose for that. He mimicked the whistles of the songbirds, as his feet met the cool, smooth surface of the marble steps, while he made his way through the garden of the Red Palace. His eyes drifted from the dragon carved fountains to the pools filled with water lilies, at last scanning the ornate pavilions through the trees.

There was still no sign of his twin.

He paused, focusing on the sounds of the birds. His father's—the Red Šar's—imperial garden was twice as big as the palace itself, so it would take someone more than two bells to find his brother. Not him, though, because he knew Levias through and through. Quietly, he left the marble steps to climb down the large, jagged rocks. Sure enough, he spotted the deeply focused head of his brother. He stood on a rock beside the pool below, still as a cold, callous crocodile while he watched his prey—a little cinnamon bird, chirping on a low-hanging branch. It was a rare gilded one, usually only seen in Ornesias, their neighbor country.

Silas inched forward, but he stepped on a twig, obliterating the silence of the moment. The cinnamon bird stretched its wings in alarm, but his brother was too fast. The blue fires of æther engulfed his black-gold wristbands and shot straight to his fingers. A flash of a moment later the bird quivered between his palms.

Lev's mouth curved into a triumphant grin as he raised his eyes to meet Silas's nearly identical ones.

"Eight sunsets and seven bells, dogan,*" Lev said as he studied the bird more closely. "But here it is, finally mine."*

Silas scoffed. He hated it when Levias called him dogan—*little brother. He was only the cry of a babe younger!*

"Reuben could catch it within a tinkling."

Lev's eyebrows scrambled into a scowl. "Not with his bare hands he can't."

"What do you want with a stupid bird anyway?"

Lev's eyes twinkled as he jumped off the rock.

"Mother said Ornesias' cinnamon birds have the most alluring song of all birds, but they're too fast to be caught by even father's fastest vigiles." Lev turned to Silas and his eyes grew dark. "Yet here it is, caught by me."

Silas shook his head. His mother was right when she complained how much Lev was turning into Father. They became enthralled by anything rare and desired within a snap of a finger and didn't stop their obsessive hunt until it was theirs. It was the reason Father's imperial harem was the most coveted of all šars in the lands of Lemuria.

"Mom hates caged animals; I doubt she'll want this bird."

"I know. It's mine." Lev licked his lips. "I hunted and caught it fair and square; the rest of Lemuria no longer has a claim to it."

Silas crossed his arms and studied his brother. The youngest of twenty-four princes and twins to boot, they always stuck together. They were two sides to a story, the tragedy and comedy masks in a play. It was no coincidence they were born during Sin and Shamash's reign over the heavens. Yet with every passing sunset they were pushed more and more into diverging paths.

"What are you going to do with it? Everyone knows how quickly you get bored."

Levias glanced over his shoulder, pools of darkness devouring his eyes.

He never answered Silas.

Silas twisted and turned in his drenched cloak. From somewhere nearby he heard his friends' voices as they fussed over him. Rē's short, clipped words as he lifted him from the saddle of some creature, Naila's sweet siren voice as she told him to be careful, Onyx's sassy warning they had to buckle up because more of *them* were coming, and Tryce snarling to 'let them come.' The gate to the netherworld was close, the prince knew that. They say life flashes before one's eyes the moment death sinks its claws into one's flesh, but none of that came to him.

Only this long-forgotten memory.

Lethos was more menacing than its name suggested.

Perhaps that had to do with Naila and her friends being surrounded by Crishirian sentries, all of whom pointed their æshefied scimitars at them. Some stared open-mouthed at Naila's phæralei, while others watched each of them with suspicion. As if they were the enemy.

The shadowreapers had long since disappeared into the far distance, but it seemed they had walked straight into another conflict. Naila clutched Silas's unconscious form tighter to her chest. We have to save him. We have to, she repeated in her mind, over and over again. A tall, imposing man walked through the crowd of city guardians. All made way for him as a pride did for its lion.

"State your name and purpose," he sneered.

The man was surprisingly young. He was clad in expensive-looking crimson robes, with a loose turban on his head. His skin was a deep bronze and his angular features looked cut out of marble. He wasn't handsome, per se, but still attractive in his own rugged way. Naila glanced from her friends, who held the reins to their camodas, to the man in question. Tryce glanced around sneakily, no doubt already looking for ways to escape. It was useless. Whether they fought to their last breath or no, escaping Lethos was not on the cards.

"We are pilgrims from the Empire of Isolon," Rē lied. "We seek no conflict, only shelter."

The man tutted. "Do you take me for a fool? You were chased by a horde of shadowreapers." He uttered his last sentence as he walked into Rē's space. "And I want to know why that is."

"I tell no lies," Rē said stoically.

Before the man could answer, or worse, talk with violence, Naila said, "We're looking for the Red Šar. Our plight will be told to him alone."

Silence overcame the crowd. Then everyone laughed. *Actually laughed.* The man came forward, his mouth curved into a mocking grin and his eyes lit up with amusement. "You've come to the wrong city, nergayla. The Red Šar is in Irkalla."

He watched her with his nose stuck in the air, frowning slightly when his eyes met Silas's pale face. Naila instantly pulled the prince's face to her chest. Chances were slim they'd recognize the lost prince from ten winters before, but she wouldn't risk it. She didn't trust any of these men with Silas's identity.

The man spoke aloud. "Even if the šar was here, what makes you think pedesters are worthy of seeing His Majesty? Even a nergayla as comely as you?"

"It's a delicate matter, but I promise it's worth his time," Naila said with more confidence than she felt. "Please, I'm telling the truth."

The man's eyes narrowed.

"Lord Gorgo." A sentry stepped forward.

Lord Gorgo's hand shot up for silence. The folds in his face morphed into a sneer. "You're wasting our time, my beaut."

He inclined his head to the sentries. "Throw them to the rattlejacks, but bring the nergayla to the summer palace."

Rattlejacks? Whatever those things were, it couldn't be good.

The sentries stepped forward at the same time Onyx arched her bow, Rē unsheathed his scimitar, and Tryce swung his ax from the holster on his back.

"Wait, no!" Naila said and snatched the hem of Lord Gorgo's robes.

The lord scolded, looking at Naila as if she were a mere cockroach dirtying his pristine floor. But then his eyes widened. Naila followed his gaze toward her hair clip. The ruby beads Reuben had given her sparkled like unspoken promises in the soft beams of the afternoon sun.

Lord Gorgo halted his men and rubbed his stubbled chin. For a few moments, he said nothing, only stared at her in wonder.

"Who told you to seek the Red Šar?" he finally asked.

"A man called Reuben."

Naila tried to decipher an answer from Lord Gorgo's expression, but his face was unreadable.

"We shall see if you speak the truth." The lord smiled cruelly. "If you don't, nergayla, I promise you'll wish you'd had to deal with me instead of His Majesty."

So, Lord Gorgo had lied, and the Red Šar was in fact there... Nerves clenched her stomach. It was too late for second thoughts. She would have to see this through. The sentries shackled them and pushed them toward the gate. One of them made to grab Silas, but Rē shot the man a glare and threw the prince's limp body over his own shoulder. Naila winced.

Onyx snapped at Rē, "Be more careful. He's not a ragdoll!"

With a signal from Lord Gorgo, the wooden-and-bronze gate reopened with a resounding snap. What awaited them at the foot of the volcano were no monsters or other such threats, not even markets or people. It was a true Fata Morgana, a mirage of enchanting flora and fauna.

The lovely fragrance of blossoming trees spread over the waves of a soft breeze. The trees were scattered over fields of pale grass and desert flowers, like the ones beyond the gate. A woolly *elephaunt* and its calf stared curiously at them, but then went back to their business, eating hidden leaves between thorny acacia branches. The sentries pushed them toward a pebblestone path that led to a camoda stable. Several ornate litters were parked there.

"Get in," Lord Gorgo ordered. He pointed at a litter already fastened to two camodas.

Naila's eyes shot to her friends who were forced into another litter.

"You have to the count of three to get your paws off of me or you can kiss them goodbye," Onyx sneered at a sentry.

"What about my friends?" Naila said.

"You're in no position to negotiate. If His Majesty so wishes, you may see them again."

A sentry smashed the door closed behind her. Almost instantly the camodas grunted and the carriage started its journey.

Naila opened the embroidered curtains. To her surprise, the litter moved into the volcano, where a steep path was carved into the slope. The scent of sulfur stung her olfactory bulbs. Up and up the litter wobbled, the camodas grunting now and then. The limited view outside was an immense pit of darkness. The only light came from the wall torches' flames dancing between the shadows of the rocks.

Finally, after what seemed like ages, the litter, at last, entered the spiraling city Naila had seen from afar. Donkeys brayed and horses whinnied amid the murmurs of the busy marketplaces. The beats of goblet drums and melodies of flutes blared all around the litter, whilst several merchants attempted to scream over their notes.

Up and up, they went, until the camodas finally came to a stop before a grand palace. Naila was no expert on architecture, but by the looks of it, the limestone ziggurat covered at least two thousand acres; even more if you counted its stunning terraced gardens.

A young sentry opened the door.

"Welcome to the summer palace," the lad said.

He couldn't be more than sixteen winters old, yet his attire spoke of a far more lavish life than that of the gate's sentries. His caftan was made of satin and his outer robe was lined with fur. Atop his head rested a high silk-lined cylindrical hat, a stark contrast with the messy curls peeking from underneath it.

Naila didn't answer him, but instead, pushed her shackled hands forward. The lad chuckled but unlocked the manacles. Apparently, he didn't think it possible for Naila to run away.

"Follow me, *feylana*," the sentry said.

He spoke excitedly as they climbed the bronze-lined limestone steps, "Usually, His Majesty won't come here until the Firefalls festival, so imagine our surprise when he—"

The boy's eyes widened, and he abruptly closed his mouth. Naila couldn't help but smile. She resisted the urge to ruffle his black curls. He reminded her of Tryce. "Where are you taking me?"

"Lord Gorgo ordered to have you cleaned up." He shot a pointed look at Naila's garments, which now more resembled dirty rags than traveling attire. "You cannot show up to His Majesty in your present state."

Naila bit back a snap. She didn't care what Levias thought of her. She just wanted him to give Silas iscias. Annoyance, however, made way for nerves. In just a few moments she would finally meet the infamous Red Šar, and she would have but a single chance to convince him to save his brother instead of killing him.

Her shoulders were heavy with worry; she scarcely noticed the grand hall they walked through, with its intricate wall reliefs depicting scenes of battles and rituals, and the carved ivory pieces inlaid with gemstones and gold. The boy led her to a spacious courtyard underneath the ziggurat's open ceiling. Palm trees and several basins filled with turquoise water framed a hammam in its very center.

Several stunning women sipped herbal tea as they basked in the sun's light, some of them petting the animals—Guinea fowls, ostriches, and dik-diks among others—that wandered about. Unlike the popular caftan gowns in Havenmor, these *feylanas* wore colorful kaunakes, an ankle length skirt-dress cut into leaf scalloped shapes that wrapped around one shoulder. Floral motif headdresses and exquisite hair clips like Naila's *fayalobi* adorned their shining locks.

Naila snapped out of her daze when they halted before a regal woman seated upon one of the marble benches. Several hierodulas sat on the well-groomed grass at her feet. The woman's beauty shone in an otherworldly way. Like an elf or a water spirit, or a faery, perhaps. Her glowing skin was but a shade removed from African blackwood and although she looked no older than five-and-twenty, her long butterfly locks were as pale as the ivory kaunake draped around her.

Peculiarly, a lying crescent moon adorned her forehead. It gleamed the same indigo as the peacock fan in her hand. This couldn't be anyone else than the revered nergayla Nova.

"Lady Nova," the boy bowed. "I bring to you lady, er—"

He looked at Naila helplessly.

"Naila Groenhart," Naila said.

Nova's heart-shaped lips tightened into a disapproving line. "Junior eunuch, you may leave us."

Naila blinked.

Eunuch?

With a last bow the boy left.

Nova rose, as did her protégés. Her eyes drifted from Naila's dirty slippers to her half-torn attire, finally resting on her phæralei, all the while leisurely fanning herself. Finally, she smiled, although Naila had a hard time deciphering whether it was genuine. Heat stung her cheeks when she realized she had drawn the attention of the other *feylanas* in the courtyard. They stared at her with calculated gazes, as if assessing 'new meat.' Was this the Red Šar's imperial harem?

"Very well then," Nova said. "We have much to do and very little time. Come, we must not keep His Majesty waiting."

One of the hierodulas gently pushed Naila to a door that led to a private hammam with cobalt tiles. The moment Nova left them, with not so much as a word, excited whispers broke out. She was quite certain she heard the words 'nergayla' and a questioning 'concubine.'

A hierodula pulled at the hem of Naila's tunic. "Off these go."

They rinsed, exfoliated and, to Naila's guilty protests, massaged her with lush, fragrant oils that smelled of oud and jasmine.

"You have such beautiful hair," one of them said as she brushed Naila's ebony curls until they were shiny.

Naila twisted a curl around her finger, pondering the girl's words as she said, "Thank you."

She remembered when she was younger and all she wanted was 'good hair.' How she had damaged her curls with chemical hair relaxers and flat irons, when now she couldn't imagine herself with anything but her natural hair.

The ripples in the clear turquoise water smoothed to make way for her reflection.

Before the lands of Lemuria, she had been lost, eager to please others in order to gain their approval and acceptance, all the while losing herself in the sacrifices this brought with it. She brushed her fingers over the smooth sienna of her cheeks. There was a confidence in her gaze that hadn't been there before. Without knowing it, somewhere in this wild quest, she had blossomed from a girl to a woman. Perhaps she had even started to find herself.

"*Feylana*?"

A hierodula entered the hammam with a silky dress.

Naila sucked in a breath.

The burgundy kaunake, embedded with tourmaline gemstones, was a dress for a long-lost princess in an Arabian fairy tale, not for a middle-class girl from Rotterdam, who simply wanted an audience with the šar to get a cure.

Naila raised a hand. "This is really unnecessary. I'm just a simple, ah, pedester."

The hierodula shrugged and said, "Nova's orders." She smiled. "Besides, you're no pedester. You're a nergayla."

Naila sighed but didn't argue. In better circumstances she may have valued the worth of such a gift.

Exactly one chime later the young eunuch returned. His eyes glinted appreciatively, almost proud. He bowed to her for the first time, before leading her back into the grand hall. This time Naila paid attention. Due to burning sandalwood and frankincense, it smelled as divine as it looked. She realized many of the wall reliefs depicted Suzano Stormhold and the twelve, battling what looked like legions of winged warriors. The Unspokens. *The Ænunaki.*

They stopped at a door that reached the ceiling.

The boy whispered, "My family is powerful... We could be allies. Remember me in Irkalla. Saladin Amar-Sin is my name."

Before Naila could ask whatever he meant by that, he bowed and retreated.

A sentry opened the door, revealing an immense throne room. Like the corridors, the walls were carved with brightly painted reliefs, but this time of šars and serpentine creatures akin to the Azag of Helath. At the far end of the room, stood a grand empty throne. No Red Šar.

Another pair of open doors led to a vast terrace, giving Naila the chance to view Lethos in all its glory.

"Bow to the ground," the sentry ordered. "You do not rise until you're told to."

This one wasn't young with a boyish smile, but hard and stern.

Naila did as she was told.

And waited...

Footsteps padded softly on the lush rugs. With every closing step, Naila's breath quickened, her heart thumping in her throat.

The sentry thumped his staff several times to the tiles.

"His Imperial Majesty, Levias Dayamon vi Iliyas, Lord of Dragons, Flame of the Burning Sands, and Red Šar to Crishire and Ornesias."

Naila did not dare raise her head, waiting instead for the Red Šar to address her. This was it. Silas's life hinged on the following conversation.

After several long moments, he finally spoke. "You may rise."

A sharp, unpleasant feeling squeezed her throat like a vice. Was it fear or was it horror? Naila couldn't tell. Even so, she ordered her body to rise; dreading what she would see.

Gilded brown eyes met a midnight oceanic gaze.

One she had seen mere nights before.

Her mysterious stranger, who had helped her, guided her... Reuben, but that wasn't his name, was it? It couldn't be. Because standing in front of Naila was the dreaded Red Šar. The man who saved her in the redwoods, who haunted her every dream... and Silas's twin brother.

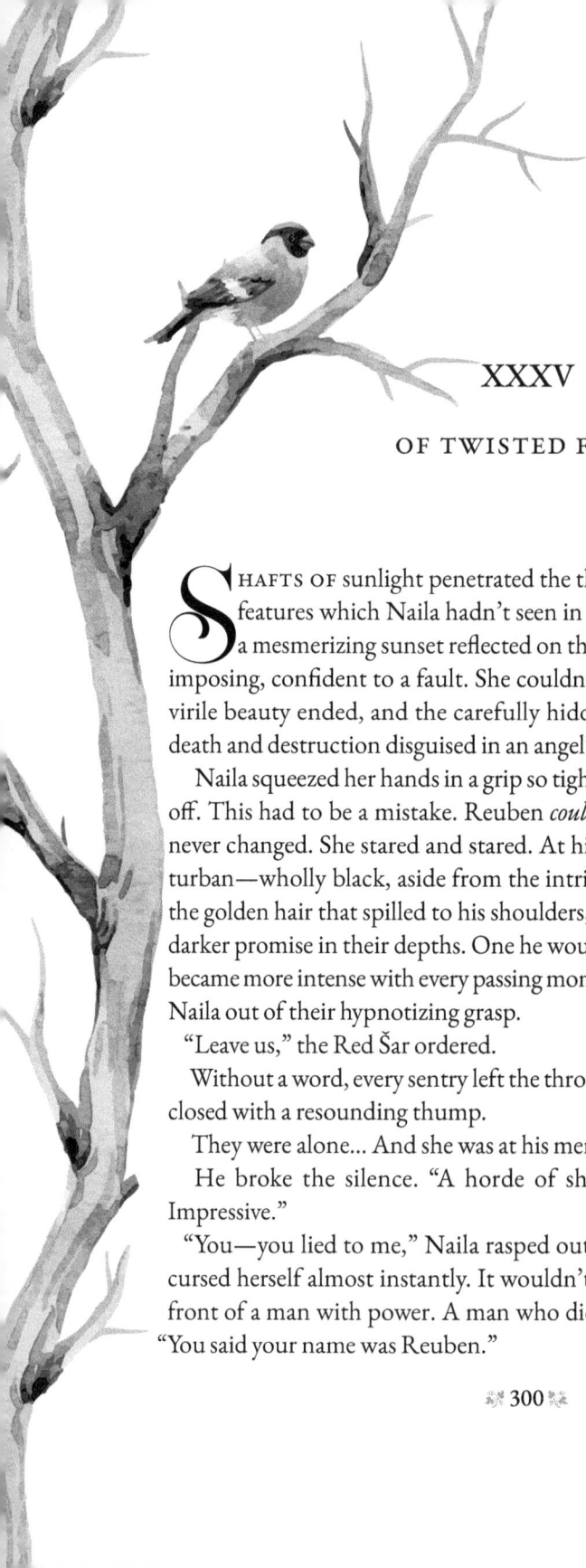

XXXV

OF TWISTED FATES

SHAFTS OF sunlight penetrated the throne room, unveiling the šar's features which Naila hadn't seen in daylight until that day. He was a mesmerizing sunset reflected on the waves of a ruthless sea. Poised, imposing, confident to a fault. She couldn't begin to make out where his virile beauty ended, and the carefully hidden lethality began. A spirit of death and destruction disguised in an angel's clothing.

Naila squeezed her hands in a grip so tight the blood in her veins was cut off. This had to be a mistake. Reuben *couldn't* be the Red Šar. The sight never changed. She stared and stared. At his finely woven robes and loose turban—wholly black, aside from the intricate crimson embroideries. At the golden hair that spilled to his shoulders, and his dark eyes with an even darker promise in their depths. One he would no doubt see through. They became more intense with every passing moment, refusing to let a squirming Naila out of their hypnotizing grasp.

"Leave us," the Red Šar ordered.

Without a word, every sentry left the throne room. The doors behind her closed with a resounding thump.

They were alone... And she was at his mercy.

He broke the silence. "A horde of shadowreapers on your heels... Impressive."

"You—you lied to me," Naila rasped out. She stepped backward... and cursed herself almost instantly. It wouldn't do good to show weakness in front of a man with power. A man who didn't hesitate to kill or conquer. "You said your name was Reuben."

"I said I *went* by Reuben. And I do. It is my road name."

She shook her head in disbelief. He was right, technically, but there was no doubt he had deceived her.

"Follow me," he said.

The šar sauntered to the open terrace doors, never looking back to see if she followed. With a sigh, she did exactly that and followed at a safe—for her—distance. Limestone steps led to a terraced garden with a smallish lake. The scent of raindrops on freshly cut grass spun through the wind.

Reuben, *no*, the Red Šar, descended the stairs, his hands folded behind his back. His midnight robes so at odds with the garden's delicate flowers. He came to a halt beneath a floral arch, and turned so suddenly Naila would've smacked into him if she hadn't kept her distance. She lifted her head to meet his eyes. He was just as tall as Silas. His brother. *His twin*.

All this time, whenever Levias was mentioned, she had imagined a near identical version of Silas. Ironic how Levias had his mother's coloring whereas it was Silas who likely took after his paternal family. In the pale sun, Levias's eyes simmered like dark sapphires. Even their eyes were different, for Silas's were a shade or two lighter.

The šar gave her his arm. Naila wanted to refuse, if only to spite him. She lifted her chin defiantly. Levias's lips curved into a cocky smile, but his eyes left no room for argument. For all means and purposes, she was at his mercy, and he didn't shy away from making that fact clear. Naila nuzzled on her bottom lip, but at last tucked her hand into the crook of his elbow.

He led her through the garden, on a mosaic path around the lake. Perhaps if Naila weren't so shocked by the nightmarish turn of events, she would stand to admire the desert roses in the neatly kept garden or the lotus flowers in the lake, or mayhap she would have asked which important people the many sculptures scattered about represented.

"I have the strangest tale to tell..." Levias broke the silence as his fingers stroked the back of her hand. Large, warm, calloused. The hand of a warlord, not one of a pampered king. Strong enough to kill but lean enough to wield the most elegant of swords. An involuntary shiver thrilled through her, leaving a field of goosebumps in its wake. "I was visiting Jodrir when a dream came to me. Can you guess?"

"No, but I'm sure you're going to tell me."

"It was you. Wrapped in a tunnel of the night's sky."

Naila's eyes widened, and she abruptly stopped.

What?

The Red Šar's gaze drifted over the smooth lines of her face. Curious. *Calculating.*

He continued, "You cried out to me."

"I didn't," Naila breathed.

Levias cocked his head and studied her stricken face. "Did you not?"

The enchanting melody of an oud instrument twirled its way from somewhere at the back of the garden. A pair of swans whistled as they swam through the clear waters of the lake, whilst colorful butterflies fluttered through the soft midday breeze. The šar's finger curled underneath Naila's chin and he inched her face upward.

Their eyes clashed. Ebony-blue to gilded brown. Dark to light.

"You were frightened," he continued, "Lost. Your soul called out to me."

Naila held in her breath, both eager and terrified to hear his words. Try as she might, she couldn't tear her eyes from his face. Halfbeard was right. Here was a devil hiding behind the mask of an angel.

"And I, *Evening Star*," Levias whispered as his thumb trailed her cheek, "could not stop myself from answering."

Did she haunt his dreams the way he did hers?

"What does this mean?" Her voice was barely a whisper.

She suppressed another shiver, but she couldn't stop her lips from opening slightly. His eyes followed the movement—endless pools of seductive darkness. Stay away, a voice whispered in alarm. But it was faint, weak, too soft for her ears. The šar's scent engulfed her, overwhelmed her; a beguiling blend of leather, the earthy smell of an uncharted forest, and something all man.

"I don't believe in fate but for you I'll make an exception," said he.

"My dreams… they warned me to stay away from you."

His eyes twinkled. "As did mine, but I've never been good at following orders."

So there was some kind of connection between them. Something dangerous that should be avoided at all costs. Was he the evil the šaltana alluded to? The one they had to conquer to bring balance to the worlds?

The swans in the lake honked again.

Naila blinked.

Somewhere, somehow, in the short time they'd been there, their bodies had inched closer. She could feel his heat, the tickle of his breath against her skin. The treacherous šar, Silas's despised brother, was but a hair removed from her... *Silas*.

Naila pushed her hands to Levias's chest. She had to get away from him.

"Silas," she said.

The smile melted off his face.

"Silas, *your brother*," Naila repeated, "Please, he needs iscias."

For several moments only the birds could be heard in the picturesque garden. Then the šar's lips curved into his mocking half-smile anew. "Here I thought nothing in the lands of Lemuria could surprise me. *Silas...?* Silas fell to a shadowreaper's blade? Surely you're playing me for a fool?"

"'Tis the truth. He got hurt protecting me."

"He should have done so without falling into their trap. It's what we were trained to do from the moment we could walk. Old Möndör Softsword rubbed off on him."

Naila's eyes widened. Silas was dying, and Levias mocked him for getting hurt. "This is your brother we're talking about. Your *twin*."

His expression grew colder than the Arctic. "So?"

"You must save him!"

"No."

She shook her head in disbelief. "You're a villain."

"Villain is... relative," he said, completely unfazed. "To a butterfly a bird is a villain. To a bird a cat is a villain. To us a cat is no more than a furry companion on a lonely winter's night."

"Reuben... Levias, he's your own flesh and blood. Whatever happened with your mother... Look, he had nothing to do with it." Naila's fingers dug into his finely woven robe. "We can't change the past, but we can shape the future. You two are family."

One by one, he unfolded her fingers off his robe as he studied her through hooded eyes.

"If I do not aid him, Skeldor falls into my hands by default. I am a man of business first and foremost." His dark eyes glittered with something unrecognizable. "Tell me, what will I get in exchange for Skeldor? And what will I get to replace my bottle of iscias, of which there is only one in all of Crishire?"

Naila's lip trembled. She had failed to get through to him. If he had any love left for his brother, it was buried underneath layers of heartless ice. "Please," she said as a tear tumbled down her cheek and fell to the grass like an unopened letter. Her eyes begged him for mercy she knew he wouldn't give.

He thumbed her tear away. "If you want to save him, you will have to do better than that."

"What do you want?" Naila whispered in defeat.

She had no property to her name. No means to strike a bargain. Something told her he wouldn't even be interested in the Unspokens' gauntlet they had found.

His fingers brushed over the length of a raven curl. Something shifted in his eyes. Was it admiration? Longing? Greed?

"Here you are, by far the most exquisite being I ever laid eyes on. You burn brighter than *Iluna* in the empty night, as if the stars shed their ethereal coats and gifted them to you. Ishtar come to life. Is this why the Shadow Šar wants you so?"

"I'm not following."

"Become my consort."

Naila's brows shot into her hairline. That was the last thing she expected him to say. "What?"

"It's a good deal, is it not? I have something you want and *you* are what *I* want."

Naila forced herself to breathe. Trade her freedom for Silas's life. The very thought of becoming a šar's property repulsed her to the bones. For him to do with her as he wanted, and when he tired of her to cast her aside as he so pleased. For her to be left at this ruthless man's mercy. Someone who didn't bat an eye at letting his own brother die.

"You want me to join your imperial harem," Naila hissed, "But what number woman does that make me?"

"Ah, is that what bothers you? Many a lord has gifted me their daughter as a concubine, yes, but you would be my very first consort."

The third highest rank within the imperial harem, below the imperial nergayla and the šar's mother only. Due to the strained state of affairs with Levias's mother, the latter fell away, which would make her the second most powerful woman in Crishire.

"You don't even love me!"

He looked at her as if she were an adorable bunny stuck in a fairy tale where a fox was a friend not a foe. "What does love have to do with this? It's a fickle emotion that fades with time. The position of consort, however, brings security, power, and more importantly strengthens with every day. I cannot give you love, but I promise you will want for nothing else."

Once upon a time in Rotterdam, Naila had been a shy girl who dreamed of her own fairy tale. She'd never been fierce or outspoken, was far from a born leader. In her journey to acceptance, she had even changed herself into what she thought her peers wanted to see. But what was it *she* wanted to be? A difficult question, but anything that involved Silas dying was not the answer.

"If I accept, you must heal Silas. He *must* live. You must also free my friends, Onyx, Tryce and Rē. Lastly, the Mehari are stuck at Gomorra because of the shadowreapers… You must help them."

He smiled.

"Upon my word."

Naila would let Levias think she'd accept his terms. However, as soon as Silas was healed, she would find a way to escape. Life was not a fairy tale and there were no guarantees for a happily ever after, but she would not let hers end imprisoned in a gilded cage. She was done conforming to others, done seeking approval. She, Naila Groenhart, would live the life she wanted, on her own terms.

"Then, I accept."

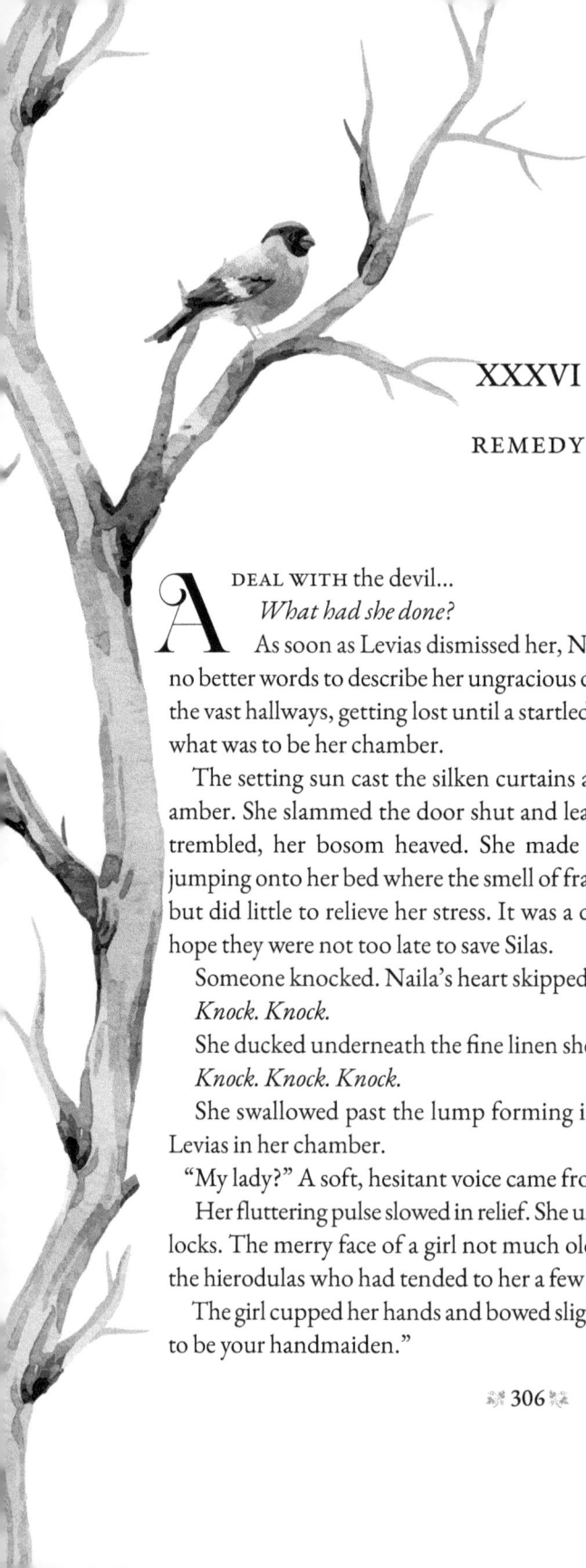

XXXVI

REMEDY

A DEAL WITH the devil...

What had she done?

As soon as Levias dismissed her, Naila fled the garden. There were no better words to describe her ungracious departure... She dashed through the vast hallways, getting lost until a startled eunuch showed her the way to what was to be her chamber.

The setting sun cast the silken curtains and cushions of her bed in soft amber. She slammed the door shut and leaned against it. Her fingers still trembled, her bosom heaved. She made sure to lock the door before jumping onto her bed where the smell of frankincense poked at her nostrils but did little to relieve her stress. It was a done deal. Now she could only hope they were not too late to save Silas.

Someone knocked. Naila's heart skipped a beat.

Knock. Knock.

She ducked underneath the fine linen sheets.

Knock. Knock. Knock.

She swallowed past the lump forming in her throat. She did *not* want Levias in her chamber.

"My lady?" A soft, hesitant voice came from the other side.

Her fluttering pulse slowed in relief. She unlocked the door's heavy bronze locks. The merry face of a girl not much older than Naila met her. One of the hierodulas who had tended to her a few bells earlier.

The girl cupped her hands and bowed slightly. "Lady Nova appointed me to be your handmaiden."

The girl unveiled her pearly teeth in a grin. Her features were delicate, her skin the palest shade of brown. If they were on Earth, Naila would have guessed her ancestry to be Inuit with a dash of Middle Eastern.

"Handmaiden?"

"*Yana.* My name is Crestal. I am the youngest daughter to my lord father, steward of the city Vigrid."

Crestal stared at Naila expectantly. Her doe-like eyes were wide with hope. Naila gifted the girl a weak smile. It was likely a great honor to become handmaiden to a šar's consort. Little did Crestal know she had no intention of staying.

"Crestal, uh, right." Naila's eyes shifted from the door to the girl. *Subtle, Naila.* Still, she just wanted to be left alone. "I'm a little tired right now."

The girl's smile faltered. "Oh, I'm sorry. It's just that Lady Nova gave me an urgent message, but I'll return a little later."

Naila's hand shot out to stop the girl. "What message?"

Crestal's face lit up again. "His Majesty's twin brother has returned to Crishire. Can you believe it?" Crestal didn't wait for Naila's response but clasped her hands together. A dreamy look glazed her eyes. "Whisperers say he's as handsome as the šar, but much more likely to give you a smile."

Naila blinked.

Whoever thought this girl to be hierodula material had a severe lapse in judgment, considering they were supposed to be more chaste than a nun.

"He is very ill, however. Lady Nova is tending to him now. She wanted you to know."

Naila grabbed Crestal by the arms. "Take me to her."

She hadn't realized that Nova, *the* Nova, would be Silas's chosen healer. He would be safe! Levias had made good on his promise.

"Our visit can't be long," Crestal chirped as she led Naila through one of the endless hallways. "There are many things to do before *tsimora* tomorrow."

Tsimora... The mating bond.

Naila arched a brow. "What do you mean tomorrow?"

Crestal added hastily, clearly unable to rein in her enthusiasm. "The šar's too impatient to wait until we reach the capital. He means to do it tomorrow and have the proper festivities at a later date in Irkalla. You must be thrilled by how much he covets you."

A coldness shuddered through Naila's body. She thought she had time...

"What about my friends? Onyx, Tryton, and Rē they're called. Has he released them?"

"The other foreigners at the gate? From what I understood, he will. After *tsimora*."

Levias had her cornered. There was no way to escape without jeopardizing her friends.

"What happens at the bonding ceremony, anyway?"

Crestal shuffled back a step, surprise etched on her face. "You don't know?"

She let silence be her answer.

Crestal scratched at her cheek. "*Tsimora* is sealed with sacred wine made from pomegranates grown in the Elysian Fields and blessed by a nergayla. It releases the consorts from all previous shackles and from henceforth binds them by blood. Not a bond as strong as that of star-fated, mind you, but strong nonetheless."

An æther-infused blood oath? The more Naila thought it over, the worse her bargain sounded. She still didn't know why she had those frightening visions of Levias... swearing a blood oath seemed like begging for trouble, yet she didn't have a choice. Not really. Silas had to be safe. Same for Onyx, Tryce, and Rē, and the poor Mehari stuck at Gomorra. At least Naila would be rid of the bond the moment she got back to Earth. She hoped.

Naila's fingers tingled with anticipation when they entered the quarters Levias kept Silas in. Framed with gold and gemstones, it was lush and decadent, more so even than the rest of the summer palace. For all of Levias's vicious talk, he had put his brother in quarters worthy of a man of status. Worthy of a šar. Maybe he did care a little...

Two sentries stood watch outside Silas's chamber, armed with silver kandshar daggers and staffs. Without a word, they opened the door. Several oil lamps provided a dim light in the spacious chamber. A Moorish screen was folded in front of what Naila could make out was a king-sized bed. Feminine whispers came from behind it, as they fussed over someone lying on the bed. *Silas.* Silas was there.

As if in a daze, Naila stepped forward, her feet moving of their own volition. He lay nearly bare upon the bed, as unconscious as last she'd seen him, although the green pallor had disappeared.

She rushed to the bed.

Behind her, the door clicked to a close.

She snapped out of her daze, her gaze sliding to the hierodulas hunched around Silas's bed. Several maidservants stood at the feet of the bed, whereas Nova, draped in an ivory toga, sat next to the prince. Æther engulfed her forearms. The same indigo flames were spread over Silas, like his body was on fire. Yet not a single burn appeared on his flesh. An empty bottle of iscias stood on the table next to Silas's bed. Small and insignificant... yet it had demanded such a steep price.

Nova's guarded eyes met Naila's. The same azure ones as the Mehari's. They held a wisdom within them that suggested an age far older than her youthful skin suggested.

Naila didn't sit. She grasped her compass as she watched Nova work. The woman's brows crunched in concentration. The day had long since lost its light when Silas's pallid skin blossomed with the faintest hint of rose on his cheeks.

"H-how is he?" Naila asked.

"Weak. Very weak," Nova said. "But, he will live. Iscias is the most powerful antidote in existence."

Naila's vision blurred with tears. She perched on the mosaic tiles next to Silas's bed and let her tears fall down her cheeks. It hadn't been for nothing. Her gamble had been right.

"Naila," Silas mumbled.

She squeezed his hand. It was cold and trembling. She rubbed it within her own to warm it. Silas's eyes moved rapidly underneath his eyelids.

"Give him the night," Nova said, "By the morrow, he will awaken."

Naila smiled gratefully at the nergayla. "Thank you."

Nova hesitated before she spoke. An unreadable look consumed the depths of her azure eyes. "For the šar to spare his brother... I—" Nova glanced at the hierodulas still in the chamber and shook her head. "It is you who deserves my thanks."

Bitterness laced Naila's next words. "Levias didn't do it for free. Everything for him has a price."

"Still, if it were another, His Majesty wouldn't even entertain bargaining. It's nothing short of a miracle he agreed to your terms."

"More like *his* terms."

But Nova said no more. She continued to work her æther on Silas until the whole of his body had absorbed the iscias. Naila stayed by Silas's side, even after Crestal and the other hierodulas had left. Nova, however, stayed with her. The owls outside hooted well into the night, but the prince never opened his eyes. Finally, she couldn't fight her sleep any longer. Her eyes fluttered to a close.

THE SUMMER palace was quiet, except for the echoing footsteps in the hallway leading to the šar's wing. Levias Dayamon vi Iliyas trotted toward his destination, an impatient expression etched on his Adonis face. He barely spared his ancestor Suleyman Chad vi Iliyas's sculpture a glance, nor the infamous scimitar clenched in the hands of the first Red Šar. On the surrounding walls, the history of his paternal family was told through countless murals. The Red Šars basked in glory and victory in those depictions, oblivious of their progeny who walked about their halls centuries afterward.

Levias's footsteps slowed as he reached his destination. His sentries cupped a fist within their palm and bowed before opening the door.

"Red Šar," Nova said from the doorway. "Here I thought you were too busy scheming and wreaking havoc."

Levias smirked at the way the nergayla tilted her chin in defiance, showing him he did not intimidate her. He'd never tell her this, but it was something he admired in Nova. Most people feared even the mention of his name, and those acquainted with him knew that fear was justified. Nova did not care.

"Does your gift never sleep, nergayla? Not even in the death of the night?"

Levias stepped inside, not waiting for an invitation. His lovely consort-to-be was asleep, her head resting on a table next to his estranged brother's bed. Her long spiral curls hung like a curtain over her delicate hourglass figure. Even in her sleep, Naila's face emanated innocence and sweetness. Everything he was not.

"It's not a gift, Your Majesty. To make near-accurate premonitions, nothing more is required than the use of one's æther to connect with Mother Nature and her celestial sisters. They have been here long before us and will be here long after our bones have turned to dust," Nova said matter-of-factly as she closed the door behind him.

"So, you say," Levias said as he took seat on a chair next to the bed.

The paleness had left his *dogan's* skin. Silas mumbled something incomprehensible and twisted in his bed. The prince hadn't awakened yet, but he would live. Nova never failed Levias. He reached for his twin before pausing at the last moment. He squeezed his fingers into a fist and retracted his hand.

"You let him live," Nova said as she clasped her hands before her.

Her eyes were prying, hungry to snatch any hint from his face, but he gave her none.

"I did," was all he said.

She sighed and took a sip from some herb tea. "What is it you came to seek?"

"Do not insult my intelligence by pretending you do not know."

Nova looked him straight in the eye. She had the regal countenance of a queen—one who didn't bend to pressure, be it from king or peasant. And she was a queen, in anything but name. To Levias, she was the closest thing to a mother. "She is no ordinary nergayla."

"Then pray tell me what she is, because the shadowreapers seem adamant about getting her."

Nova seemed to hesitate for a moment, opting to peer at the yellow liquid in her cup instead. When Levias tapped impatiently on the rail of the chair, she let out a sigh. "Her phæralei are vivid, complete. I've seen nothing like it before... Although I once had a vision..."

Levias leaned over Naila to brush a lock covering her forehead away. The pendant that dangled around her neck gleamed in the light of the oil lamps.

Nova continued, "There are rumors, legends, written in scrolls long lost to us. They speak of a power that rules over life and death."

Levias brushed his finger over his lip in thought. "You think she holds this power?"

"I'm not sure."

"What of my visions? The ones she shares?"

Nova's expression turned grave. For the first time, she seemed uncomfortable.

"We must be star-fated."

"Levias..."

"What else could it be?"

"The Legends do not work this way. Star-fated are guided toward one another, never driven apart. For the visions to warn you away from each other means something bigger is at play."

The šar let the words sink in.

"You know my old man leveled cities to the ground, just so he could collect the rarest *feylanas* as gems for his harem. But even father's most radiant consorts were but shadows in the light of her beauty."

Nova's lips tightened into a thin line. She stared at him sharply. "It would grieve me to see you follow in Jericho's footsteps. Abducting exotic, pretty women just to show them off and pad your ego wouldn't make you any better than the ruthless villain your father was, Levias. Do not challenge the stars, for they are wise and all-seeing."

The šar flashed Nova a smirk; the mischievous boyish one that made women feel weak at the knees. Predictably, her countenance softened.

"Father's legacy died with him. You know full well I have no intention of setting forth with his customs."

Levias reached for her hand over the bed and planted a soft kiss on her palm. He might be confident in his belief he was different, and Nova might be easily swayed by his charm as a mother was blind to her babe's faults, but Levias Dayamon was very much his father's son. More than even he himself realized.

No woman, no man, no being celestial or no, would ever tell him what to do. He lived by one rule and one rule alone: fate is what you make it to be.

XXXVII

AN OATH INKED IN BLOOD

“Will you tell me when he wakes up?” Naila asked as a maid sewed her into a ceremonial dress.

“We will,” Crestal said, “but *after* the ceremony. You must focus on *tsimora* now. The prince can wait.”

Several maids had fretted over every inch of Naila the whole morning. They brushed away a stray curl, pressed the last rumple out of her gown, and dabbed an extra layer of rosy stain on her lips. Rose powder and the pristine aroma of fresh fabric filled the whole of the chamber.

“You must be over the moon, my lady,” Crestal gushed, “For you to become His Majesty’s first-ever consort.”

“Indeed,” said the maid from behind Naila. “Many a lord has offered him their daughters as consort, but he has always refused. All of nobility were complaining, you know. Saying the šar is too enchanted by the arts of war, never allowing for the softness of a *feylana’s* touch.”

Naila scoffed.

She doubted Levias had any plans to renounce his warlord ways.

“If you play your cards wisely, you may well surpass Nova in power,” Crestal added, her eyes sparkling as she grafted the fayalobi hair clip in Naila’s updo.

Play her cards right?

“And how do you suggest I do that?”

“Well, you must satisfy His Majesty, of course.” Crestal blushed, and a few maids giggled. “And you must bear him an heir. Quickly, if I may say so.”

Naila scrunched her nose. The poor babe would become a disaster.

Crestal studied Naila's face. "Do not see this as an obstacle, my lady, but rather as an opportunity. Many would die to be in your place."

A maid rolled a mirror stand before her. Naila frowned. She had been so occupied with thoughts of an ailing Silas, it hadn't registered how exactly they were dressing her up.

"What do you think?" Crestal grinned.

Before Naila could stop herself, she blurted, "I look like a lady of easy virtue."

A collective gasp resounded throughout the room. The maid's mouth stood ajar, while the tailor got into a coughing fit.

Naila swiveled around to take in her gown. Burgundy gossamer barely covered the lower globes of her chest. She was fairly well-endowed, so every movement of the dress could cause a potential scandal. *This gown was not her.* Fake marriage or no, it had to go.

"Isn't there something else I could wear?"

"His Majesty ordered this dress. It would do you no good to disobey him," the tailor stuttered.

Now, Naila really rolled her eyes. "Well, *His Majesty* has no say over what I wear. I want another dress."

The maid's eyes widened, but with an encouraging nod from Crestal, she bowed and thrust forward the clothing rack. Naila brushed her fingers along the sumptuous gowns until she stumbled upon a deep green gown made of silk.

She caressed the material with reverence.

"'Tis a lovely one, isn't it? They bought it from one of the Ice Šar's consorts, Baosi, I think she was called. She made it as a love note to her beloved daughter, who was lost to her when shadowreapers raided her village."

Naila's heart strutted.

What? *Baosi?* Onyx's mother? All this time she had been locked up in the Ice Šar's palace in Jodrir!

Naila pointed absentmindedly at another dress, a tulle dress in shades of blush and ivory, trying to collect her chaotic thoughts. "This one, but I'd like to keep the green one if possible?"

"As you wish."

She would give the dress to Onyx, alongside the message of where to find her mother.

Crestal patted a tear away as she and the maids stared at Naila, newly dressed. "You look ethereal. Like a goddess of spring."

Someone knocked on the door. A bundle of nerves burst inside Naila's stomach.

Nova entered the room, whilst two sentries she arrived with remained outside the chamber. She was, again, dressed in a kaunake the same color as her hair. The nergayla's phæralei shimmered a pearly silver against her dark skin instead of the indigo of the night before. Just like Naila's burned gold when she used her gilded flames.

Nova pushed Naila gently toward the door. "Come, it is time. Your arrival surprised us. If we had known the šar would choose a consort, we would have prepared accordingly."

"Meaning what?"

"All imperial eunuchs are at the palace in Irkalla. It will take fourteen sunsets to get them here. I've already sent word to Lord Kizlar, the chief eunuch. But do not worry, the sentries at the summer palace are instructed well, and it's only for a few weeks at the most."

"Eunuchs? Goodness gracious, how many balls did you cut off?"

A maid giggled from behind Naila whilst a blush crept up the sentries' cheeks.

Nova clucked her tongue. "Language."

"How can Levias do this to them?" Naila hissed.

"It's not *His Majesty*"—Nova shot her a pointed look—"who orders it so. It is a longstanding tradition in all lands of Lemuria and a great honor to be an imperial eunuch. They are of equal status to the low-ranked lords. Sometimes even higher." Nova rubbed Naila's upper arm soothingly. "It will do you no good to frown upon our ways. Eunuchs guard all imperial harems. It's the way it has been since the time of the juhrators and it will be so long after your grandchildren's grandchildren."

"Stay strong, my lady," Crestal whispered.

Nova led her back to the throne room. This time it was furnished with a floor table with four seating cushions, all adorned with Crishire's black serpentine crest. Atop the desk were a glass-and-tin carafe and two jeweled goblets.

"Leave us," Nova ordered the sentries.

Without argument, they left and closed the door behind them.

"What's going to happen now?"

"You will fulfill your side of the bargain, as His Majesty did his."

"Where are my friends?"

"They aren't in the dungeons, if that is what worries you. They are kept and fed in proper rooms. You shall see them *after* the blood oath."

"What is expected of me?"

Nova tutted. "So many questions. All you have to do is drink the pomegranate wine and speak the oath. It is a brief ceremony."

Nova studied Naila's face. "You truly did not know? Where do you come from, *feylana*?"

"I'm from Earth. I've told everyone that a thousand times."

"Earth? *Earth*, you say? Surely—"

The beating of a guard's staff was the only warning before the door flung open and the guest of honor arrived.

The Red Šar entered with a familiar man by his side. Lord Gorgo, the haughty man who arrested Naila and her friends. When the lord's eyes fell upon her, he grinned. The audacity!

Levias was dressed in black and crimson, as if he were attending a funeral instead of a wedding.

The šar took in her appearance. "I could have sworn I ordered another dress."

Naila tilted her chin in defiance. "I liked this one better."

"Ah, so she does have a bite..." A hint of a smile tugged at Levias's lips. "I like that."

Naila had a faint urge to wipe the cocky smirk off his face.

Nova interrupted. "Everything is set in place."

As soon as they took their seats, Nova started the ceremony. The imperial nergayla unveiled a jeweled dagger from her cloak.

Nova first pricked Levias's finger and squeezed his finger above the carafe until a drop of blood splashed into the already wine-red pomegranate liquor.

Then it was Naila's turn.

She winced when Nova made a slight cut on her finger and immediately looked away. The sight of blood always made her queasy and light-headed.

Nova clasped the carafe and closed her eyes. Indigo flames burst from her fingers and the sweet burn of æther spread through the chamber. The flames licked at the metal of the carafe and crawled inside, where they spread over the liquor. Just as quickly as the flames arose, they vanished. The nergayla poured the liquor into Levias's and Naila's goblets.

Finally, she handed them the goblets and hummed,

"Forged by honor, sealed by blood,
This is no bond thou can rend.
Bound by hatred, bound by love,
No man can break it until death's cove.
Witnessed by the sacred moons,
Our souls are bound to forever attune."

With every phrase, the goblet in Naila's hand burned fiercely. At the last word, the liquid sizzled anew with flames. This time, the flames were crimson. Not the color of the Lemaian's æther, but the color the Ænunaki's were rumored to be.

"You may drink," Nova said.

The room was quiet. Only the crackling flames trembled through the air.

A prickling sensation shot up Naila's neck.

Was she really going to do this?

Her eyes latched onto Levias's and she knew it was too late. The time for breaking off the pact had long since passed. If she wanted to keep her friends safe, she had to see this through. She drew the heated goblet to her lips. Levias took a sip from his, his eyes never leaving hers. Hesitantly, she tasted the liquid. It was tangy-sweet, with the fruity edge of pomegranates. It was also hot...

The moment the liquor entered her throat, it consumed her body. Like an avalanche of fire, it scorched its way through Naila's flesh, her veins, her nerves.

She gasped. Levias squeezed her hand. She saw a fire blazing behind his eyes. She knew that very same fire burned behind hers. Her body turned feverish, as if the liquor forced her body to purge... something hidden within her. A déjà vu of something she almost remembered.

From somewhere afar, Nova said, "It is done."

But Naila didn't see her, for the room had turned dark. It was only her and Levias. And the purging flames within her body.

"Witnessed," Lord Gorgo said.

Hot. Naila was so hot. Her breath hitched in her throat. She couldn't breathe. Couldn't move. Her eyes widened in panic.

"Calm yourself," Levias said as he palmed her cheek.

A drop of sweat slipped down her neck.

"Well, I'll be. Someone has chained her mind with æther," said Nova.

What? But Naila knew it to be true. Even as she spoke the words, the purging flames were attacking an invisible chain around her mind, melting it shackle for shackle.

"I—" Naila tried again, but she couldn't utter any further words.

A thousand stars sprinkled across her vision and her limbs weakened.

Levias frowned. "What does this mean?"

A vision flickered on Naila's retinas. It came with the force of an avalanche. Nothing she did would stop it.

Wings of crimson.

A palace in the sky.

And many lifetimes before, a little girl waddled over a pearly floor in a pale, lavish room. She was young, no more than four winters. Although where she was no winter ever visited for it was a paradise of eternal summer.

A beautiful woman sat on the sparkling floor and opened her arms for the girl. The woman's skin was a luminescent brown, her curly hair black as night and her lips stained ruby. Her slanted eyes were kind, a smoky quartz purer than the gemstone itself.

On the woman's forehead was something achingly familiar. A diamond, but without the crescent moon. Low on the woman's neck swung a compass pendant. But there was something unusual about it. A golden stone shone from its center. It pulsed strangely. Like a gilded heart outside a body. How familiar it was. Not unlike the depictions of the murals of Gomorra.

The girl pushed out her brown chubby little hands. "Momma."

"Yes, little angel." The woman beamed.

But then something happened. The gilded stone pulsed faster and faster until it shattered into a thousand pieces. The golden dust spread through the room.

"Naila," the woman said, her eyes wide with fear, as she edged to the little girl.

The gold dust particles whirled into the air and before the woman could utter another word, they darted to Naila and enveloped her in their grip.

Tighter and stronger, their grasp became.

Little Naila was afraid.

The dust was hot, so hot. She couldn't breathe.

Finally, it sank into her flesh, and her skin cooled down until nothing remained. Except Naila and her mother. But the golden dust wasn't gone, for the Stone of Songs and Souls had awakened within her. Had claimed her mind, body, and soul.

"Naila," the woman said as she drew the girl into her warm, safe arms.

The girl stared at the woman in wonder, until she finally spoke, "No, I..."

"...am Ishtar," Naila said.

The last thing she remembered was falling into Levias's arms. Then the world faded into shades of black.

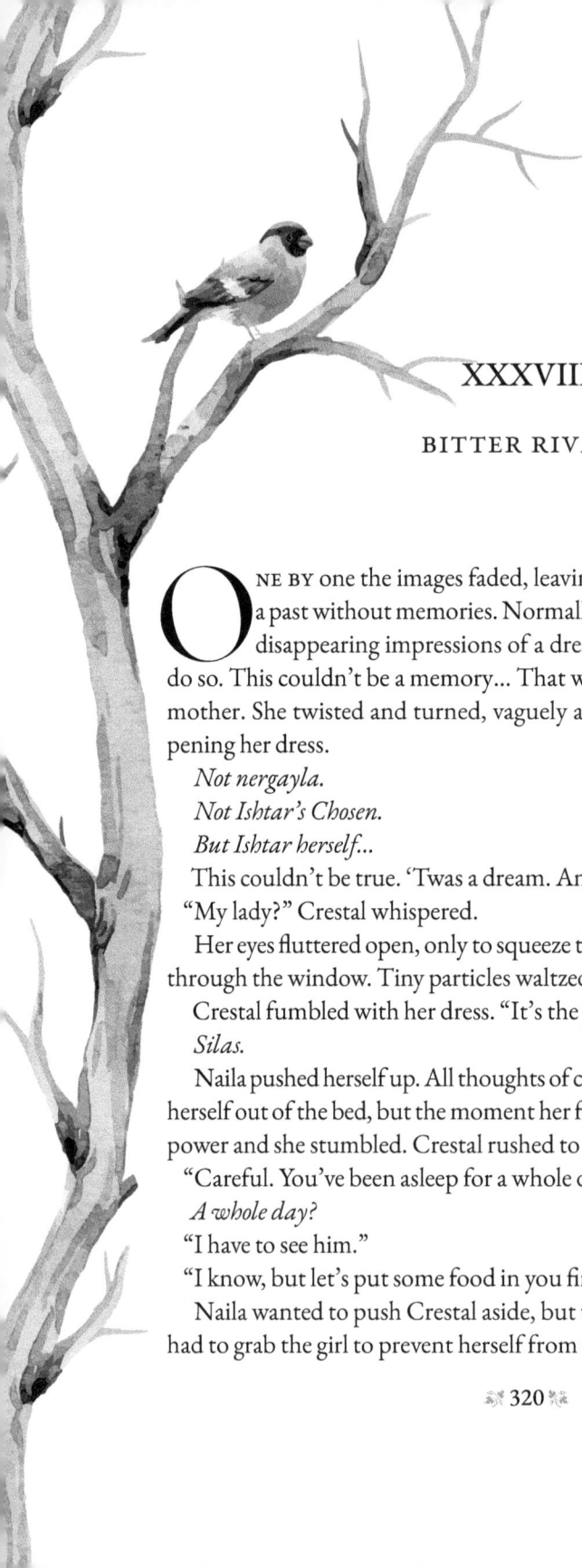

XXXVIII

BITTER RIVALS

One by one the images faded, leaving nothing but the remnants of a past without memories. Normally, Naila would grasp the swiftly disappearing impressions of a dream. Now, she was too scared to do so. This couldn't be a memory… That woman in her vision was not her mother. She twisted and turned, vaguely aware of the feverish sweat dampening her dress.

Not nergayla.

Not Ishtar's Chosen.

But Ishtar herself…

This couldn't be true. 'Twas a dream. An illusion. No more.

"My lady?" Crestal whispered.

Her eyes fluttered open, only to squeeze them against the sunrays wafting through the window. Tiny particles waltzed through the light.

Crestal fumbled with her dress. "It's the prince! He woke up."

Silas.

Naila pushed herself up. All thoughts of confusion evaporated. She forced herself out of the bed, but the moment her feet hit the tiles, her legs lost their power and she stumbled. Crestal rushed to steady her.

"Careful. You've been asleep for a whole day."

A whole day?

"I have to see him."

"I know, but let's put some food in you first."

Naila wanted to push Crestal aside, but the world spun around her. She had to grab the girl to prevent herself from falling.

"Okay," she sighed. "Food it is. But hurry!"

When they arrived at Silas's chamber, she didn't wait for the sentries, instead, she pushed the heavy door open and dashed into the room. Her legs froze on the spot. *Silas.* Silas sat at the edge of the window, dressed in his travel leathers, his face tan as if it had never lost its color. As if he'd never been ill. Just like Levias had promised...

Onyx sat next to him whilst Rē and Tryce leaned against the wall. They had all their limbs attached and not a single scratch marred their skin.

"Naila," Onyx gasped.

Tryce jumped from his place. "There she is."

Rē inclined his head in acknowledgment, but even he couldn't hide the smile forming on his face. Naila's chest swelled with emotions. Her friends were safe. They were all safe.

She forgot how to walk but somehow her feet still carried her. Silas met her halfway, lifting her into his arms, his precious face warm like the day's first sunrays. She burst out in full-blown sobs. Her nose ached with the unpleasant swelling of her mucosa. She hated ugly crying but she couldn't hold back. Silas was here. *Alive*. Everything hadn't been for nothing.

Naila whimpered. "W-we did it! You're alive."

Silas's lips curved against the crook of her neck. "I told you I wouldn't die so easily."

Onyx threw her arms over both of them. "By the stars, that was close."

"He let you out," Naila grinned through her tears.

Onyx scoffed. "They threw us in a dungeon. I could've sworn we were about to be a lion's meal."

"But whoop!" Tryce waved his arms dramatically, "All of a sudden they let us out and Silas was healed."

Naila beamed. "I hoped... I'm so glad he kept his word."

Silas put Naila down, his brows furrowing. She let out a little whimper of protest. She wasn't ready to say goodbye to the warmth of him. To his comforting scent.

The expressions on Onyx's and Silas's faces grew serious, while Tryce just eyed her curiously. And Rē, well, he always looked solemn, although there was a darkness in his eyes she couldn't decipher.

"What happened, N?" Onyx asked.

Silas clenched his jaw. "And what's with your clothes?"

Naila followed his gaze to her kaunake. It was made of the finest salmon silk with edges of lace, complimenting her brown skin to perfection.

Someone cleared their throat.

Like one, they turned. Standing in the doorway was the last person Naila wanted to see. A mocking half-smile and midnight eyes met her horrified gaze…

The Red Šar. He leaned against the wall, dressed in all black, whilst twirling a crystal glass.

Levias hadn't bothered to button up his blouse. As if they weren't worthy of the barest decency to see the šar properly dressed. Soft sunrays kissed the velvet tan of his skin. The exact same color as Silas's. How hadn't she realized they were brothers?

"I was looking for you," he said, his words aimed at Naila, but his eyes burning on Silas instead.

The chamber deafened to a deadly silence.

"What?" Tryce cough-laughed humorlessly.

Silas's hands balled into fists, his face a kaleidoscope of emotions: surprise, confusion, anger. Then his eyes flicked from Naila to Levias, understanding dawning. "You better not have touched her," he growled.

"He didn't," Naila said hurriedly before Levias had the chance to open his mouth.

Levias pushed himself off the wall, his eyes never leaving Silas. The room crackled with an invisible current, as if the air itself braced for this unwanted reunion of the twins. "If I did, *dogan,* it would be well in my right. You see, Naila is my consort."

Silas's head snapped to Naila.

"Huh?" Onyx spluttered; at the same time Tryce's jaw dropped.

Rē narrowed his eyes on Naila. For the first time since she knew the silent seaman he showed a hint of emotion. He was not happy. But nothing, absolutely nothing, compared to Silas's reaction.

A devastated expression bled over Silas's face. "What?" He breathed out.

"Silas…" Naila began, reaching for him, but he only stepped backward. Away from her.

Teardrops wetted the fan of her lashes, clouding her vision as they dropped to her cheeks. "I—" her voice broke, "I wanted to save you."

"By swearing tsimora to *him*?" Silas shook his head in disbelief.

Onyx shuffled her feet uneasily while Tryce balled his fists, venom leaking from his face as he eyed Levias.

Naila brushed a tear away. "There was no other way."

"Naila..."

Her eyes dropped to the floor. "I couldn't let you die. I just couldn't."

"Silas, N did it to save you." Onyx grabbed for his arm but the prince twisted out of her grasp.

He wasn't faking the pain. It was real and raw. In his eyes she saw any hope for their love crumble to dust.

Levias cocked his head, studying Silas. Any thoughts he kept carefully tucked away. "You should be thanking her, Silvanus."

Silas's face grew dark. "I'd rather be dead than have anyone I love at your mercy."

Naila shivered.

Love?

Levias chuckled. He sipped from his glass, before speaking. The warning in his words could not be misread. "Be careful what you wish for. On a whim, I decided to spare your life... And on a whim, *dogan*, I may just change my mind."

"No, you promised!" Naila stamped her foot at the same time Onyx reached for her quiver, momentarily forgetting she was without weapons.

"And I shall keep my end of the bargain as long as *you* honor yours," Levias warned. He sauntered toward her, eroding the distance. Without a word he pulled off his outer robe and tugged it over Naila's shoulders. "Which means, no more sneaky visits to other men."

"Levias," Silas growled. "She is under the Silver Šar's protection. She's to be *his* imperial nergayla!"

Naila's eyes widened. *What?*

Naila stared from one brother to another, as they glared at each other, her breathing accelerating with every second. Levias's eyes... They were cold and dead as the shadows behind a tombstone. Yet, they still conveyed a thousand messages with a single look. Piercing messages of a promise, a warning. Of a threat. And every last one of them was aimed at his brother.

"Are you blind, Silvanus? Or perhaps your incompetent swordplay with shadowreapers turned you daft? Tsimora severed all other bonds and obligations."

"She is a nergayla," Silas spat. "Tsimora is prohibited for them. You know the code of honor."

What?

It made sense, however. If hierodulas were locked to a life of chastity surely nergaylas would be all the more. Yet Silas had kissed her… Naila's eyes shifted from Silas to Onyx, who shrugged.

Amusement crept up the Red Šar's face. "I'm sure you would hold yourself to that old-fashioned code, would you now, *dogan*?"

Silas gritted his teeth. If looks could kill, his twin would be at the bottom of the Sea of Helath speared with a thousand scimitars. To the prince's credit, he refrained from strangling Levias. "Is that what this is about? Another one of your petty mind games? Fine, you have my attention. Tell me what you want. Just. Release. Naila."

Levias waved Silas's words away. "A game is for those who yearn to taste the nectar of freedom, all the while forgetting the chains that bind them to its rules. *I* make my own rules. I do not need to play silly games."

"There are shadowreapers after her. The Shadow Šar is after her." Onyx broke her silence. "She is too much of a hassle for you, Red Šar. Please… let her go."

Levias corked a brow. "Ah, Nehemia, so you have returned as well, I see?" Onyx blinked in surprise. She obviously hadn't expected Levias to recognize her. "But you see, unlike my brother and his mother, I do not run from my problems. I face them head on. Let those shadowreapers come." Levias took another sip from his glass as if they were talking about the weather.

"Don't be a fool," Silas hissed. "You don't find it weird shadowreapers crawled out of the Shadowlands to hunt Naila down? Think, Levias, think. They are up to something, and it may well have to do with the Unspokens. For all we know, they need Naila to bring them back."

Levias put his glass down on the night table next to Silas's bed.

"The Unspokens are never coming back."

Silas opened his mouth, but Levias continued, "When Suzano defeated the Unspokens' king, Arakiel, a thousand winters ago, every single one of them was executed. Our forefathers killed the men, the women, the elderly, and the children. None of the Unspokens, and I do mean none of them, were left alive."

"No!" Naila covered her mouth. "How could they be so cruel?"

Levias, Silas, and Tryce looked at her without a hint of pity or remorse. Only Onyx looked uncomfortable.

"The Unspokens met the fate they tried to impose on us. We simply beat them to it in self-defense," Levias said matter-of-factly. "If a prey spares its hunter, it will not have the chance to make the same mistake twice, for it will be dead."

Naila shook her head in disbelief. She didn't care what they said to justify the actions of their ancestors. It was genocide no matter how you spun it. Children should never pay for their parents' mistakes.

Silas watched his brother, deep in thought. His look wasn't one of surprise, but rather one of contemplation. "Shadowreapers are chasing us over land and sea to get to Naila. Grandfather's vigiles report their numbers are rapidly increasing. They are up to something."

"Perhaps old Möndör Softsword is lying."

"Careful." Silas bared his teeth.

"What? You don't think he is capable of withholding information from you?" Levias's mouth curled into one of his sardonic half-smiles. "From deceiving you? Skeldor loves to paint itself as a utopia but make no mistake, like all of Lemuria, your carefree life is built on the back of lies, theft, and not to mention blood slaves."

Silas scoffed. "Thanks, but no thanks for your little lecture. The Empire of Skeldor thrives with her head high. We don't need the approval of tyrants who rule through chaos and anarchy."

"Anarchy knows no ruler," Levias said, his voice dangerously low. "And it would do you well to remember that I am Crishire's šar, *dogan*, and you are at my lair."

Naila balled her fists. "Stop it. Just stop."

The twins looked at her in unison, Silas frowning, whilst Levias crossed his arms.

"Please, not another word. You'll have me questioning whether I should run to the shadowreapers instead."

"Naila..." Silas began as he reached for her, but she stepped backward.

Someone knocked on the door, followed by the heavy door creaking open. Lord Gorgo stormed into the room, but instantly halted at the sight before him. He looked at Levias and then at Silas and then back again. "Levias, a word please."

Levias sighed and rubbed his temple, "I am busy, Idris."

"It's urgent." Lord Gorgo shot the šar a pointed look.

Levias narrowed his eyes but then flicked his finger. The sentries that kept watch outside the door entered the chamber.

"As much as I would like to indulge you, Silvanus, I have an empire to run. Take Nehemia and your little band of trespassers, and leave Crishire while I'm still in a good mood."

"What?" Naila gasped.

But Levias raised his finger to silence her. "I am feeling rather generous right now, so be grateful that I'm not issuing an order for their heads. Next time I may well change my mind."

Then the šar beckoned his men. "Escort them out of Lethos."

He turned to Naila, the look on his face unreadable. "Now would be the time to say your goodbyes."

Naila's breath hitched in her throat. *No. No. No.* This couldn't be happening.

Silas glared at Levias but reached for his satchel. As he walked past his brother, he threw out, "This isn't over Levias."

Naila dashed after her friends, not wanting to waste the last of their precious time. Just as she was about to step through the door, a hand tugged at her sleeve. Levias drew her back, until her back pressed flat against the hardness of his chest.

"Let me go," Naila hissed. "You said I could say goodbye, so keep your word and do some good for once."

"Oh, I do some good deeds from time to time."

Naila scoffed. "Like what? Not killing someone every now and then?"

Levias chuckled. He turned her around, twisting one of her curls around his finger. "I left you alone at the Shores of the Blood Moons, didn't I? And again at the oasis?"

Naila tilted her chin in defiance. "Well, what do you know? Two good deeds. Looks like you can retire."

A hint of a smile tugged at his mouth. "Do you remember my warning at the hot spring?"

She thought back to how he told her he couldn't be trusted. The šar pressed her raven curl to his lips. "Next time, when someone shows you their true face, don't mistake it for a mask that is more to your liking."

XXXIX

AN UNEXPECTED GUEST

THE MORNING had barely said its goodbye, but the sun already scorched the clouds into an air stifling heat. Wayward curls stuck to Naila's neck as she and her friends rode in a heavily guarded litter to the east exit of Lethos—the opposite entrance from the way they had gotten in a few days before. The road spiraled around the length of Lethos' namesake volcano, of which they got the full scenic view, albeit in less than fortunate circumstances.

Through the split of the curtains, she saw a group of sweaty, bare-chested *lugals* wrestling. Several *feylanas* cheered them on, patches of sweat also soaking their simple tunics—kaunakes, apparently, were reserved for the wealthy. Normally, Naila would be eager to learn more about these peculiar citizens of Lemuria, but no sparkle of interest occurred. Everything felt bleak, with cracks of desperation threatening to implode into something more... hopelessness.

"We'll get you out, N, don't worry." Onyx squeezed Naila's hand, her eyes sympathetic.

Tryce snorted from next to Silas, a matching sullen look on his face. "Yes, whatever can the Red Šar and a thousand imperial sentries do against the four of us?"

Onyx rolled her eyes. "Aren't you a ray of sunshine?"

Naila squeezed Onyx's hand back. At least one of them was optimistic. She peeked through her lashes at Silas, but the prince said nothing. He just stared outside at the caravans hobbling into Lethos, his jaw clenched tight.

"How though?" Naila sighed. The city is better guarded than a prison.

The carriage lurched viciously over a stone. Quick as the wind, Silas steadied her before she fell through the curtains.

"Th-Thanks."

He ran his fingers through his hair. "I can't believe you swore tsimora to Levias."

Naila pursed her lips. "If I didn't do it, you'd be dead right now. Compared to that, I really don't think it's that big a deal."

"No big deal?" He laughed humorlessly. "*No big deal*? It's harder to undo tsimora than to obtain iscias, Naila. You're bound by blood until you die."

"In a few weeks, *I* will be back home." She finger-counted. "*You* will be alive and well in Skeldor, and this whole oath thing will be forgotten."

"Let it go, Silas," Onyx said, whilst shuffling the arrows in her quiver. Apparently, Levias didn't consider them that big a threat to confiscate their weapons. That, or his arrogance knew no bounds. "Don't you realize what she did? She made your brother, of all people, save you. I say our little Earthling did a wonder."

Silas shook his head. "It's to spite me and grandfather of course. Things are always personal with him."

Naila glanced sideways. "I don't know if that's the reason."

She told them all that had happened. How Levias had saved her in the redwoods. How she had dreamed of him ever since, frightening dreams though they were. All but Rē gaped at her, although the latter's ethereal face was every bit as serious.

"Are you certain?" Silas shifted uneasily in his seat.

Naila fumbled with her compass, unsure how to answer his question. Finally, she sighed. "It's very strange, these dreams, I mean."

"What do they show you?" Rē urged.

His interest surprised Naila. There were many layers to the stoic man she had yet to unfold. "They warn me away. He said... Levias said he's been having the same dreams."

Silas rolled his eyes. "He only said that to lure you into his trap."

Ignoring Silas, Onyx mumbled in wonder, "When we get back, we should ask Mr. Thoth and Zarqa whether the scrolls have ever mentioned such a thing."

Tryce shot up. "Listen. What if... the Shadow Šar put some spell on Naila and Levias?"

"For what reason?" Naila asked. "He has no control over Levias."

No one did, that much was clear.

"The Red Šar could be working with the Shadow Šar, you know?" Tryce suggested. His words hung in the air for several moments.

Naila went back to staring at the donkey-led wagons on the road. A bird of prey called high in the sky, circling their litter with keen eyes.

Silas crossed his arms, his eyes burning on Naila's face. "I'm beginning to think this Earth may not be your home."

"But it is," Naila protested. "I lived there my whole life! I was even born there."

But was she, really? What was her mother hiding? What had *Philly* been hiding? She now knew her mother's explanation of her phæralei had been false. And then there was that memory where she had absorbed the dust of a gilded stone... What was that thing?

To her surprise her breathing remained calm. No telltale signs of panic pricked her fingers.

"It's all speculation at this point, isn't it?" Onyx concluded.

Tryce's eyes gleamed with mischief. "Unless we talk to the shadowreapers."

Silas flicked the boy's head.

"Hey!"

"Let's focus on getting Naila out of Lethos as a first step," Onyx said as she patted her arrow-filled quiver.

"It will have to be tonight," said Silas, determined. "I won't leave you there any longer."

"It's going to be mighty busy in Lethos tonight." Onyx smirked, eying the caravans crowding the road.

"The perfect opportunity for a little chaos." Tryce cracked his knuckles.

"We just have to cook up a plan." Silas nodded. "I want to avoid coming across Levias again."

That was something they could all agree to. The tension between the brothers had been too much for her to bear, so she really wasn't looking forward to another confrontation.

"If I can sneak out of the palace, I could pretend to join a caravan," said Naila.

Onyx said thoughtfully. "That could work, but it must be one who will leave Lethos tonight before Levias gets wind of your disappearance."

"Do you have enough crystals on you?" Rē looked at Silas.

Silas patted the heavy pouch on his belt.

"The good thing about šars is, they may try to steal your woman, but they swim in enough gold not to rob you."

"You think I can pay someone off?" Naila asked.

"Everyone has a price." Silas winked.

Naila's heart grew lighter as they concocted the finer details of their plan. She was relieved Silas's anger abated. And maybe, just maybe, this idea of theirs could work.

The moment the litter halted, the door jerked open. "You got another half a bell, but then I must escort you back to the palace, my lady," said the sentry.

Naila smiled at him, and a blush crept up his cheeks. He obviously didn't want to answer her smile but couldn't help from responding. She glanced at her friends, and a cloud of sadness descended upon her. Only half a bell... So little time to say a—maybe—goodbye.

The sentry whispered conspiratorially, "The šar's meetings with his generals tend to run long. No one will know if you, say, would be away for half a bell longer."

Naila beamed at him. "Thank you."

The plaza in front of the gate burst with life. Wealthy Lemaians pranced about craft workers' stores to empty their pouches and showcase their latest robes from the finest Perusian wools and Citronian silks. Two people stood at the corner of a baker's shop, their faces hidden by the hoods of their dark cloaks.

"Let's go," Onyx said. She pulled Naila to a busy market road that led to the gate, following after Silas, Tryce, and Rē. "Your guard here can fetch you himself later."

"Onyx, wait," said Naila.

At Onyx's questioning look, she thrust a package into the young woman's hand.

"What is this?" Onyx eyed the gown curiously. "I mean, it's pretty, but you know I'm not a dress type of girl."

"Your mother made it."

Onyx's eyes flicked to Naila. "What?"

Naila told her what she had learned.

Emotion welled in Onyx's eyes. She caressed the dress with reverie, finally pulling it to her chest, breathing the scent in. "*Māmān,*" she whispered, closing her eyes. "Thank you for telling me."

"What will you do?"

"When this is over, after we find Nebiru, I'll stop at nothing to save her."

Naila nodded. Her chest constricted. She wished she could be there for Onyx. To help her friend, as she had helped Naila.

Squawk.

The bird Naila had seen earlier circled the crowded plaza. At first, she figured it was just a bird on the hunt for its midday meal. When she saw the faint golden sheen between its feathers she tugged at Onyx's sleeve. Ro-Ro had returned.

Onyx, however, paid no mind to the bird. The huntress sneaked a glance behind, taking in the sight of two shadows creeping behind them. The men glanced behind as well, a dark look painted over their faces. Silas nodded to them before he and the others turned around the corner. Naila and Onyx heeled them into the alley. A little mouse looked up from a half-eaten banana and skittered away. The acrid, damp smell coming from the garbage in the alley made her stomach lurch in disgust.

"Who do you think they are?" Naila whispered to no one in particular as she pushed herself to the stone wall behind a store.

It would be suicide for shadowreapers to enter the Red Šar's city with so many sentries walking about. Still, Naila grasped her dagger, just to be sure. Silas unsheathed his scimitar, Tryce his battle-ax, Rē blew at the razor-sharp edge of his sword, and Onyx already had an arrow in hand.

The two hooded figures emerged out of the shadows around the corner. Ro-Ro flew above them, squealing excitedly.

"No, Ro-Ro!" Naila said.

She clutched Elgafar securely, ready to prevent the strangers from hurting the bird.

Onyx strung an arrow on her bow when one of them pushed back the hood of their coat.

Flaxen locks fell atop the coat and a familiar woman smiled at them. The other woman followed suit and revealed herself to them as well. Naila didn't know the latter personally but had seen her once or twice in Havenmor as a lady-in-waiting.

"What in the—" Silas breathed out as he rushed to the šaltana. "Mother? What are you doing here?"

Silas pulled his mother into a tight embrace. The šaltana took his face into her hands and kissed his cheeks.

Naila sheathed her dagger. How could the Silver Šar allow the šaltana back into the Empire of Crishire after all that had happened?

"When Naila wrote you got poisoned by a shadowreaper's blade..." The šaltana's voice broke with unshed tears. "I had to come, Silas. And my dearest here was such a sweet, selfless soul to help sneak me out."

The šaltana stroked her son's face. "I took with me a bottle of iscias I hid from Jericho ten winters ago, I didn't send it with Roc because you needed me to activate it... but I see you healed already. Do not tell me"—the šaltana's lips trembled—"Did Levias give you it? Nova...?"

Silas's body stiffened. "It's a long story. But first, we need to make arrangements for Naila."

"What?" The šaltana's brows rose high on her pale face.

Onyx sighed. "She made a deal with Levias to save Silas's life. She's sworn tsimora to him."

The šaltana's eyes widened. "Oh, dearest kittling. But that is against the code of honor. Nergaylas are not to be bonded."

Silas's eyes flashed. "We will get her out." He didn't look at his mother, but straight at Naila. Against herself, despite knowing the odds were against them, Naila's spirit soared. "Upon my word, we will. Tonight."

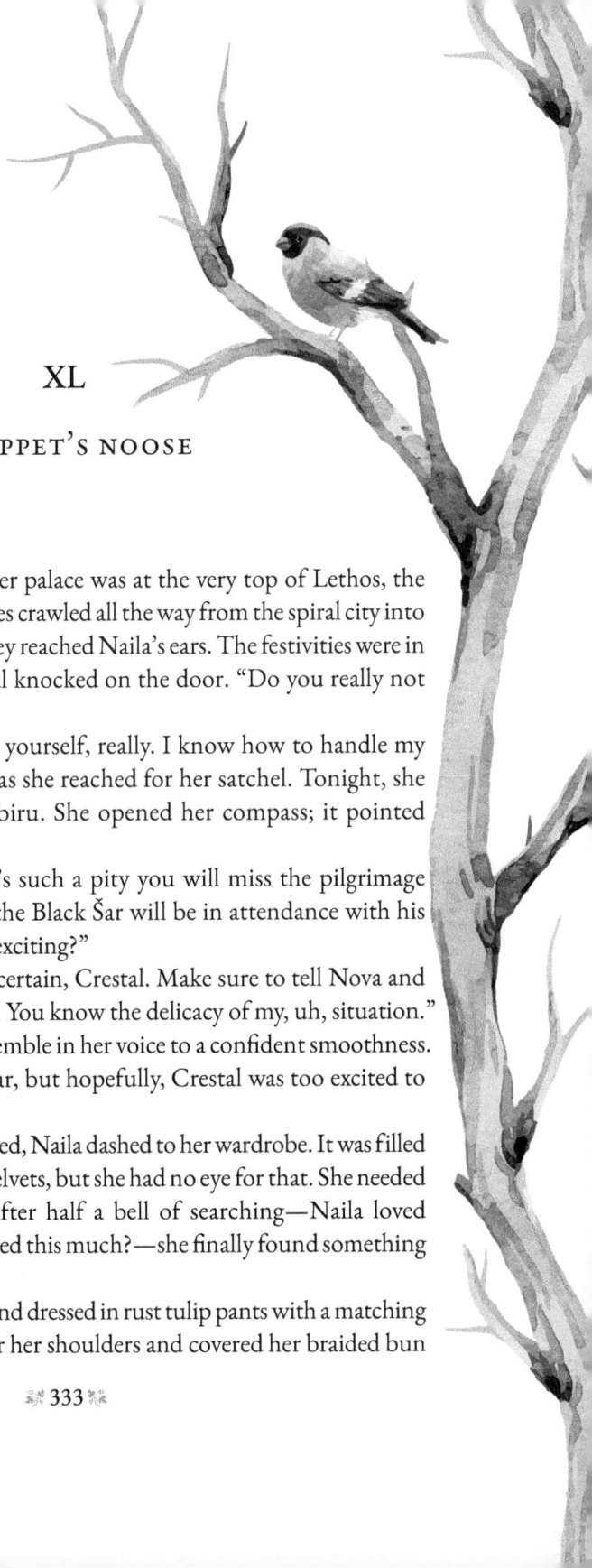

XL

A PUPPET'S NOOSE

ALTHOUGH THE summer palace was at the very top of Lethos, the noise of drums and flutes crawled all the way from the spiral city into its endless halls until they reached Naila's ears. The festivities were in full swing. "My lady?" Crestal knocked on the door. "Do you really not need my help?"

"It's okay, Crestal, go enjoy yourself, really. I know how to handle my monthly cramps," Naila lied as she reached for her satchel. Tonight, she would leave, straight for Nebiru. She opened her compass; it pointed southwest as ever.

"Well, if you're certain... It's such a pity you will miss the pilgrimage festival. Whisperers say even the Black Šar will be in attendance with his favorite concubine. Isn't that exciting?"

Naila rolled her eyes. "I'm certain, Crestal. Make sure to tell Nova and the Red Šar not to disturb me. You know the delicacy of my, uh, situation." Naila tried to ease the slight tremble in her voice to a confident smoothness. She'd always been a terrible liar, but hopefully, Crestal was too excited to notice something was amiss.

When Crestal's footsteps faded, Naila dashed to her wardrobe. It was filled with lush silk and the softest velvets, but she had no eye for that. She needed something inconspicuous. After half a bell of searching—Naila loved shopping, but did she really need this much?—she finally found something that would do.

She discarded her kaunake and dressed in rust tulip pants with a matching top. She draped a poncho over her shoulders and covered her braided bun and phæralei with its hood. No one would recognize her. *She hoped.* Somewhere outside, Ro-Ro cawed. The signal the others were waiting outside of Lethos. All she had to do was sneak out of the fortified city. This was no mission impossible... right?

Naila opened the door, which creaked to her annoyance, and stuck her head out. She exhaled in relief. The hall was empty. She tiptoed through it, quickly hiding behind a sculpture or in an empty chamber whenever sentries neared, until she came across a large wooden door. Naila had seen many a maid and manservant enter those doors. She puffed her chest and slapped some confidence into her cheeks before she shoved the door open as if it were her every right. Delicious savory aromas hit her.

Several servants strolled around the kitchen with baskets filled with onions, figs, and goat cheese. Lentil soup bubbled in a cauldron whilst barley bread and pastries filled every wood-fired oven.

"You."

A large, beefy woman dressed in an apron waggled a spoon at Naila.

Soup splattered all over the limestone floor. Naila froze. She grabbed the strap of her satchel to make a run for it, but the woman interrupted her.

"They've called all dancers to gather at the Crescent Plaza. You're a slacker, *feylana.* Make haste and leave before you make a mess of my kitchen."

Naila glanced about, like a deer cornered by wolves.

The cook huffed and pointed at a door behind her. "That way."

She didn't have to tell her twice. Naila swore she could hear the cook mumble something akin to "Youth these days."

The door led to a darkish stairway, lit by oil lamps. She rushed down the stairs until her feet cramped in protest. The laughter of Crishirians and beats of music grew louder and louder. Just as her pace slowed, she finally reached the exit.

Naila's eyes bugged out in delight at the sight of the Crescent Plaza. It was a humongous plaza in the shape of a crescent moon, outlined by torches of shimmering fire. Bright lampions illuminated colorful market stalls set out around a temporary stage where veiled fire dancers had already started their show.

She adjusted her veil and trekked through the crowd. Like Mort Nor's market, this one sold exotic things not even her wildest imagination would have come up with. There were candy fountains in every color, and rows of caramelized fruits from small to large. Some were boxed in rusty kettles, whereas they sold others per piece.

“Fifty blue crystals for this prime male hellhound. Do I hear more?” A man chanted from a stage nearby.

On top of the stage, a two-headed wolfen creature paced behind a cage. Shimmers of æther hinted that more than just bolts secured the canine’s cage. Several people crowded around the stage started shouting higher amounts.

Why anyone would want that vicious-looking animal was beyond her.

“Coming through,” a man barked.

Naila glanced over her shoulder. To her shock, the familiar crimson and black armory of the imperial sentries appeared. She swiftly shielded her face with the hood of her poncho. She retreated backward but accidentally stepped onto something soft.

Shhhh.

A black fanged, vicious-looking Venus flytrap hissed from next to a market table. She jumped back just before it snapped at her leg. *Where did all these creatures come from?*

Thankfully, the sentries already left.

Aside from some lecherous comments now and then, no one seemed to realize the object of the Red Šar’s questionable interest walked in their midst. Naila peeked over the heads of the pedesters, but she couldn’t identify any caravan.

She was about to wander to the other side of the Crescent Plaza when the seductive melody of a pipe and strings called to her. It pulsed like a beat, the same way the portal had done.

Memories of happier days swam to the surface. When she had visited Philly to see what he was up to, when her mother had saved for over a year so they could visit Suriname again—how she had roamed barefoot through the white sand of the Amazonian rainforest.

She had to grind her feet together to stop herself from answering the melody. Despite diseases, poverty, and the grumpy sentries wandering about, people weren’t cranky or on edge like where she was from… Earth. They laughed and gossiped while emptying their pouches for the latest in-demand object. All thrilled. All awfully unaware of the horror that laced itself through their world.

Did the lack of rights mean nothing to these people? And what of the blood slavery the Red Šar had spoken of but everyone else kept awfully hushed? Her throat grew thick with emotion.

"Little one..." An elderly woman stuck out her bracelet-enveloped arm. Behind the woman, two teenage girls sat in front of the brightly colored wagon with musical instruments. They were the ones creating magical notes that had spoken to her soul. She locked gazes with the woman. Her eyes were liquid silver set in wrinkled tan skin. The woman had dyed her graying hair black, which did nothing to reduce her aged appearance. She couldn't pinpoint what, but something was familiar about her.

"Such a vision you are. Don't wrinkle your face with sorrow and pain."

"I cry for those who can't." She lifted her chin. "For those who are forgotten... Those who are unrightfully ignored."

The woman smiled. "Cry for them, yes, but don't forget to smile as well, or you might become someone others will end up crying for."

Naila looked away. "How can anyone here be so happy when there's so much wrong with this world?"

"Don't be fooled by appearances, little one. You don't know what sorrow people carry with them. Still, without a smile on your face, you might as well stop living." The woman waved her hand in the general direction of the people. "People of Lemuria know that all too well. We are survivors."

The woman walked toward the caravan and beckoned her to follow. "Come, little one, I'll fetch you some spiced wine to soothe that aching heart of yours."

No. She couldn't. She had to escape...

But before she could protest the woman poured the liquor into a goblet. "Where is your bond-mate? Surely a *feylana* such as you is sworn to a powerful man?" said the woman.

She took her time to sip on the sweet, steaming wine. "I, uh," she said when she'd waited so long to answer it'd almost become rude.

"Ye sneaked out, huh?" The woman winked.

Naila cast her eyes down to her goblet and nodded nervously.

"My lips are sealed," the woman said in a conspiring tone. "Even the meekest birds need a bigger cage from time to time."

Except she was not someone's bird. The Red Šar's watchful, dark gaze flashed before her eyes. Naila wrangled her hand out of the woman's grasp.

"I have to go."

She stood to leave, but the spiced wine made her a little dizzy and a lot giddy. She felt happy. Carefree. The music was hauntingly beautiful. The woman sang,

She spreads her wings and takes her flight,
Answers her calling and takes on this plight,
Off she goes, to the world wide and far,
Off she goes, bearing each cherished scar,
For the Legends of the Sky await in sight.

She hummed to the notes. Word after word about tales of a songbird captured by a wicked king. The woman's eyes glittered and encouraged her to continue. She lost all control of her body. It felt as if she were in a trance. First, one foot stepped out of line and then another. Her hips swayed to the melody and moved into a slow dance. The woman clapped in excitement as the girls amped up the beats of their instruments.

She was vaguely aware of the small group of spectators forming around her. They cheered her on and clapped in unison. A small voice whispered she should quit drawing so much attention to herself. She ignored it. It felt so good to be carefree for once. Normally, she didn't like attention, but the wine had snatched all her worries and locked them tightly inside a vault. Somewhere in the back of her mind, she knew that vault would reopen with a vengeance when she was sober again.

Naila closed her eyes and felt a pair of eyes burning on her face, gliding to her chest, her wasp waist and then to her toned legs. A stare so intense it felt like she caught fire. Droplets of sweat dampened her face and her body. She knew who those eyes belonged to. She turned in a slow swirl toward the crowd. Their cheers became louder. She reopened her eyes, and the burn of the gaze faded into nothingness. He wasn't there. She nearly fell to her knees in relief.

The woman shoved Naila toward her wagon. "Come, little one," she said. Then her voice turned to steel. "Come, *Ishtar.*"

Naila turned frigid.

She at last saw what at first, she did not see. The woman's silver eyes gleamed with æther flames, and her smile turned cruel. Morgana. The wrinkles on Morgana's face melted into the sickly gray so unique to shadowreapers.

"No," she protested weakly as she tried to wriggle out of the shadowreaper's grasp.

But all the strength had left her body, and the little energy she had left was not enough to even keep her eyes open. The wine... Morgana must have spiked it.

The shadowreaper pushed her into the dark wagon.

"We meet again, Stormhold," Daena said.

Her black-gold gloves sizzled with flames. She seized Naila by the neck.

Naila screeched out as a horrible pain split through her head.

The last thing she saw was Colios, appearing from out of the shadows. He reached for her with thick, black-gold ropes in his hands.

SCROLL IV

A LEGEND IN THE SKY

Hers is a tale of awe and woe,
Of secrets kept and promises thrown,
Like a newborn babe with violence and a cry,
Her long-awaited voice comes out with a pry,
Exhaling a song of legends in the sky.

XLI

A SHADOWREAPER'S TALE

"HOW MY *heart weeps to see this day come,"* a woman said.

An angel picked up little Naila from her bed and squeezed her tight to his chest. No, he couldn't be an angel. Angels didn't have wings that bled crimson. He was cloaked in shadows, so she couldn't see his face. A familiar compass hung around his neck. The one that belonged to her father...

"They *know the Stone of Songs and Souls awakened. It's only a matter of time before they find her." A familiar woman lurked behind the man. She gazed upon Naila with sad eyes. Naila raised her tiny hand to brush the woman's tears away. She didn't want to see her sad. It made her sad too.*

"It must be done tonight," the woman whispered. "It cannot be delayed."

The man shook his head. "No... There must be another way."

The woman pressed her finger to the man's lips. How young she looked. How beautiful. Words of anguish ripped out of her chest, laced with a longing unspoken. "If there were another way, I would do it in a heartbeat, you know I would. But rest assured, when I am done, I will be no more than a memory long forgotten. You will go on with your life, you will take your daughter and move somewhere far away, and you will forget there was ever a man called Stormhold."

Drip.

The vision drifted away like déjà vu.

Drip.

The roof leaked again... Naila made a mental note to tell her mother to hire a plumber instead of their hobbyist neighbor. By the stars, was it cold. She turned to reach for her bedsheet. Only, it wasn't there.

And why was her bed so hard?

Drip. Drip. Drip.

She squeezed an eye open. A midnight sky met her, brushed with strokes of moonlit clouds. Leafless, coal-colored branches hung over the snowy path like a spider grappling at its web-covered victim. Sleet dripped onto the wagon's wooden deck and upon her face.

Her eyes flashed open.

She lay atop a straw mat in the middle of a wobbling wagon. Bleeding heart flowers filled every corner. Its sweet, seductive scent hid its poisonous nature quite well from an untrained eye. What was it the hierodulas had taught her? *Ah.* They were a potent suppressor of æther.

Naila's eyes squinted to make out the shapes in the dark. Aside from *Iluna,* hidden behind the clouds, only flickering candles made for light, their dim rays dancing around two hooded figures seated opposite her. Ice-cold sweat trickled down Naila's neck. The shadowreapers... they had captured her. Everything rushed back.

"She's awake." Colios's raspy voice sounded.

The shadowreaper sat next to Daena atop a pile of cushions, sharpening his scimitar on a whetstone. Morgana and a few other shadowreapers framed their wagon, riding upon doran horses, as they threaded through a dark, endless forest. Naila pushed herself up. The tree trunks were barely distinguishable from the midnight sky. Their hanging branches, so similar to weeping willows, held violet leaves so dark, they imitated a shade of black.

Her throat turned bone-dry. "You..."

Daena regarded Naila through emotionless eyes. "You had your fun, Stormhold, but our little game of cat and bird is done."

"Wh-what do you want from me?"

No hint of emotion danced upon the shadowreapers' faces.

Naila continued. "I know I'm a nergayla. But so what? Why do you want me so much?"

"It is not you we desire, but the fruit born of your choices."

What? Naila regarded Daena and Colios through hawk-eyes, taking in their expressions for any sign of a lie. She chuckled humorlessly, while the two continued watching her with solemn expressions. Her laughter died out into hiccups. She clenched her fists. "The fruit of my choices? You chase me across two worlds but give me nothing but a vague explanation!"

Suddenly it didn't matter that the Shadow Šar's lackeys were murderous villains that had hunted her through space and time. They pissed her off and hell if she didn't make her feelings known. She snatched one of the bleeding hearts and threw it at them. Daena caught it with little to no effort.

"I hate you," Naila spat.

"So you have made known," Daena said dryly.

"Are you at least going to explain to me what you mean?"

The shadowreaper cocked her head, her eyes calculative. "There is little more to what I have said, but I will try to appease your senses."

Colios shot her a warning look.

The woman ignored him. "The Shadow Šar is wise and all-knowing. He knows what even the great Suzano Stormhold did not... The reason the Ænunaki came to this world."

A deadly silence followed suit. Something rustled in the bushes, a deer mayhap, oblivious to the centuries-old secret to be told but a few feet away.

"According to the Legends of the Sky, long before the birth of time, there was nothing. And then there was æther. Out of this energy, worlds took shape, and life took its first breath. Eventually, the first sentient beings came into existence. Some call them titans, the high gods and goddesses of the sky. The Ænunaki, however, call them Edenians, after the world they inhabited.

"Edenians were both beautiful and intelligent creatures. But they were also greedy and envious like a snake. They stole all æther and imprisoned it into the fruits of a fig tree, which shriveled into stones—one for every Edenian, each with their own power.

"The most powerful of all stones held within it the æther of life. What the Edenians didn't account for, was that life energy consisted of two contrary interdependent forces—one dark and rational, the other bright and passionate. During the incarcerating process, the two forces navigated to opposite stones, just like they did in their natural habitat. And so, one stone became two.

"Cut away from each other, the power of these stones both lessened and intensified. Over time, one stone became the Stone of Songs and Souls, and the other the Stone of Shadows and Darkness. Legend would call them the Gemini stones."

Naila's heart thumped wildly. The gilded stone she had seen in her memory... the one she had absorbed.

Daena continued. "No crime can go unpunished, however. The Edenians and their world perished under unknown circumstances, but some of their offspring survived. They became—"

"The Legends of the Sky. The last bearers of the stones," Naila finished. "One of them Virgo... Ishtar."

"So you know the tale."

"No, I just put two and two together. What happened to them and their stones?"

"Something grave. Something even the Ænunaki do not speak of. A long, long time ago, the stones were spread across the worlds, and what was history became nothing more than a legend. Until one day, the Ænunaki caught whispers of a stone found in a distant world.

"The Stone of Songs and Souls was already within the Ænunaki's possession, but separated from its other half the Gemini stones are useless, for they stay in a dormant state. For ages, the Ænunaki traveled from world to world in search of the other stone. You see, the combined power of the stones was what they truly coveted, for the Stone of Shadows and Darkness brings death where the other stone gives life. Together, there is nothing they cannot do. In the end, they found the world the stone was hidden on: Lemuria."

Naila shuffled on the pillows in unease. "So, you think I possess these Gemini stones?"

Colios finally spoke. "No, little Ishtar. You do not hold both stones. We wouldn't be having this conversation if you did."

Naila lifted her chin in defiance. "But I do have one, don't I? The Stone of Songs and Souls? That is why you want me. I won't give it to you. I won't!"

Colios's eyes narrowed. "You are in no position to negotiate. Do I have to remind you that you are at our mercy? The Shadow Šar never specified which state he wanted you in. As far as I'm concerned, I can throw you in a pleasure house and take you back the next day. I assure you; you will be well used by then."

She glared at him with equal hostility.

"What do you plan to do with the stones? Colonize everything like the Ænunaki?"

"I told you before that we are not the enemy. The Gemini stones hold a power that rules over life and death."

A shadowreaper riding near Morgana broke his silence and whispered, "Imagine a world where none had to die. A world where sickness no longer wrote your destiny."

"Careful, Morpheus," Morgana warned her comrade.

Naila's eyes softened. She took in the sickly gray of their skins—the scars of *ut mortes nero*. "Is that what the Shadow Šar promised you? What makes you so sure he's not deceiving you?"

"You do not know of whom you speak," said Colios.

"If you want a world where none die then why do you kill?"

"There is no heaven without hell. No world where victory does not require sacrifices."

Naila scoffed. "Well, if you want the stone so much then you'll have to pull it out of me."

Daena pulled off her black scarf. "The stones need hosts to awaken, but not any host will do. That's where you step in. Yes, Stormhold, you are Ishtar in flesh and blood and so the Stone of Songs and Souls awakened within you and you alone."

The wagon bumped over a stone on the dark forest road, which caused *her* compass to fall out of Colios's lap.

"That's mine!" she gasped.

The corner of Colios's mouth lifted in a mocking smile. "The stone is not the only reason the Shadow Šar wants you, little Ishtar. There is much we need, knowledge to gain. He presumed, correctly may I say, that you would be the key to unlocking the Ænunaki's secrets."

It finally dawned where they were.

The Dark Forest.

And the shadowreapers had somehow discovered her compass pointed at Nebiru. But how?

Daena advanced to her, playing with her scarves as she did. From the corners of her eyes, Naila saw Colios pushing himself up too. Just like that, she forgot how to breathe. Colios was quick like a cheetah. Before she knew it, he held her hands behind her back, tight like a vice. Daena held her scarf up high, and she knew she was going to stuff her mouth with it.

"Who knows what Nebiru holds? Aside from historical scrolls from the Ænunaki and every world they ever encountered, that is," Daena said. She lowered her face. Naila felt her breath as she moved her lips next to her ear.

"And did I mention it has the key to unlocking the most powerful portal in existence? One that can form a bridge to Arbatros, the Ænunaki's world? You, Naila Stormhold, are going to give us entrance to Nebiru."

XLII

THE DARK FOREST

DARK CLOUDS made place for *Iluna* like peasants made way for their king. The moons bloomed among the stars like enchanting roses: beautiful and melancholic, with endless whispers of unkept promises. Watching and waiting as the scene of the Dark Forest unfolded.

The forest itself was as silent as any woodland if one overlooked the howling of awakening night dwellers and the rustling of leaves on the few trees that still had them. The squelching of hooves in muddy snow told the forest had other visitors too. In the shadows of the night, another wagon trudged behind Naila's. There was something big and round inside, but the shadowreapers had covered it with blankets.

She blinked in confusion.

Colios followed her eyes. "That is none of your concern."

"*Hnng, hnng.*"

A shiver ran through her body.

After casting the shadowreapers one last glare, she continued going about what she'd done before: ignoring their existence and trying to deny the cold. A thick layer of sheepskin covered her, but the dusting of snowflakes chilled her cheeks and bound hands to icicles. And her rear... she couldn't feel it after sitting for what seemed like ages.

"Dampen the lights and stay quiet." Morgana, who led their unmerry band of captors and captive, whispered.

To Naila's surprise, Colios put out their candles without questioning. Morgana probably read these woods like a bear did the seasons.

Aside from the moonlit path, she couldn't see a thing through the thick mass of leafless trees. The forest looked as dead as a graveyard, yet she felt the faint pulse of life hidden in its shadows. Dark and savage life, just roused from its slumber, confident and ready to strike and take away that same life from its unsuspecting victims.

A deer drank from the black waters of what could only be Lake Hathor, unaware of the people traveling half a kilometer away... unaware of the dangers that lurked underneath the lake's surface. The rustling of the forest grew quiet. Too quiet. The deer scrambled back in alarm, but it was too late. Fast as the wind, a forest-green, scaled creature snapped its razor-sharp teeth around the deer's neck and yanked it into the dark water. And just like that, the sounds of the forest sizzled around her again.

Her bosom rose and fell raggedly. What was that thing?

"A kreekan," said Daena as if guessing her thoughts.

Two words only with no other explanation. She tried to remember anything Mr. Thoth had mentioned about the Dark Forest but came up empty. These kreekans and whatever else dwelled in these woods surrounded her, and there was nothing she could do about it. How she wished she could go back to Lethos. Facing Levias was by far the better option.

"We should have taken the longer road," Colios mumbled to Daena. "This one is too dangerous."

For once, Naila agreed with the shadowreaper.

"The longer we stay outside the Shadowlands, the more risk we take of being detected by the Red Šar's *ut Asanatæ*. We have no choice," Daena hissed.

The woman turned to Naila. "Ah yes, it seems like you have been quite busy, *yana*?"

Naila strained her neck to meet the shadowreaper's gaze.

"Whisperers say you've done the impossible and seduced both the war-hungry Red Šar and his rake of a brother. Who knew the Dragon Lord would ever want for something other than bloodshed?" Daena lowered her voice. "You know, the stones are like magnets. It has come to the Shadow Šar's attention that Skeldor has been hiding some rather interesting tales about Prince Silvanus." Her eyes latched onto Naila's. "Whispers of the prince summoning flames of shadows upon his birth. You wouldn't know anything about that, would you?"

Naila sucked in a breath. Both the šaltana and Nova were convinced Silas was part of the ancient foretelling. Flames of shadows… Powers the complete opposite of hers. Could it be?

Soon, far too soon, they arrived at the lake. Thick drifts of mist hung over it, making it impossible to make out much of its surface. Daena ripped off the scarves around her hands and mouth. She immediately started coughing.

"Ugh."

Naila grabbed a flask and gulped. Water never tasted so sweet. Morgana and the other shadowreaper, Morpheus, dismounted their dead-looking horses, whilst Colios took out her stolen compass. To her bitterness, her compass unveiled its secrets.

They were here.

Nebiru was here.

"What now?" she rasped out. Her mouth still felt dry as a desert.

She glanced about, but nothing more than a misty lake in a snow-covered forest revealed itself.

Morgana sauntered toward them. "Now, we wait."

Naila's eyes skirted over the lake and back to the forest. Going back into the Dark Forest wasn't an option—yes, she wanted away from the shadowreapers, but something told her they weren't the worst dwelling in these woods.

Time ticked away.

Gradually, the mists exposed its lake.

A bolt of nerves hit her. She'd been through so much to find Nebiru, had lost and gained so much, but now that she was so close, she didn't want to find it. Not when she'd yet to think of a plan to lose her captors and hadn't even said goodbye to her friends, or told Silas… told him what exactly? Her stomach knotted. She really liked Silas. Next time she saw him, she would tell him, sworn to his brother or not.

"It is time," said Morgana.

The mists dissolved into nothingness, releasing *Iluna* to find its mirror twins on the calm surface of the lake. For a few moments, nothing happened. The forest grew quiet again, save for the whistling of winds through the trees.

She held her breath.

Inch by inch, shafts of moonlight crawled over Lake Hathor until they reached the lake's center. Within its depth light twirled, spreading its tendrils throughout the water. It was breathtaking. The lake glowed like a fallen star surrounded by tufts of mist, its light spotted by small shadows. The scene hypnotized her so that, at first, she didn't notice how Daena pushed her toward the shore.

"Quick," Daena urged.

When they reached the shore, she realized who the flashing shadows belonged to. Kreekans. The light in the water flickered several times before it extinguished like a candle. For a few moments, none said a word until Morgana let out a deep breath and confirmed what she feared.

"The path is clear. Those were the lights of Nebiru... at the bottom of the lake."

"The bottom of the lake? But it's crammed with those kreekan creatures," said Naila.

"Thank you for enlightening us," Daena sneered, but the slight quiver to her fingers told her the shadowreaper was as anxious as her.

A doran horse neighed.

Its owner reached past it into the second wagon. The shadowreaper pulled a huge translucent ball out of the wagon. It was as wide as Colios was tall and glowed like diamonds in the rays of *Iluna*. Something told her this had once belonged to the Ænunaki.

Colios's darkened teeth glinted. "It is a good thing we came prepared for all options."

An ominous feeling gripped her by the throat. "What is that thing?"

"A water-wheeler. It will take us to the bottom of the lake," said Morgana. She fumbled with the belt of her coat. When she raised a brow in question, Morgana continued, "Take off those sheepskins, else we won't fit inside."

"That won't be necessary." Daena held up her hand to stop Morgana. She snatched the compass out of Colios's hand. She beckoned Naila with her head and added, "I will go with the girl."

"Huh?" Naila gaped at Daena in disbelief. "You're out of your mind. There's no way you're getting me into the water. The lake is filled with those kreekans!"

"You will do as I say," Daena snarled. "And you best hurry. The longer we wait, the more our hovering about the lake will draw out the kreekans."

Daena pushed her toward the water-wheeler, but Naila stuck her heels into the wet snow. "Let me go, you jerk." She scratched at Daena's face, who unleashed her with a shriek. She didn't give the other shadowreapers the chance to meddle and made a go for the woods. She changed her mind. The Dark Forest or not, she'd rather take her chances there than with those kreekans.

Someone tugged hard on her braid. With a squeal, she fell backward. Icy wetness spread across her frame as the sleet soaked her drapes in its moisture. Colios looked down at her with an icy coolness. "You have more chance with a water-wheeler in the lake than by foot in the Dark Forest, little Ishtar."

"That witch," Daena screeched as she stomped toward them.

Colios pulled Naila up and Daena raised her hand as if to smack her, blue sparks at the tips of her black-gold gloves. Then she froze mid-movement. Naila followed the shadowreaper's glowering gaze.

Out of the shadows of the forest, Silas, Onyx, Tryce, the šaltana, and her lady-in-waiting appeared. A gentle rainfall met the light from their lanterns in a halo around their frames—like her very own guardian angels. Angry guardian angels. Her heart swelled with warmth.

Silas narrowed his eyes to dark slits as he crossed his arms.

"It looks like we missed the invitation."

XLIII

THOSE THREE SACRED WORDS

It is true what they say, how much the heart wells for a lost treasure found.

They found her! Through land and forest, perhaps water and mountains too, they somehow did.

Naila broke out in a tearful smile. "Well, that took you long enough. Hey, wha—"

Colios pushed her back into the sleet and pulled out his twin blades. Their sharp edges blazed with flames.

An æshefied arrow flew past them, into the shoulder of an unlucky shadowreaper.

"*Aargh*," he bellowed.

Silas arched his brow. "What happened to waiting for my signal?"

"Oops," Onyx shrugged. "Guess my hand slipped."

The shadowreaper pulled the arrow out of his shoulder, unsheathing his scimitar with a murderous glance on his face. It dawned on Naila her friends were on a suicide mission. *For her.* What in the stars could they do against the shadowreapers and their poisonous blades?

"Prince Silvanus," Colios bared his teeth. "This time no iscias will save you."

"Hmph," said Silas, his own æshefied scimitar already in hand. Through the faint beams of the moons, Naila saw no tension in his stance, nor any hint of anxiety in his smirk. "For a shadowreaper, you really do talk a lot."

She barely made out Silas's and Colios's forms in the dark of the night, but the swift whoosh in the air followed by metal clashing told her they came to blows.

Lightning cut through the black of the night, illuminating the eerie trees looming over Lake Hathor as if curious about their rare visitors. Something whined in the woods. The doran horses whinnied piteously, but their owners paid them no heed. Instead, the shadowreapers trudged toward Colios, swords at the ready. They kept their distance, however, respecting the code of the dance of flames.

Naila would never forgive herself if Colios hurt Silas again. She pushed herself out of the sleet to do... something. *Anything.* If only she had better control over her fledgling powers. If only she had had more time with Zarqa.

"*T'ilaa ni gloria*!" Onyx cried. Arrows flew by, one after another.

Tryce swung his ax at a shadowreaper, crying out too.

The šaltana and her handmaiden scurried toward Naila. Two darts, tips basked in flames, missed the women by mere inches, blocking their path. Like a snake catching an unwary bird, Daena clasped a hand over her mouth and dragged her toward the water-wheeler.

"You and I have another appointment, little Ishtar."

If her lips weren't sealed, she'd tell Daena exactly where to take her appointment. She tried to push her away, but the woman's grip was tight as a vise.

"Naila," the šaltana gasped as she tried to evade the shadowreapers.

"In, you go." Daena pushed Naila into the water-wheeler. Its crystal folded around them like enchanted water, before solidifying back into the glassy substance.

Surprisingly, the inside of the sphere was like a fairy tale carriage, with pale leather seats and a silver steering wheel. A faint aroma of iron hit her, but she couldn't discern where the scent came from.

Daena pushed her flat against the window whilst taking the seat next to her. Raindrops pattered against the crystal, the force of the storm growing with every passing breath. Daena thrust her hand into some sort of gauntlet stuck to the water-wheeler, much like the one they had found in Gomorra. The shadowreaper winced slightly, and the tang of iron weaved through the air.

"What is that thing?"

"You ask too many questions."

"Does it have needles inside or something?"

"As a matter of fact, *leachers* do."

Naila gaped at her.

Daena's grayish face grew a shade paler. The *leacher* tapped on her blood... as fuel? It must harvest æther out of blood.

Outside, ever so close, Onyx threw herself upon another shadowreaper. They rolled through the snow, the tip of a dagger gleaming in the shadowreaper's hand.

"Onyx!"

"Silence," Daena barked.

Naila shot up, but Daena pushed her back into the seat.

The šaltana and her handmaiden gawked at the spectacle unfolding before them. Naila exhaled slowly. They weren't used to battles. She had to remind herself of that before she'd scream at them in vain.

The water-wheeler lurched forward. One by one, tiny lights pulsed in its shield of crystal.

The šaltana glanced at them in alarm. She looked about frantically and picked up a stray branch before she made her way to them. As if that would stop a shadowreaper.

It was too late either way.

Daena steered the water-wheeler toward the lake. The crystal sphere waded through the cordgrass—peculiarly, the seats remained upright despite its motion—before it hit the water with a splash.

Naila yelped.

She massaged the sore spot where she'd hit her head. "Ugh, besides being a dreadful person, you're a dreadful driver too."

Daena's lips narrowed, but she made no reply.

Slowly, the vehicle sank into the water. Within the teal water, long tendrils of seagrass and aquatic flowers moved with its waves. A school of deep-red fish swam above rows of coral and violet anemones.

Naila's mesmerism didn't last long.

Something crashed against the water-wheeler, pushing them off course and twirling straight into the translucent tentacles of a giant jellyfish.

"What in the—"

The jellyfish encased the water-wheeler, leaving trails of slime all across the windows. After a few moments, it probably decided the water-wheeler wasn't edible and let them go with a jerk. She landed flat on Daena's lap. The water-wheeler twirled at a frightening speed toward the bottom of the lake.

Daena twisted the steering wheel aggressively, but nothing gave. She had completely lost control.

They smashed from wall to wall. Naila hit her head so hard tiny flashes filled her vision. By the time the vehicle came to a stop, she had to force herself not to retch all over its ivory seats.

A bank of seaweed encased the crystal sphere. Daena turned the steering wheel, but to no avail. Disoriented, Naila groaned.

"What happened?"

Daena gnashed her teeth. "May the stars show us mercy."

The sound of nails sharpening against glass echoed through the water-wheeler.

Her heart thundered with the force of a horse's galloping hooves. The alarmed look on Daena's face did little to calm her nerves. Ever so slowly, she turned to the origin of the noise. A pair of ebony slits in yellow irises stared back at her.

No, not one pair, but dozens of them.

"Kreekans," Daena hissed.

They were unlike anything Naila had ever seen. At least seven feet tall, seaweed-green scales covered their bodies, their arms, and their legs, whereas their faces were an eerie mixture of a piranha with something human-like.

With every scratch of the kreekans' elongated claws, Daena winced and Naila pressed farther into her seat. If those creatures frightened a deadly shadowreaper, then how was she supposed to feel? Their odds did not look too great.

One of the creatures cracked the window with its claw—a slight fissure, but a crack, nonetheless. The kreekan screeched, its voice high-pitched like a banshee's, and bared its razor-sharp teeth in a malicious grin. Water trickled through the crack.

The other kreekans gauged them for several moments before they stopped scratching the glass and opted to swim circles around the water-wheeler instead. They knew she and Daena had nowhere to escape to. It was only a matter of time before they could sink their teeth into their flesh. So, they waited. Like patient hunters.

"Listen, and do as I say," said Daena.

"Why should I? You're the one who got us into this situation," Naila snapped.

Blazing blue eyes met pools of molten gold. Without a word being spoken, the two came to an agreement. *Ah, yes. The enemy of my enemy is indeed my friend.* The thought left Naila with a bitter aftertaste.

"Kreekans are skilled predators, especially now that we are in their territory. They will not let us escape, so we only have one chance to force them to."

More and more kreekans joined the circuit around the water-wheeler. The already dark lake was filled to the brim with their shadows.

"All right, what do you have in mind?"

Daena pushed the compass into Naila's hands. "Nebiru is here. These kreekans"—she cocked her head toward the creatures—"are guarding it. Find it, open its gate. I bet they will leave us be if you do."

Naila frowned at the compass, its needle hidden in the lake's darkness. "And how am I supposed to do that?"

"That is what *you* need to figure out."

Naila scoffed.

"Don't you have it easy?"

Her eyes shifted between the ever-growing crowd of kreekans to Daena. The shadowreaper was right. If they didn't find Nebiru, they would end up as fish bait, or whatever those things were. She squinted but couldn't make out anything except the army of kreekans between fluorescent aquatic plants.

"We don't even know where Nebiru is located."

"The Ænunaki do not think like the Lemai. Their communication with each other, with their tools, transcended the flick of a sword. The answer is made known to whoever they allow it to be."

"And if it isn't to me?"

Daena's flaming eyes flashed icy blue. "If it isn't... then we at least died trying."

A sense of resolve soothed Naila's nerves. Somewhere in the back of her mind, she realized she had yet to endure a panic attack despite the direness of the situation. How much she had changed in the little time she had been in Lemuria.

She sucked in a deep breath.

She could do this.

Yes, she could.

Naila closed her eyes, reminiscing about Philly, her mother… The compass. The scroll. *Iluna.* Her eyes fluttered open. Just as she did so, a faint shaft of the moons' light cut through the waves.

Crimson markings appeared at the edges of her compass. A riddle in the Hædur. One that hadn't appeared in Iluna's light on the surface. Only when Daena mumbled the words did Naila realize she spoke the riddle out loud.

Utilize the instrument we hear but never see,
Unlock the path to the end we're meant to be.

"Think," Daena whispered. "What message would they want to leave you?"

Utilize the instrument we hear but never see…

"My voice," she heard herself mumble. Her mind swirled in fleeting thoughts and images. Completely entranced, she said again, "They mean my voice."

"Your voice?" Daena urged, her expression eager. "What more? Tell me."

Unlock the path to the end we're meant to be.

The path to the end… *think, Naila, think.* Path to the end as in final destination, perhaps? If I were an Ænunaki, she thought, what would I think to be the end of my journey? A colonizing species who perceived themselves superior in all ways. What would they think?

She gazed ahead, in the distance, between the swimming kreekans. But a few hundred feet before the water-wheeler stood Nebiru. Why she felt it, she didn't know. She only knew it to be true. Yes, come to think of it, she noticed the kreekans bypassed something large in that place. Something hidden.

"Unlock the path to the end we're meant to be," she said. "They are legends. And all legends have a… legacy. They are the Ænunaki, heirs to the mighty Edenians."

Naila sat up straight. "Nirihim no Nalahai."

Nirihim no Nalahai? They were words in the language of the Hædur. The language she had never heard, yet completely understood.

Nirihim no Nalahai. Heir of Elysium.

The water trembled.

Lake Hathor burned anew. Bright with the lights of the fallen city of Nebiru.

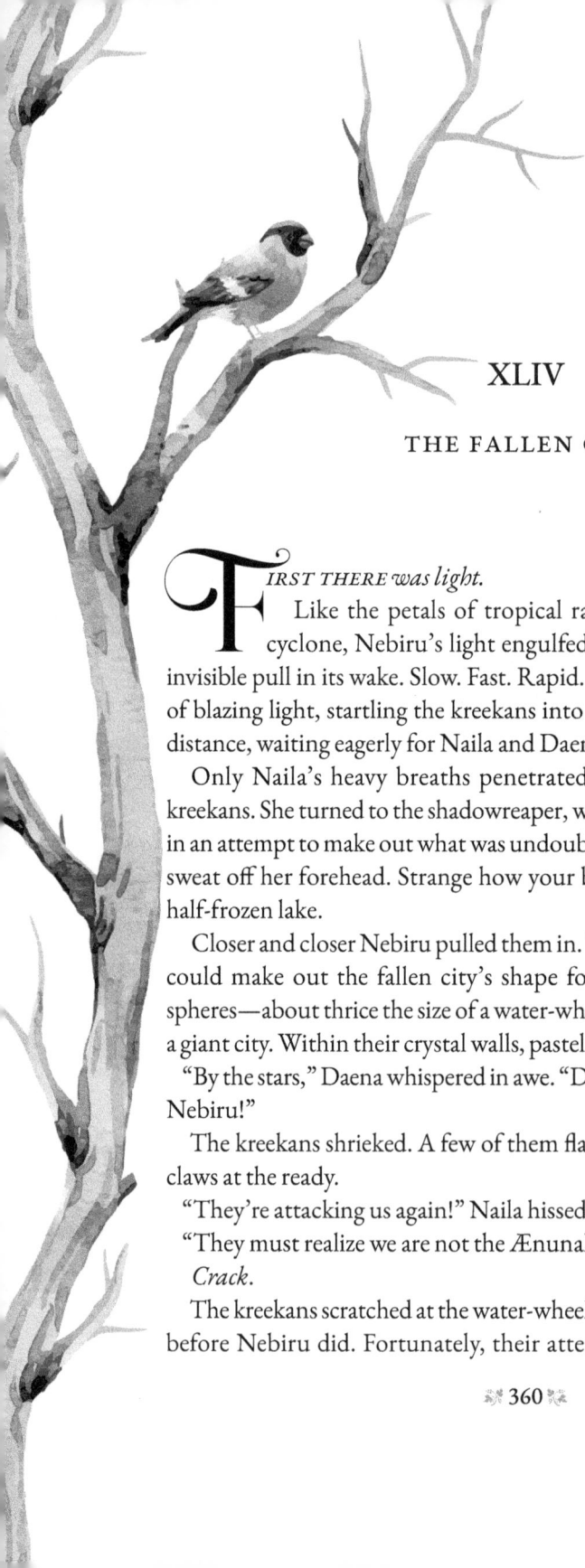

XLIV

THE FALLEN CITY

FIRST THERE was light.

Like the petals of tropical rain birthing the whirling of a cyclone, Nebiru's light engulfed the water-wheeler, leaving an invisible pull in its wake. Slow. Fast. Rapid. It pulled the sphere into a core of blazing light, startling the kreekans into retreating. They glared from a distance, waiting eagerly for Naila and Daena to make a mistake.

Only Naila's heavy breaths penetrated the indignant shrieks of the kreekans. She turned to the shadowreaper, whose flaming eyes were pinched in an attempt to make out what was undoubtedly Nebiru. Naila rubbed the sweat off her forehead. Strange how your body can boil in fear, even in a half-frozen lake.

Closer and closer Nebiru pulled them in. Through the shafts of light, she could make out the fallen city's shape for the first time. Hundreds of spheres—about thrice the size of a water-wheeler—were fused together into a giant city. Within their crystal walls, pastel lights shimmered like tiny stars.

"By the stars," Daena whispered in awe. "Do my eyes deceive me? Nebiru... Nebiru!"

The kreekans shrieked. A few of them flashed toward the water-wheeler, claws at the ready.

"They're attacking us again!" Naila hissed.

"They must realize we are not the Ænunaki."

Crack.

The kreekans scratched at the water-wheeler in desperation to get to them before Nebiru did. Fortunately, their attempts proved fruitless. Nebiru opened like a crystal rose, pulling the water-wheeler inside as if hauled by an invisible rope. A blinding, crimson light pulsed out of the gate. A light so similar to æther. The nearby kreekans froze mid-movement, their eyes widening in surprise as they took in the last thing they would ever see.

She yelped in horror. First the kreekans' scales, and then their flesh, melted off their bones. Her stomach twisted and turned, and before she knew it, she threw up its contents.

"Nebiru... It must have attacked them," Daena said in admiration, shifting to the side to avoid Naila's vomit.

When the last waves of nausea left her body, she sank back into her seat. The remaining kreekans watched them from a safe distance.

"Stormhold..."

But Daena didn't have to say anything. Naila was on full alert.

And then there was nothing.

The abyss of Nebiru swallowed their water-wheeler, extinguishing every glimmer of light.

For a few dreadful moments, she could see nothing, could hear nothing except for the fluttering heartbeats in their raggedly moving chests.

A noise, growing softer and softer, buzzed from somewhere deep inside the city. Like a switch, Nebiru lit up again. Everything was made out of the crystalline material. The floor, the curved walls, the wave ceiling. She took a tentative step outside the water-wheeler, the crystal ebbing and flowing over her frame like liquid. Pastel lights shimmered at her footsteps, as if awakened by her touch. The air smelled stale with the hint of something sweet. The remnants of æther.

"This... this isn't a city," Naila whispered. She eyed her surroundings in confusion. They were in a hallway of some sort. Naila gazed back to see Daena stepping out of the water-wheeler carefully, her poisonous dagger in hand. She pressed her hand to a wall, so warm to her touch, and again tiny lights shimmered like stars. "This is a vessel... a highly advanced one."

Naila shook her head in disbelief. "All this time, I thought... I thought those Unspokens of yours were wizards or demons or spirits or something." She remembered the šaltana's words: *They came from the sky*. The Legends of the Sky spoke of foreign worlds. Not magical realms or fairylands, but real worlds. Planets. But of course, the Ænunaki... they were aliens!

"Stormhold—"

"No," she smacked the wall, all the while glaring at Daena.

She knew the shadowreaper didn't deserve her wrath for this particular reason—although other reasons she had aplenty—but she was angry. Angry at everyone for being fooled. Angry at herself for believing in their fairy tales.

Apprehension marred Daena's scarred face.

Outside, a thousand angry kreekans still attempted to break in. She shuddered as the faint cries crawled at her skin.

Naila shook her head.

"Magic and prophecies don't exist. This æther"—sparks ignited on Naila's fingertips—"there must be a rational explanation for it."

Daena's eyes narrowed on her.

Naila glanced around the crystal hall. It was vast and spotless, housing countless water-wheelers in crystal branches. Despite its solid look, the floor was soft like sheepskin, muting any sound her wet slippers made. At the very end of the hall stood an immense round door with no handle or any hint of how to open it. Naila turned to Daena, her mouth opening and closing.

Naila pressed her hands to the door, the lights twinkling underneath them. Somewhere behind this door could be a portal that took her back home... Her gut clenched with unease. When she glanced over her shoulder, she saw Daena fast approaching, her pupils dilated with eagerness. In the catastrophe of the kreekans' attack, she forgot who Daena really was. A shadowreaper, her hunter.

She chewed on her cheek. "*Nirihim no Nalahai.*"

Without a sound, the door melted over her frame, letting her in, just like the water-wheeler.

"What did you do?" Daena said. She was only a few footsteps away.

"Close the door," Naila said aloud. To her relief, her words came out in the Hædur. She wanted it, and it happened. Just like that.

"What?"

Daena's face scrunched in fury as she made a run for the door.

Naila tipped her chin and stared her dead in the eye. "Don't take this personally. I'm not on the Shadow Šar's payroll after all."

Daena smacked against the door.

Naila's hands trembled as she leaned against a cool, smooth wall. *Did I just do that?* She coughed up a laugh. When her breathing slowed, she forced herself upright and studied her surroundings.

The hall was a long narrow one framed in black gold. With every step she took, lights lit up, revealing more of the hall's endless path. After several moments of walking, the hall widened. Behind the crystal walls, the kreekans' screeches grew louder and angrier.

She scurried through the broadening hall, but the cries of the kreekans followed her every step. Although she couldn't see inside Nebiru from the outside, she could see every detail of Lake Hathor from inside, including the blood-thirsty kreekans. Both she and the kreekans knew only a wall—albeit a very powerful one—separated them.

Even in her hurry to find the portal, she noticed the ethereal grandeur of Nebiru. The crystal halls were colossal and imposing, with breathtaking ornate ceilings depicting stars and moons and other worlds.

She rushed through the hallway, lights automatically brightening the space with every step she took, and stumbled from one place to another. No matter where she looked, the walls shined as if new, and the floors exhibited no sign of weariness. It was as if the vessel had been there for only a few days, even though she knew it was, in fact, over a thousand winters.

Finally, she stumbled into a magnificent hall adorned with precious metals she'd never seen before. Not even in Lemuria. They were azure blues and flamingo pinks and crimson reds. Marble-esque statues from no doubt great Ænunaki warlords lined the walls, all in some kind of battle pose, with two fingers from each hand held in front of their masked faces.

Her heart pounded fiercely when she opened another round door, even though she knew the ship was abandoned. Nobody met her on the other side. Well, aside from more breathtaking metals, gems, and intricate embroidered textiles. She willed herself to calm her breathing. The chamber was empty aside from a floating black-gold bed in its midst, cornered by floating triangular tables made from what looked like a mosaic of gemstones. She gulped back her disappointment and made to leave when she saw a scroll resting on the bed.

Step by step she neared the bed, nervous somehow, for what she might find inside of the scroll. She tried to open it, but it didn't budge. She turned it around. A circular seal was stamped upon it. A circle her compass might just fit in. What were the odds? She pulled off her necklace, huffing in frustration as it tangled in her wet curls. After pulling it out of her hair impatiently, she pushed the compass into the circle.

A perfect fit.

Peculiarly, her compass shimmered with light of its own. The seal broke.

With trembling fingers, she opened the scroll. It was a diary of some sort, written in the language that was rapidly becoming an acquaintance. Just like the inscriptions in Mr. Thoth's scroll, the words automatically translated in her mind. The first page read, *Scroll IV by Arakiel the Destroyer, juhrator.*

Juhrator… the leader of the Ænunaki legions? The journal was filled with maps, formulas, and logs she could only read when her compass's light shined upon the inscriptions. She rolled out the scroll, skimming but not really registering the juhrator's words. He had written countless logs about his observations whilst traveling to an unknown world.

She almost put the scroll back on the bed when a log near the end caught her eye.

This marks the first moon since we have arrived on this world. It is the birthplace of a sentient species much like our own. We have learned they are capable of considerable intellect, but also of undeniable cruelty. As we resumed our quest for the Stone of Shadows and Darkness, we came to a startling discovery—

Interesting.

She stashed the scroll inside the top of her wet clothes and resumed her search for whatever could help her.

"Naila Stormhold." A masculine voice boomed behind her.

She swirled around, the scroll in hand as if she could use it as a weapon. The image of a man shimmered before her.

It was *that* man.

The man she had seen in many a Lemaian statue. With glowing skin of fallen autumn leaves and tightly coiled curls spun of ebony. Tall, muscular, and handsome to a fault, he was dressed in black from head to toe, except for the violet threads in the cape that fluttered behind him. There was something peculiar about him, something she hadn't seen in the statues: he had phæralei like her.

Her hand shot to her mouth. "Suzano Stormhold."

She didn't see a warlord, however. His amber eyes were soft. Kind.

The brown skin around his eyes crinkled. "That I am."

"W-where did you come from?"

He pointed at her compass.

Naila gazed at her pendant in wonder. All this time Suzano's... essence... was hidden inside it?

She smiled nervously.

"Who are you?"

He smiled. "A friend."

She smiled back awkwardly. "We seem to have the same surname... are we related?"

He cocked his head, perhaps contemplating his next words. "I think you can say that, yes. Although time and space separate us."

"I-I am looking for a portal. I'm looking for a way back home. To Earth, I mean," said Naila nervously, unable to pull her eyes from Suzano's formidable frame. Even though he was an illusion, there was no doubt this was a man who commanded respect.

He frowned. "Earth?"

"Yes, it's where I'm from. Shadowreapers abducted me and brought me to Lemuria. I've been looking for a way home. I've been told Nebiru holds a portal that may take me back."

A pitying look appeared on his face. "I'm afraid I don't know what you mean. You see"—his shimmering hand waved to his surroundings—"Lemuria and Earth are one and the same."

Time stopped.

Sound stopped.

Everything and anything stopped.

"You are already on the world once called Earth."

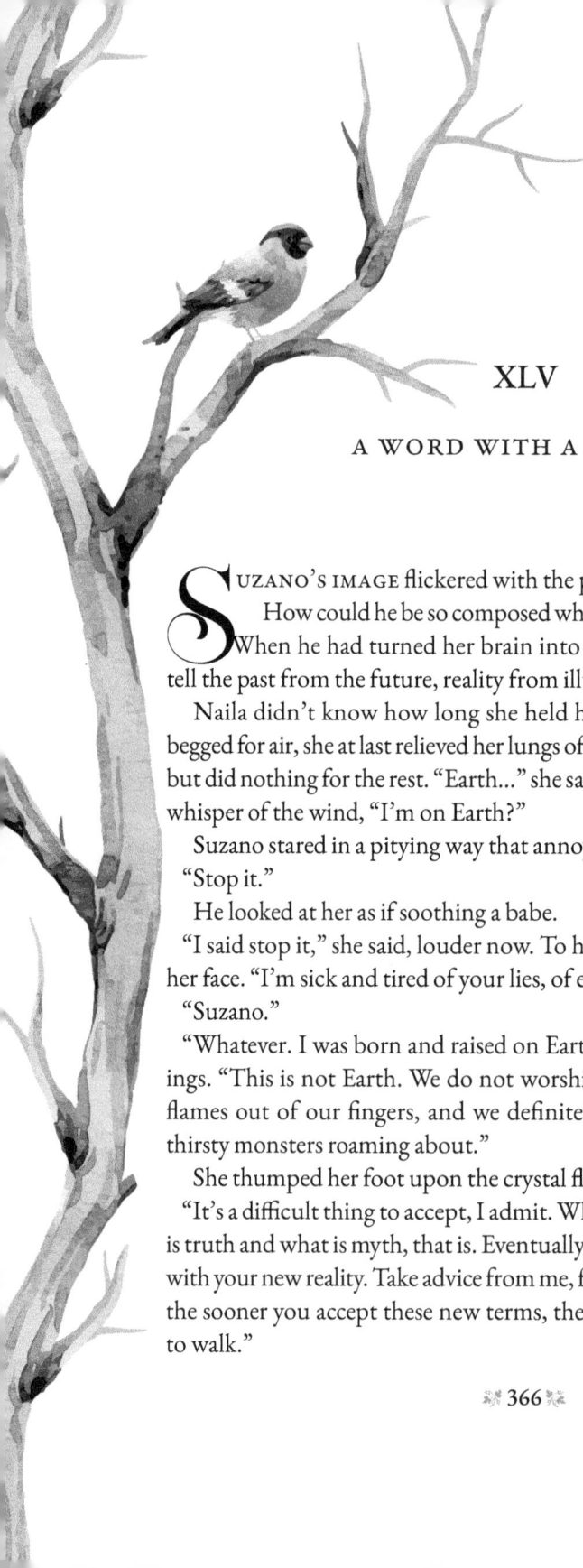

XLV

A WORD WITH A LEGEND

SUZANO'S IMAGE flickered with the pulsing heat of Naila's compass. How could he be so composed when he just obliterated her world? When he had turned her brain into mush and she could no longer tell the past from the future, reality from illusion?

Naila didn't know how long she held her breath, but when her body begged for air, she at last relieved her lungs of their misery. It helped her lungs but did nothing for the rest. "Earth…" she said, her voice little more than the whisper of the wind, "I'm on Earth?"

Suzano stared in a pitying way that annoyed her.

"Stop it."

He looked at her as if soothing a babe.

"I said stop it," she said, louder now. To her horror, tears streamed down her face. "I'm sick and tired of your lies, of everyone's lies. Look, mister—"

"Suzano."

"Whatever. I was born and raised on Earth." She waved at her surroundings. "This is not Earth. We do not worship the Legends, we don't spew flames out of our fingers, and we definitely do not have all these bloodthirsty monsters roaming about."

She thumped her foot upon the crystal floor for good measure.

"It's a difficult thing to accept, I admit. When you're left wondering what is truth and what is myth, that is. Eventually, you will have to come to terms with your new reality. Take advice from me, from one Stormhold to another: the sooner you accept these new terms, the less painful this path you have to walk."

Naila jumped off the bed and rushed to Suzano, but when she tried to grasp his shoulders, her hands slid through his body. Her eyes widened in a tango of horror and wonder.

"You're really just an illusion."

"*Lai*. I put my essence into your compass. You see me as I was, as I walked and talked."

"Why?"

"To lead you, to guide you, in the event our plans failed, and the Ænunaki got a hold of you."

Her head dropped. A few dreadful moments passed, wherein only the soft shrieks of the kreekans prevented silence.

"What happened?" she sniffed.

"You're in shock... I don't think you'll believe what I have to tell you. So, instead, let me show you."

Before she could protest, the gemstones of the spacious chamber turned into the dark of a starless night. A tiny light appeared in its midst: that of Earth.

"Humans overcame excruciating hurdles in their past. Battles with nature, battles with diseases, battles with themselves. Leading to three world wars. But the biggest one was yet to come," Suzano began as images passed by them from Earth during its many wars.

The destruction Naila had seen when she had traveled through the portal... it made sense now.

All at once she found herself in an illusion where she walked once more on the streets of *her* Earth. Where she tucked herself tightly into her coat, protecting herself from a cool breeze in the rainy Dutch weather, as she waited for the tram to take her to home.

"Many ages ago, the Ænunaki arrived on Earth in peace. At least, that is what they convinced mankind of. They infiltrated their homes, their technology. Their hearts. But soon, they revealed their true intentions. Earth harbored something they wanted: the Stone of Shadows and Darkness. And there would be no such thing as sharing."

She remembered her last days on Earth. How the news had announced a mysterious stone in Genghis Khan's grave was found... could it have been? An Ænunaki spy must have picked up on this, prompting them to send a fleet of warriors to Earth.

How shocked people must have been to have the answer to a question long asked: are we alone? To find that truly there are other worlds with their own sentient species and one of them had decided to visit Earth. Did they welcome the Ænunaki with open arms? Meet them with apprehension? She could only guess.

The starless night turned into a spectacle of twinkling stars. No, a battlefield.

Crimson shadows depicting the Ænunaki battled with humans. The world once called Earth, flattened to a map. Weapons of mass destruction sizzled through the chamber as if they were in there with her and Suzano. She let out a gasp when one shot straight at her, but exhaled in relief when it went through her, just like her hands had slid through Suzano.

Suzano shook his head. "Humans never stood a chance. How could they, against a species born and bred for battle? A species that had conquered world after world, at the time humans first discovered fire? A species so advanced they had little use for weapons of mass destruction because they themselves were the weapons? They took out Earth's armed forces with little to no sweat wasted."

Naila found herself walking along a road in the distant future—now in the past. People ran into hiding, parents cried, their children clutched to their chests. The concrete roads shuddered. Skyscrapers split in two. Fighter jets filled the sky, attempting to delay what was to be their doom.

A map of Earth appeared again, this time with several crimson targets, among which were the United States, China, Russia, India, France...

Her face scrunched in pain. She wanted so desperately to look away from what she knew was to come.

In one swift flash of crimson flames, the whole of the Americas was obliterated, leaving nothing but ruins in the oceans. Gone. From one moment to the next. Like the fabled Atlantis. Only charred, barren lands left in their place.

The Lost World... Once upon a time, those lands had been North and South America.

"No." Her voice cracked as her heart shattered in a thousand pieces.

"Over two-thirds of the human race perished at the Ænunaki's hands." Suzano paused, melancholy entering his stance. "Perhaps all of them perished, not in body, but surely in mind."

Shackles appeared around the hands of the human shadows, who were left standing amid mountains of bodies.

A second moon was born out of crimson flames, like a phoenix rising from the ashes of slaughter. The Ænunaki molded what was left of the world into several lands, which one day would become the empires of Crishire, Skeldor, Isolon, and so on.

Naila stared at Suzano with a new sense of awe. To think this man had led to the Ænunaki's defeat. A mere human. She whispered the words she knew would come. "But then, a thousand years later, one man stood up and made them believe in themselves again. Believe that this was their home, and if they didn't fight for it, nobody would."

Suzano Stormhold's figure rose, his fist held up high, between the shackled bodies of his brothers and sisters. Behind him were the twelve figures of his generals—the first šars.

"The War of the Fallen was officially a fact," said he.

A battle between the shadows broke out in the chamber, leaving countless illusionary casualties scattered on the shimmering floor.

"After many winters, the war ended, and we earned our bitterly fought for victory. Took twice as long before our wounds and pride healed. Like all other obstacles in the past, we picked up our pace and attempted to move on."

Silence engulfed them as the lands floated in waves around the juhrator's imposing room. "In the ashes of an Earth long gone, a new civilization was born. Pure humans were no more, for the people also carried the blood of their past enslavers. No longer were they shackled to the dark, no longer forced to bend to the night. They were the Lemai, and theirs were the lands of Lemuria. The lands of the everlasting sun."

A long time ago, when her ma went to sleep, Naila had secretly watched a ghost movie she had forbidden. While she hid behind her tattered teddy bear as the ghost feasted upon its victims, a fleeting thought passed. What would it be like for your soul to leave your body?

Now, she knew. Her body felt numb, and she had no control over the movements of her fingers as they brushed over her quivering lips. No control over her feet as they stumbled back, away from Suzano's imposing form.

Earth's images dissolved.

The crystal floor was exquisite as before, as if the biggest war ever fought on Earth... Lemuria wasn't just shown on this very flooring. As if she didn't just see how the Ænunaki crushed Earth beneath their feet. Killed billions of people with a snap of a finger.

War.

Genocide.

Enslavement.

They took everything from humans. From the Lemai. Their homes, their cultures, their honor; leaving mankind behind as only a shell of their former selves. The Ænunaki did all of that.

The Unspokens...

An enemy so feared none dare to speak their names...

For the first time, Naila understood the pain that came with that name, with that heritage. They would never know the Earth she had known. See the heights humanity had once upon a time reached. These Lemaians, these children of men... *this* was their cross to bear.

"How was it possible?" Naila breathed. "How could one vessel of what, a few hundred Ænunaki? How could they destroy a whole world?"

Suzano folded his hands behind his back. "Imagine technology so advanced it challenges everything you know. A civilization so developed, humanity is but ants beneath its boot. If history teaches us anything, the victor is usually the one with advanced weapons on their side."

"Yet you defeated them."

"No, not defeated. *We* won a battle, but the war, Naila, is yet to come."

"They are dead!"

"They are hidden in the shadows, biding their time until they can grasp what drew them to this world in the first place."

She sucked in her breath, couldn't possibly breathe. "And what is that?"

"You know what they want..."

"But that has nothing to do with me... It's the Stone of Songs and Souls that resides in me."

"No, they want the Gemini stones as a whole. And the Stone of Songs and Souls is half of it. The other half is lost to us: the Stone of Shadows and Darkness."

He watched her, studied her.

"You know where it is."

She nodded.

Oh, did she know.

Her fingers caressed the carefully sculpted walls, before she opened the door, to get far away from the juhrator's chamber.

Suzano's voice whipped behind her. "I can assure you I tell no lies."

She didn't turn around, but only stared at the grandiose hall with its mosaic ceiling, glistening walls, and marble statues. "I know," she whispered, "but that's exactly my problem."

Her lips tasted the salt of her tears. She stumbled into a statue. Having no strength left in her legs, she fell to her knees, sobbing loudly as her eyes rested upon the unapologetic face of an Ænunaki warlord.

In her hurry, she didn't look at the statues properly before, but now she saw it all. Whilst some wore masks of horror, others were unmasked! That Ænunaki face... it was *exactly* like that of a human. More symmetrical, yes, ethereal in its beauty without a doubt, but human, nonetheless.

How could this be?

Her eyes drifted to the center of the Ænunaki's forehead: twin crescent moons drifting next to each other, the second smaller than the first. Phæralei like hers. Her fingers skimmed over the marks on her forehead.

"It's called phæralei," Suzano said behind her.

"I know... but what do they stand for?"

"We don't know exactly, for it is a secret kept locked by the Ænunaki. We do know they give the Ænunaki the innate ability to speak the Hædur. Just like a bird understands its parents' songs from the moment it hatches. When activated, it also gives its host the ability to promptly understand any language it encounters. The Ænunaki knew the importance of mastering communication."

Was that how she understood Tierratongo? A language derived from ancient human languages and the Hædur? More importantly, was that why she understood the Azag? Under normal circumstances, she'd be impressed, but now she felt... nothing.

Naila glanced back at Suzano's illusion. Upon his forehead were the same markings as that of the statue.

She rubbed her tears away. "Why do I have phæralei? Why do *you* have phæralei?"

"It is, Naila, because we are direct descendants of powerful Ænunaki bloodlines. Bloodlines that are claimed to be descendant from the Legends of the Sky. Whether myth or truth, I cannot tell you, however."

She rubbed the damp wool of her sleeves, as she tried to process Suzano's words. An overload of emotions overtook her: confusion, apprehension, and a hint of fear.

"Suzano... does Nebiru hold a portal to take me back home?" she whispered.

A pregnant pause reigned.

"It does."

"Take me to it."

A flicker of disappointment crossed his face. Or mayhap it was her imagination. Yet he beckoned her to follow him.

He took her to a spacious hall at the very center of Nebiru. Within it was a humongous portal. The chamber was filled with crimson light. When she took in the crystal ceiling, she realized why. Somehow it concentrated the light from the moons far above the surface, casting it in a beam to the portal's center. The portal already pulsed with its seductive song.

"By the stars," she whispered. "It's already activated!"

"If you concentrate on your destination, try to feel it with your heart, it will take you back home," said Suzano.

Naila stepped toward the portal, reaching for it. She just had to step inside, and all of this would be over. The Ænunaki? She'd never encounter them in her lifetime.

"What will you do, Naila Stormhold?" said Suzano. "Will you go home and forget all of this? It's a one-way portal. Any decision you make is final."

"I..."

She thought of her Ma and her cat, Tigri.

Her hand grasped at her chest.

Images of Silas and Onyx and Tryce and Rē flashed by. They had come for her. Endangered their life to save hers.

She only had to step inside the portal, and all of this would be over. No more danger, no more fear, no more destiny unknown. She'd be a fool not to... Wouldn't she?

"I"...

This was it.

The final destination of her journey.

The whole reason she traveled over sea and land. Had endured vicious creatures and her never-resting hunters.

"This may be your last chance to get back home," said Suzano. "Nebiru is granting you mercy, it may not do so the next time. Choose now and choose well. The past or the future?"

"I..."

Tears streamed down her face.

She backed away from the portal, her heart breaking with every step she could never undo.

"I can't." She straightened her back, forcing her trembling chin to meet Suzano Stormhold's gaze. "The past is set in stone. The future is my playground."

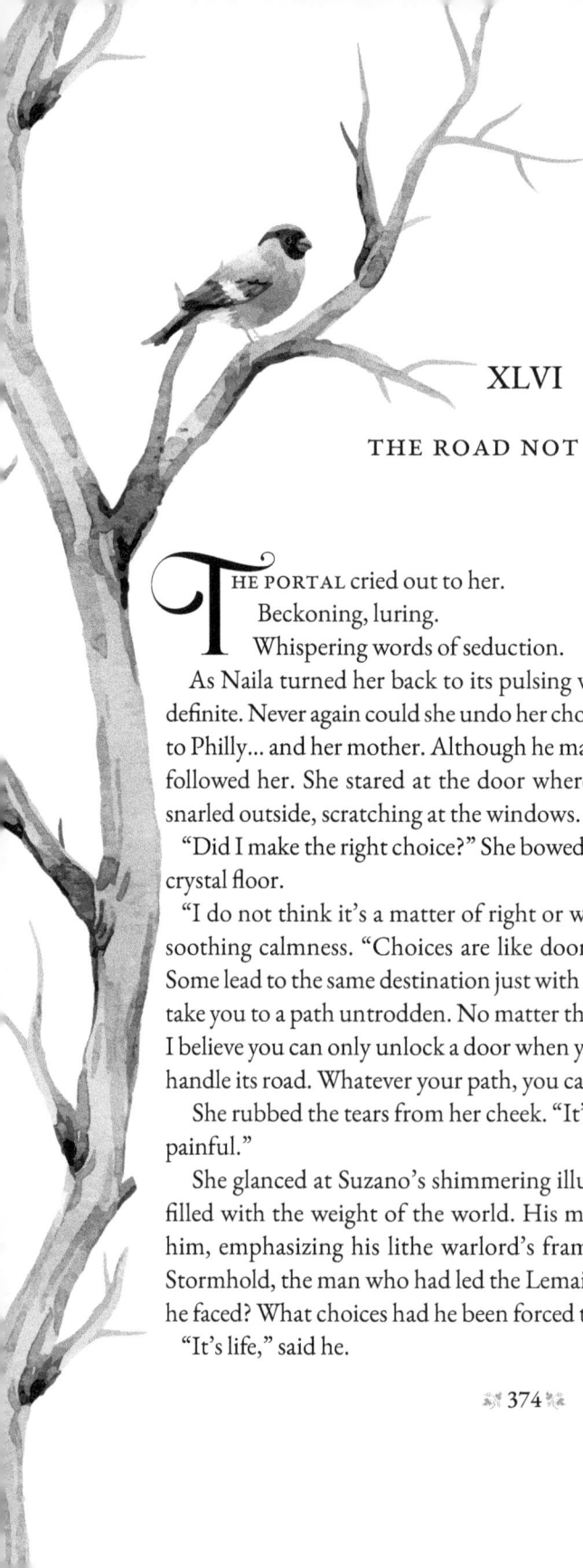

XLVI

THE ROAD NOT TAKEN

THE PORTAL cried out to her.

Beckoning, luring.

Whispering words of seduction.

As Naila turned her back to its pulsing void she knew her decision was definite. Never again could she undo her choice. This might well be goodbye to Philly… and her mother. Although he made no sound, she knew Suzano followed her. She stared at the door where Daena waited. The kreekans snarled outside, scratching at the windows.

"Did I make the right choice?" She bowed her head. Tears dropped to the crystal floor.

"I do not think it's a matter of right or wrong," said Suzano, his voice a soothing calmness. "Choices are like doors that open to different roads. Some lead to the same destination just with another detour, whereas others take you to a path untrodden. No matter the door you open or close, Naila, I believe you can only unlock a door when you have the right equipment to handle its road. Whatever your path, you can do it."

She rubbed the tears from her cheek. "It's hard." Her voice broke. "And painful."

She glanced at Suzano's shimmering illusion. He smiled sadly, his eyes filled with the weight of the world. His magnificent cape flowed behind him, emphasizing his lithe warlord's frame. This was the great Suzano Stormhold, the man who had led the Lemai to freedom. What horrors had he faced? What choices had he been forced to make?

"It's life," said he.

In the past months, her entire life was torn apart, with not a single brick left standing. Her eyes met Suzano's warm ones. In that moment, she realized nothing scared her anymore. Fear felt as alien as serenity did.

What was there to fear, anyway?

She had the Stone of Songs and Souls, after all, and if their suspicions were true, Silas had the other half of the Gemini stones. Whatever happened, they could face it together, and afterward... Afterward, she would lick the wounds of whatever was left of her.

She spun around. "Okay, first things first—"

"You and your companion need a way out of the lake," Suzano finished.

She nodded.

"Leave the lake through another water-wheeler. It will be a challenge, mind you. The extraterrestrials will not let you go without a fight."

Her mouth fell open as she took a step back. "Extraterrestrials?"

"*Yana*," said Suzano, "They are one of the enslaved species the Ænunaki captured on another world. Their favorite *pets* so to speak; lethal enough to outbattle the Lemai, but dumb enough to control."

"I, uh, what—"

Her words died out mid-sentence. Another screech sounded behind her, from one of those beings that *shouldn't* be there. And apparently, they weren't the only ones the Ænunaki had dabbled in. All these strange creatures walking about Earth, no, Lemuria... were species from other worlds?

A muffled voice echoed behind the door.

Daena.

"Stormhold? You had better come out!"

Naila lowered her voice. "Quick, hide, I don't want her to see you."

Soon, *far* too soon, Suzano's figure fractured into a million pieces like tiny stars. A sense of deflation slithered down her spine. "Suzano, sir... will I ever see you again?"

"Do you want to?"

"Yes. No." Naila turned to the door, ready to open it, but then looked back. "Maybe."

She swore she saw the corners of Suzano's mouth lift ever so slightly, but when she blinked his face was back to a solemn expression.

"*Nirihim no Nalahai*," he said. "Speak those words and I will appear anew. Whenever you need me. As long as you need me."

Several tiny stars twirled to the compass, encasing it to give its rusty surface a golden glow. The rest of the illusionary sparks dissolved into air, just like the lights inside Nebiru had flicked off and on.

She slapped her cheeks. *Buckle up, Naila, this will be a rough ride.*

"Nirihim no Nalahai."

The door disappeared before her, leaving nothing between her and a disheveled looking Daena. She stepped into the hallway. The door instantly solidified. Daena's mouth thinned to a hard line. She closed the gap between them with big steps.

Smack.

The sound echoed in the lofty hallway before she felt its impact. Naila skimmed her fingers over her stinging cheek but schooled her features to indifference. "There is nothing of value in there."

Daena's gloved hands clenched into fists, but Naila didn't let the woman's angry countenance deter her. She met Daena's gaze straight on, refusing to be the first to look away.

"Why should I believe you?" said the shadowreaper.

"Because you have no choice."

The women stared at each other, neither wanting to bend. At last, Nebiru's lights interrupted them.

"If we want to make it out alive, we need to get into another water-wheeler."

Naila strutted to one of the spheric vehicles, choosing one twice the size of the shadowreapers' broken one. She glanced back at Daena. "Are you coming or what?"

Daena narrowed her eyes. "This isn't the last of this."

Naila opened the crystal door and waved at Daena to get in. The woman chuckled humorlessly. "Next you will tell me you will steer this thing?"

"Well, you kind of suck at it so I might as well give it a try."

A hint of surprise and, dare she say it, admiration entered the shadowreaper's eyes. It was over before she could blink. "The Shadow Šar is never mistaken," the woman mumbled to herself.

Naila pushed her hand toward the leacher, but Suzano's voice halted her. Like the Azag, she could feel his words within her. *"You do not need that."*

"What—" She looked around the impeccable crystals of the water-wheeler but his face was missing.

"I am in your pendant," he said.

You almost gave me a heart attack, Naila murmured.

"Your phæralei, Naila," Suzano said, "All you have to do is *will* æther. Nothing else is necessary. It will give you more control over the water-wheeler than the leacher will. You will need it against the kreekans."

Naila stared at her glowing compass in wonder. Suzano was right. She had faced the Azag and that wind-slasher with no tools. If she did it then, she could do it again. She took a deep breath and closed her eyes.

Deep inside her belly, something tugged at her navel. Hot and raw. Something uncontrollable. It engulfed her in the flames of its power, consuming her inch by inch. Her body was her temple, and she was its one and only queen. Right that moment, she knew she was in control. She willed the flames to do *her* bidding. It wasn't her begging æther, no, æther was the one at her mercy.

Her eyes fluttered open and æther poured out of her pores like ethereal lava. It took over every piece of the surrounding crystal until the water-wheeler was under her control. Her entire body burned in gilded flames, and so did the vehicle.

Despite the situation, she couldn't help herself from smiling. She did that. She, Naila Groenhart: reject, social outcast, sufferer from anxiety. Now, controller of a power many killed for.

"Hold on."

The water-wheeler started rolling. With a last glance at Nebiru, the gate opened, and the lights lit up the entire lake again, scaring the kreekans away.

"Get to the surface quickly, the kreekans will not stay away for long," Daena ordered.

"Tell me something I don't know."

The water swirled, unwilling to let them go without a fight. Sweat rolled down Naila's temples as she willed æther to move the water-wheeler upwards. It cost all her energy. Like someone let her blood.

Screechhh.

The ear-piercing sound of sharp nails against glass resonated above, below, and all around them. The kreekans crowded the water-wheeler as moths did to a flame. She couldn't see a thing through the many bodies crawling about the sphere.

"By the stars," Daena hissed as she unsheathed her dagger.

How Naila wished the shadowreapers hadn't confiscated Elgafar.

Something leaked out of her nose. Was it sweat? She wiped it away, only to see her fingers stained with blood.

One.

The tip of a claw cracked the crystal near Daena, leaving a spurt of water in its wake.

The kreekan snapped its jaws at them, unveiling row after row of jagged teeth.

Two.

"Hold on," Naila said.

She summoned all her energy, focused her æther. Up, up, up, she ordered.

Three.

With a rough tug, the water-wheeler swirled to the surface of the lake, even as the glass's crack spread like a spider's web.

She met Daena's eyes, reading in them what she had come to realize herself.

They wouldn't make it.

"In life," Daena said quietly, "some are born to rule, and others are born to be their catalysts."

The water-wheeler shattered into shards, just before it could take them to the shore. Dozens and dozens of kreekans flashed through the lake, their screeches victorious.

Daena eyed the kreekans, a sense of resolve on her face. She turned to Naila and for the first time smiled. She mouthed, "The wind blows to move us forward, not so we can stand still. Go, now."

Naila stared at the shadowreaper. She knew her mind was made up, whether she protested or not. The best gratitude she could give Daena was by respecting her choice: to choose the way she wanted to die. Daena had her role to play, and Naila understood that so did she.

She nodded to the shadowreaper in thanks and swam to the shore.

Light flashed behind her. Then the cutting of flesh, and a horrible, painful screech. A kreekan or two had met their end. She didn't look back. The kreekans would only be temporarily distracted before they followed her. She swam and swam until at last she met the misty, freezing air.

"Naila," the šaltana rushed toward her.

Naila glanced at Lake Hathor, but Daena never resurfaced.

The princess pulled her from the cordgrass onto the sleet-covered ground. Her flaxen hair was plastered all over her face and the wetted wool of her coat. "Goodness, dear." Her expression turned to one of confusion. "What happened? No, that can wait for later. Come, Silas ordered us to go into hiding."

Naila chewed on her cheek as her eyes skimmed the small valley. Her friends were in a fierce battle with the shadowreapers. In the middle of the snowy field, Silas dodged Colios's twin scimitars, each one trailing flames that crackled in the sinistrous forest. His own scimitar, Valkarian, flared to life as he blocked a slash that threatened to cleave him in two.

"Onyx, right flank!" he barked, his eyes darting toward her for a breath of a moment. She loosed an arrow, catching Morpheus's arm just as he closed in on Tryce.

Colios's blades came down in a vicious arc. The prince spun, swinging Valkarian with an elegant precision, steel meeting steel as he drove Colios back. Their movements were so fast, æther replaced their shadows in their deadly dance of flames.

"We must help them," Naila squeaked.

"No, we will only be in their way. Come now, kittling, we must go," urged the šaltana.

Naila almost tumbled into the snow.

The šaltana grasped her by the arm. "Are you all right?"

Her head felt featherlight. The æther she'd used had drained her. Worry knotted inside her stomach. Now was not the time for her flames to abandon her.

"Tryce, cover me!" Silas called out, leading the way.

"Gotcha!" Tryce, with a grunt, swung Māru with all the force he could muster, nearly cleaving through another shadowreaper that lunged at Silas. The shadowreapers, however, had reflexes sharper than a cat's.

Her heart nearly stopped its beat when the shadowreaper attacked Tryce with a vengeance. Just how were they supposed to defeat a foe who was as fast and strong as the poison upon his blade was deadly?

But Silas's lips curved into a dangerous grin, as if he wasn't fighting for his life. Onyx, who stood with another arrow ready, shook her head. Naila was sure the huntress mouthed something close to '*lugals*' and, to be honest, she very much thought the same.

Silas's and Colios's swords met once more in a storm of flames. Colios pressed in, but the prince's movements, though reckless, were swift and untamed, like the fire itself.

Colios cried out when Silas cut off his arm. He swung the flaming sword in his good arm at Silas, but Silas was too fast.

"Behind you," Naila screeched, right as Silas aimed to slash his throat. He missed the other shadowreaper's blade by only a few millimeters. Colios took advantage of his distraction to take another go at him, but Onyx jumped on his back and tackled him to the ground.

By the time Naila and the šaltana reached them, the snow was stained red all around Colios. Blood spurted out of his stump. The shadowreaper beckoned to his comrades before, as one, they retreated into the shadows of the Dark Forest. Somewhere, in a far recess of her mind, Naila knew that couldn't possibly mean any good, but for the time being she had other pressing matters.

Pity marred the šaltana's face. She kneeled beside the villain. Blue flames lit her forearms. Colios shuffled away from her, but he was too weak to fend her off. The flames traveled from her hands to his bloodied flesh. A moan escaped Colios's mouth as the gushing of blood stopped, and crusts formed on his stump.

Onyx pulled Naila into an embrace. "You're still here..."

Silas frowned. "What happened to Nebiru?"

Naila filled them in with everything that happened, from the moment she sneaked out of the hut—which earned the shadowreapers several curse words from Silas—to the reason Daena, and Colios kidnapped her—which earned her a confused frown from Onyx—to her escaping the kreekans and finding the fallen city of Nebiru—which earned the lake a starving look from Colios.

"Wha...?" said Tryce. He looked as if someone had stomped him on the head.

"So, you're saying that you're from the past?" Onyx's eyes widened. "Can you believe that Silas? Someone who has lived in ancient times."

"Incredible," said Silas.

The prince's hands rubbed gently over Naila's upper arms. His voice turned soft, his ocean eyes gentle. "Was there no portal?"

Naila leaned her forehead against the hardness of his chest.

"There was."

He squeezed his arms around her. Resting his cheek against her hair he whispered. "But you're still here."

"I'm still here," she affirmed.

"Eeeeeek."

"Mother!"

"Stand back or I will kill your precious šaltana."

Colios had his good arm around the princess's torso with a poisoned blade pointing to her chin.

"So, this is how you thank me?" the šaltana whispered, an edge of disappointment laced through her tone.

"I never asked you to save me," Colios snarled through gritted teeth.

"Give me the nergayla, and you will get your mother back. What say you?"

"I'll end you," Silas gritted through his teeth.

His scimitar already blazed anew with ice-blue flames.

"Wrong answer," Colios chuckled humorlessly.

A twig snapped behind them followed by the sound of footfalls from horses and men. Whatever hopes or fears had taken Naila captive, those feelings melted faster than ice in a fire. She was yet again thrown into a kaleidoscope of disaster.

Out of the shadows of the Dark Forest, a horde of crimson and black-clothed *vigiles* appeared. Some rode horseback while others were already unseated and shielded with blazing æshefied scimitars, spears and bows and arrows. But that's not what grabbed her attention. In their midst was a man more unnerving than the forest itself.

The Red Šar.

He took off his helmet; golden strands stuck to his neck with rain dripping off the ends. A streak of lightning stressed the icy darkness in his eyes. His following words were even icier.

"I believe you have something that belongs to me."

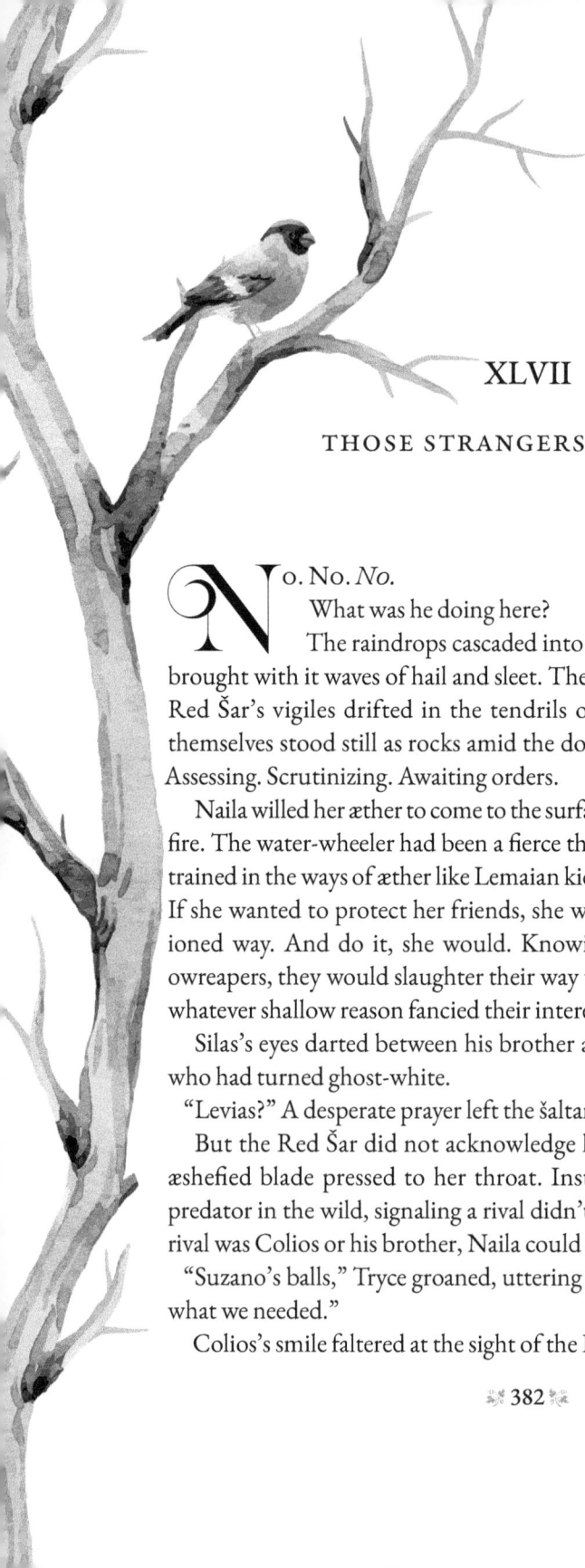

XLVII

THOSE STRANGERS WE KNOW

No. No. *No.*

What was he doing here?

The raindrops cascaded into a full-blown storm as the wind brought with it waves of hail and sleet. The opal-and-crimson robes of the Red Šar's vigiles drifted in the tendrils of the freezing wind, but they themselves stood still as rocks amid the dormant trees of the Dark Forest. Assessing. Scrutinizing. Awaiting orders.

Naila willed her æther to come to the surface, but it sizzled out like a dying fire. The water-wheeler had been a fierce thing to control, and she was not trained in the ways of æther like Lemaian kids from the day they could walk. If she wanted to protect her friends, she would have to do it the old-fashioned way. And do it, she would. Knowing the Red Šar and the shadowreapers, they would slaughter their way through everyone to get her for whatever shallow reason fancied their interests.

Silas's eyes darted between his brother and Colios holding his mother, who had turned ghost-white.

"Levias?" A desperate prayer left the šaltana's lips.

But the Red Šar did not acknowledge his mother's presence, nor the æshefied blade pressed to her throat. Instead, his stance loosened, as a predator in the wild, signaling a rival didn't intimidate him. Whether that rival was Colios or his brother, Naila could only guess.

"Suzano's balls," Tryce groaned, uttering a few more vulgar words. "Just what we needed."

Colios's smile faltered at the sight of the Red Šar and his vigiles.

With a little shove he let the princess go. Shadowreaper or no, he was no match for two dozen highly trained vigiles. Silas pulled his mother into a brief hug before pushing her gently behind him.

"Red Šar," said Colios, "we do not seek a conflict."

The Red Šar affixed his black-gold helmet to his horse. Like the shadowreapers' doran horses and the Mehari's camodas, the magnificent stallion's hooves burned with flames of æther, the tips dancing like shadows. If there was beauty in the underworld, the stallion would be it, so out of the world was it in both its sin-seducing allure and fear-inducing countenance. He and his master truly were a match made in hell.

"I find that hard to believe, shadowreaper. You are seas removed from the Shadowlands, in a hostile confrontation with an imperial heir, and more importantly, in the possession of my consort," said the šar.

"Your Majesty," Morgana said, peeling herself from the shadows behind a nearby tree, her voice smooth like a snake's forked tongue.

Naila blinked at her, stunned. She had been hidden there all this time!

"I did not give you permission to speak, woman," the šar snarled.

"Perhaps we can come to an agreement," Colios said swiftly. His eyes flicked to the Dark Forest as if he expected someone. Naila couldn't help but wonder if he was stalling until his comrades returned.

"What could you possibly offer that isn't mine for the taking?" The šar narrowed his eyes.

"This *feylana* here is kin to our master. We wish for nothing more than to return her to him. Do not believe her stories. She has a rich fantasy, as you may have noticed."

"Liar," Naila hissed, but Colios ignored her.

"She fled the Shadowlands with a precious scroll of the Shadow Šar's," he continued. "He wants both his relative and the scroll back."

A swell of panic constricted her throat. So Colios had realized she had the juhrator's scroll. She shouldn't have told the others in front of Colios what had happened in Nebiru. Why had she been so stupid? Although she didn't know what secrets the scroll held that could interest the Shadow Šar, she knew she had to keep it away from him. Perhaps this was why Daena had consented so easily to leaving Nebiru.

"Grant us this and the Shadow Šar shall reward you richly. Is it black gold you want? We have aplenty. If you wish for power, we will gift you doran horses or *anteleosts*. Or perhaps it's beauty you covet? We will fill your imperial harem with the most beautiful *feylanas* the lands of Lemuria have ever seen."

The Red Šar stroked the angles of his jaw. "A rather abundant offer for a stolen scroll and a relation of the Shadow Šar. It begs me to wonder why they are so precious to him."

"I am but a simple servant," said Colios smoothly. "I do not know my master's mind."

"Said every liar before I hanged them by their treacherous necks." The šar crossed his arms. "Let the Shadow Šar explain it to me himself and we shall see whether we have an agreement."

"Oh, for all that is holy, Naila is no kin to that damned Shadow Šar, Levias," Silas spat. "You've dropped to a new low if you're actually thinking about working with that backstabbing snake."

Levias's expression remained indecipherable. "Foolish *dogan*," he said as he paced toward them, two vigiles armed with blazing maces on his heels. "Ever so clueless, ever so witless."

He stopped several feet before Silas. As one, Onyx and Tryce formed a barrier around the prince. Silas pulled Onyx behind him, hissing, "What do you think you're doing?"

Levias paid them no heed and focused on Naila instead.

A shiver crawled through her at the sight of his imploring eyes, and instinctively, she rested her hand on the scroll hidden in her drenched cloak. From the outside, the pocket couldn't be distinguished from the rest of her attire. It hid the juhrator's scroll perfectly. Levias sauntered toward her as if he had all the time in the world.

When he stopped in front of her, she had to raise her head to meet his gaze. He was as tall as his twin. Silas made a move toward her, but the Crishirian vigiles kept him at bay with their æshefied maces, which in turn prompted Naila's friends to æshify theirs. One move and this would turn into a bloodbath.

Levias pulled her hand away. Her heart thumped loudly as she drowned in the shadows of his beguiling eyes. His fingers brushed over the lower part of her belly, leaving featherlight tingles behind. His eyes never left hers, as his fingers paused when they found her hidden pocket. His hand slid inside to uncover the Ænunaki's scroll.

The scroll held high, he pulled his eyes away toward a fuming Silas. "If and only *if* you ever become šar, you may entertain me with your ideas, but until then leave the speaking to those who know what they're talking about."

"Please," Naila's voice broke, "don't give it to them."

Levias considered her silently.

"As you know, I'm a man of trade. No matter how sweet a deal, I can be persuaded to a better one."

Naila lowered her gaze to his obsidian armor. Her mind's wheel spun, fabricating scenario after scenario on how she'd get out of the dire situation but came up empty.

He tucked a finger underneath her chin and lifted it so she met his eyes once more. "What say you?"

She forced her eyes into steel and pushed his finger away.

"I don't belong to the Shadow Šar, nor do I belong to you. I refuse to be a part of this pissing game between you and your brother. Give me back *my* scroll."

A sliver of a smile passed over his face.

"The world does not revolve around my brother, Evening Star. I'm too busy a man to indulge myself with childish rivalries."

Naila didn't believe a word coming out of his mouth.

"Levias, please," the šaltana said as she stepped forward.

"Please what, šaltana?" He laughed humorlessly. "You lost the right to ask me anything the moment you threw me to the lions."

Princess Sayana winced, agony washing over her face.

"It was a mistake, my love. Please believe me when I say not a day went by without me regretting it." She grabbed him by the arm, but he rejected it. "I tried to get you back, Levias, I did. Your father refused."

"And why wouldn't he?" He snipped, but Naila could have sworn she saw a hint of melancholy in the depths of his eyes. "Healers have to make instant life and death decisions, only to live their entire life with the consequence of their choices. You made your choice, šaltana. What's done is done."

"I was withering there, Levias," Sayana begged, but her words fell to the snow, as weightless and forgotten as autumn leaves. "I would have died under Jericho's cruelty if I stayed there a day longer. What use could I have been to any of you dead rather than alive? I would have failed you both."

Levias shook his head. "Don't worry, you only failed one of us."

"What would you have had me do?" Her voice cracked. He finally allowed her to grasp his arms.

"Be a mother," said he. "To have been a mother instead of taking the cowardly, easy way."

"You sound just like your father," Sayana whispered bitterly as she let his arms loose.

"He at least was in the vicinity, pity though his presence was."

Tears spilled down Sayana's cheeks, but her son exhibited no hint of pity. Naila's heart broke for her beloved šaltana, but for once, she understood where the Red Šar came from. To feel rejected by your parents, the two people in the world who were supposed to cherish and protect you. He had withstood his mother's betrayal and his father's cruelty. Had worked hard to earn the respect of his people and build a prospering empire.

She feared that Sayana's chances with her son had evaporated the moment she chose a better life for Silas and herself at the expense of her other son. The hardness in his eyes, as he regarded his mother, told her he would never forgive her. The šaltana's shoulders sagged. Her flaxen hair clung to her delicate frame. She looked so small in front of her son. So broken next to his warlord frame. Sometimes in life, there were no happy endings.

"*Māmān*, leave it be," said Silas. His eyes shot daggers at Levias.

The šaltana stepped backward. Back to the son who did want her.

A flock of winter jays flew out of the forest in a rush, cawing loudly as they skated over the lake. At first, Naila thought it was a figment of her imagination that the ground underneath the sleet trembled. Before she knew it, the tremor threw her toward the ground. Fast as lightning, the šar caught her by the arms and steadied her, his eyes narrowed on a spot behind her. He beckoned his vigiles to get to the front, but an ear-deafening screech stopped any movement.

Naila covered her ears, doubling over in pain. She'd do anything to get away from those excruciating shrieks. In the eighteen years she'd been alive, she had never heard a sound so piercing. The high-pitched notes scratched like claws at her eardrums. The kreekans' screeches were child's play compared to this.

"As touching as this reunion is," a hauntingly familiar voice, stoic and colder than ice, echoed when the shrieks dampened to an unpleasant hum, "I have a lengthy journey to continue and two stones to harvest."

Rē's tall frame emerged out of the Dark Forest, several shadowreapers close behind him. Next to them, two giant worm-like creatures broke out of the sleet. They were as big as a redwood tree, with a face two times wider than that of an *elephaunt*. Their scales were crimson, like the blood staining the snow, and they didn't seem to have eyes. Instead, a round, humongous mouth, with countless rows of jagged teeth, took up most of their faces.

"Screechers," a vigile barked out.

The Red Šar ordered his vigiles into a fighting position. He pushed her to the back and called two vigiles to protect her. Naila let it happen without protest. She was so shocked, words escaped her.

"Rē?" said Silas.

His voice held no anger, only disbelief.

"Sack of wine," Tryce spat.

His ax blazed with flames. He stomped forward, but Onyx pushed him back with a warning hiss.

Colios ignored the confusion around him and pressed forward with determination. Morgana smirked triumphantly and followed suit.

They bowed to Rē, cupping a fist in their palm. "I welcome thee, His Imperial Majesty, Sariel, son of Samael, He Who Walks Between the Worlds, Warden of the Starless Skies, and Shadow Šar to all the Shadowlands."

XLVIII

THE SHADOW ŠAR

Did her mind concoct an image that held no roots in time or place? Naila shook her head in disbelief. She couldn't take her eyes off Rē. No—*the Shadow Šar*. This wasn't happening. Rē couldn't be the man who abducted her to this forsaken world; the notorious leader of the shadowreapers who had so thoroughly ripped her life to pieces.

He sauntered toward them, casting off an air of indifference only the Red Šar could match. His skin gleamed pale gold in the snow's light, or perhaps his obsidian suit absorbed all its color. Like his shadowreapers, a leathery mask, laced with black-gold fangs, covered his jaw. A flicker of crimson ignited in his dark, dark eyes.

Naila inched forward. A vigile tried to pull her back, but she cast him a glare and shook him off.

"Rē," Onyx hissed, her fist blanching around her bow. At the same time Silas said, "Why?"

The Shadow Šar regarded them with disinterest.

"By the twelve's holy bones, answer him," Tryce demanded. His body was wired tight and his face was folded in anger… and pain.

She could only imagine the emotions going through him. Rē had been part of his father's crew. Had been there all those summers when Tryce grew from a boy to the cusp of manhood. Where Onyx had taught Tryce how to hunt, Rē had taught the boy how to navigate the sea. Together with Halfbeard, he had planted within him the seed of a seaman's love.

"You were a means to an end," the Shadow Šar finally answered. "A way to monitor the Silver Šar's heir"—his dark gaze shifted to the šaltana who had blanched to an impossible paleness—"the bearer of the Stone of Shadows and Darkness."

Silas chuckled, but there was no humor to it. "I don't have the patience for this." He pushed a vigile out of the way and pulled his scimitar out of the melting snow. "Say what you want to say and be done with it."

Naila ignored her sore muscles and trudged through the field to join Tryce. The snow was so ethereal, it almost felt like sacrilege to see it marred with blood-red stains. She winced at the sight. How much more blood would be shed in her name?

She took Tryce's hand, stroking circles on his palm to soothe him. She felt his stance loosening slightly, although agony still filled his dark-brown eyes. Tryce wasn't faking the pain. He had lost a surrogate brother. Somehow that made her angrier than the fact the Shadow Šar had ripped her from her home.

Lord Sariel sauntered toward them. The Red Šar's men drew their æshefied scimitars, maces, and shields. He paid them no heed, his eyes remaining fixated on Silas. "I must admit I had my doubts when you refrained from using those accursed flames of shadows. I tried to test you, šargon, but even against the Azag of Helath you did not use your powers."

Naila clasped her mouth in horror. Rē had summoned the Azag? Had forced the serpent to attack the Chimera?

"Murderer!" Tryce cried.

His ax blazed blue as he ran toward the Shadow Šar.

"Tryce, no!" Naila screamed.

She ran after him, hoping to intercept him.

Rage blinded the boy. It made him twice as fast and doubly less susceptible to reason.

"Tryce," Onyx cried.

She and Silas also rushed after him, but Tryce reached the Shadow Šar first.

With a furious roar, he cut his ax through Lord Sariel's body. Her eyes hadn't fooled her. It went through him like a knife through butter. Sariel's body burst into crimson flames, disappearing into nothingness...

"What?"

And reappeared behind Tryce.

"Aargh," Tryce choked.

It happened too fast.

The Shadow Šar withdrew his blade of crimson flames. Tryce fell to his knees, blood seeping out of his back.

"No, please, no..." Naila's voice broke.

The Shadow Šar turned to them, the ethereal planes of his face schooled to indifference. In the light of the moons, he looked every part the dark prince. His hair and eyes were darker than the abyss, with the leathers covering his muscles an equal match in coloring.

The forest grew quiet, only the whooshing of the snowy wind breaking the silence in the moments to follow. Naila didn't dare breathe. The moment Lord Sariel left Tryce in a growing pool of blood-covered snow, the šaltana rushed to the boy and, to Naila's relief, started the healing process. If only she hadn't used all her æther in the lake. She was of no use to Tryce right now.

"You failed the test," Sariel continued, eying Silas, as though he hadn't just stabbed a lethal hole through Tryce. "But then I couldn't deny your attraction to the Ishtar. The stones calling to each other. Come heaven or hell, šargon, I will draw that power out of you."

She could feel the confused stares burning in her back. She hadn't had the chance to tell them about the Ishtar revelation.

The Red Šar frowned. "The stones...?"

"The Ænunaki's birthright: the stones of life and death."

Levias quirked a brow. "That fairy tale about their origins?"

In the shock of the moment, Naila had forgotten Levias. He and his men watched the Shadow Šar through skeptical though alert eyes, and with good reason. Even she knew the Shadow Šar's use of æther was beyond exceptional. To use it to create an illusion... To bind the minds of screechers and even a karuiles siunes to his will. This would not be a battle easily won.

But first things first. Naila swallowed her pride. She knew the Red Šar came prepared. He must've had a healer or two with him. She brushed a tear away and begged Levias. "Please... Please help Tryce. He's an innocent boy."

To her surprise, without bargaining, the šar gestured to his crew. A dark-skinned woman appeared from the back of his group. Her forehead held a vague scar—a priestess who'd been one of the Mehari. Without a word, she went to the šaltana and Tryce.

When blood stopped pulsing out of Tryce, Silas glared at Lord Sariel. "So what if it's true? What do you want with those stones, anyway?"

The Shadow Šar closed his eyes for a moment. Just then, Naila saw a hint of the old Rē again. The grumpy right hand of Halfbeard, who had no patience for questions he deemed silly. The one who had been their friend.

"The stones of life and death..." Levias answered in his stead. An unknown emotion gleamed in his oceanic gaze. "Let me guess, they give you the power to rule both?" His narrowed eyes rested upon his brother. "And you think my *dogan* possesses such a stone? Come now, Shadow Šar."

Before Silas could banter with his brother, an ear-piercing screech echoed anew.

"Wha—"

The snowy ground shook and crumbled. A screecher sped underground, no doubt on the Shadow Šar's orders. Before anyone could react, it burst out of the sleet and caught a vigile in his rows of jagged teeth.

"Aaargh."

The sour scent of panic spread through the icy winds. Everyone scattered and fled like headless chickens into the Dark Forest, far away from the bloodthirsty worms. In the chaos, someone pushed Naila to the ground, almost trampling her.

"Wait, stop!" she said.

When it came to flight, fight, or freeze, the latter still held over twelve thousand years of intellectual evolution within its icy claws.

Levias strutted to the front, a murderous expression carved on his face. He beckoned his vigiles and barked, "Back in line, men. Between the beasts, the Dark Forest, and me, you do *not* want *my* wrath."

And just like that, order returned... for the Red Šar's vigiles, at least.

"Let's get out of here," Silas said as he pulled Naila out of the snow.

He scanned her body as if to make sure she had no injuries.

"B-But what about your brother?"

"He's the one who wants to compare sizes. Besides, R—the Shadow Šar is after us, not him."

"But..."

"No buts, Naila." Silas squeezed her shoulders gently. He captured her gaze with his, his eyes pleading. "I need you, mother, Onyx, and Tryce to be safe. I'm not risking your lives."

She swallowed, but nodded. Silas pulled her into a hug. He planted his soft lips on her forehead. Even amid the chaos, she couldn't help but sigh.

She closed her eyes, listening to his feathering heartbeat, until the agonizing screams of people ripped apart pulled her out of her haze. Peculiarly, a needlelike pain stung her feet, but it was over before it began.

"Here," he said, thrusting her dagger into her hand. "I got it back for you. Come on, let's go."

Hand in hand, they rushed toward Princess Sayana and Tryce. Naila couldn't spot Onyx anywhere. Tryce groaned, but there was some color in his cheeks. His wound had even scabbed over.

"Oh, Tryce," said Naila.

She hugged him tightly. When he protested with a weak, "Ye're killing me." She couldn't help but tear up in relief.

The šaltana rubbed the tiredness out of her eyes. "He's going to be all right. Thank you for your help, dear friend."

The Crishirian healer bowed and took her leave.

As Silas checked on his mother and Tryce, Naila's worry shifted to her other friend. She frantically looked around for a dash of fiery red hair.

"Silas," she squeaked, "I can't see Onyx anywhere."

"What?" Silas stopped fussing over his mother. His eyes darted around as well. "Seven hells, Red, why are you always so reckless?"

"Wait here," he commanded, before they could object. He scurried back to the battlefield where his brother and his men fought the giant, worm creatures.

She huffed.

"Let us go to the trees," Sayana said. "We'll find shelter there."

Naila had no doubt about that, but she had made up her mind.

"You go, and take Tryce with you," she told the princess. "I'm going to look for Onyx and Silas."

"Naila, wait!"

But Naila had rushed back to the field, even though her body ached with exhaustion. She may not be a fighter, but this was her fight.

She pushed herself between the vigiles, who fired æsh-arrows and spears at the screechers. Blood oozed out of the wounds of a worm, but it didn't deter the creature from attacking. Instead, its attacks gained even more vehemence.

She glanced about, desperate to capture a hint of her friend, but she didn't see Onyx, and she had lost Silas now too.

"Naila!" she heard from afar.

The šaltana. Oh no, why was she following her?

"Princess, go back!" she cried. "Please, I'll join you soon."

The šaltana, however, seemed a woman on a mission. She waded through the thick snow toward Naila. Time stood still when Naila caught a screecher eying Sayana. Ignoring the surrounding warriors, the screecher went straight for the attack.

Desperate, Naila willed her æther to appear, but the vault was utterly empty. Her whole life, she had wished for those flames to disappear. Now that she needed them the most, they decided to stay silent. There was nowhere to run, nowhere to hide. Not anymore. If she survived this, she had to learn to master the ways of æther.

"Eeeek," the šaltana shrieked as the screecher bolted lightning fast toward her.

"Šaltana!"

Fear shot through her. Naila dashed toward the princess. She hadn't thought about what she'd do now that her æther had abandoned her. All she knew was that she had to save the šaltana. Had to save this precious woman from undergoing even more suffering. She was halfway toward Sayana when she realized she wouldn't make it. The screecher was too fast.

It snapped its fanged jaws at Sayana, ready to rip her apart.

"No," she breathed, her voice hoarse with agony. She squeezed her eyes shut. She couldn't bear to see the inevitable.

Suddenly, the piercing shrieks grew quiet. The only sounds were those of the vigiles' screams and the other screechers' infuriated shrieking.

Slowly, she opened her eyes. She fell to her knees in relief at the sight before her.

A pair of æshefied scimitars, one from Silas and the other from his twin, perforated the screecher's neck. Blood gushed out of the wounds, splattering all over the brothers as the screecher's scarlet body grew limp.

The twins pulled back their swords in unison. Levias cut off the screecher's head with one fast blow.

"Show off," Silas huffed.

"Hmph," his brother answered, but she swore the hint of a smile tipped at the corner of his lips.

"I... I," the šaltana hiccupped.

Naila got back to her feet and closed the gap between her and the others. She let out a breath in relief when she saw no harm had come to the princess. "Šaltana, are you all right?"

Sayana's face had lost all its color. Her eyes were full to the brim with tears.

"Mother." Silas caught the šaltana's face between his big hands, his eyes skimming over every inch of her face. The princess's trembling fingers clasped his coat. She rested her forehead against his broad chest.

"Thank you," Sayana whispered. She raised her head and peeked over Silas's shoulder.

The Red Šar stared at the blood-red scales of the giant lifeless corpse with disdain. He wiped off his bloodied sword against it.

Sayana made to reach for him. She almost fell to the sleet, but Silas steadied her. "You too, Levias, thank you."

The šar didn't turn to them. Instead, he looked far into the distance, a frown wrinkling his face. What he'd say Naila would never know because an arm encased her body. The sharp end of a shadowreaper's blade pressed to her neck. *Morgana*. A drop of blood warmed her skin as it streamed from her neck to her collarbone. The poisonous blade had cut her.

The princess gasped in horror.

Silas and Levias instantly turned, their scimitars at the ready.

"I wouldn't do that if I were you," Lord Sariel's voice boomed.

Morgana's black-gold dagger pitched its flames of æther even deeper into her skin. Naila didn't dare swallow. Her gaze drifted over the field, but she didn't see the Shadow Šar.

Levias beckoned his men in the back. From the squelching of footsteps, they were well on their way toward them. Then his darkened eyes locked on something above her.

The air above her left swirls of wet snow in its wake.

First, his feet descended.

Then the rest of his lithe, warlord's body.

Sariel had been flying above them all this time. Literally flying.

His golden, luminescent skin was now joined with bleeding flames. Stunning feathers of crimson flames sprouted out of his back to gift him a pair of large, powerful wings. He was magnificent, like something not at all from this world. So powerful his build, so bewitching his beauty. A statue of an ancient deity come to life.

She held her breath, her heart thumping so loud she was sure Morgana could feel it.

The Shadow Šar descended upon them like an angel of death.

"Impossible," Silas mumbled.

"Æther," the Red Šar whispered, as if not believing his eyes, "can only enhance that which is, not create. At least not for the Lemai."

Lord Sariel's flaming boots crackled atop the snow when he landed. "Why don't you say it, Red Šar?" he said, a ghost of a smirk on his face. "Why don't you speak the words aloud?"

Naila frowned in confusion, but then her eyes traveled over the angles of Sariel's stoic face. Her breath hitched—causing Morgana to tighten her grip—when her eyes landed on that which she hadn't seen before. There, in the center between Sariel's eyebrows, were eerily familiar markings. Markings like hers, burning crimson.

Phæralei.

To be specific, two crescent crimson moons.

Then it clicked.

"*You*," she whispered, the tips of her fingers sizzling with what could only be the return of her æther, "You are an Ænunaki?"

XLIX

MERCILESS

THE SNOW seemed to melt underneath Naila's feet, leaving her in a mud of untruths and deception.

Rē... Her once-thought friend was one of the feared. One of the legendary Unspokens who had colonized her Earth, had enslaved humans, had destroyed everything they stood for. Suzano was right. The Ænunaki had been among them all this time, feeding them lies like trusting lambs until they became complacent enough to walk willingly into the slaughterhouse of their master plan.

She clenched her fists.

The scent of burning honey interlaced with the notes of frozen pines. Like a long-lost friend, æther sparked in her fingers—those gilded flames she used to love to hate, but somewhere in the past moons began to hate to love. Lord Sariel's eyes followed the sparks with a hint of approval. Is this what he wanted? To see her angry enough to embrace her childhood tragedy? Well, he just got his wish.

"*T'ilaa no gloria!*" An æsh-arrow shot through the frigid air. Its target, a shadowreaper, jumped out of the way, but not fast enough. It sliced through his bicep.

"Onyx!" Naila exhaled in relief.

Onyx nocked another arrow and unleashed it upon a shadowreaper. She wasn't alone. Shadowing her were some of Halfbeard's crew. Two-Toed Teddy, Bubba, and the others! Naila's heart soared. They were alive. So that's what Onyx had been doing—getting reinforcements.

"Took ye long enough." Tryce grinned, hefting his ax.

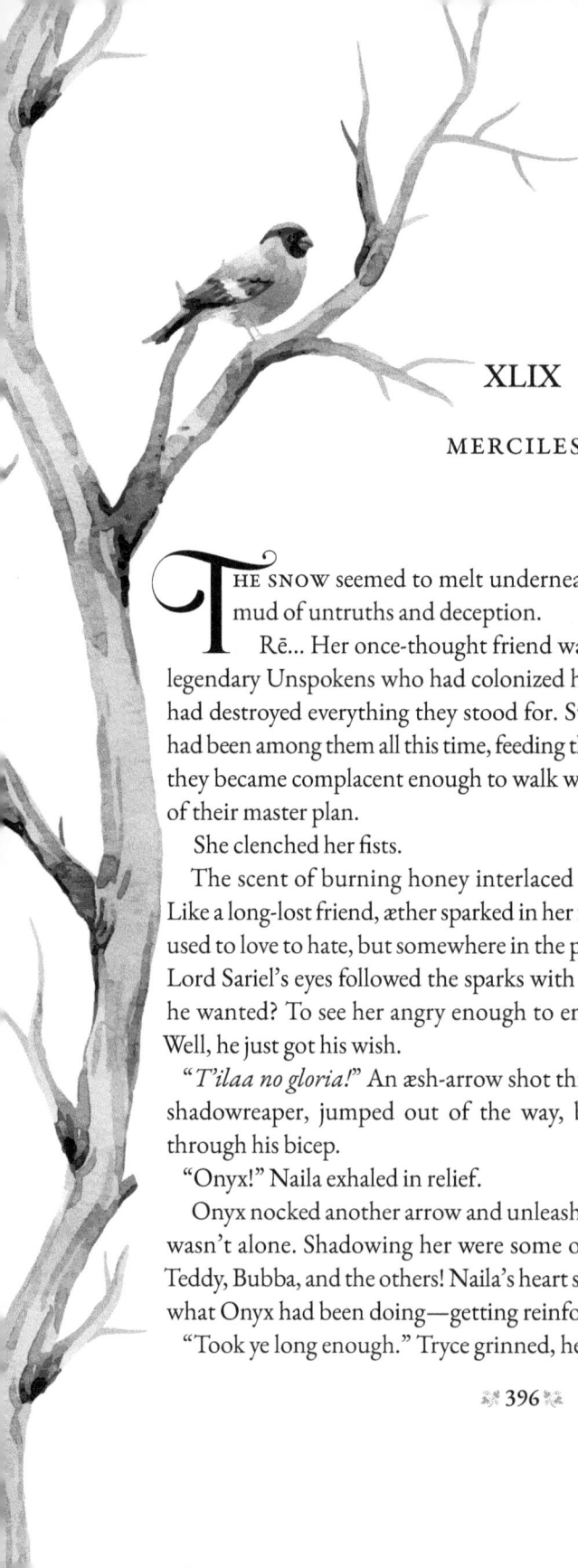

Bubba ruffled the teen's curls. "Wouldn't miss this party for anything, aye?"

"Aye," cheered the crew.

Bubba clapped the boy on the shoulder, his laugh booming like thunder. "We would'na let ye have all the fun now, would we?"

The crew roared their agreement, raising their weapons high. "Aye!"

Sariel nodded his head toward Onyx and the crew, ordering his shadowreapers, "Get them."

Everything happened at once: Onyx unleashing arrow after arrow, Silas and Levias throwing themselves upon the Shadow Šar with blazing scimitars, the shadowreapers attacking both vigiles and Halfbeard's crew alike. Not to mention the two remaining screechers eying the field like a Christmas meal come early.

Chaos turned into a bloodbath.

Naila willed æther into her hands. She squeezed Morgana's forearm as hard as she could. The smoky odor of burned flesh stung her nose. The shadowreaper pushed her away with a hiss. Naila didn't wait for a reaction, but focused on gathering æther. The flames were so close to the surface she could feel it, smell it.

Morgana's poisonous dagger blazed with flames. Blood dripped from the corners of her humorless smile. "Give up, Stormhold. Do not be ruled by your lust for a prince. There is more at stake than a doomed romance."

Anger shot through her. How dare she treat her like a lovesick teen who can't think for herself? Her body burned, the punctum maximum forming in her fingertips. Morgana's eyes narrowed. Another shadowreaper appeared to the woman's side, blazing scimitar at the ready.

"Get her, Morpheus," Morgana ordered.

Without warning, Morpheus pushed forward, his sword pointing toward her. She refused to be at their mercy. Not again.

She pulled Elgafar out of her cloak. Out of the tips of her fingers, two golden spirals curled around her dagger until it grew into a scissor-tipped sword of gilded flames. A golden crescent atop a half-moon adorned the hilt's center. She had no time to think how in the worlds she'd done that.

The corners of Morgana's mouth bent into a satisfied smirk as her lackey circled Naila. "To think I doubted you. It pleases me to see your colors."

Naila swung clumsily at Morpheus, but he met her blow easily with his own. To everyone's surprise her sword went through the tip of his like melted butter. Stunned, he threw his ruined blade away. Morgana threw him another scimitar. He dove to the side and picked it up. "I will not stop, Stormhold," he warned. "This either ends with you conceding or with my death."

He threw himself upon her. She barely missed his blow. He was fast, yes, but the long preceding battle had demanded some of his stamina. On the other hand, æther filled her to the brim. It strengthened her, made her faster. A high unlike anything.

She would *not* lose.

She had no sword fighting prowess, but her flames gave her an advantage she had to make use of.

Morpheus swung his scimitar without so much as a grunt. This time, she blocked his attack, shattering his blade with her own. She pressed the twin tips of her sword underneath his chin, leaving blood trickling down his neck. She swallowed, but didn't budge. Looked him straight in the eye.

Morgana narrowed her eyes but Morpheus held up a hand to ward her off. "Do you have it in you to kill, Stormhold? Do you hold true to your forebear's name?" he mocked.

"I… I do."

A lie.

He smirked knowingly.

"Yet you could not do it to save your Philippe," said Morgana sweetly.

Naila pushed the sword deeper into his skin, whilst glaring at the woman. "Don't you dare speak his name."

Why did her hand tremble so? Why couldn't she force it to press a little deeper? A drop of sweat formed on her temple, but it instantly cooled in the icy wind.

Morgana stuck out her palm as if trying to soothe a frightened bird. "Philippe Jang is alive. Did you know? You can still save him. Come with us and no harm will come to him."

Her breath formed little clouds in the frozen air. "You're lying."

Morpheus eyed her gilded sword, shadowing its length until they reached her face.

"Am I?" said Morgana.

There she stood in the middle of chaos, yet it seemed a room desolate of sound. Could it be?

"The Shadow Šar is wise. He knew we needed leverage if you proved to be... difficult. Your life for Phillipe Jang. What say you, Stormhold?"

Morgana's eyes gleamed with something dark. She knew better than to fall for another of their traps, yet she couldn't shake off the doubt. If Philly was alive, she *would* save him. No questions asked.

Morpheus took advantage of her shocked state and slammed her hand aside. The sword fell with a thump to the snow. The gilded flames sizzled until the blade crumpled to its original form. They both reached for the dagger, but Morpheus was faster. He picked it up and raised it high above his head, a mocking gleam in his flaming eyes.

The sound of bones crushing preceded the ripping of skin and splattering of blood. Morpheus's eyes bulged as blood trickled from the corner of his mouth. His eyes lowered to the flaming fist protruding from his stomach and then met her gaze again. Dark flames scorched the freshly formed wound.

"The wind blows to move us forward, not so we can stand still."

Those were the last words that ever left his mouth.

The fist retracted from the man it had just killed. The shadowreaper's lifeless body fell next to her on the once pristine snow. The Red Šar loomed over the spot where Morpheus previously stood, his eyes as dark as the shadows that engulfed his bloodied fist. For a moment, he watched her. Then he turned back to the battle.

Morgana slowly retreated, back to her master's side.

Naila bent over Morpheus's corpse. With shaking fingers, she closed his eyelids. Like Daena, Morpheus had been her enemy. He had done horrible things. Still, death was something she wished on none. She knew now that she wouldn't have killed him. Yet, if Levias hadn't interfered, the Shadow Šar would have gotten his wish. "The wind blows to move us forward, not so we can stand still," Naila whispered. If there was a next life, she wished he'd get to forge a different, better path.

She pried her dagger out of Morpheus's fingers and rushed to the field.

Screechhhh.

Onyx's arrow put an end to a screecher's life. Its scaled tail whipped around. It smacked Onyx, throwing her several meters away.

"Ugh," Onyx grunted. She pushed herself off the muddy snow. A shadowreaper sneaked up behind her, a flaming blade in his hand. Naila didn't have time to think. She æshefied her dagger and threw it at the shadowreaper. It went straight through his hand.

"Aargh!" the shadowreaper screeched.

Onyx instantly turned around and fired an arrow at the shadowreaper.

"Are you okay?" asked Naila.

She stuck out her hand to help Onyx up, just as the huntress had done when she'd saved Naila in the redwoods.

Onyx gaped at her, awe marking her face. She grasped Naila's hand. "You saved me..."

"As you saved me. Come on, Silas has his hands full."

But Silas had just slashed Colios's throat, marking the end to their third and final dance of flames.

They barely made it halfway to the prince before something red flickered before them. Inch by inch, crimson flames solidified into mighty wings. They stretched open to reveal the Shadow Šar's formidable frame. His eyes flashed scarlet. "Resistance is futile. Give up, Ishtar."

"By the seven hells, she won't," Onyx snapped. "Not on my watch."

Onyx tuned up her bow with another æsh-arrow.

"Ah, Onyx, ever the hunter, are you? You have caught yourself some big prey in the past. I will give you that."

"The same way I'll skewer you alive, and then boil you into mush, traitor," Onyx spat.

Sariel chuckled. He sauntered toward them, his crimson wings flapping behind him. "Do you know why the hunter and the scorpion never simultaneously grace us with their presence in the night's sky?"

Onyx narrowed her eyes as she followed Sariel's every move with her arrow. "I'm sure you're about to tell me." Her æsh-arrow unleashed, but Sariel caught it. The flames of æther died in his fist. The arrow cracked in two.

"The Legends put their graves as constellations at the opposite ends of heaven, because the scorpion's stinger brought upon the hunter's death. Do not challenge me, huntress, or you'll see the same fate as your namesake."

Onyx huffed. "The sky is fickle. It births new stars and buries dead ones. It's not the stories of the past you should swear on, but the ones of the future."

Onyx nocked another arrow on her bow but Naila put her hand atop it to stop her.

She had to know the truth.

"Philly... Philippe Jang. What have you done with him?"

Lord Sariel cocked his head. A secretive smile formed on his face. "You ask me, but you already know."

She almost fell to her knees. Philly was alive! He was alive and there, in the lands of Lemuria.

"Please let him go. It's me you want, not him."

"Surrender, and I will take you to him."

"There will be no surrendering of any sort. Leave or die," Levias's stone-cold voice cut through the conversation.

The end of his scimitar pressed into Sariel's back. Like Tryce, however, it cut through flames, leaving no wound behind in the Shadow Šar's body.

The corner of Sariel's mouth turned up ever so slightly. "I will leave when I have my due."

An ear-deafening screech bellowed through the air. The last screecher broke out of the snow. Levias swung his sword, blazing in flames almost the color of a darkening sky, but he was too late. The screecher snapped his jaws, swallowing him whole.

Desperation marred Silas's face. "Levias!"

"Levias, no!" Sayana cried as she rushed toward them, tears streaming down a face crumpled in agony.

A dreadful chill permeated Naila's skin.

What just happened?

It... it couldn't be. The Red Šar couldn't be dead.

L

OF SHADOWS AND DARKNESS

GONE...

Just like that.

The creature's piercing shriek slashed at Naila's eardrums but she made no move to cover her ears. Frozen in shock, she gaped at the screecher, not quite believing it had just eaten the infamous Dragon Lord.

Lord Sariel dusted off his black suit. "Now, where were we?"

"You—" Silas began.

The creature's shriek pitched into one of agony. Its belly split open from the inside out. A sword covered in midnight flames cut it open until it fell, limp and dead. There, covered in purple slime and blood, was the Red Šar himself. Alive, intact. Angry.

"Your Majesty," a shadowreaper warned.

Sariel caught sight of the šar, astonishment plastered over his face.

Levias stepped out of the nest of intestines, rubbing slime off his black armor. The flames of abyss sizzled out, only a few remnants dancing on the tip of his scimitar.

Sariel's gaze honed in on the šar's approaching frame. The crimson flames of his eyes burned with vehemence, as did his wings. Some of the feathers molded into razor-sharp javelins.

"Watch out," she yelled, but the javelins of æther unleashed on Levias so fast none could stop them. The šaltana, only steps removed from her estranged son, dragged herself up from the snow. Water dripped from her blond strands, soaking the pale wool of her clothing until it stuck to her body. She looked like a fallen angel whose wings had just been ripped off—

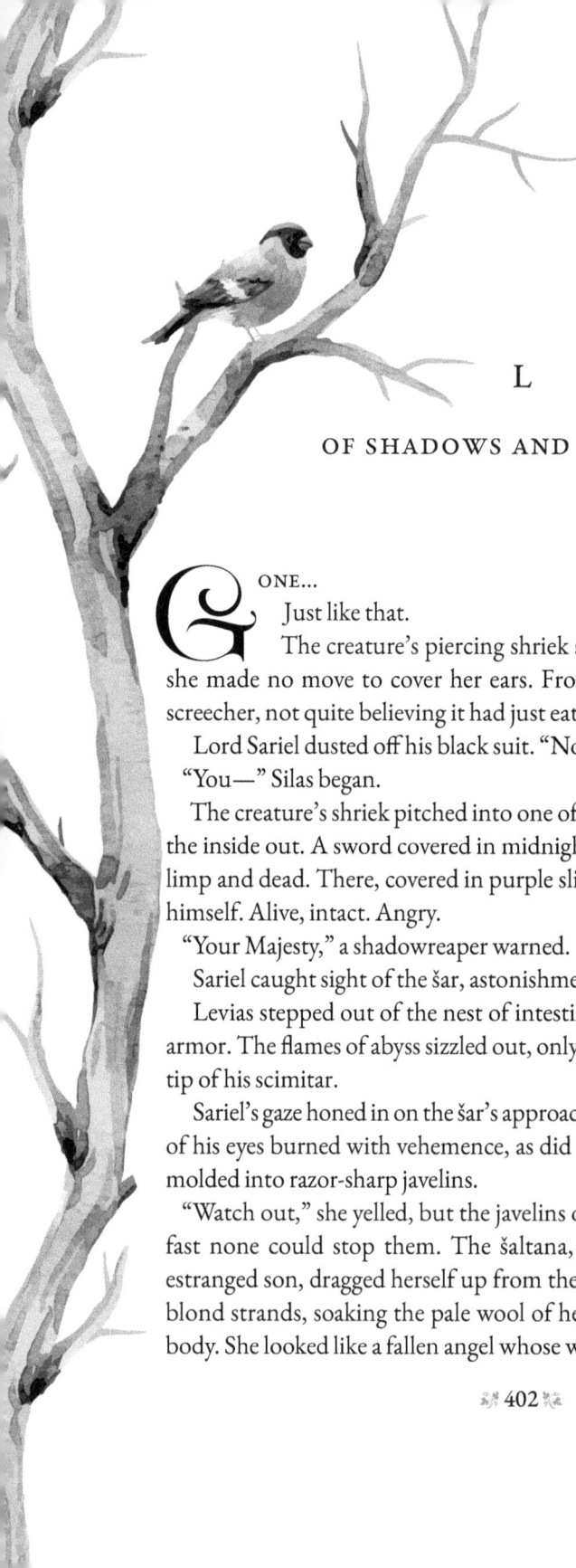

one still determined to get back to heaven. There was no doubt in her expression, no hesitation in her stance.

Everything seemed to unfold in slow motion. Right before Sariel's javelins hit Levias, Sayana jumped in front of him. The šar reached to push his mother aside, but it was too late. Sayana fell into his arms, hissing javelins covering her torso. The clothing of her chest was soaked with blood.

"Mother!" Silas dashed to them.

Sayana's trembling fingers stroked Levias's cheek. The šar's eyes were wide in shock, his stricken gaze darting over the soft curves of his renounced mother's face. No doubt he felt as Naila—no pain, no sadness, nothing. A body and mind wholly numb.

This was a dream; it had to be.

He gently cupped the princess's cheek. "Why?"

"Forgive me, Levias," Sayana whispered. "I… Please forgive me."

Her hand fell from his cheek to her broken body. As her last breath left her body, the light dulled in her gentle eyes.

"Mother," Silas's voice broke. He pulled her out of Levias's hands—he still stared, dazed—and cradled their mother's body to his chest with a careful gentleness. Silas kissed her face, his tears wetting the šaltana's lifeless face. "Mother… Mother…"

The šaltana had been a gentle soul. A being perhaps too sensitive for this ruthless world. Even as life threw her tragedy after tragedy, after the wounds of her heart had lured her into making decisions she came to regret, she had gazed forward to the everlasting sun. Naila knew Sayana's death had been on her own terms, yet she couldn't help but wish the sweet princess had met a happier ending—one filled with light and joy.

She and Onyx approached the twins hesitantly.

Agony bled on Silas's face. He whispered, he murmured, his words utterly broken. Onyx hugged Silas, stroking his back. Naila squeezed his shoulder gently. She knew their gestures brought no comfort.

"*You*," Silas hissed. His eyes spat venom at Sariel. He æshefied his scimitar.

Sariel sighed; his eyebrows creased in sorrow, but Naila felt no pity for him. He was a traitor, a *murderer*.

Within a blink of an eye the Shadow Šar jumped backward. Where he just stood, flames of shadow flickered atop melting sleet. Sariel flicked his gaze to the Red Šar.

Levias pointed his sword at Sariel. Black flames flickered over its sharp edges. "You are a dead man."

"Black æther?" Onyx whispered.

Sariel's lips tightened to a straight line. "Black æther," Sariel repeated. It seemed like he talked more to himself than to them.

His train of thoughts dawned on her. Surely, he was wrong?

"Well, I'll be," Sariel continued, as Levias's vigiles gathered around him. "I thought nothing could surprise me, yet your mere existence proves me wrong."

Naila's gaze went from Sariel to the šar, to the šar's sword and back again. She clasped her hand over her mouth.

Sariel was right.

"No," she gasped.

"After all our calculations, all our careful planning, fate decided to test our limits," Sariel said as he eyed the šar greedily. Then he said the words she so feared in her heart. "I should have known it was you, Red Šar. After all, you were born with a soul many a shade darker than the Stone of Darkness itself."

The šaltana had been mistaken; everyone had been mistaken. Silas wasn't the carrier of the Stone of Shadows and Darkness, it was his ruthless, war-hungry brother. Some of the flames must have rubbed off on Silas, deceiving Nova and Sayana into thinking it was him.

The šar's eyebrows shot up as he finally took in the dark flames sprouting from his sword. His stone-cold expression melted into one of boyish wonder. The dark flames retracted from the tip of his sword into the palm of his hand. "What is this?" he whispered.

All the vigiles from the battle ground had joined them now. Yet Sariel smiled as if he had the upper hand. He turned to Naila and said,

"A palace lies in a heart of earth and shadows,
Beyond a forest frozen and cursed meadows,
When the last leaf of the second autumn falls,
Death awaits your Philippe,
Should the Gemini Stones fail to answer this call."

"Wha—" she began, but crimson flames started swallowing the Shadow Šar whole.

"Sack of wine," Levias hissed. Sariel had his full attention again. "You're a fool if you think I'll let you slip out of my fingers alive."

He swung his burning sword at Sariel.

"No!" Naila screeched.

Without thinking she jumped before the Shadow Šar, thrusting her own dagger forward. Like before it morphed into a double-tipped golden sword. No harm could come to the Shadow Šar, not until she'd saved Philly. Levias's scimitar stopped less than an inch before her own.

Both gilded and night-dark flames fizzled out in the air.

Sariel's mouth edged into a satisfied grin as he saluted Naila. His body blasted into a million scarlet shards. They hit the snow with a hiss creating fumes of steam.

"What kind of witchery is that?" one vigile whispered to another.

"Hush, boy, do not tempt the Dark Forest with tales of witchery."

"The shadowreapers are taking to the forest," another cried.

A shadow fell over the Red Šar's face.

She didn't dare look at him, opting to stare at his boots instead. They were dirty with bloodied snow, as crimson as the crest on his cloak. His finger curled underneath her chin, and he forced her to meet his stormy eyes.

"Never stand in my way again."

"I have to save my friend," she rasped out.

"You are a fool to think him trustworthy, woman. Mark my words, your friend is either dead or in a state you'd never wish to lay eyes on."

He let go of her chin and turned so abruptly his black cloak wafted with the winds before he stormed to his black steed. "Hurry, they cannot be far."

The vigiles rushed to follow their šar, but he didn't wait for them to gallop through the Dark Forest.

"Naila..."

Naila fell into Onyx's arms. What had just happened?

"It's been a long night," Onyx whispered.

Silas stumbled over to them, carrying his mother's corpse, Tryce and Halfbeard's men close behind him. The raw pain on his face spoke volumes. "He'll be busy combing through the Dark Forest. Let's go before he returns. I want to be on the first dhow that leaves for Havenmor. I refuse to bury mother in a place that's not her home."

EPILOGUE

A KINGDOM IN RUINS

THE LONG night faded into dawn, but it might as well have stayed pitch-black. All Naila could see was the lifeless body of the princess, not the eerily calm waters of Helath's sea she'd sworn to never sail again. Ro-Ro soared through the cloudless sky, cawing now and then, his feathers as golden as the burning sunrise.

Just a quarter of a moon ago, Rē betrayed them and killed the šaltana in front of their eyes. It was still unreal. Every time a door opened, she expected the šaltana to walk upon the dhow's deck with her gentle smile, assuring her it'd all been a joke. She'd run to her and hug her and cry and scold her for playing such a cruel trick on them... on Silas.

Her hand stroked her throat absentmindedly. No sign of battle remained. Even the cut of Morgana's poisonous blade had healed without the use of iscias. Somehow, those gilded flames had burned any trace of poison out of her body. She promised herself that one day she would figure out how she'd done it. No shadowreaper's blade would ever threaten another... and maybe, just maybe, she'd be one step closer to battling *ut mortes nero*.

The deck creaked behind her.

Naila met Silas's eyes. They were filled with small red veins. Even with his face lined with worry, even with his linen shirt creased and half-buttoned, he still looked devastatingly handsome. He joined her at the rails. At once she became aware of the needling pain in her feet that had been intensifying these last days. The curse of a blood oath broken.

For a moment they just stood there, watching the sun illuminate the cobalt sea waves in shades of orange and pink. They listened to the first birds chirping, whilst breathing in the sea's saltiness. The night had been long, but it was over now. Come victory or tragedy, the everlasting sun would still be there, thousands of winters after their passing, to laud a new day.

A lump formed in her throat. "When I started this journey, I didn't realize the sacrifices it would demand. If... if it weren't for me, and you guys didn't work so hard to protect—"

Silas slid his arm around her shoulders and pulled her to him, his spicy scent of timber soothing. He kissed the top of her head. "It's not your fault. You needed help, and we would not abandon you. I'd do it all over again, no questions asked."

She rested her head against his broad shoulder. Somehow, he always knew the right things to say. But...

"Will your grandfather say the same?"

The prince studied the sunbeams lighting up the sea with a frown on his face. He rested his face atop her head. "Leave grandfather to me."

His words didn't ease the knot in her stomach. She could only imagine the Silver Šar's reaction when they brought before him his favorite daughter's corpse, not to mention the news that her mere presence in Skeldor brought war with Crishire to his door. And then the scheming Ænunaki Shadow Šar who wanted her for whatever reason. She had more than enough reason to believe she wouldn't be his favorite person.

"I'm going to find Rē and I'm going to kill him," Silas said in a deadly calm voice.

She swallowed. "Silas..."

"And I will show him no mercy."

She studied her nails, a deep unease coiling within her. "I don't think revenge is the answer."

"I will not let Mother's murder go unpunished," he said simply.

The coldness in his tone brought shivers to her skin. "Please don't let revenge consume you."

A faint, bitter smile played on his lips. "We come from different worlds, Naila."

"Yet here we are, standing together in the same one."

His gaze drifted to the horizon, shadowed and distant. "Sooner or later, we'll have to face Rē, either way. If we want to save your friend."

"I know," she whispered.

Silas's face closed off. "I'll figure something out." He seemed so far away, like a distant star she couldn't reach.

"*We*," she stated.

"Hmm?"

"We," she said more firmly. "We will figure out something. As a team."

His eyes softened. "Ever so stubborn."

Yes, ever so stubborn. But the stakes had become too high to depend on others. She had to carry her own weight.

"All right." He smiled; sad and small, but a smile, nonetheless. "Then we'll do this together. As a team. Every step of the way."

The crew stomped to the deck one by one. From the cooking smell tickling her nose, she could tell Bubba was already up making their breakfast—barley porridge flavored with onions and garlic. When the last patches of the night's sky made way for a promising new day, she finally looked up.

There above them, high atop the ship's mast, was a nest made of what looked like cinnamon. A nest of cinnamon birds. A puffy golden-brown fledgling fluttered its little wings and sprang bravely to the edge of the nest. Its siblings chirped loudly as the baby bird fell, but just as it was about to hit the sails, its wings took strength, and the bird entered its first flight.

"But know, Naila, that saving your friend will be difficult," Silas said, lost in thought. "You saw the Shadow Šar. He had perfect control over æther, it was like he was a flame himself. Compared to him, we're only embers."

She smiled at the brave little bird and turned back to Silas. "Don't forget," her voice gained strength with every word. "Embers can ignite an entire forest."

She straightened her back and interlaced her hand with Silas's.

Her path was clear.

Home would have to wait.

JODRIR
The White Mountains
Greykeep Mountains
The Frozen Sea
The Enchanted Tides
The Sea of Helath
ISOLO
The Ocean of Lost Souls
THE LOST WORLD
Riolos
The Arctic Waves

SKELDOR
SYEON
NUMIDEA
Daggedor
Elysian fields
The Shoreless Ocean
Esyleron
CRISHIRE
Lethos
Irkalla
The Black Desert
THE LAND OF THE GIANTS
The Wild Lands
The Shifting Sands of the Red Desert
Taegras
The Island of flames
The Black Waters
The Jade Sea
CRISHIRE (PREVIOUSLY ORNESIAS)
Goriana
The City of Gold
The Endless Sea
The Sea of Mists
THE SHADOW LANDS
THE LANDS OF LEMURIA

ACKNOWLEDGEMENTS

I'm filled with gratitude for the people who walked beside me on this journey. To my mother–thank you for being my anchor and my light. To my family for your patience and unwavering support, Susanna, Carol and Joel, especially. I also want to thank all my friends for their continued excitement.

A special thanks to my editors C.B. Moore and Melanie Underwood for your insightful feedback that helped shape this manuscript.

My illustrators Cynthia Conner, and Moreno Paissan & Angela Gubert deserve an applause. Thanks to your talent and creativity, this story has come alive with a breathtaking cover, a beautiful fantasy map, and heraldic crests. I couldn't have asked for a better visual team. Also shout-out to Nebraska J.C. illustrations for the multiple beautiful character illustrations she created for me.

Heartfelt thanks to my beta readers, Regina, Elise, Heather, Sara, Troy, Krys, Amy, Christina and Raluca, whose critiques strengthened this story in ways I cannot thank them enough for.

Finally, to you—the reader—thank you for picking up this book and stepping into this world with me. Your time is the greatest gift an author can hope for.

It would mean the world to me if you could leave an honest review before you move on to your next book adventure.

ABOUT THE AUTHOR

FAYE OLIANDER is an Afro-Surinamese author of Fantasy & Science Fiction. Her books transport readers to non-Western settings, weaving epic adventures with a touch of romance. Currently residing in a small European country with her beloved cat, Faye enjoys reading, practicing yoga, and indulging in her love for old-school music and movie soundtracks. A true foodie at heart, she's always on the lookout for her next culinary adventure.

A Legend in the Sky is the first in a breath-taking new fantasy series.

Join Faye Oliander's Newsletter or follow her on TikTok, Instagram, Threads, and Facebook at @fayeoliander.

www.fayeoliander.com